From Here to There and Back
by
Robin Blake

Dedication

This book is dedicated to my parents, Hildur and Bob Blake, and to my granddaughter and fellow writer, Ellie Blake.

First published in 2012 by Robin Blake and printed by the University of Missouri Book Store.

The second edition was published in 2018. Anyone wishing to share one or more pieces in this book with someone else is welcomed to do so, as long as appropriate credit is given to the author.

The cover scene is from a watercolor painting by Bob Blake.

Table of Contents

Nonfiction

Short Fiction

Betrayed

"Doc, my stomach's killin' me."

He sat hunched forward in the exam room, his eyes peering out from a sun-leathered face, a face that spoke of hard living over 41 years. Although I had not seen Clarence Walker before, I had seen his type for the past two years: the stoic, self-reliant Appalachian farmer who would rather be almost anywhere than in a doctor's office on a sunny day in May. In his sweat-stained yellow shirt and faded bib overalls, with his anxious eyes and hesitant voice, he told me why he was sitting in the clinic instead of planting tobacco in his field.

His symptoms worried me: increasing abdominal pain, loss of appetite, a feeling of fullness after a few bites of food, baggy clothes from weight loss, unaccustomed fatigue. He had even vomited, something he had not done since being wounded in Vietnam, and he still carried the shrapnel in his back, a hint of pride in his voice. The relatively normal physical examination did little to mitigate my concern about something serious.

Unaccustomed to sickness, Clarence made his agenda clear: He wanted medicine to make the symptoms go away. In contrast, I wanted to figure out what was causing the symptoms. It was a challenge I had often encountered; I had learned that flexibility was the key. We negotiated a deal: He traded a tube of blood for a bottle of pills. He left the clinic with the futile hope that he would never see me again.

In a week he returned, his face etched with worry, his eyes like pebbles sucked into a dry river bed. His wife Molly accompanied him, a thin, worn woman, like so many of the mountain women, her youth succumbing to the toll of life at the edge of subsistence. Sitting next to her husband, staring at the floor and saying little, she seemed insubstantial.

The blood tests revealed anemia and abnormal liver enzymes, ominous findings. Several days later, gastroscopy and x-rays performed at the VA hospital near Asheville confirmed my worst suspicion: Clarence had stomach cancer that had spread to his liver. The VA specialist told him that medical science had little to offer.

A few days later, I met with Clarence and Molly in the clinic while their ten-year old son and eight-year old daughter waited outside in the pickup truck. I tried to explore with him how he was coping with this tragic turn in his life, but he sat depleted, folded into himself, leaving Molly and me to discuss his diminishing future. Understandably distraught, she cried intermittently, but she also seemed strangely energized, as if the spirit of her once robust husband had been transfused into her. She asked appropriate questions and appeared to absorb and understand the bleak answers. When we finished she stood up, turned to her husband and helped him rise. She steadied his body with one hand and with her other swept a strand of brown hair from her face. Our eyes met. I had underestimated her.

Over the next month, I saw Clarence and Molly twice in the clinic. He was declining rapidly. Oral narcotics controlled the pain, but there seemed little else that I could do. Emotionally, Clarence had withdrawn into his sickness. Molly seemed to be drawing on some core of resilience to manage the day-to-day challenges.

As was common among the mountain folk, they were strongly opposed to hospitalization, so I arranged for home health care through the county health department. After her first visit to the Walker home, Peggy Spence, the home health nurse, stopped by the clinic to give me a report.

"It's so sad." She sat in my small office by the desk, cluttered with unfinished patient charts, her hand gently on my arm. "He's given up."

"Yeah, I know."

"Molly's in agony, but I think she'll be able to handle it with our help." Her gaze moved from my face to the window behind me. "She's tough. She reminds me of my sister Claire."

I had just recently met Claire and her husband and three kids, who lived on a farm in a little valley, three mountains removed from town.

Peggy made frequent home visits over the next few weeks. When the oral medications no longer relieved the pain, she taught Molly how to give injections of morphine. Peggy and I had taken this approach with an earlier patient who died at home, and it had seemed to work. But I didn't want to think what some of my professors in medical school would have said about it.

Peggy had grown up in a mountain hollow. Somehow, she had avoided the barefoot and pregnant fate of her peers and had attended nursing school in Asheville. Claire had had a lot to do with that; their mother had died when Peggy was little, and she had been raised by her older sister.

When I moved into the community and became the clinic doctor, Peggy was finishing her first year as the county home health nurse. We settled into a comfortable professional relationship fairly quickly; the personal relationship took much longer to develop. I became interested early on. There was the physical attraction and also a level of empathy and compassion evident in her day-to-day care of patients that I had rarely seen.

6

But she hung back from me, kept it all professional. Later, I realized that she had been testing my commitment to her people. Would I stick it out, become a part of the community, or would I be a two-year transient, like my predecessor at the community clinic?

A few weeks before Clarence's first clinic visit a breakthrough occurred: Peggy consented to attend a music festival in Asheville with me. Picnics on the banks of the French Broad River and walks on the Appalachian Trail followed. Soon, the town gossips were buzzing about the blossoming romance between the doctor and the nurse. I was ready for something more sustaining than the evanescent relationships that had plagued my medical school and residency years.

Late one night in June we lay on a soggy sheet, sweat drying on our bare bodies, John Denver's "Rocky Mountain High" softly serenading us from Peggy's stereo. I felt her damp hair against my face, her warm breath on my ear, her arm light on my chest.

"Do you want to stay the night?" She murmured.

Life was good.

In the morning over coffee and pancakes, with Willow, her golden retriever, nuzzling my foot, we talked about life in the mountains. Peggy talked about why she had come back to a place that so many had yearned to escape. I talked about how a guy from the suburbs of Charlotte had ended up practicing medicine in rural Appalachia. We touched on the hard work, the frustrations, the satisfaction of helping people in need. It seemed easier than talking about the meaning of the night before.

Just before I climbed into my Jeep, Peggy hugged me and said, "You fit in here. You care about us. You're a good doctor and a good man."

The following weeks pulsated with the joys of discovery and celebration.

On a late afternoon in August, I made a home visit to Clarence and Molly. Peggy had told me that the end was near. Following her directions, I turned at Moore's store in the Pine Creek section onto a dirt road, baked hard by the sun. As it wound higher into the dense pine forest, the road deteriorated. I passed occasional houses and small plots of tobacco. After a mile of uncomfortable bouncing in the Jeep, I recognized the unpainted house that Peggy had described. It stood on a shelf of land that jutted out from a hill. High grass partially concealed the rusted carcass of a car at the edge of a cluster of stunted corn. Clarence's pickup was squeezed between the house and rows of tobacco plants that extended up the hillside. Somehow, the crop had been planted.

I pulled the Jeep into the dirt yard, scattering chickens and attracting the attention of two hounds that emerged from underneath the front porch, barking aggressively. Having made enough home visits to be ever cautious of strange dogs, I waited for someone to come out and restrain them. Soon, Molly and a boy came onto the porch and yelled at the dogs. They ignored the yelling and continued to circle the Jeep, growling. The boy came down and wrestled them back under the porch. With the dogs subdued, I got out of the Jeep and crossed the dusty yard to the porch steps. The dogs grumbled but made no menacing moves.

"Don't worry, they won't bite." Molly spoke from the porch.

I looked up at her from the bottom of the stairs. She wore a green dress that ended at her knees; her bare legs were pale in the shadow of the porch. The afternoon breeze blew brown hair around her face. I climbed the steps and shook her hand.

"Thank you for comin', doctor. We really 'preciate it." Her voice effaced the cackling of the hens and growling of the dogs.

Inside, the house was cool. I stood in a small room furnished with a sofa and three stuffed chairs arranged to face an old TV with rabbit ears on its top. On good days, maybe it would pick up the ABC station out of Asheville. An unlit floor lamp stood by the sofa. A rug partially covered the wooden floor. A picture of Jesus and a calendar hung on one wall. On the opposite wall hung a photograph of a young man in a World War II-vintage uniform. A Bible lay on a small table in a corner.

I heard murmuring behind me and turned to find a man and woman standing in the doorway of an adjacent room. Behind them, in the bedroom, I caught a glimpse of a little girl. Molly introduced me to Clarence's mother and father, who also lived in the home. They each had wrinkled, leathery skin and gray hair; they seemed frail and decrepit. The woman mumbled something, and I could make out "my boy" but little else. I spoke briefly to them, and soon they shuffled into the bedroom; I did not see them again.

Clarence lay in a back room, down a short hallway. Before I reached the room, I smelled him, the familiar odor of dying. The detritus of illness and implements of futile treatments littered the bedroom. Medicine bottles and tubes of cream covered the top of a bedside table. A bedpan and urinal lay on the floor. In a corner, a bedside commode sat beside a chest of drawers. Curtains drawn across the single window preserved the gloom of sickness.

Inert and silent, Clarence lay on a bed that occupied most of the room, his body covered by a sheet. A yellow strip of fly paper hung motionless from the ceiling in the moribund air above him. As I moved around the foot of the bed to the other side, I saw bodies of dead flies stuck to the gum of the paper. I leaned over Clarence; fetid breath greeted me. Pallid eyes sunken into a corroded face stared past me.

"Clarence, the doctor is here." Molly spoke from the other side of the bed.

"Hello, Clarence." Squeezing a bony shoulder, I watched his eyes blink and his face grimace. He looked at me and groaned. His mouth moved, but he uttered no words. I watched his cracked lips struggle, but soon he seemed exhausted and gave up the effort to speak. He closed his eyes and receded from me, a stick sinking below the surface of still water.

Lowering the sheet to examine his body, I encountered the emaciation. Parchment-like skin covered a protruding rib cage, which barely moved with each shallow breath. I could see the rapid rhythm of his heart pulsate the wasted flesh. A cancer-filled liver bloated his abdomen. I wrapped the blood pressure cuff around his once muscular arm. The low reading portended death. Clean skin and the absence of bedsores testified to Molly's good care.

Back on the porch, I went over things with Molly. She confirmed Peggy's latest report: Clarence had stopped eating and drank little fluid. He slept most of the time and often seemed confused. Urine output had virtually ceased.

"Is he having much pain?"

"I make sure he doesn't have pain."

"How much morphine are you giving him?"

After a pause, she replied, "A shot about every three hours."

"That's quite a bit."

"He seems to need it. That's what it takes."

"Okay. Peggy gave you a new supply yesterday."

"Yes."

"You're recording each shot in the notebook."

"Yes."

The sun had disappeared behind a mountain, leaving the yard encased in shadows. Molly's son stood by the Jeep kicking at something in the dirt. The hens had settled down; the dogs stirred under the porch but did not bark. The breeze had picked up, diluting the heat of the day. Like a welcomed visitor, evening approached through the pine forest beyond the yard.

"How much longer?" Molly brought me back to it.

I felt the air stir from the movement of her body beside me. "Not much longer, I think." I looked at her; a strand of hair fell across her down-turned face. "But it's hard to predict. It may be a day or two, or it could be as long as a week or so." I stopped and waited for her to respond. When she didn't, I said. "Peggy has talked to you about what to do when he passes."

She shifted beside me but continued to look at the floor. "Yes, I'll call Peggy; she said she would come out." Molly stopped and peered into the distance. She hugged her sun-browned arms to her body like she was clutching a small child. "Sometimes, I wish it would go ahead and happen, and then I feel so ashamed. It's a terrible thing to wish for. I know I shouldn't." A tear fell from her down-cast face; she fumbled in the pocket of her dress for a tissue. I handed her one from my pocket, and she dabbed at her eyes.

I reached out and touched her arm; her skin felt like winter sunshine. "It's okay to feel that way. It's natural. It's difficult to see him like this." I removed my hand from her arm. "You're doing a good job of taking care of him. Peggy has told me how impressed she is with your care, and I can see what she means." I stopped and waited. When she said nothing, I continued. "I know this is very hard for you, for the kids, for his folks. I think you're doing the best that anyone could do under the circumstances."

We stood on the porch and I watched her son throw stones at a pine tree behind the Jeep. She told me that the kids were taking it hard. Oren was angry a lot, difficult to handle, at times. Rhonda was afraid and cried frequently.

"Do the grandparents help?"

Molly gazed into the woods and seemed to ponder the question. "They're old and sick. They can't do much."

Molly told me that her mother came over to help on occasion, but she lived on Buck's mountain and didn't drive, making it hard for her to get here. Her sister tried to help also, but she had two little children and a husband who didn't like for her to be away from home. Eunice Hogan, who lived down the road, brought food. Neighbor men tended to the tobacco. Pastor Wiggins and his wife came by on Sunday afternoons to pray.

"It's important to take care of yourself. Joan, the home health aide, could come over to help with housework, to give you a break. Maybe, you could get away for an hour or two."

"I know; Peggy mentioned that. I'm doin' okay. When Peggy comes, she sits with me in the kitchen for a spell, and we drink coffee and talk about things, and that helps a lot."

I stood with her, feeling the breeze and watching the shadows deepen. I could have stayed on the porch, listening to the evening insect chorus, but I knew it was time to leave.

"Is there anything else I can do?"

"No, you've done so much. I 'preciate it."

Savoring her gratitude, I turned to her and extended my right hand. "You know how to reach me." I started down the steps and heard a growl from under the porch.

"Oren, you come mind the dogs for the doctor."

The dogs obeyed Oren, and I drove back down the dirt road, hoping that Clarence Walker would die soon.

He did, three days later. Peggy called me with the news. Molly had found him dead when she awoke that morning, and Peggy had driven over to the home. She told me that his family seemed to be doing okay, considering. Boyd, from the funeral home, would be picking up the body soon and would swing by the clinic to have me sign the death certificate. Services would be the next day at Burning Bush Faith Church. Peggy suggested that she and I visit Clarence's family some evening a few days after the funeral to see how they were doing. That sounded like a good idea to me. As usual, Peggy seemed to have everything covered.

Late that afternoon, as I finished up at the clinic, I got a frantic call from Molly. Clarence's father was sick, and she needed me to come quickly. He refused to go to his regular physician at the VA and insisted that only I could help him. Over the phone, I could get little additional information from Molly.

"Come quickly, doctor, please." She pleaded.

Before I left the clinic, I tried to contact Peggy, but she was tending to Maggie Fuller on Indian Bluff. I left a message with her office that I would be late for dinner at her place.

The rain started as I passed the gas station and turned onto the narrow pavement that would take me around Booker Mountain to Pine Creek and the dirt road up to the Walker home. Two years before, when I had first traveled the road as an untested doctor, I had become sick and had almost vomited. Part of the nausea had been an effect of the winding road, but part had been caused by fear, fear of the unknown, fear of failure.

On the left, I passed Wally Henderson's two-story brick house, flowers blooming in the front, lush tomato and bean plants standing tall in the side yard, a TV satellite dish flanking the two-car garage, a sea of green tobacco plants stretching over the floor of the valley. I always experienced a sense of achievement whenever I passed the Henderson homestead. A few weeks after I started practice, Wally's wife drove him to the clinic because he had chest pain. Soon after he arrived, he suffered a cardiac arrest. I saved his life, administering CPR in the clinic and keeping him alive in the rescue squad ambulance during the one-hour ride to the hospital in Asheville.

On the backside of the mountain, the country music on the radio degenerated to static, and I listened to the steady drumming of rain on the Jeep and the rhythmic thumping of wipers on the windshield. Yes, I had weathered those fears, and my anxieties had been gradually replaced by self-confidence, as I had dealt with the challenges of a demanding practice. Peggy was right, I was a good doctor. Whatever awaited me at the Walker home, I would deal with it.

The downpour had converted the dirt road to mud, but my Jeep was up to the task. By the time I turned into the Walker's yard, the rain had diminished to a drizzle. Vehicles occupied the yard; I found a spot between a beat-up Chevy station wagon and a pickup. I saw no sign of the dogs. Three men huddled in the drizzle by the edge of the tobacco field, their cigarettes glowing under wide-brimmed hats. The women-folk would be inside, consoling the new widow. By the time I stepped into the mud, Molly appeared on the porch. She waited until I reached the top of the steps, black bag in hand.

"Thank you so much for comin', doctor. Papaw is so sick. I don't know what we would do without you."

Standing beside her on the porch, I sensed her desperation. She didn't need this on top of Clarence's death.

Inside the house, I found a table covered with food, dominating the room. The sofa and chairs had been pushed against the walls, and the TV was gone. About half a dozen women

14

crowded around the table; all eyes focused on me. A thin middle-aged woman rushed forward.

"Praise the Lord. Thank you for comin', doctor. The poor man has taken a frightful spell. To lose a son is a terrible thing."

Beside me, Molly spoke. "This is my momma. Momma, the doctor will take care of Papaw." She turned to me. "He's in here."

Molly opened the door of the room in which I had glimpsed the brown-haired girl three days before. Recoiling at the smell, I hesitated and then followed Molly. She closed the door and switched on the overhead light. Clad only in long underwear, the old man lay on a mattress, moaning; his thin body curled into a bunched-up urine-stained sheet. His wife sat in a chair on the other side of the bed, folded forward, crying. When the light came on, her body jerked up, her eyes flying to me.

"Please, doctor, give him the needle, please."

I turned to Molly. "What's she talking about, a needle?"

Impassively, Molly stared past me. I could not read her. When she did not respond, I stepped past her to the bedside, placed my bag on the mattress and leaned over the sick man. A vision of Clarence's skeletal face wavered before my eyes, his mouth struggling to tell me something. The image vanished, and I peered into dilated pupils and a face of agony.

"Give me the morphine. I must have the morphine. I'm dyin'."

Suddenly, I understood. Turning from the old man in the throes of narcotics withdrawal, I glared at Molly. Silently, she looked into my face, a pleading in her eyes. After a few seconds, her face turned downward, disheveled hair falling over her face, but not before I saw the tears.

15

Movement on the mattress drew my attention back to Clarence's father; he had contorted his body and was reaching for my bag. As he grabbed the handle, I slapped his hand away. The bag fell to the floor, spilling my blood pressure cuff and stethoscope. He rose onto his knees, his hands clutching at me. I pushed him away, and he crumpled onto the mattress, where he lay gasping for breath. His wife shrieked.

After gathering the things from the floor, I picked up the bag and moved to a sobbing Molly. I turned to take one last look at the man, who lay motionless, moaning into the soiled sheet. I grabbed Molly's arm and propelled her from the room, closing the door on the abject wails of the old woman.

Impervious to the stares of the shocked women, I moved Molly out to the porch and let go of her arm. She continued to sob. Turning away from her, I watched the rain pucker the puddles between the cars. Mist hid the mountain I had admired three days before. Gloom permeated the pine woods across the yard. The men still clumped by the tobacco, oblivious to us.

"So, you gave him morphine, too." I struggled to speak calmly.

She said nothing. Staring at the mud-covered wheels of my Jeep, I waited. The sobbing decreased. She wiped her eyes and blew her nose into a tissue she pulled from the dress pocket. I looked at her again.

"Why did you do it?"

After a while, she told me about it: how he had been wounded at Pearl Harbor, how he got some kind of dope in the military hospital. It was the only thing that helped the pain. He had become addicted, but he'd finally kicked it. He had not had any for a long time, but he still remembered what it was like, what it had done for him.

"He's such a pitiful old man. He begged me so much. 'Just one time,' he said, 'One time.' Mamaw took his side. 'Give it to him,' she said. 'He's so miserable. Give him some peace before he dies.'"

Her sobs returned. I could barely hear her. I felt my fury subsiding, draining out like a plug had been pulled, leaving me empty. I began to realize what had happened in the bedroom, what I had done.

Molly started up again. "Clarence said 'no' not to do it. But then he got weaker and weaker and stopped carin' 'bout anything. I couldn't take it any more, so I gave in. I gave him a shot. 'Just one,' he said, but then he wanted more and more." She paused and looked at me through the tears, her body still trembling. "I didn't know this would happen. I never would have. Please, believe me."

I did.

I wanted to leave, to get in the Jeep and escape from this mess. However, there was a medical problem to deal with. Narcotics withdrawal was terrible, but it didn't kill people; it just made them wish they were dead. Still, Clarence's father was old and probably had some health problems, so he needed medical attention over the next few days. I began to feel ashamed of the way I had behaved. I had been blind-sided by a shocking surprise, but that did not excuse my actions.

"When did you give Clarence's father his last shot?"

She seemed surprised by the question. "Two o'clock this mornin'. I wrote it down in the notebook, like I always do."

"So you recorded each shot, whether you gave it to Clarence or to his father. Some of the shots recorded for Clarence actually went to his father?" I remembered Clarence's futile effort to tell me something.

As she grasped the implication of my question, she turned to face me, her mouth tight, her eyes lashing out. "I made sure Clarence got enough morphine. Don't you dare think I skimped on that."

"Okay." The drizzle had stopped. The mountain had emerged from the waning mist. "I know you took good care of Clarence."

She turned to gaze into the mist. "Peggy took the leftover morphine and the record of the shots when she came this mornin'." She paused and then continued. "If I'd known this would happen I would've kept some of the shots."

"That would have just delayed the inevitable. He has narcotics withdrawal. It was bound to occur whenever he stopped getting the shots."

My anger had dissolved; I needed to be a physician. "He's going to have a rough time over the next few days as he goes through withdrawal. He would be better off in the hospital. The rescue squad can take him to the VA." Then I added. "Of course, the doctors are going to want to know how this happened."

She looked out into the misery of her muddy yard. "I know I done wrong. I'll tell them what happened." She hesitated. "What will they do to me?"

"When they hear the whole story, I don't think they'll do anything to you." But they will have a low opinion of me, a thought I did not share with her.

For the first time since we left the bedroom, she looked at me, our eyes met. There was something in hers. I wanted to comfort her.

"So, he'll still be real sick tomorrow, havin' withdrawal?"

"Yes."

18

"But if he had morphine from now until then, he'd be alright for the funeral?"

I didn't reply.

"It'd mean so much to all of us if he could be there."

When I realized what she was saying, it all boiled up inside me again. "What you did is illegal. What you are asking me to do is illegal, and I will not do it." I spit it out and turned and descended the stairs and entered the mist. Without looking back, I climbed into the Jeep and made my way out of the muck and the mist.

Late that night, Peggy and I sat on her porch swing, listening to the sound of Bluegrass pulsing through the open door, Willow snoring on her pallet and water dripping from leaves in the yard. The lasagna and wine had been delicious.

Peggy had been surprised about the morphine. We tried talking about other things, but the specter of an old man in the throes of opioid withdrawal permeated the evening.

I felt the warmth of her body against mine.

"You're still thinking about it, aren't you?"

"Yeah." I said.

She was quiet for a while, and I listened to her breathing and smelled the fragrance of her body. Nothing stirred. After a while, she reached down and touched something that had been hidden beneath my sadness and anger, something I did not want to know about.

"Poor Molly."

"Poor Molly?"

"Everything she's been through, losing her husband, and now this."

"Do you think I should have given him morphine?"

"I don't know." Slowly, she expelled a breath. "Yes, I guess I do."

Soon after that Peggy faced me and kissed me on the cheek. "Good night. Drive carefully."

Later, Peggy told me that Clarence's father had been in the hospital during the funeral. She visited the Walkers several times over the ensuing weeks and reported that things were going as well as could be expected.

I never saw Molly again. Peggy and I tried, but things were never quite the same for us after that night.

The next spring, I left the mountains and joined a group practice in Charlotte. Peggy invited me to her wedding three years later, but I didn't make it. I got married too, and we had a son, but that didn't work out either.

Sometimes, late at night, when sleep eludes me, I see Molly standing on her porch in that green dress, but she soon mutates into an old man crumpled onto a stained mattress. I am lost in a mist of sorrow.

Gone

As he does six mornings a week, Hiram Fowler stops by the post office on the way to the store. He enters the one-room building thinking of Margaret Benson, reminding himself that he needs to check on her and chop some wood for the winter. His thoughts of the young woman are eclipsed; for the first time in five weeks, an envelope with the familiar writing awaits him. The post mark is Salina, Kansas; Caleb is making his way westward. His last letter had been sent from Neosho, Missouri. Later this evening, Hiram will look on the map for the new place. As he leaves the building on the cool autumn morning, his fingers fumble open the envelope and remove a piece of paper.

> I'm cutting wheat in Kansas. It sure
> is flat. Not a mountain in sight. I'm
> doing fine. Don't worry about me.
> Hope you are doing well. Caleb

He turns the sheet over; it's blank on the other side. Approaching the store, he reads the penciled words again. He feels relieved but also disappointed. Up ahead he sees Grover Ramsey standing on the stoop of the store, squinting into the sun that has just emerged from behind Broken Pine Mountain. Hiram places the letter in his coat pocket.

Grover turns to him. "I was beginnin' to think you was sick or somethin'."

"It's not eight o'clock yet, Grover. I don't open 'til eight, you know." Hiram speaks as he unlocks the door and stands aside for the old man to enter. The empty right sleeve of Grover's shirt brushes Hiram's coat. Grover left an arm at Gettysburg; Hiram's father was not so lucky at Chickamauga.

Before he turns to follow his customer, the store-keeper glances at Grover's mule and unpainted buckboard parked in the dirt street. Wally Hogan's Ford kicks up dust as it chugs past the indifferent animal.

While Grover rolls a cigarette with his only hand, Hiram gathers the things that the old man calls out that he needs.

"This enough molasses for you?"

"Yeah, I reckon."

"Whatcha need these nails for?"

"Gotta patch up the barn."

"Would you like for me to come over and help you with it?"

"Nah, Jasper's oldest boy's comin' to help on Saturday."

"How old is he now?"

"Don't know for sure, 'bout seventeen or so, I think."

"You don't say." Hiram lifts the bag of flour onto his shoulder and watches Grover draw on his cigarette. "How many grandchildren you got, Grover?" Sometimes late at night, he finds himself thinking about grandchildren.

Grover blows smoke through his nose and seems to study the question. "Over a dozen, I'd say." He pulls on the cigarette again and releases a smoky breath. "I was over at Jasper's a few days back."

"In Knoxville?" Hiram carries the stuff out and loads it onto the buckboard.

Grover follows him outside, flicks the glowing stump of the cigarette into the dirt and hitches up his bib overalls with his hand. "Yeah, I can only take it there for a coupla days, you know, the big city, the noise, the kids runnin' 'round the house alla time."

"Did you happen to bring back a newspaper?"

"No, sorry. I forget you like to keep up with things. Jasper did read me somethin' outa the paper, though, 'bout the war they got over there. You know that Kaiser, who's stirrin' things up. You wouldn't believe what Jasper told me 'bout how they're fightin' in that war, aroplanes and poison gas."

Hiram waves to a traveling salesman who has come out of Maude's boarding house across the street. "Did Jasper mention anything about whether we're gonna get into it?"

"He did say that head feller in Washington seems dead set against it."

"That's good. We don't need our boys getting killed over there." Hiram's older brother had died of fever fighting in Cuba.

"Yer right about that, I reckon."

The old man looks at Hiram, and the store-keeper braces for a question about Caleb. Instead Grover turns away, informs his mule that it's time to go and climbs onto the seat of the buckboard. As he picks up the reins he says, "Put it on my bill. I'll take care of it when the tobacco's in."

Hiram is busy all morning. Between customers, he pulls out the letter and reads it. By late morning, he has put together the weekly batch of groceries and supplies for Margaret Benson. He calls Harold from the back of the store. He had waited for three months after Caleb left before he hired someone to help him with the store. Of course, Harold hasn't replaced Caleb. Hiram doesn't give Harold half the responsibility that Caleb had, and he only teaches the new man enough so that he can do little things around the store. He certainly isn't going to start training someone else's boy to run his store. Most of the time, Hiram is confident that his son will take over when the time comes.

"I want you to run this bag of food out to the Benson place. See if you can give it to her directly and not leave it on the porch."

Harold is bigger than Caleb but not as old. He dropped out of school a few years back. For a while, he hunted deer and bear and trapped beaver in the mountains, but there wasn't enough money in that anymore. He worked on the railroad for a time, but his widowed mother didn't want him gone so much. Hiram turned him down the first time Harold asked for a job after Caleb left, but then he realized Caleb would be gone for a while, and he needed somebody to help with the work. Harold was as good as any of the other young fellows who hadn't left town.

"She don't come to the door when I knock. I can't force her to come out."

"Okay, you just be sure you knock and wait a spell; give her a chance to get there before you leave. You can do that much."

"I told you, that's what I done the last time."

Hiram believes him. When Hiram had taken the bag of groceries out to the house on the edge of town in mid-September, he had knocked on the door and waited. Because he had not seen Margaret for over a month, he had stood on the porch and called her name. He had heard sounds inside the house, but the curtains had been pulled tightly across the windows, and she had not come to the door. Later that day when he walked by to check, the bag he had left on the porch was gone. That had reassured him, but he was still worried.

Harold picks up the bag. "When does she pay you?"

"That's none of your concern."

Harold starts for the back door, carrying the bag to his bicycle. "This is a lot of food for one person." He stops and turns back to Hiram, who stands behind the counter. "I've heard people talk that there's somebody else that lives in that house besides her,

24

a feller who's got somethin' bad wrong with him. But then some say he died a long time ago, and others say there never was such a one."

"Harold, aren't you old enough and smart enough not to believe what folks 'round here say about other folks?"

"Yes sir." He turns to the door. "I'll knock real loud and wait a long time, like you told me."

Later in the day Harold tells his boss that he knocked real loud, called her name over and over, and waited a long time, but Margaret never came.

Margaret's father Paul had been Hiram's best friend all though childhood and right up to the time he had come to him one night and said, "I can't take it no more, Hiram." Together, they had hunted in the mountain forests, fished in the creeks, swum in the French Broad River, played hooky from the one room school house, pulled the girls' pigtails and worked in the rocky tobacco fields that extended up the hillsides. They had even catted together in Knoxville that time before they got religion at the river bank revival and were baptized proper. Each married a woman he'd known all his life and settled down, Hiram to help his grandfather with the store, Paul to cut timber on mountain sides. But Paul's burden had been greater and, perhaps, his faith weaker.

After Paul took off, Hiram never saw him again, but from time to time he would get an envelope in the mail with a bit of money. He had known what to do with it. The last money had arrived years ago; Caleb and Margaret had been seven, and Phronia and Ruth had still been alive.

Phronia was the first to die. Caleb was twelve, and only Margaret could console him. "Consumption," the doctor in Knoxville pronounced, and she came back to Newport to wither away, like the mountain laurel in winter. Hiram buried her beside his Ma on the hill overlooking the creek.

When Ruth died four years later, Margaret sent word to Hiram, who went into the Benson home to bring out the body. He had not even known she was sick. It was his first time in the house since Margaret had been born. Margaret stood in the hall, silent and wet-eyed, watching him carry her mother over the porch and onto the wagon in the yard. He expected that Margaret would go live with Ruth's sister in Nashville. However, a week after the funeral, the sister was gone, and Margaret remained in the house.

Some of the town women had been stirred up about a girl that age living by herself. Hiram had reassured them that he and Caleb would look after her. The talk had subsided, and after a while, it appeared to Hiram that most of the folks had pretty much forgotten about Margaret.

Hiram is not one to be overly curious about others. Valuing his own privacy, he respects the privacy of his neighbors. But in the weeks following Ruth's death, sometimes he would replay in his mind that brief time he had been inside her home. He could not keep himself from brooding about what he suspected was behind the closed door of the other bedroom.

Late in the afternoon Rebecca Shelton cheerfully enters the store to buy some sugar and flour.

"Gonna bake a cake?"

"Yes sir, goin' on a picnic tomorrow."

"Hope it's a good day for it."

"Me too."

Hiram plans to show her the letter, if she asks about Caleb. But she doesn't. She has not come into the store for several weeks. For the past two Sundays, he has seen her sitting in church with the pastor's boy, Jeremiah.

After he eats dinner and washes the dish and pan, Hiram sits in his chair in the small circle of light from the candle and picks up his Bible. Opening it to the first page, he removes the four other letters he has received from his son and reads each one. None is any longer than the new one, which he reads again. It has been five months.

He had been sitting in his chair, reading the Bible. Caleb had entered from the kitchen, where he had cleaned up from the dinner, and was standing before his father, tears in his eyes.

"Pa, I'm going away for a while."

It took Hiram a moment to register what he had heard. He laid the Bible on the table and stood to face his son. What do you mean, you're going away? I have to go. Why? Why do you have to go? What's happened? Are you in some kind of trouble? I can't talk about it now, Pa. I just have to go. I'm sorry. If it's something you've done, tell me. We can pray. We'll kneel right here before God and pray, my son. I can't. I have to go. Tell me, son, please. I can't. What about Rebecca? Does she know? Rebecca? I thought you and Rebecca would be... I can't. I must go.

Alone, Hiram sat in a circle of despair, his life upended like a tree in a tumultuous storm. Later he went into his son's room, stood in the dark and thought of the night he was born. He lit the lantern that Caleb kept by his window. Nothing was gone; everything was in its place, except Caleb. He walked over to the chest and pulled out the top drawer to see if it was still there. That's where Caleb kept it, the 1894 silver dollar. It was gone; he had taken it with him, his prized possession.

"This is for you." Phronia had said from her bed so many years ago. "It was coined the year of your birth. Keep it to remember your mother."

Hiram lays his son's letters on the table and studies the names and dates written on the first page of the Bible. He reads his grandfather's scrawl, his father's name, the name of a man he has no memory of.

Paul's Pa he does remember, a broken man who returned from the war with only one leg and a jagged scar on his head where no hair grew, to sit on the porch, the jug at his side, chunking rocks at the dogs and chickens, and sometimes the children, while his wife and kids struggled to deliver subsistence from the rocky soil. Until one, day he died. By the time Paul was a man, his Ma was dead, and his brothers and sister were gone, to Knoxville and beyond.

Hiram scans the column of births; Caleb's is the last one recorded.

Phronia had suffered pains for hours by the time Aunt Jete arrived. "Must be a night for birthings." She muttered as she set the water on the wood stove for boiling.

"Have you been at the Benson's?" Hiram asked.

"That's right, and a long time, too." She looked at him. The big wart on her chin bobbed up and down when she spoke. "Now you go sit in that chair and read the Bible while your woman and me take care of things. You menfolk can start things up fine, but ya ain't no use when it's time to finish it."

But Hiram was persistent. "What do they have, a boy or a girl?"

Aunt Jete stopped pulling things out of her bag and looked at him. She reminded him of the old school teacher they had one year, the one who wouldn't let him and Paul get away with anything. "One of each. Now you git outa here and let me git ready."

"Twins, Paul and Ruth have twins!"

"That's what I said, and I aint gonna say no more 'bout it. You git on outa here."

It was not until late the next morning, after the midwife had left and Hiram had held his son and his exhausted wife and then had seen them both sleeping, that he made it over to the Benson place. He should have suspected something was wrong when, instead of inviting him inside, Paul had come out on the porch. He did not look like a man who was celebrating two new children, but Hiram, immersed in his own joy, did not notice this initially. Hiram told him at once about Caleb, and his best friend managed a smile and found his right hand.

"Congratulations, Hiram. That's wonderful. The Lord has blessed you and Phronia."

"I hear you've got yourself two at one time."

He watched Paul look past him to stare at something in the distance, and he saw the grief in his friend's eyes.

"Only got one now, Hiram. The little boy's dead."

They stood silently together on the porch until Hiram said, "I'm mighty sorry, Paul. Can I do anything for you and Ruth?"

Paul looked at him. "Hiram, all I ask is that you never say nothin' about the poor little feller to me or anybody else again. He's gone from the world."

Four years later, when Paul had come to him and told him that he couldn't take it anymore, Hiram had almost broken his promise.

Hiram finishes his review of the births and deaths recorded in the Bible. As a breeze carries the chirping of crickets through the open window, he wonders if some day there will be another birth to record, and he ponders who will be there to write his name in the book when his time comes.

After laying the letters in their place, he turns the pages to Luke, Chapter 15 and begins to read.

Still restless after reading the parable of the prodigal son, he decides to take a walk. Under the half moon and the canopy of stars, the valley is peaceful. As he walks, he breathes in the comfort of the dark mountain in the distance and absorbs the familiar calls of the bull frogs in the creek. Most of the houses are dark. Soon, he finds himself standing in the dirt road in front of Margaret's place. Through the darkness, he can barely discern the swing on the porch, and he recalls the music that they had played on that porch many years ago, before the kids had been born: Byard Ray on the fiddle, Paul on the banjo, Hiram on the guitar. Paul had never again played his banjo after Margaret came along, and Hiram had not touched his guitar since Phronia had passed.

As he stands contemplating the silent house, he hears the whistle from the ten o'clock freight train in the distance. When the train passes through town, it slows down enough that a man could hitch a ride on it, if he wanted to leave town in the night.

After Paul ran off, Ruth rarely left the place. Neighbors would see her tending to the garden or hanging wash on the line or collecting eggs from the hen house, and every so often she'd be observed sitting on the porch swing in the evening.

Sometimes, Phronia and Hiram would come over to sit with Ruth on the porch and watch the two children chase the chickens and dogs in the yard and play hide-and-go-seek. But then Phronia became too weak to go out. She and Ruth did not see each other during those last few months.

In the fall and periodically through the winter, Hiram would go over and chop wood for Ruth and Margaret, and in the Spring he would plow up the garden plot behind their house. When Caleb got big enough, he took over these duties.

One summer day when the kids were about ten, Hiram went over to the Benson's to get his son for dinner. Caleb and Margaret were playing in back, and when he walked behind the house he saw something on the back porch.

Later that evening Hiram and his son sat on their porch, watching the sun fade. Phronia was finishing up in the kitchen.

"Caleb, who was that on the porch?"

Caleb shifted in his chair and waited a while to answer. "I can't tell, Pa. I promised Margaret." The boy stood up and went into the house. They never spoke of it again.

After her mother died, Margaret quit going to school and rarely left the house. Like her mother, she could be seen working in the garden or hanging out the wash, but folks rarely saw her sitting in the swing. Caleb would deliver the groceries every week.

"She's doing alright." He would tell his father.

Hiram had always been proud of Caleb. He had tried to interest his son in the state college in Knoxville. He imagined his son coming back to Newport as a lawyer or doctor or real preacher. All along, the teachers told him the boy had an aptitude for learning. Caleb said no to college. He loved the forests and streams of the mountains, the eagles along the river, the deer in the meadow. His future was the general store that his great-grandpa had started after the war and his father ran.

Caleb had been content to live among his people, until something had happened, something momentous. Hiram agonizes over what it was; it gnaws at him like a hookworm. His son's absence is a hole at the very center of his life.

The sound of the train empties into the distance. In the partial moonlight, rumpled remains of corn stalks form dark skeletal shapes in the exhausted garden between the house and the creek.

Two summers back, Hiram had found Margaret on a late afternoon picking beans in that garden patch. He had walked between the rows of plants and squatted beside the kneeling woman. She turned to look at him, a faded straw hat partially concealing her face. Sweat pooled at the base of her neck. He recognized one of Ruth's dresses.

"Good afternoon, Mister Fowler. Out for a walk?"

"Yeah, it's a good day for it." He looked into the large bucket, almost full of beans. "That's a right mess of beans you've got there, Margaret."

"Yes sir, it's a good crop."

He listened to the bees buzzing in the tassels of the near-by corn. "Are you doin' okay, Margaret? Do you have everything you need?"

"Oh yes, thank you. I'm doin' just fine." She dropped a pair of plump beans into the bucket.

He watched her pluck a handful from low-lying vines, her callused fingers moving deftly. "Caleb and me would be pleased if you'd join us for supper tomorrow night." It was a frequently offered invitation.

She paused and looked at him again. "Thank you, Mister Fowler. I'm much obliged, but I reckon I'll stay 'round here." It was her usual polite refusal.

"It might do you good to get away for a spell. We'd be mighty happy to have you eat with us."

"I'm doin' fine here; I don't need to get away." She returned to her picking.

Hiram shifted on his haunches. Now was the time; he was going to do it.

"How's he doin'?" He asked softly.

She turned to him, her eyes hidden, her lips quivering. "What... what... how? Did...?"

"Caleb didn't tell me, Margaret. He's kept your secret. I figured it out myself." He looked into her shadowed face and saw Paul. "Let me help, please."

She gathered the bucket, stood up and turned away from him. "I've got to get these beans snapped." He watched her climb onto the back porch and enter the house.

Later Caleb said, "Pa, I know you mean well, but there ain't nothin' we can do."

"Why?"

"I don't understand it myself."

Hiram starts home, his boots crunching dead leaves in the dry road. When he looks back at the house, he thinks he sees an orange glow slivered between the curtains of a side window. Is Margaret still up? He considers knocking on the door, but quickly realizes that she would be frightened by such a late-night intrusion. Still, he knows that soon he must see his old friend's daughter. It's been far too long. Aware of his fatigue, Hiram makes his way home in the partial moonlight, ready for bed.

Awakening to a noise, Hiram lies in bed momentarily disoriented. It is still dark outside his window. Suddenly, he recognizes the ringing of the church bell; something bad is happening. Within a minute he is dressed and in the road, where he sees figures with lanterns, running. He smells it before he turns eastward and sees the red glow silhouetted against the blackness of Broken Pine Mountain. Instantly, he knows what it is and starts running, his fifty-six-year old legs fueled by fear. A moment later the horse-drawn fire wagon rattles by. When he is in sight of the burning building and can see the flames tearing at the wood and the smoke belching into the night sky, he starts yelling, "Get 'em out! Get 'em out! Get 'em out!"

He's still yelling it when Harold and his cousin Rollie grab him a few feet from the flames. "We've got to get 'em out. We've got to save them." With futility, he thrashes at the restraining hands.

"Mister Fowler, we don't know that she's in there. She might've got out. We don't know. You can't go in there; you'll get burnt up." Harold clutches Hiram tightly.

Winded from the run, Hiram struggles to talk. Harold continues to hold him; Rollie relaxes his grip.

"She's probably got out. Some of the women folks are looking 'round for her. I bet they find her soon, but we need to work on the fire. You don't want that dry grass over there to catch fire."

Hiram breathes through molasses, and his legs feel like fifty-pound sacks of potatoes. The wisdom of Rollie's words sinks in. "Okay Harold, let me go. I ain't gonna go in there."

"Good." Harold releases him. "They're puttin' on the water from the wagon, and there's a bucket brigade formin' from the creek. Let's go over and help out."

Hiram gains control of his heaving chest. "You boys go help with the buckets. I'm gonna look for her."

"You ain't gonna go in that fire, are you, Mister Fowler?" Rollie peers at him.

"No, don't worry 'bout me. You fellows go get the fire out."

Rollie leaves to join the bucket brigade. Harold stays, facing his boss, his face black against the red flames, his voice emerging from the crackling of the fire and shouts of the men.

"Them. You said get them out. Who else was in that house, Mister Fowler?"

Hiram studies the dark form of the young man before him. "That doesn't concern you, Harold. You go over and help with the fire."

Hiram walks through the dead corn stalks and dried up bean and squash plants, calling for Margaret. He walks down by the creek, repeating her name. Finally, he walks among the trees on the other side of the creek, but he doesn't find Paul's daughter.

He stands in the road and watches the flames. He remembers the time that Caleb was laid up in bed with a broken arm from falling out of the willow tree, and how Margaret came over every day and petted him. She seemed to know just what to do to cheer up a miserable boy.

By dawn, the remnants of the house are merely smoldering. Most of the folks have gone home. After Harley Nelson finishes winding the water hose on the wagon, he comes over to where Hiram stands.

"No sign of her?"

"No."

"It's a crying shame." He removes his smoke-grimed hat and rubs the sleeve of his filthy shirt over the side of his face. "She had a rough life."

Hiram doesn't respond to that, but when Harley starts to go back to the wagon, he says, "I'm gonna go have a look around in it?"

"It's still mighty hot."

"I have my heavy boots on."

"Alright Hiram, if you're set on goin' in now, I'll go with you. Don't go touchin' nothin'; you'll get burnt for sure."

35

Following Harley, Hiram walks through the rubble of the front porch into the smoldering ashes of the living room. The heat penetrates his boots to embrace his feet, but he keeps on walking. He recognizes charred bits of tables and chairs. The stench and smoke make him cough.

"You alright, Hiram?" Harley looks back at him.

"Yeah."

Moving cautiously, he picks his way through where the hall had been and past the kitchen. Up ahead, he sees that Harley has stopped in the room where Hiram had found Ruth's body years before. Harley is starring down into the ashes. Hiram moves over to him, looks down and sees it too. He has seen other burned bodies, the white bones amidst the ashes, the congealed blackened flesh, and he knows he is looking at Margaret. She seems to be lying on her side.

"Who the hell is that?"

Then Hiram sees the other one. Beside Margaret, there is someone else, much smaller than her, a charred form, a twisted deformity that defied the fire. To Hiram the two burned bodies seem to blend together, the secret finally exposed.

"That's her twin brother." Hiram speaks with calm certainty.

"Her brother! I'll be damned. I'd heard rumors 'bout that, but I never put no stock into it. If that ain't the damndest thing." The town constable removes his hat and with it fans misty smoke from his face. "It don't look like they even tried to get out at all. They just lay there together and burned up."

Hiram doesn't say anything. He bends forward into the odor of burned flesh to get a better look at something that he has just noticed, something very small and very black in the dark crevice between the sister and brother. Harley sees it, too.

"Damned if that don't look like a little baby there, laying between the two of 'em. Did she have a baby?"

Hiram doesn't answer. He straightens up and gazes at Broken Pine Mountain, where fingers of the natal sun streak the sky a fiery orange. How could he have allowed this to happen?

As Harley moves away from the scene, muttering to himself, something catches Hiram's eye, a glint of metal through a layer of ash beside what remains of Margaret's arm. He removes the handkerchief from his pocket. When Harley's back is turned, he quickly bends down, reaches into the hot ashes, picks up the round flat object with the handkerchief, and drops it into his pocket. Immediately, he feels its heat pierce the cloth of his pants and burn his thigh. He stuffs the handkerchief between the hot metal and his leg to ease the pain.

"I've got to get home, Harley."

At home, Hiram dunks the coin in a bucket of water to cool it off and get rid of the soot that cakes most of it. When it is clean and shiny, he inspects it more carefully to discover what he already knows: It is an 1894 silver dollar.

Hiram sits in his chair and picks up the Bible. He dips the pen in the ink well, opens the book and inscribes a name followed by the day's date at the bottom of the list of births. He dips the pen again and adds the same name and date to the list of deaths. For the last time, he dips the pen in the black ink and adds the name of his beloved son to the column of deaths. He sets the book and the pen down on the table and strikes a match across the sole of his boot. One by one, with the flame, he lights the letters that he removes from the Bible and watches them turn to ash on the floor.

What the Box Held

Aunt Hattie died in church on a Saturday evening. Maw said that's the way she'd have wanted it, but I was still sad. Then three days later I was sad in a different way.

Aunt Hattie was my great-grandmother, but everybody called her Aunt Hattie. Until she died of cancer when I was nine, Mamaw called her own mother Aunt Hattie. Once, when I was little I asked Maw why folks called her Aunt Hattie when she wasn't really aunt to any of them, and she said that had been her name for as long as she could remember.

It was getting on towards the end of April when Horace and I went over to Aunt Hattie's to help her finish putting in her garden. She lived down the road from us; you could see her house across the field from ours. In the summer it was a tobacco field, and that Saturday Paw was plowing it up. Horace was fourteen and I was twelve. The potatoes and lettuce and spinach and peas and onions were already coming up in her garden, and we were going to help her plant pole beans and sweet corn and butter beans and okra.

Soon after we got to her house I could tell things weren't right with Aunt Hattie. She moved slower than usual. Sure enough, when we were standing on her back porch watching Horace lug the hoes and seeds and bucket of manure out to the garden plot, she said, "Emmy Sue, I feel kinda puny this mornin'. I reckon you chil'ren will hafta do mosta the work."

She puttered around a bit in the garden, showing us where to lay out the rows, and she shooed away the chickens so they wouldn't eat the seeds. But mostly she sat on the back porch and watched. I'd look over there often, and sometimes I'd see her pass her hand over her chest and make a face. Other times she was fanning herself, even though I knew it was cool in the shade of the porch.

It felt real strange not having her out there with us, putting the seeds in the ground. Every once in a while, she had us come over to the porch to drink some ice tea and rest a spell. Towards noon I noticed her knitting on a blanket she was making for Sadie Pritchard's baby that wasn't born yet.

The best thing about helping Aunt Hattie put in her garden was the coconut cake we got to eat for lunch dessert. She could bake a cake better than anybody I've ever known, and coconut was my favorite.

After lunch and before Horace and I went back to the garden, Cale Forbes brought Aunt Hattie's groceries from his daddy's store up at the head of the road. Cale was in Horace's grade at school, and on Saturday he would deliver groceries on his bicycle to old folks in Little Branch. Horace told me Cale was sweet on me, and I saw him give me the eye when he carried the bag into the kitchen that day, but I paid him no mind.

On Saturdays, people always dropped by Aunt Hattie's to visit with her. That morning Jake Colburt came by while Horace and I rested on the porch, so I heard what he said.

"Aunt Hattie, you have these young-uns puttin' those beans in too early this year. They gonna come up, and the frost's gonna bite 'em off for sure."

Aunt Hattie rocked easy in her chair and looked at her cow that grazing on the other side of the fence; her hands kept on working the knitting needles. "I don't reckon it's too early, but if the frost knocks 'em out, we'll just plant 'em again."

Horace and I looked at each other and giggled. Nobody knew better about when to plant a garden than Aunt Hattie. Everybody said that she grew the best vegetables in Little Branch.

She'd been dodging the frost since before Jake Colburt was born, and he wasn't a young man.

After a while Mister Colburt said "Guess I'll see you folks in church this evenin'," and left.

We were in the garden when Beulah and Bertha Hocks came by after lunch, so I didn't hear what they said to Aunt Hattie. I figured it was something about the quilt they were making with Aunt Hattie, or Jesse Porter being drunk, or Bonnie Pratt being laid up with a broken hip in the hospital, or Harvey Forbes shooting at Able Hawke's hound dog, or Rennie Ramsey's daughter being in the family way without a husband, or most likely all those things and a lot more. I watched Aunt Hattie; she just kept on rocking and knitting. I knew she'd rather be out working with us than listening to those busy-body sisters. I hoped she'd feel better soon.

By the middle of the afternoon, we had finished. Horace went home after eating another piece of cake. I scrubbed the dirt off my hands. I could tell Aunt Hattie wanted me to stay for a while, nothing she said, just the way she acted. I could tell that she still felt poorly.

"Emmy Sue, I'm gonna lay down for a spell. If anybody comes, tell 'em I'm restin'."

For her to lie down in the daytime was real unusual, and I got worried. I remembered when she had been sick in bed the winter I was ten. Maw had stayed over at her house almost all the time. Preacher Hall had come by twice a day to pray over her, and a bunch of others had come to pray and to help Maw mop her brow and feed her broth and to bring food. I never saw so much food. Maw said some of them had come to see for themselves that Aunt Hattie was really sick in bed. Nobody could recall that happening before. Usually, it was Aunt Hattie who tended to the sick.

Maw had been worried and kept asking Aunt Hattie if she wanted her to call the doctor from Marshall. But Aunt Hattie said no, she'd trust in the Lord, and if it was her time to go, there's nothing a doctor could do. Mary Coke Lukens sat up with Aunt Hattie one night so Maw could get some sleep. Aunt Hattie got better in a few days. But now she was lying down in the middle of the day, and I was scared. I thought about calling Maw, but Aunt Hattie hadn't told me to do that, so I didn't.

I sat in her living room on one of her old chairs with the hard back. Maw said all the furniture was ancient, probably seventy years old, which was about how long Aunt Hattie had lived in the house. She'd grown up on Sandy Bottom Creek. My great-grandpa married her and brought her to the home he built on the other side of Bone Mountain near Cracked Rock Creek. She'd been eighteen.

With the breeze coming through the window, it was cool in the room. I looked at the picture of Jesus on the wall and then at all the pictures of family on the table. There was an old yellow one of Mamaw as a little girl, and another old one of her brother Riley who died in the first World War. There were pictures of Maw and her brothers and quite a few of me and Horace. In my fourth-grade picture, I had on the blue dress Aunt Hattie had made for me. The big Bible sat across the room on the smaller table by itself; my birthday was written in it, February 5, 1950.

Aunt Hattie's dog barked outside, and I heard somebody on the front porch. A woman's high-pitched voice calling Aunt Hattie followed the knock on the door. I opened the door to find Preacher Hall's wife. I told her Aunt Hattie was resting.

"Is she sick, Honey?"

"No ma'am, she got a mite tired plantin' the garden."

She looked at me suspiciously, and I figured she'd heard from the Hocks sisters about how Aunt Hattie had been sitting on the porch instead of working in the garden. But she didn't say anything about that; she just looked at me a while. I figured she was waiting for me to invite her in and go get Aunt Hattie, but I didn't. She finally said, "Hope to see you-uns in church this evenin'," and left.

Aunt Hattie had these books of poetry. "Emmy Sue," she had told me, "poetry opens up a whole new world." Emily Dickinson was our favorite. That afternoon, while Aunt Hattie rested, I turned on the lamp and read some of Emily Dickinson's poems. I read the one about somebody dying in a house and the mattress being brought out. It gave me goose bumps.

About time for supper, I heard her stirring in the bedroom, and soon she came out and told me to go home to eat. I didn't like the way she looked and offered to fix her supper. She said she would heat up some pork meat and turnip greens, and she shooed me home.

While Maw fixed our supper, I mentioned that Aunt Hattie had taken a nap. She turned and looked at me real serious. Then she told me to tend to the cooking and hurried over to Aunt Hattie's house. She came back about the time we were sitting down to eat. She told Paw that he'd need to take Aunt Hattie to church in the pickup, but she didn't say anything else. Horace and I looked at each other; we knew that Aunt Hattie must be bad off.

Even though the church was just down the road from the house, we all rode to prayer meeting that evening, with Aunt Hattie squeezed between Maw and Paw in the cab, and Horace and me in the back. Folks looked at us funny. The only other truck at the church was the Hobgood's; they lived up Henry's Fork and always rode to church. Walking to church on Wednesday and Saturday evenings and Sunday mornings was something we did in Little Branch hollow unless it was raining or snowing or bitter cold.

The sun had set behind Craggy Mountain when Maw and Paw helped Aunt Hattie descend from the truck into the shadows of the church yard. She clutched the Bible that she always brought to church. Folks gathered around her, speculating and inquiring about her health.

She kept patiently saying hello to the folks in the church yard. "I'm doing fine, just a little tired this evenin'." She repeated several times.

Frowning, Maw steered her around knots of the curious and concerned to the church door. Horace and I followed them. Paw lagged behind, talking to Hap Pickett about whether it would rain that night. I looked up at the darkening cloudless sky.

As we entered the church, I heard Aunt Hattie say to Maw, "I thank the Lord that He's let me live long enough to come to church today." I couldn't see Maw's face. I shuddered.

The church was a simple wooden building with a dirt floor worn smooth by generations of worshipers. The two windows on each side were open. Three big overhead lights lit the room. Benches with no backs were arranged on either side of a central aisle. At the front stood the piano that Mary Coke Lukens played while we sang. We had no hymn books; we sang the songs we knew by heart over and over. A lot of folks couldn't read anyway. There was no pulpit; the preacher stood up front to address the congregation and the Lord.

The church was the center of life in Little Branch when I was growing up. Aunt Hattie had been married in the church, and her husband, dead from the 1919 influenza epidemic, lay in the graveyard behind it. She loved that old church.

On the evening Aunt Hattie died, we sat as we always did on our bench on the right side, with Paw's brother, Uncle Eddie, and Aunt Rachel and our three cousins. Aunt Hattie sat as usual at the end next to the aisle, with Maw beside her and Paw beside Maw and then Horace and then me, with Aunt Rachel on the other side. The church was full that night, so when Aunt Hattie got in the aisle along with the others to praise the Lord and pray, I couldn't see her.

Even though it was called prayer meeting, Preacher Hall still preached a sermon on Saturday nights. Horace said it was to rev folks up for Sunday morning, but I don't think he ever told that to anyone else but me. That night the sermon was about Daniel in the lion's den, and Preacher Hall talked a lot about trusting the Lord and fighting the devil and keeping yourself pure.

Some of the folks got worked up along with the preacher, and they started in with "praise the Lord" and "hallelujah" and "yes brother" and "preach the word." Then the Hocks sisters and Elmer Jordan were in the aisle throwing their arms around and shouting and speaking those words that you couldn't understand. And soon others joined them, kneeling and praying. It became the usual Saturday evening prayer meeting.

But then something different happened: Aunt Hattie got up and stepped into the aisle. I saw Maw grab for her arm, but Aunt Hattie ignored her and moved forward up the aisle. Maw started to go after her but Paw reached out and stopped her. The look on Maw's face is something I will never forget. I couldn't see Aunt Hattie anymore; I started to cry. Horace shushed me and said that Aunt Hattie was kneeling to pray. People clustered in the aisle where I thought she was. They all sang and prayed and chanted, and the preacher paced back and forth up front, shouting about being saved and defeating Satan.

After a while, the tumult died down, and the preacher spread his arms high in the air for the final prayer. We stood at our bench. I still couldn't see Aunt Hattie. I tried to stifle my sobs. Tears streamed down Maw's face, and Paw had his arm around her.

As soon as Preacher Hall finished, Maw rushed forward. I reached the end of the bench and looked for Aunt Hattie. A bunch of people stood in the aisle looking down at the ground. Maw pushed between two men, calling for Aunt Hattie. I heard the voices.

"Get up, Aunt Hattie, the service is over."

"She's mighty still."

"The spirit got hold of her tonight."

"Hollis, she ain't moving none."

"She's uncommonly blue."

"Is she dead? Is Aunt Hattie dead?"

Maw had disappeared into the mass of people, and then I heard her shriek, and I saw Paw dive into the pack. Soon, he came back out pulling Maw, who was beating on his arms and crying. I was bawling, and Horace was holding me back.

Jake Colburt came up and put one hand on my shoulder and the other on Horace's shoulder and said, "Let's go outside."

Crying, I turned and looked again at the knot of people. The men were peering down; some were squatting as country men do when they're studying on something. Women sobbed. Beulah and Bertha Hocks clutched each other and wailed. Preacher Hall prayed loudly. On the ground, I could see a small patch of Aunt Hattie's gray dress between the bodies, where she lay dead, surrounded by the people with whom she had lived, the people who had made up her world.

Three days after we put Aunt Hattie in the ground I sat on the bank of Carved Rock Creek with the old box Aunt Hattie had entrusted to me in my lap. I had only seen the box one other time. Around Christmas, she had asked me to dig down in the bottom drawer in her bedroom and bring her an old shoe box she kept there.

We sat at the kitchen table near the wood stove to stay warm. The light outside was fading fast, and the wind howled through the back porch, rattling the wash tub. I dreaded the walk home; I knew I would freeze despite my heavy coat. Bundled in her sweater, Aunt Hattie sat with the box in her lap and looked at me real serious, like when she told the story of Ruth and Naomi from the Bible or told me how I had to be nice to Sally Pickett, even though she wasn't right in the head and couldn't talk normal and slobbered all the time.

"Emmy Sue, when I die I want you to get this box and destroy what's in it."

I wasn't thinking about the box at all; I was fixated completely on the idea of her dying, and I couldn't stand it.

She knew what I was thinking and said "Now don't worry none, I'm not plannin' on dyin' any time soon. But we both know I'm not gonna live forever, wouldn't want to." She looked at me and smiled a little. I tried to smile back. "What's in here are things important to me, but not to another livin' soul. When I'm gone they should be gone too. You understand?"

I trembled. "Yes ma'am," I stammered.

"I don't want you burnin' this unless you're full grown enough to handle matches. You can tear the things up into little bitty pieces and throw them in the creek." She was looking right into me. I was swimming in her eyes. "I don't want nobody else to see what's in here." She stopped and peered intently at me, and I realized that she was letting me know that it was okay for me to look at what the box held.

That's how I came to be sitting on the creek bank late on a spring afternoon, discovering Aunt Hattie's secret. Except I didn't know that's what it was at the time; it took a while for me to figure it all out. What I saw at the time was a bunch of letters written over a forty-year period by Your Dearest Gladys. The oldest were yellowed and brittle and crumbly, and I couldn't read many of the words written in black ink that had faded into the decaying paper. The last one was dated June 10, 1951. I could read most of the more recent ones, from the 1930s and 1940s. Some of them had lines from poems that I recognized. From studying the letters, I was able to put it together that Your Dearest Gladys had moved away from where Aunt Hattie lived, to Asheville. She had been real sad to leave. Later, she had moved to Greensboro where she taught school for a long time. The last letter told how she was sick.

As I read what I could of the letters, a strange feeling stirred deep inside me and began to build. I felt something I'd never felt before, a type of fear I guess. I felt like Aunt Hattie was slipping away, was dying again, and I was scared, but also angry. It was like I didn't know the woman who had received and saved these letters. I didn't want to know her. But I had known her, and loved her, as much as anyone I knew. It seemed that Aunt Hattie wasn't Aunt Hattie any more.

I couldn't read any more of it. Tears streaming down my cheeks, I stood up and started tearing the letters into little pieces, my hands going hard and fast, ripping the old yellow pages and throwing them as fast as I could in the flowing water of Cracked Rock Creek. In a fury, I ripped that old box to shreds and heaved it in after the pieces of paper. And I watched the little pieces of great-grandma's letters float down the creek, bounce against the rocks, swirl around in the little eddies and whirlpools, and finally disappear down the clear water that coursed through Little Branch hollow.

I reckon I've thought about that afternoon on the creek bank more than I've thought about any other day of my life. I gradually came to accept that Aunt Hattie had a secret world apart from the world of Little Branch, a world of desire and love and poetry. It was a world that brought suffering, but a world that she cherished. It was a world that she shared with me. I would give just about anything to have those letters back, to be able to read them and to feel in a small way the pain and the joy that they brought my great-grandma.

At first when I wondered why Aunt Hattie had chosen me, I was confused and frightened. As I grew older, I began to realize that even then she knew something about me that it took me a long time to learn about myself. After I graduated from high school, I went off to train to be a practical nurse in Greensboro. Maw couldn't understand why I didn't go study at the hospital in Asheville, which was so much closer. I wasn't able to explain to her my need to get away and the pull that Greensboro had on me.

I've never gone back to Little Branch to live, but that life is a part of me, and I visit Maw from time to time. Paw's dead; Horace and his family live in Atlanta, and Maw lives alone in our old house. But she's not alone; there are people all around her whom she's known and loved all her life. Yet, I've wondered if Maw has a secret life that she protects at the bottom of some drawer.

Me? In Greensboro I looked for Your Dearest Gladys for a long time. I finally found her; only her name is Beverly.

Faith

I inched along in the jammed traffic on the Raleigh Beltway, watching the crimson streaks slowly dissolve in the western sky. On the radio, NPR started an interview with some fundamentalist preacher, who insisted that the survival of Western civilization depended on the defeat of Bill Clinton in the upcoming election. I found Conway Twitty on another station, not my favorite music but still a big improvement. By the time I turned into the driveway, darkness had infiltrated the yard. Dry leaves rustled beneath my feet, and I saw the black coil of the water hose under the oak. Brandon needed reminding of his responsibilities. Wearily, I stepped into the light of the porch, thankful that I was not on call.

"Daddy." My daughter's voice welcomed me as I closed the door. "I'm in the kitchen."

I found her leaning over the center counter, spooning warmed up chili into her mouth and watching something on the TV across the room. While I poured a glass of Chardonnay, she told me that Brandon was eating at Lorie's house and that I had just missed their mother.

"Good."

"Now Daddy, don't be like that." She turned from the TV, strands of blond hair falling across her face. I saw Becky around her green eyes and her wet lips. "She wanted to talk to you but couldn't wait any longer."

"Sorry." I swallowed some wine. "Things were busy at the hospital. What did she want to talk about?"

"Several things, I think, but mainly she wanted to see if it was okay to do the hand off later, nine o'clock or maybe even ten. She's going to the mountains for the weekend with Greg." Karen stopped to drink from her can of diet soda. "I told her there wouldn't be any problem with us. I'm sure Brandon will be at Lorie's, and I'll be at the church making signs for the rally."

The pro-life rally at the capitol, I had heard so much about it already. I didn't know which irritated me the most, my ex-wife's weekend get-away with her boyfriend or another reminder of my 16-year old daughter's obsession with religion. Actually, neither should have bothered me at all; I'd had enough time to get used to each.

Not surprisingly, the kids had reacted to the divorce differently. Brandon had been fourteen at the time. His anger had slowly moved from explosions of rage to prolonged silences grounded in brooding resentment. In recent months, as far as I could tell, he had settled into a tenuous acceptance. While it was still touch and go between us, we could have conversations about sports and even his schoolwork that didn't end in shouting matches. I was encouraged that he seemed to be seriously considering colleges, although he avoided talking with me about it.

Faced with the divorce, Karen had turned to religion, something that her life had been mercifully free of for the first thirteen years. With the vigor of a convert, she had immersed herself in the religious fundamentalism of her best friend's church. Three years later, what I had hoped would be a brief phase showed every sign of solidifying into a long-term affliction. I still struggled to adjust to a daughter who prayed daily for my soul.

After the divorce, which we told everyone was amicable, Brandon and Karen continued to live in the house. I lived downtown near the hospital, and Julia moved into a condominium near the new country club. We took turns living with the kids, usually a week at a time, occasionally longer. I once did it for a month while Julia romped around Europe. We handed off the kids on Sunday night. At first, we made a special effort to eat Sunday supper together, like a family Karen had said, but this occurred less and less. Julia and I still tried to meet face-to face at the hand off, to discuss the kids, deal with any issues, she would say. Returning later than usual to my apartment would pose no problems for me; it wasn't as if I had a lot to do on Sunday nights.

"Nine or ten o'clock is okay with me. I'll give her a call tonight."

"Good. Call her late. She said something about going to a concert."

I watched my daughter place the empty bowl in the sink, toss her soda can in the recycle bag and turn off the TV. She moved confidently, like my sister at the same age.

"Maybe, I should remind you again what it was like in this country before Roe versus Wade." My voice was shaky. I finished the wine.

She made a face. "Don't waste your breath." No anger, just righteous certitude. She glanced at the clock on the wall. "Do you want me to pop something in the microwave for you before I go get ready?"

"Get ready?"

"Jennie and I are going to the church. A missionary who has been spreading the gospel in Russia is giving a talk."

"A missionary, I didn't know there were any missionaries left."

"Daddy, don't be that way." She turned from me, walked to the refrigerator and opened it. She was small, like her mother; the jeans and t-shirt reminded me that she was now a woman. "There's turkey, lasagna, and tuna. What's your pleasure?"

My pleasure? "Turkey."

Once, Julia consoled me that worse things than religious fanaticism could befall a daughter. I told her that I wasn't so sure of that. I knew of one consolation: My daughter's wide net of disapproval included her mother's year-long thing with a fellow teacher.

When she turned back to me from the refrigerator, her face reflected something that I had not seen there in a while.

"Daddy, I want to ask you something. It's important to me."

"Okay." I noted the slight tremor around her mouth.

"I'm leading prayer meeting next Wednesday night. It's my first time. Mom and Brandon are going, and it would mean a lot to me if you came too."

She had never asked me to go to church before, even when she had been baptized. I set the wine glass on the counter and looked past her to the large calendar on the refrigerator door, where the stick figures and lollipop trees she used to draw had hung so long ago. I steadied my voice. "I don't know; I'll need to see if I'm on call that night."

"I know, that's why I'm asking you now, so you can get someone to cover for you for a couple of hours if you're on call." Her voice was stronger; my self-assured daughter was returning. "I'm hoping we could all eat supper together at Antonio's before the service."

She had it all planned. Becky used to do that. I looked at Karen. Prayer meeting, I hadn't thought of that in years. Every Wednesday night, Reverend Kirkland, droning on, Becky and I, side by side, sneaking peaks at each other, making faces, each trying to make the other laugh while stifling our own giggles.

"I don't know, Honey. I'll need to think about it. You know about me and churches."

52

She came over and hugged me. "I know about it, but I don't understand it." I felt her arms tight around my chest. "Thanks for thinking about it. I hope you'll come."

Later, I poured myself another glass of wine and carried it through the dining room and into the den. I turned on the light. The faint scent of Julia lingered in the room, which I expunged with a bolus of wine. I found the newspaper on my chair underneath a glossy religious tract, placed by my always hopeful daughter. I laid the devotional on the arm of the chair, picked up the paper and sat down. It occurred to me to turn on the TV, but the remote was on a bookcase across the room. The wine tasted good. Karen moved around in her room overhead.

Suddenly, memories of another bedroom arose, and I saw Becky again lying unconscious amidst the bloody sheets of her bed. It was spring of our senior year; she and I had been accepted by Duke. After it ended, it was easy to see the signs that we had missed, even I, her twin. She'd been sick and acting differently for a couple of weeks. A torn uterus, the emergency room doctor told us. Nothing they could do by the time we got her there. We never found out who did it.

The church said no funeral. The church where we had been baptized, where our mother sang in the choir and our father was a deacon, the church of youth groups and picnics and hayrides, that church, no funeral for my sister. So, we stood in the sunshine and watched my sister put in the ground while a stranger uttered vacuous words into the April breeze. Mom and dad found another church.

Now, Karen wanted me to go to a prayer meeting.

The phone rang; it was Julia, on her way to the concert. I told her the late hand-off would be fine. But I knew that wasn't really why she had called or come by earlier.

"Did she ask you about next Wednesday night?" I could hear the tension in her voice.

"Yeah."

After a pause, "Well, what did you tell her?"

"I told her that I'd think about it."

"Well, that's better than an immediate rejection."

"Rejection?"

"John, you know that I think you're a good father to the kids, but you really should consider whether you want to continue to exclude yourself from such an important part of Karen's life."

I suppressed my initial response and then said, "Thanks for the advice about my daughter." I let that sink in. "Have fun this weekend; I'll see you Sunday night."

I didn't like my mood. I returned to the chair, swallowed the last of the wine and picked up *The News and Observer*. Most of the front page was devoted to the impending Clinton-Dole debate. I grunted and turned the page, looking for respite. On the way to the comics, a small headline caught my eye, and then I was in another place.

Shadows from the nearby mountains enveloped the former farmhouse cloistered amidst tobacco plants. In the back room, I was writing the last patient note, eagerly anticipating the evening ahead. Alma entered the room, interrupting my paper work with the bad news.

"There's a woman here with a sick kid. Do ya wanna see 'em?"

I looked up at her from the table. "Damn, who is it?"

"Don't know. Don't recall seein' 'em before,"

That surprised me. Having grown up and lived almost all of her life in the little Appalachian community, she knew virtually everyone who came to the clinic and was kin to many of them.

"What's wrong?"

"She says he's got a fever. Looks to be about two. There's two others with her, a girl who's older and a baby." The lines of Alma's face suggested fatigue. It had been a busy day. "What should I tell her?"

I sighed. "I'll see him. Put him in the room and take his temp."

"Okay, after that I'll need to leave. I've got to fix dinner and then get Betty Ann over to the school for a play. Can you lock up everything when you're through?"

"Yeah, I can manage." Alma could be a mother hen; sometimes, she acted like she was the only one who could take care of things. But I had practiced medicine in the clinic on Tuesdays and Thursdays for three years. I figured I could lock up the place.

She left the room. I resumed my writing, reassuring myself that this would only be a minor delay. I heard the murmur of voices and a child whimpering in the hallway. Several minutes later, Alma came in and handed me a sheet of paper.

"Temp's 102," she announced. "Mother seems frightened. I could stay a little while longer, if you want. None of my bunch will suffer much if they have to skimp on a meal."

"No, that's okay. I'll see you on Tuesday."

"Okay, have a good weekend."

"Weekend starts tonight."

She smiled. "Oh, hot date?"

"Hope so."

"Have fun."

I looked at the paper she had handed me. The boy's name was Joshua Colwin, with a birth date that made him almost two. Colwin, the name was familiar, but I couldn't place it. I retrieved my stethoscope from the bag and headed to the exam room. I tapped on the door before opening it.

A young woman stood by the table, holding a baby with her right arm and a larger child with her left. The baby slept; the other child, clad only in a tan t-shirt and cloth diapers, had red eyes and tear-streaked cheeks. He peered suspiciously at me. Beside the woman, a thin girl with curly blond hair stood, clutching a fistful of the woman's shabby gray dress, a well-used diaper bag at her feet.

"Hello, I'm Doctor Bingham." I smiled at the little girl and then at the boy. "Who's sick here?" I tried to be cheerful. The boy buried his face against his mother's neck. Turning her face to meet his, she whispered to him. I waited for her to speak. When she didn't, I squatted and faced the curly-haired girl. "What's your name?"

She stared at me in silence. A cow mooed in the nearby pasture. After a time, I heard a soft voice above my head. "She's Ruth. Her name's Ruth."

"Hi Ruth." There was no response. Her hair adorned a somber sun-browned face. Barefoot, she wore a faded green dress that extended to her knees. She appeared to be about four. "Are you a big sister?"

She turned her face up to her mother and shyly said, "Yes."

"I see that you have a baby. What's the baby's name?"

"Jacob." Whiteness of teeth blinked behind quivering lips. A cutie!

"Jacob. That's a good name." I patted a bare arm and stood up to face the mother and her burden.

56

"Is this Joshua?" I nodded towards the whimpering boy, whom she clasped to her body with one arm. His head continued to burrow into the side of her neck.

"Yes." She responded in a weak voice, and then a little stronger, "He's sick."

"I'm sorry to hear that. How's he been sick?"

"Feelin' hot, not eatin' much, layin' 'round." She paused and studied the floor. "They've all had colds, but he got worse."

"Has he been hurtin' anywhere?"

"His ear's been botherin' 'im."

"His ear?"

"Yeah, he's been cryin' with it mosta the day and night."

"I'm sorry. Anything else?"

"No."

"Is he usually healthy?"

"Oh yes, he don't get sick much. This is the sickest he's been."

Something in her dark eyes troubled me; I needed to reassure her. "Well, it's good that he's usually healthy. I'm sorry that he's sick now. Let's see what I can do to help."

She bent her head, rubbed her cheek against the top of his head and whispered something to him. Ruth stirred below.

"Where do you usually doctor?"

It was still in her eyes. She looked down at Ruth, huddled at her side. I could barely hear her. "Nowhere. We don't use doctors."

Don't use doctors - I encountered this on occasion. "Okay." Usually, this frustrated me. I watched her gaze shift from her daughter to the wall behind me. "Has he had his baby shots?" When there was no response, I added, "Shots, at the health department?"

She looked at me and spoke softly, "No, we don't believe in 'em."

"Don't believe in them." I stopped, waiting for the irritation to coil inside. Studying her, I was struck by how pretty she was, no make-up, a simple beauty common to the mountain women, an evanescent bloom.

"Okay, have a seat there in the chair. I need to check him over. You can hold him while I examine him. It won't take long."

She sat in the chair. Ruth held tightly to her mother's leg through the long dress. I sat on the rolling stool facing the four of them. The examination didn't take long and confirmed what I suspected, an ear infection. Joshua was fearful but passively compliant during most of the process; he cried when I looked in his ears. Ruth watched me intently. The crying woke up Jacob, and he squirmed and fretted. While trying to console Joshua, the mother shifted the baby to her lap and bounced him on a thigh.

I started on my explanation. "He's got an ear infection. That's what's makin' him sick." I stopped to wait for her response. The fear that Alma had sensed hung like a curtain between us. I resumed, "Has he had an ear infection before?"

"No."

"Well, it's common in children, and we can treat it. There's medicine you can give him to help him get better."

Determined eyes peered at me from her pale face. "No."

"No?"

"No medicine."

She looked at her sick son, who quietly eyed me and then at the baby, who whimpered in her lap. Instinctively, I wanted to reach over and assist her with the balancing act, as I customarily did in such situations, but I sat immobile, stymied. Outside the window, insects droned incessantly into the languid summer evening.

"I can't give him no medicine." She said, nostrils flaring slightly.

Arousing myself from the momentary passivity, I shifted on the stool. "Why not?"

Tightening her grip on Joshua, she focused on Ruth, who was caressing Jacob and whispering to him. Just before I repeated the questions, she said, "It would disrespect his daddy." Tears appeared in her eyes.

"Mommy."

"It's okay, Ruth. It's okay; tend to Jacob."

It hit me; I knew who she was, who the kids were. Colwin, yes, that was the name. I should have put it together sooner, recognized the name. It had been about four months earlier, in the spring, a church near the Tennessee line. The story had been all over the news, a young man, early twenties, named Colwin. So, he had left a wife and three little kids, the son of a bitch!

A tear clung to the widow's cheek. Both boys cried in her arms. Ruth fastened to her mother's leg, distraught. I sat there before them. While I struggled for something to say, a knock on the door rescued me.

"John, it's Alma." The welcomed voice came from outside the tension-filled room.

"Excuse me, it's the nurse. I'll be right back." I left the room and met Alma in the hallway. "What are you doing here?"

She touched my arm. "I figured out who they were half way home. I'm sorry I left you."

"Yeah, I just realized it myself. She basically had to tell me." We moved down the hall away from the exam room.

"What have you found?"

59

"Well, he has otitis media and needs ampicillin. She refuses. That's as far as it's gone. I don't know what to do." I knew how unfamiliar that admission must sound to her, but I didn't care.

She peered down the hallway at the closed door. "She brought him here; that's a good sign."

"Yeah, I don't know why she brought him when she won't let me treat him. I don't know how they got here."

"There's a man in a truck out front, a young guy. I don't recognize him. I figure he brought 'em."

I was glad Alma was there. "Well, what do we do? You're the expert on these religious fanatics."

She looked at me, and I was immediately sorry I had said it. This was not the time to provoke her. "Now, don't get off on that." She nodded towards the exam room. "Do you think they're fanatics in there?"

"No. You're right. I'm just frustrated as hell."

"Me too." Her face softened. "He needs ampicillin. She's torn, that's why she's here. Let's see if we can convince her to give it to 'im. All we can do is try."

"Okay."

We went back in the room. The woman had stopped crying. Ruth was sitting on her lap, holding Jacob. Joshua stood by the side of the chair, his body pressed against his mother. They appeared to have compacted into as small a space as possible. The children were quiet; their mother watched us with defiant eyes.

Alma spoke first. "Hello, Mrs Colwin, I'm sorry Joshua has an ear infection." She stopped, and the woman nodded slightly. "Ear infections can make a child feel bad." Alma paused again; there was no response. "Fortunately, we have an antibiotic that helps get rid of it, that can make him better." She paused again, still no response. She sat on the stool, facing the huddled family. "I understand that you don't want him to have medicine."

"No, not doctor medicine." Her voice remained firm.

"Because of your husband?" Alma spoke softly, looking into the woman's face.

"Yes, and our beliefs. We trust in the Lord."

"That's good. I trust in Him, too." She leaned forward. "It's good that you brought Joshua here to see the doctor." She stopped and waited. Jacob cooed and gurgled in his sister's arms.

Mrs Colwin broke the silence. "My brother brought us. He lives over by Greenville. He came up to see us today. Said we should bring 'im here to the doctor. Some of his wife's folks doctor with y'all." She shifted Joshua on the chair. "His folks would never forgive me if they knew I was here."

"His folks?"

"My husband's Maw and Paw. They live down the road from our trailer. They don't believe in doctors. They leave it to the Lord. They'd think I was dishonorin' my husband and his faith." She stopped and released a sob; tears reappeared. Alma touched her arm.

Alma and I glanced at each other. She rolled the stool to the side, and I squatted in front of the mother and her children. I had thought of something.

"Mrs Colwin, you don't dishonor your husband by taking care of his son. Joshua is sick. He has an illness that I can treat, help him get over. God gave doctors knowledge and skills so that we can help people when they're sick. He shared a little bit of his healing power with us." I tried to maintain eye contact with her. "After all, Luke in the New Testament was a doctor."

Alma shifted on the stool beside me. Mrs Colwin glanced briefly at my face but didn't say anything. Joshua put his arms around her neck. His movement knocked awry the gray scarf that concealed her hair; a few brown strands escaped from under the cloth. I was struck again by her fragile beauty.

Alma broke the silence. "I'll go get the ampicillin." She left the room.

The conflicted mother listened as I gave the usual instructions about the medication. She had no questions. There seemed to be less tension, but the kids were restless. I left to check on Alma. I found her in the back room, shaking a bottle of pink liquid.

"How is she?"

"Don't know. Can't tell."

"She's terrified."

"Yeah, she's afraid of those in-laws. What a shame. I think if was left up to her, she'd give him the stuff."

"Yeah, I expect you're right." Alma stopped shaking and stuck a label on the bottle. "What a spot to be in: grievin' for your husband, wantin' to do what's right for your boy, not wantin' to cross your in-laws. Poor thing." She stopped and looked at me; her tone changed. I knew what was coming. "You ole hypocrite."

I grunted. "I'm not above a little hypocrisy when I need to persuade someone to do something for a kid."

"I agree. I thought what you said was fine." She smiled. "How'd you know about Luke bein' a doctor?"

"My folks tried to make a Christian out of me. I know more about the Bible than you think."

"Well yes, I see that. Maybe, there's hope for you yet."

"Don't waste your hope on me. Hope that poor woman in there gives her kid the ampicillin."

Alma handed Mrs Colwin the bottle of antibiotic and reiterated the instructions. Peering at the floor, she asked what she owed us. Alma told her there was no charge. Alma was like that; we didn't make much money at the clinic.

Standing on the porch of the old house, Alma and I watched the mother and her children squeeze into the cab of the pick-up. The man behind the wheel gave us a wave. As the truck started up the dirt driveway, two crows ascended from the tobacco field, moving dark blotches against the yellow twilight.

I practiced in the mountain clinic for another two years, but I never saw the Colwins or heard anything about them again.

The hot date had been a bust.

I heard a car honk outside and looked up from the newspaper. A figure stood in the doorway to the dining room. It took me a few seconds to realize this was not Becky.

"Daddy, Jennie's here. Your dinner is cold. Do you want me to heat it again before I go?"

As I stared at her from my chair, I knew that sometime soon I had to tell Karen the truth about Becky. Holding the paper in my hand, I stood up. "No, I can take care of it, thanks."

She moved across the room towards the hall. When she passed close to me, I reached out to her. She came to me, and I wrapped her in my arms. She felt warm and smelled fresh. The top of her head was just below my chin, where Becky's used to be.

"Be careful, honey."

She stepped back, her face turned up to me. "Are you okay, Daddy?"

I let go of her. "It's been a rough day, but I'm fine."

"You're thinking about it?"

"I'm thinking about it."

She walked into the hall. "I'll be home by ten."

I heard the front door close. I turned to the newspaper in my hand and read the article again.

Colby County Man Dies of Snake Bite

Joshua Colwin, 23, of Cornhill, N.C. died two days after being bitten by a diamondback rattlesnake during a church service. After suffering multiple bites, Colwin had refused medical care and had been attended by church members, including his wife, mother and sister, who prayed for him. Colwin had been arrested twice in the past for handling poisonous snakes. According to Colby County sheriff, Chester Potter, "This type of activity is now very rare in the county, but if someone is determined to handle snakes, there's not much we can do about it." In 1975, Colwin's father, Jonah Colwin, died after being bitten by a poisonous snake during a church service. In addition to his wife, mother and sister, Colwin is survived by a brother, a son and a daughter.

I laid the paper on the chair and went into the kitchen, where cold turkey and more wine awaited me.

Note: The following four stories are connected. In the first two stories and another later in the collection, I have used a racially derogatory word that is deeply offensive to decent people. Unfortunately, I encountered this word not infrequently while growing up in North Carolina in the 1950s. In my efforts to represent racial conditions of those times in fiction, I faced the dilemma of whether or not to include the word in my writing. I decided to do so in pursuit of verisimilitude. I cringed every time I wrote it, and I hope you cringe every time you read it.

Helen, 1948

Helen was not excited about it; in fact, she didn't want to go. But Will was set on going. He had been following the campaign on the radio and in the newspaper, and he wanted her to go with him. So, by the time she opened the door to Mrs. Burton's knock she had resigned herself to the unavoidable. Billy's shout of joy behind her did little to ease the guilt that had floated like a cloud through her day. Her 3-year old and their nearest neighbor in the apartment building were buddies. Several times recently Helen had almost asked the woman to stop giving her son candy, but her children were one of the few sources of pleasure the old woman had. No, it was not Billy who concerned her; he would be fine. She worried about Janet. Stranger anxiety, a normal phase the book said, but Janet seemed to be lingering in it longer than Billy had. The best Helen could hope for was that the 14-month old now being diapered in the back room by her father would quickly cry herself to sleep.

They could still hear her after the front door of the building closed and they stood momentarily in the porch shadow. Will touched her arm. "She'll stop soon."

"I hope so."

They stepped onto the sidewalk and turned towards town. Sunlight slanted diagonally through the leaves of the oaks along the street. Heat hung in the stagnant air, late summer in full force. At the corner Helen peered through an opening in the canopy. Clouds clung like cotton candy to the purple sky. In the west, over the roof of the textile mill, a round orange sun painted onto a lavender background recalled the pictures her former second-graders had created.

"Should we go back and get the umbrella?"

For the first time her husband gazed upward. "I don't think we'll need it." He paused and looked at Helen. "And we'll just get Jan riled up again."

Hand in hand, they walked by familiar houses, a Baptist church on one corner, a Methodist on the next. In pleasant weather Helen walked this way with the kids; the Piggly Wiggly was only six blocks from the apartment. When they had to go further, into town or to the library, they caught the bus. The kids rode free. Early in the evening the buses ran infrequently, and Helen and Will had decided to walk to the armory downtown.

Soon, Helen saw the tobacco warehouse ahead; in the still air the scent was faint. Sometimes, with a brisk breeze it would reach the open window of their bedroom. When they visited from Philadelphia, her parents complained about the smell. "How can you stand it?" They would ask.

"Do you think there'll be trouble?" She broke the silence. Not for the first time, she posed this question.

Will walked beside her. "It'll be alright. There'll be some protestors probably, but the mayor and the police chief made clear statements yesterday about maintaining order. They'd rather not have to deal with it at all, but it's going to happen, so they have to make the best of it. Get it over with. That's their attitude."

"There's been trouble in other places."

"Yeah, and that's why the city leaders are prepared. They don't want that to happen here. They want to preserve the image of a progressive town." He looked at his wife and chuckled softly. "You know, with the university and all." Will was an instructor in the art history department at Duke University.

"Most of the folks hate Duke; you've said so yourself, a bunch of Yankee communists."

"Yeah, but the university brings in a lot of money. Bankers and businessmen run the town, and they need the university."

"But it's not like the university is going to pick up and leave if there's a riot at a political rally."

Will gently squeezed his wife's arm. "There's not going to be any riot. Maybe a few rednecks making fools of themselves, but things will be okay. You worry too much." In recent days, she had heard this several times.

As they walked, residential yielded to commercial, traffic picked up, clouds in the eastern sky darkened, the sun melted behind them, and their shadows stretched ahead, drawing them forward.

When they passed the Carolina Theater two blocks from the armory, Helen saw the line at the ticket window. *The Maltese Falcon* was showing. She wished she was in that line. The last time she and Will had left the kids with Mrs. Burton, on their anniversary more than three months earlier, they had seen the new Walter Mitty movie and had eaten at Bullock's, one of the best restaurants in town. If she had to suffer the distress of leaving her children at night, she wanted it to be for something enjoyable. As she moved with her husband up the street towards the armory, frustration flavored her fear.

A block away, Helen could see the crowd gathered on the sidewalk by the gray brick building and could hear the low bubbling of voices. This was not a welcomed sight. Two policemen straddled motorcycles at the curb. Another stood at the intersection, directing cars and pickups to the parking lot at the baseball field two blocks away. There should be more of them, she thought. As the couple crossed the street, Will's hand again found hers.

"Just keep walking; we'll go right in. We'll be fine."

Figures now had faces and voices. Helen caught individual words, words that pierced like thorns. She and Will picked up their pace, moving towards an enlarging clot of people at an entrance into the building. The air was viscous with humidity, cigarette smoke, vaporized sweat and hostility. Clumps of men glared at them from under wide-brimmed hats and Durham Bulls caps. A red-faced man waved a home-made sign in front of them. Helen read the words, 'go back to Russia' before she ducked her head and hurried past.

They reached the cluster at the door. Helen could easily distinguish the outnumbered Wallace supporters. They were the ones who silently stared straight ahead, trying to ignore the invective. She glanced at one of the policemen who sat passively astride his motorcycle, his face grim.

Then she saw her, a small woman in a yellow summer dress, much like hers, standing silently beside a hefty man, who wore a gray undershirt, his eyes black like the cockroaches she occasionally found on the bathroom floor, his mouth open in an

68

angry shout. The woman seemed familiar; Helen had seen her somewhere. Where?

The going was slow; those entering the building were funneled into a single-file line through a gauntlet of abuse. With a hand on each of her shoulders, Will maneuvered her in front of him and behind a tall stone-faced man dressed in a tan suit. She felt trapped in a can of humanity. Sweat that had slowly beaded at her hairline during the walk cascaded into her eyes and down her face. Will's hands remained on her shoulders, nudging her slowly forward until finally she stumbled through the doorway.

If anything, inside was hotter; the inert air enclosed her like a cloak. A young man and women offered those who had entered white cardboard placards inscribed with 'Wallace for President' in large blue letters. Will took one from the man and spoke briefly to him. Helen shook her head at the woman. Most of the people who entered the room accepted a sign, but some refused with varying degrees of vehemence. She realized that the protesters were inside too. Her apprehension deepened.

Will nodded towards the two who were handing out the placards. "They were students in my Nineteenth century class." He gave Helen one of the hand fans that an older woman was distributing.

Helen dug a handkerchief out of her pocketbook and wiped her face. She closed her eyes and saw Janet sleeping in her crib and Billy playing with his cars on the floor. She opened her eyes to a cavernous room, half filled with people, mostly men who stood alone or quietly in small groups fanning themselves, smoking cigarettes, in uneasy anticipation. Some held Wallace placards at their sides. She saw a few couples, but no woman who appeared to be unaccompanied by a man. Assembling along the walls of the room were men with a different demeanor. Helen fervently wished they would go away.

Near the center of the room, she observed a group of Negroes, three men and three women, middle-aged or older, engaged in conversation. The men wore suits, ties and fedoras; the women, Sunday dresses and hats. So, they had come. Admiration mixed with anxiety; she didn't want to think about what they had endured when entering the building. She could not avoid worrying about what their presence might portend.

Politics didn't interest Helen nearly as much as it did Will. She read the newspaper, kept up with what was happening in Europe, the Marshall Plan, the Iron Curtain, all of that. She knew about Truman and Dewey, and now Thurmond and Wallace at opposite ends of the political spectrum. In a way she admired Truman, a feisty guy who had some good intentions, the health insurance idea, for example. But she would vote for Wallace. She liked his commitment to peace and his stand on race.

Growing up in the North, she had gone to school with Negroes; some had been friends. Things had changed dramatically in 1942 when she and Will had come to the South for Will to satisfy his conscientious objector obligation at Duke Hospital. She had entered another world, a strange world of strict rules, compelling customs, powerful sanctions.

Segregation greeted them immediately. In the train station, Helen peered through the grime-streaked glass partition into the shabby Negro waiting area. On their walk to the hotel, Will and Helen stopped outside the court house for her to use a water fountain. As she bent to drink, she heard a voice say "Don't drink that, it's the nigger water. It'll make you sick." Helen straightened up to look at the middle-aged woman who stood nearby. She smiled and pointed to another water fountain across the walk-way.

70

"Ya'll must not be from around here. Ours is over there." That's when Helen noticed the 'Colored' etched on the concrete pedestal of the fountain. She waited until they reached the hotel to satisfy her thirst.

For six years, segregation had been a persistent presence in her life, like a nagging skin rash that itched just often enough to remind her it was there. The reminders irritated: the elderly Negro woman who relinquished her bus seat to a young white guy who had stood in the aisle and glared at her, the little boy who lived in the house on the corner and called the Negro man who cut the grass and tended the flower beds Fred.

Periodically, Will would rail in private against the injustices, and he sought opportunities to befriend Negroes. He talked to the janitor at his work about the weather and sports and even local politics. He tipped shoe shine boys extravagantly. But there was little of substance he could do.

When Helen taught school, she tried with minimal success to replace 'nigger' with 'colored' in her second-graders' vocabulary. She asked Mrs. Burton not to use the word around her children. But in reality, for Helen, Negroes were everywhere and nowhere. She would go for months without any meaningful contact with one. They blended into the background scenery.

People continued to enter the armory; it was filling up. Helen wished for a chair to sit in; she wished for a large fan to invigorate the turbid air, she wished she was home in the rocker reading Billy a bedtime story.

Will introduced her to Steve, an English instructor from the university, and his wife Annie, a nurse. The men talked about the turnout and the people in the crowd they recognized. Helen studied the nurse's face, the makeup intact, emerald eyes bright. Any fear there was well concealed. Annie smiled at Helen. 'It's exciting."

"It's stifling."

Annie frowned. "It's disgusting. At the last minute they said we couldn't use the electric fans, a fire hazard. What a joke." She paused, looking around the room. "I was here a month ago, a garden show. They had these four big fans set up. It was comfortable. This is pure harassment."

Fanning her face, Helen glanced behind Annie at the men along the wall who ringed the room like a noose. "It's not comfortable tonight."

Just then the noise from the front of the room increased; it sounded like cheering. Helen stood on her toes to get a better look. A small group of men had entered at the door in the front and were stepping onto the platform. She recognized the candidate; he was taller than the others and was waving to the crowd. Will and Steve held their placards high in the air, and Annie clapped vigorously. It was loud, but the cheering was mixed with other sounds; booing and hissing contributed to the cacophony. A wave of fear surged through Helen, almost sweeping her breath away.

After a few minutes a young man from the group on the stage stepped up to a lectern and microphone that Helen had not noticed before. After the obligatory "testing, testing, testing," he started, "Fellow Americans."

"Traitor! Go back to Russia." The shout emanated from the periphery near Helen and was followed by a chorus of agreement.

"Bastards!" Annie muttered.

Helen looked around, a lot of people, but not a policeman in sight. Her legs wobbled, her heart pounded. She placed a trembling hand on Will's back; his muscles were like boards under the damp shirt. He lowered his left arm and pulled her to his body while continuing to wave the placard with his other hand and stare at the speaker.

The man at the lectern glared in the direction of the shout and waited for the jeering and heckling to wan. When the noise level subsided to a low rumble, he said, "My name is Alan Pittman, and I'm the campaign manager for the Progressive Party in North Carolina. I was born and reared in North Carolina, and I've lived here my whole life except for the three years I spent in the Pacific fighting the enemies of our country."

Thunderous applause erupted. Annie jumped up and down like a child on Christmas morning, and Will and Steve waved their placards in the air. Helen detached herself from her husband, wiped her face with the handkerchief and joined in the clapping.

"That'll shut the bigots up." Annie announced in Helen's ear.

Maybe so, she thought.

Obviously energized, the young veteran proceeded to introduce former Vice President Henry Wallace as a "patriotic leader with a new vision for America." Cheers clearly eclipsed the jeers as the candidate stepped to the lectern.

For the next twenty minutes or so, Helen stood beside her husband and listened to Henry Wallace expound upon election issues. Her ears rang with the recurrent waves of cheering and booing, which splashed from wall to wall. When Wallace talked about the importance of peaceful relations with the Soviet Union such epithets as "dirty Red," "commie," "traitor," "Stalin's dupe" were hurled at him. But his appeal for racial equality ignited the greatest explosion of condemnation. This assault of outrage halted his speech. The chant "segregation" reached a crescendo, reverberating through the room. Helen covered her ears with her hands and pressed her body against Will's. He yelled something, which was lost in the clamor.

After a while two policemen entered the front door and walked to the microphone. They were joined by Alan Pittman, who had stood on the stage behind Wallace with other members of his entourage during the speech. One policeman spoke to Wallace, and Pittman began gesturing angrily. Wallace tried to calm Pittman. The policemen placed a hand on Wallace's arm. Wallace looked at him and then turned to the audience and waved his other hand. He bent forward to the microphone, "Thank-you for coming out tonight. Remember, this is America, the land of the free and the home of the brave." With that he turned, left the stage and exited the building, flanked by the policemen and followed by his entourage.

Pittman remained alone on the stage. He walked to the lectern, faced the crowd, raised both outstretched arms over his head and bellowed "Wallace" Then he repeated it, again and again. Supporters quickly picked up the chant. "Wallace, Wallace, Wallace...." Soon Helen could recognize the counter-chant, rising from the opponents, like billowing smoke: "Traitor, traitor, traitor...." She clung to her husband, her tears mingling with his sweat. She heard his whisper in her ear, "We're going to be okay."

Soon, through the chaos of the competing chants, she heard a new voice over the loud speaker. She separated from Will and looked to the front where a policeman stood at the lectern beside Pittman and spoke into the microphone.

"The rally's over. Ya'll go on home now. Let's be peaceable. We don't want no trouble." He repeated this several times while Pittman stood by, scowling.

Slowly, the noise diminished, and Helen noticed that several doors had been opened on each side of the room. She was pleased to see a policeman standing at the closest one, motioning for people to exit. But then she recognized several heated

74

arguments between Wallace supporters and opponents. A well-dressed woman was pulling on the arm of a man in a suit who was face-to-face with a smirking guy in bib overalls. She saw the Negroes moving towards one of the doors, being watched by menacing men. Good luck, she thought.

Will put his arm around her. "Let's get out of here."

That made sense to her. She became aware of Annie beside her.

"Well, we don't have to go to Russia now; the bastards brought Russia to us."

Helen looked at her but said nothing. There seemed to be a bit of a smile playing around Annie's mouth. "Something to tell your grandkids about some day."

Steve grabbed his wife's hand and nodded towards the front, where the crowd was thinning. "Let's go speak to Phil over there."

Annie looked at Helen. "Glad to meet you. Maybe next time, not quite as much excitement."

Helen managed an "okay" and watched them move across the floor. As she watched Annie's back, she remembered where she had seen the woman on the sidewalk, the woman in the yellow dress, the woman with the big loud lout. Last week on the bus, she sat in the seat just in front of Helen and the kids. She had a little boy with her, about Billy's age. She played peek-a-boo with Janet. The two boys climbed onto an empty seat across the aisle. Billy did not want to get off the bus at their stop.

"Hope to see ya'll again." The woman had said.

Near a door, Will and Helen joined a slowly moving line of exiting Wallace supporters. In an effort to tune out the venom being directed their way, Helen tried to envision Janet's smile. But she only saw distorted faces shrouded by a grotesque darkness.

Then she was out on the sidewalk, a night-time breeze bathing her cheeks. She looked around. Most people moved rapidly away, receding into the shadows. Others congregated in menacing clots, glaring at departing Wallace supporters and in some cases continuing the verbal attacks.

Will held her hand, and they walked quickly towards the corner where a policeman stood, observing the scene. Overhead, dark clouds hovered in a starless sky, and the air smelled of rain.

Suddenly, Helen was aware of rapid movement at her side, a fleeting flash of yellow. She turned to see a contorted face thrusting towards her, barely recognizable, eyes inflamed, lips pursed as in preparation for a kiss. But then she felt the glob of spit land on the left side of her nose followed immediately by the "Commie nigger-lover" exploding into her hearing. She staggered, and Will clutched her, keeping her upright. They both turned towards the assailant, who stood defiantly a few feet away beside a large grinning man in a sweat encrusted undershirt, her face etched with hatred. Will released his grip on Helen and stepped towards the other couple.

"What do you think...?"

"No Will, don't." Helen pulled his arm. "It's okay. Don't."

He turned back to her. "Are you alright?"

"Yes, yes, it's okay. Let's go. Leave it be."

He took her hand, and they again headed for the corner. In the other hand he still carried the Wallace placard. At the corner, Will stopped in front of the policeman, who regarded him with a look of disinterest.

"Why don't you do something about what's going on back there?"

The policeman glanced up the sidewalk in the direction Will and Helen had come. His eyes then rested momentarily on Helen before returning to Will. Disdain had replaced disinterest.

"I don't see anybody breaking any laws up there. Of course, your kind broke the law when you let them niggers in, but we let that go." He paused and then said, "Ya'll get on home now; you've caused enough trouble for one night."

Helen tugged on her husband's arm. "Let's go Will."

He hesitated and then relented. She found his hand, and they crossed the street. On the other side, Helen saw a 'Wallace for President' sign lying on the sidewalk. "Wait a minute, Will." She bent down and picked it up. With her free hand she brushed off the dirt, but gray scuff marks remained, mementos of numerous shoes.

Soon they were alone, moving in silence from streetlight to streetlight, through air pregnant with moisture. The wet spot on the side of Helen's nose felt like liquid fire, but she made no effort to wipe it. She thought of the pleasant woman on the bus, the boys sitting together on the seat, Janet's giggles as the smiling face reappeared from behind the hands. What kind of a world had she brought her children into?

Two blocks past the theater, by the icehouse, Helen felt the first drop on her cheek. Others quickly followed, in her hair, on her bare arms, on her face. Will held the placard over his head.

"Do you want to go to the bus stop at Five-Points? There's a shelter." He asked.

"No, let's keep going."

She walked beside him, carrying her placard at her side and feeling the rain on her face, feeling the fire subside and finally wash away, like a baptism. She lifted the placard over her head and held it with both hands. She walked straight ahead into the watery darkness.

Eeny Meeny Miny Mo

"Eeny, meeny miny mo,
Catch a nigger by the toe.
If he hollers, let him go,
Eeny, meeny, miny, mo."

Hank's finger was pointing at me. Ben sat beside him, grinning. From sitting on the hard wood of the porch, my butt was sore. I heard a noise at the door; Ma stood just inside the screen. I knew what was coming.

"You boys shouldn't say that word. It's not a nice word. Say tiger instead, catch a tiger by his toe."

I saw Hank and Ben look at each other just before I glared across the street and saw old Tom pushing the lawn mower in the Baker's yard, his dark body moving against the green grass, clusters of white hair below the baseball cap, like puffs of cotton.

"Would you boys like some grape Kool Aid?"

I stood up and moved down the porch stairs away from the door, but Hank and Ben wanted Kool Aid, so we went inside.

On the first day of summer vacation after the third grade, we walked to the school to play baseball with some boys who lived near Crabtree Creek. On the way, Hank asked why Ma didn't want us to say nigger. His Ma and Pa said it all the time. I told him I didn't know.

At the school, men worked in the yard near the fifth-grade classrooms. Hank wanted to see what they were doing, so we went over to where they were working. There were four of them, and they were building a small wooden house. Two of them wore undershirts that clung to their backs, and the other two had no

78

shirts. Sweat beaded on their skin, like clusters of bugs. After a while, Hank asked what they were building. One of the men stopped hammering and looked at Hank. I saw the face of a woman tattooed on his arm. He looked scary. I wanted to leave. He took the cigarette out of his mouth and spit on the ground. His hands were dirty, and his face was red and ragged under the brim of a Durham Bulls baseball cap.

"Them Communists up North say that ya'll haf to go to school with the niggers now. So, we're makin' this school for the niggers."

The man closest to him stopped measuring a board, grunted and muttered a bad word.

As we walked back to the baseball field, Hank said that he sure didn't want to go to school with no niggers, and Ben said he didn't either. Ben said that his Pa had been talking about how the Yankees were trying to force mixing of the races, but that it would never happen in the South. It was against the Lord's law. Ben's Pa was a preacher.

That Sunday, we drove by the school on the way to church. The little wooden house that the men had been working on was finished, and there was a big hole beside the school building and three stacks of red bricks beside the hole. Pa said that they were adding on to the school; it was too small.

"What's that white house for?" Janet asked.

"That's a shed where the workmen keep their tools." He answered.

"It's not where the colored children will go?" I asked.

Ma turned to look at me from the front seat. Her eyes were tight. "Why'd you say that?" Janet giggled on her side of the back seat.

79

"I just heard they'd go to school in that little house. Yankees were makin' 'em."

Ma looked at Pa who had his hands on the steering wheel, his head directed at the road ahead. A muscle jumped in the back of his neck. Soon he said, "They've got their own schools. I'm afraid that Negro children and white children will not be going to school together around here for a while. The Supreme Court says they have to, but it's not going to happen quickly. I wish it would, but it won't."

Because ours was the only family on the block that didn't have a television, I spent a lot of time on late afternoons at my friends' houses. One day we watched Sky King in Ben's living room. Polly the maid ironed clothes in the kitchen. On Tuesday and Thursday, Ben's Ma worked as a secretary at the Baptist church where his Pa preached, and Polly took care of Ben and his brother.

We went to the Unitarian church. There was only one Unitarian church, and it was little. There were a whole bunch of Baptist churches, and some of them were real big.

When a commercial came on the T.V. about chocolate flavored Ovaltine, Hank asked Ben if we could take his big brother's BB gun outside. Ben said he didn't want to get in trouble again. Hank said that nobody would know. Ben didn't say anything more. I was with Ben on this one, but I didn't say anything either.

After Sky King made a daring landing with his airplane in a cotton field to catch the bank robbers, we went into the kitchen to eat ginger snaps. But Polly said no; it was too close to supper. Hank didn't like that.

I liked to watch Polly iron clothes. She did it different than Ma. Polly was a big lady, and in the summer-time she wore a

80

short-sleeved dress. The loose brown skin of her arm jiggled as she pressed the iron down and pushed it back and forth on the clothes. Steam hissed and rose from the board, and you could sometimes hear her humming a tune.

I was a little afraid of Polly. On Tuesday and Thursday mornings, I'd see her walking up the street to Ben's house, and in the evenings, I'd see her standing at the corner waiting for the bus with the other maids, and she didn't seem like much. But when she was in Ben's house and his Ma and Pa weren't there, we had to do what she'd say, and she could be pretty strict.

"Polly," Hank asked, "do you think nigger boys and girls should get to go to school with us?"

Ben and I had been moving out of the kitchen. I gave a start, and I saw Ben jerk a little too. Hank stood in the kitchen looking up at the big colored lady who had a hot iron in her hand. She turned from the board and looked down at him.

"Don't talk that foolishness with me, chile. I got all these shirts for Mister Parker to iron and a meat loaf to get in that oven, and you askin' me some bunch of nonsense. You git outta this kitchen now."

Polly turned back to the board and thrust the iron onto a white shirt, producing a sizzling cloud of steam. Hank walked over to Ben and me in the dining room, a smirk on his face.

"And don't ya'll go messing with that BB gun, neither." Polly's voice followed us into the living room.

I went home.

Once a week, Ma would go grocery shopping at the Piggly Wiggly. On those days, Pa would ride the bus to the university where he taught summer school. I would go with her to help carry the bags. One time, Hank went to the store with us. Ma was watching him while his mother played golf. We couldn't go the usual way to the store because they were working on the street. We had to drive through Walltown, the colored section. As we rode through Walltown on the way to the Piggly Wiggly, Hank pointed to some of the children he saw playing in the yards and laughed.

"There's you over there, Billy, that nigger boy playin' in the dirt, that's you. And there's Ben, that nigger boy swinging in that ole tire. And there's Janet, that little nigger girl in that ugly green dress. You can see her underwear. Ain't she a sight?"

From the front seat Ma said. "Hank, we don't use that word in this car."

I looked out the window at Walltown School. I could feel Hank's glare piercing the back of my neck like a tetanus shot. The c was missing from the sign in front of the dark brick building, and the n was hanging up-side down and looked like a u. There was only one basketball goal in the dirt playground, and the rim had no net.

Soon, Hank started in again, but he didn't use the bad word. He had a grand time identifying colored kids who looked like our friends, but he never saw one who looked like himself. I noticed that. I also noticed the back of Ma's neck as she drove the car. She didn't say anything else, thank goodness.

After we put the bags of groceries in the trunk, Hank and I climbed in the back seat and opened the Hershey bars that Ma had got for us because we had been such a big help. As we headed down the hill into Walltown, Hank began pointing to the colored kids again and laughing. But near the bottom of the hill, the car started acting funny. I could feel this thumping up front, and I knew we had a flat tire. Ma knew it too, and she muttered something that I couldn't make out.

She pulled the car over to the curb, and the three of us sat there. I looked at Hank; he held half the Hershey bar in his hand. He had been talking and laughing so much that he had not finished it. He was no longer talking or laughing. I looked outside. Three little boys who only wore dirty underwear had stopped playing in the dust next to the car and stared at us. A woman sat on the porch of a wooden shack set back from the road, rocking in a chair. A man in bib overalls stood on the porch of the shack next door. Two boys bigger than Hank and me walked towards the car, laughing. They were all colored. Cars occasionally passed on the street.

Ma said, "I'm afraid we've got a flat tire." She opened her door and then looked back at me. "Slide over and get out on the other side with Hank."

I slid over, but Hank didn't move. He seemed frozen. I nudged his arm. "Come on Hank open the door." Then I reached across his motionless body and pushed down on the handle. The door opened. Hank and I finally got out. He was like a zombie. Ma stood on the curb and looked at the right front tire. I joined her. It was flat. She turned to me.

"Billy, we can do this. We've both watched your father change a tire."

I saw little balls of sweat on her forehead. I didn't say anything. I was shaking. The big colored boys had stopped and were standing near the front of the car, still laughing. The man in the overalls watched us. The woman had stopped rocking and stood up. She called to the underwear children, who ignored her.

"We need to unload the groceries to get the spare tire and the jack." Ma pushed me towards the back of the car to get me moving. Hank stood by the car, his face white, staring at the flat tire. I went around him.

Ma unlocked the trunk and opened it. She and I lifted the bags of food. "Just set them on the ground." I did so. Together we got out the spare, the jack and the lug wrench. I wanted to put the bags back in the trunk, but Ma said to just leave them sitting by the curb.

By that time, a crowd had gathered. Black faces were turned to us. I could hear the murmuring, like insects at night outside my window. I carried the jack around to the front of the car while Ma wheeled the spare tire in the street along the side of the car. We bent down together and worked to adjust the jack under the front of the car. I heard movement beside me and looked up to see a big colored man standing there. He had on grimy dungarees and a dirty faded blue shirt. He looked like he had not shaved in a while.

"Let me do that for you, Ma'am."

Ma stood up. "Okay, thank you." She smoothed out the wrinkles in her dress and put a hand on my shoulder. "This is my son Billy; he'll help you change the tire."

"Yes, ma'am."

He put the jack under the front of the car, and with a few jerks of his arm had the flat tire off the pavement. Looking across the front of his shirt, I saw Hank huddled by the car, his eyes focused on the man, black faces behind him.

The man squatted down by the flat tire, and I squatted beside him. He smelled like a colored man. He had short curly white hairs on the back of his dark hands. With one flip of his wrist, he removed the hub cap with the flat end of the lug wrench. Then with the wrench, he loosened the lugs, but didn't take them all the way off. When he handed me the lug wrench, his fingers touched my hand; they felt rough.

"Now, you keep turnin' 'em that way 'til they come off."

84

I put each lug in the hub cap like I had seen Pa do. Ma watched. I could hear voices behind her.

The man removed the flat tire and put on the spare. The muscles bulged in his arms. I put each lug back on until I couldn't turn it anymore, and then the man turned them until they were tight. He popped the hub cap on.

While the man was cranking down the jack to lower the car, a policeman on a motorcycle stopped in the street beside the car. The black faces disappeared. The policeman asked if we were alright. Ma said yes and told him how the man had helped us. The policeman looked at the man but didn't say anything. More like himself again, Hank helped me load the flat tire and groceries into the trunk.

Ma tried to give the man money, but he wouldn't take it. "Your boy did mosta the work," he said.

The cop stayed there until we left.

Before we climbed back into the car, Hank looked the motorcycle over. Inside the car, I saw that Hank's candy bar had melted into a black glob on the seat. All the way home, Hank talked about the motorcycle. Neither Ma nor I said anything.

At supper that night, Ma told Pa about the flat tire. As he cut his meat, he complemented me for helping to fix the flat. I gazed out the window at the neighborhood kids congregating in the summer evening. Playing outside in the prolonged twilight was a pleasure of summertime. I saw Hank riding his bike, waiting for me to come out. I turned back to the table and watched Ma and Pa eat the last bits of food from their plates.

"I'd like some more potatoes and gravy, please." I told Ma.

Payback

"Hold her tight. Don't let her move, Neville."

The spinal needle poised in a gloved hand, he glared at me across the enfolded body of the baby, who lay on her side, the antiseptic orange of her back exposed through the hole in the sterile drape. My right hand pushed the back of her neck and head, while the left pressed the underside of her thighs, bringing her knees and nose within close approximation, creating an unnatural fetal position. I could feel her heat with my hands, and could breathe it, rising from her body like steam from a wet, hot pavement.

The three of us were alone in the room, familiar middle of the night noises seeping through the bare walls. Somewhere, a child wailed, but the cry of the one I held had subsided to a whisper of resistance and then to submissive silence. I had long since accepted the "Neville," or so I thought.

"I've got her. You just hit it on the first stick."

I think we were equally shocked by the words that spurted from my mouth like blood from a ruptured artery. How could a thought convert instantaneously to spoken words, bypassing a well-developed self-protection filter? While still astonished at my temerity, I braced for his angry retort. He surprised me; he said nothing but merely continued to glare at me, his mouth twisting into the characteristic sneer. He slowly inclined the needle until it pointed in my direction. Suddenly, a dark spot streaked through the air between our faces; I was never so glad to see a fly. We both watched it land on the Mayo tray that held the spinal tap tubes.

"Shit!" He said and waved the needle towards the fly, which took off. "This place is a damned disgrace."

"Do you want me to swat it?" Despite our best efforts, an occasional fly invaded an exam room.

"No, don't let go." He leaned forward and pierced the orange skin with the needle. The baby did not react at all.

I watched Hawkins advance the needle. It was the second lumbar puncture I had assisted him with that shift. Several hours earlier, he had struggled to get spinal fluid from a comatose old man. I had seen him perform over a dozen spinal taps in the three weeks he had worked in the emergency room, and it was the only time I had seen him fail to obtain fluid on the first stick. He had filled the room with curses. I had silently celebrated.

Hawkins prided himself on his technical skills, and for good reason. He was one of the last persons in the world I would want to inform my parents of my death, but if I needed a chest tube inserted to re-expand a lung or a particularly nasty laceration sutured, he was the one I would want to do it, despite the Neville and other crap.

As I held the baby tightly and watched, he turned the needle a bit and removed the stylet. Normal spinal fluid looks like clear water. The fluid that flowed through the needle into the tube looked like milk, a sure sign of meningitis, a really bad thing.

As he collected the fluid in the tubes, he told me what I already knew we needed to do, and quickly. "Get an IV into her and give her antibiotics. We'll ship her to Children's; we don't have the nursing care she needs here." He paused and looked at me. "How did they get here?"

"Taxi." I thought of the baby's mother, sitting in the waiting room, with two other kids, who looked to be about two and four years of age. The younger one, a boy, had fallen asleep on the floor at the feet of a drunk with a belly ache.

"She'll have to go by ambulance. Who's up?" He pulled out the needle, peeled off his gloves and placed a band aid over the needle site.

"Hutch and Frank." I loosened my grip and turned the baby onto her back. "Will the mother and the other two kids get to go with her?" Why did I ask? I knew what he would say.

"It's up to Hutch and Frank, but I doubt it. Too crowded." Holding the tubes of milky fluid, he headed for the door. "Let's get that IV going, pronto."

I picked up the baby, a baby who, according to her mother, had been laughing and cooing just two days before. Limp and inert in my arms, she appeared to be asleep, or in whatever state of unconsciousness the infant brain incased in an inflamed membrane produces. The mother and siblings would be able to go in the ambulance if the doctor approved it, but expecting Hawkins to do that was a pipe dream.

Within minutes, Beth had inserted the butterfly needle into the baby's arm. The baby never flinched. After she finished securing it with tape, Beth looked at me and said, "Bill, guard this with your life." She was one of the nurses I liked working with.

I guarded the tenuous IV for the next five minutes, until I handed the baby off to Hutch for her journey through the sleeping city to Children's Hospital. I don't know if the mother and siblings accompanied her. My objective for the next three hours was to avoid Hawkins until the shift ended.

I transported a woman with pneumonia up to the ward and bought a bit more time by helping the nurse's aide tuck her in and process the paper work. She gave me a quizzical look but didn't say anything. When I returned to the emergency department, I had to mop up vomit from the floor of one of the trauma rooms. I took my time until Steve, another orderly, stuck his head in and told me to get a move on; a laceration needed repair. I knew Hawkins would be doing the sewing so I managed to make myself scarce by lingering outside the x-ray room where I had taken a man who was coughing up smelly green phlegm.

The guy with the laceration turned out to be a black teenager who was brought in by two cops. They stood outside the door in the hallway under the No Smoking sign, joking and smoking cigarettes. Beth glared at them on occasion. I gathered from the bits of expletives I overheard that the patient had resisted arrest. Hawkins would be in a particularly foul mood after finishing his handiwork on the reprobate.

During the 11pm to 7am shift that I routinely worked, two interns and a senior resident staffed the emergency room. On the other two shifts, an attending physician worked with the resident and interns. Sometimes there were medical students around, getting in the way. Residents and interns spent a month on the ER rotation, working for 24 hours and then off for 24 hours. So, when I arrived fresh for work, they had already been there for 16 hours. Tired, overworked doctors can be a pain, but in my first three months, Hawkins was the only one for whom I was counting down the hours; only two more shifts, 16 hours, and he would be gone, never to return.

Fortunately, the laceration repair took a while, and the shift ended without me crossing paths with him. Once when I was taking vital signs on a homeless man with a bad toothache, I heard him yelling at an intern, a reminder that his anger was ecumenical and not solely focused on me. Still, I feared that he would accost me after the shift ended. He usually left before I did, but he might wait and waylay me outside; I could easily imagine the venting of his rage at my impertinence. It would go beyond the usual

"Neville," "commie sympathizer" and illusions of dominoes falling in Asia.

Determined not to let that happen, after I restocked supplies in my assigned rooms of the emergency department, I went upstairs and hung out in the bathroom in the men's ward. It was one of the last places Hawkins would go. After what I thought was enough time for him to yield to the desire for sleep and go home, I ventured back downstairs, through the noisy waiting room and out the door into the autumn air. I was relieved to see that his Mustang was gone from its space across the lot. Home free! At least for a while.

On July first, I had stood on the same pock-marked pavement with my mom and dad, dark storm clouds gathering overhead, and studied the red brick building that would be my place of employment for the next two years. A month earlier I had graduated from college, and two weeks after that my draft board had decided on the St. Louis City Hospital ER as the site for my alternative service. I was to start ASAP.

After I found an apartment, my parents drove from North Carolina, the back seat and trunk of the Dodge crammed with clothes, books and odds and ends. My mom provided a crash course on how to boil water, scramble an egg and avoid food poisoning. After buying a fan, a chair, a small black and white TV and a few other things to enhance my meagerly furnished apartment, my parents shed a few tears, kissed me goodbye and headed back to Durham, where 25 years earlier my father had been sent to satisfy his alternative service obligation. Perhaps they mused on the cycles of family history.

Autumn sunshine complemented my relief at seeing the vacant parking space. I lived four blocks from the hospital, and on the way home I treated myself to a donut from Hal's Grocery. I planned to sleep at least five hours and then take the bus to Forest Park for the anti-war rally. Maybe I'd finally get lucky and connect with one of those free-love girls I'd heard so much about but not yet encountered. My only date since I had arrived in St Louis, with a student nurse, had headed south quickly when she learned I was a CO. It turned out that she had a brother in Vietnam.

On the front stoop of my apartment building, I met Mr. Thompson, who was heading to the corner drug store to buy a *Globe-Democrat*. This was a daily ritual for the old man. He lived with his wife in one of the other two apartments on the third floor. I rarely saw her; she had Parkinson's. He was a rather sad case, so I would humor him by listening to his complaints about how the neighborhood was deteriorating and how "the coloreds" were taking over the city. For forty years, he had run a shoe repair shop. Disappearing business rather than advancing age had occasioned his retirement. For the past few days, Mr. Thompson had been in a better mood; his beloved Cardinals had clinched the pennant, which he reminded me of that morning.

"They're peaking at the right time." I agreed, moving towards the door and chuckling to myself that it was his baseball team that had been taken over by coloreds. I didn't want to linger to hear about the latest exploits of Gibson, Flood, Brock and his other ironic heroes. And I certainly did not want an update from the Parkinson's front. Early on, I had explained to him that just because I wore scrubs and worked at a hospital, I was not a doctor. I had pointed to my attire, "Orderlies wear gray, doctors wear green and usually a white coat." I think he grasped the distinction, but that did not deter him from proffering periodic medical reports and fishing for advice.

The third apartment on my floor was occupied by a young woman and her two small kids, whom I heard more frequently than

91

I saw. Their apartment was often the scene of noisy congregations of women and children, particularly on days when I highly desired sleep. Once after I had helped her navigate a stroller up the stairs, I asked her to keep the noise level down in the mornings, explaining my work schedule. She batted ample eye lashes at me, and her freckled bosom rose and fell suggestively, as she apologetically promised to do so, a promise that was as evanescent as breeze on a St Louis July day. Adaptable I proved to be, soon becoming expert at falling asleep serenaded by a chorus of child noises intermittently punctuated by maternal explosions of anger. Silence probably would have induced insomnia.

After five hours of restorative sleep, I found myself on that Saturday afternoon sitting alone but in proximity to several hundred other folks whom Hawkins would, at his most charitable, characterize as malcontents or dupes, on a hill in Forest Park, listening to a local band of hippies do their best to imitate the music of Joan Baez and Peter, Paul and Mary. I stood up to stretch and peered over trees into the nearby zoo. In the distance I could make out the head of a giraffe. While I watched, it disappeared.

I debated whether to stick around for the speeches or to walk up the road to the art museum. I caught a whiff of marijuana and decided to stick around. I sat down again and studied the backs of three teenage girls who sat nearby. One had brown hair that reached her butt. She reminded me of my sister Janet.

"Hey, Bill."

The voice came from above, and I looked up at a figure silhouetted against the sun. Beside him I could see a woman, mini-skirted, tanned legs, bare arms, tight t-shirt sporting a green peace symbol, beaded neck, dark hair, and eyes like the purr of a cat. But the guy, I couldn't make out.

"George Walters. Dr. Walters, from the ER."

I tilted my head and peered at him. Sure enough, an intern from the ER.

During a rare slack time in mid-August, I had gone into the supply room for a sterile suture set and found Dr. Walters sitting in a chair, a cup of coffee in his hand. In the ER, we grabbed brief breaks wherever we could: in vacant exam rooms, hallways, stairwells, even bathrooms, and apparently, supply rooms.

He had given me a smile. "Bill, isn't it?"

"Yes."

"I've been wondering where you're from."

I had found the set on a cluttered shelf. "North Carolina."

"Thought so." He had sipped the coffee and grimaced. "Your accent."

No one in the ER had commented on my accent, at least not to me. "Do you know North Carolina?"

"Went to school there, Duke."

That had caught my interest. "College or med school?"

"College. Went to med school here at Wash U. Graduated in June."

I could not resist. "I went to Duke, too. Graduated in June."

It turned out that he had finished in '63, the year I started. We had spent the next few minutes exploring mutual college experiences: The Dope Shop, Anna Maria's, the Donut Dinette, Joe College weekends, basketball victories, football Saturdays, East Campus prick-teasers. We had known only a few of the same professors; he had majored in chemistry, and I in English. He had been in a fraternity; I had not.

"So, what brought you to St Louis and City Hospital ER?" He had asked.

I had hesitated and then decided to take the plunge. "I'm a CO. My draft board figured moving me 900 miles to satisfy my

93

alternative service obligation was a sufficient hardship. The only time I'd ever been in an ER was when I broke my arm as a kid."

As I talked, I had watched carefully; his face brightened momentarily. "A CO, good for you." Then he had frowned. "This damn war is stupid. If I didn't have a deferment, I'd seriously consider the CO route, or even Canada."

Then Beth had stuck her head in, interrupting us. "Ha, I found your hiding place. This is an emergency room, guys. We have patients."

We did not have an opportunity to resume this discussion, and I had been sorry to see Dr. Walters finish his ER rotation.

I stood up and shook his hand and said hello to Liz, his fiancée. She gave me a big smile.

"May we join you?" He asked.

"Sure. I motioned to where I had been sitting. "Have a seat." Thirsty, I looked hopefully at the cooler he carried.

I was not disappointed; we sat drinking beer and listening to speakers denounce the war and its makers. I learned that Liz taught high school math in north St. Louis. With a mixture of determination and resignation, she talked about the challenges that entailed. I told her that my sister, a junior in college, aspired to be a teacher.

After the speeches were over and the music resumed, Dr. Walters turned to me, a smile playing around his mouth. "How do you get along with Dr. Hawkins?"

The alcohol had not completely loosened my inhibitions. "Do you know him?"

"Sure, we're in the same surgery residency. He's four years ahead of me. I scrubbed on a few cases with him in July."

"How's he in the operating room?" I wanted to gage his attitude about Hawkins.

94

He chuckled and Liz grunted. "He can be unpleasant."

"He's a bastard." She quickly amended his reply.

"Easy there, honey." He squeezed a bare thigh, but she was not to be quieted.

"You complained about him constantly."

"That's a bit of an exaggeration." He looked at me again. "Does he know you're a CO?"

"Yeah, I don't know how he found out. I don't advertise it. Only a few folks in the ER know it."

"He has a way of finding things like that out." He paused. "I bet he hassles you about it."

"Yup, every chance he gets." I had not told anyone about my persecution by Hawkins. Now seemed the time to ventilate. "I'm not Bill, I'm Neville."

"Neville?" Liz gazed at me, perplexed.

"Yeah, for Neville Chamberlain. You know, Munich, Czechoslovakia, appeasement. I want another Munich in Southeast Asia, according to Hawkins."

Dr. Walters laughed. "Oh, that Neville. How original." His words bubbled with sarcasm. "He does tend to obsess about communists. He fits in well with the John Birch Society. But you don't have too much longer to put up with him. Rotations change in a few days."

"Two more shifts. But who's counting?" I laughed.

"Okay guys, no more shop talk, especially about that Neanderthal. I'm hungry." Liz stood up, leg muscles rippling.

I shifted my gaze to the sun in the western sky. Coolness flavored the air.

"Bill, why don't you join us for dinner on the Hill. We're getting our weekly fix of spaghetti."

His offer was tempting. I had heard about the Italian Hill and the great food. Now was my chance. But I had little money in my pocket, and I didn't want to be a third wheel. They had already spent over two hours with me; I figured they'd rather dine alone, have a romantic meal.

"Thanks, but I should be getting back while the buses are running on a reasonable schedule. Also, I'm going to stop at Children's Hospital to check on a patient."

"A patient?" He expressed surprise.

"Yeah, a baby with meningitis we transferred this morning."

He clapped me on the shoulder. "That's commendable." He collected the cooler and blanket. "Until the next anti-war rally." He said jovially.

Liz smiled a good-bye, and I watched them walk down the hill, hand in hand.

Children's Hospital is at the eastern end of the park. I found the baby in a room of her own. She lay motionless in a crib, an IV bottle hanging, a monitor recording the rapid beating of her heart, and no sign of her mother. A nurse stood beside me and said that it was touch and go. The Gram stain of the milky fluid had shown pneumococcus. I didn't know what that meant, but it sounded bad.

The nurse was impressed that I had stopped by. "We get a lot of sick kids shipped from City; you're the first one from there that has come by to check on a patient." She was young and rather pretty. Perched on her neatly coiffed hair was one of those silly white triangular things that no nurse in City ER would be caught dead wearing.

"We're pretty busy." I said, observing the pictures of Mickey and Minnie Mouse and Pluto on the wall, silver stars surrounding a yellow half-moon on the blue ceiling, a teddy bear on the crib-side table and the bright mobile hanging over the baby. "It's a different world over there."

On the bus I tried to recall what I had in the refrigerator that might qualify as supper, certainly not spaghetti. It was dark when I got back to the apartment building. Before opening the door, I checked my box and found a letter from my mom. I entered the building and almost collided with Mr. Thompson, standing in the hallway, as if waiting for someone.

"He's back." My neighbor urgently reported.

"Who's back?"

"The colored man."

I didn't want to hear this.

"You know, the one I told you about last week. He's up in her apartment, with her and the kids." He stopped, breathless; he seemed to expect me to spring into vigorous action.

"There's no law against it. Maybe there used to be but not anymore. She can have any visitor she wants."

"But think about what might happen."

The door of apartment 1A opened, and a man's head stuck out, noise from a TV billowing around him on a cloud of cigarette smoke. I nodded to him and maneuvered past Mr. Thompson. In a few seconds the down-stairs man closed the door without saying anything.

"Shouldn't we call the police?"

I headed up the stairs. "No, we should not call the police. We need to mind our own business. Why don't you go upstairs and listen to the Cardinals game?"

"They already played this afternoon. They lost to the Cubs."

"Sorry to hear that. Goodnight, Mister Thompson." I left him sputtering below.

Fortunately, the fridge yielded one beer. Savoring it, I sat in my easy chair in the dark, looking out the open window and hearing the soft flicker of feet overhead, faint voices from the alley, a distant siren from the city, and from the woman's apartment, silence.

I finished the beer, turned on the light and opened my mom's letter. I received a letter from one or the other parent at least twice a week, and we spoke on the phone several times a month. Being connected provided comfort.

The letter contained the usual. She was concerned about Janet's new boyfriend. Dad had a heavy teaching load. The church picnic was a success. She hoped I had opportunities to play the trombone. I glanced over at the gray case in a dusty corner where it had resided since the move. I returned to the letter. Mom had seen Sally Rogers the day before writing; she still seemed sad. I folded the letter and looked out the window.

At one time, Hank Rogers had been my best friend. We had gradually drifted apart, and after his family moved across town at the end of the fourth grade, I rarely saw him. We reconnected a bit in high school, but we moved in different circles. He excelled on the baseball diamond; I participated in the chess club and band. He dropped out of Carolina after a year and joined the army. One evening we drank cider and split a pizza at the Rathskeller in Chapel Hill. A few days later he shipped out to Vietnam. Six months later he was back, in a body bag. I stood at the graveside, listening to the soft sobs of his parents and brother, gazing at the flag-draped casket, and reflecting on the workings of fate.

At the end of the letter, my mom asked how Rachel was doing. That, I didn't know. We had last talked on the phone a month earlier. Apparently, law school in New York City demanded much time and energy. Steady contact with a college semi-

98

boyfriend seemed expendable. Mom liked Rachel a lot, investing considerably more hope in the relationship than either of the direct participants ever did. Such was life.

Later, I ate a peanut butter and cream cheese sandwich and a salad assembled from the last of the lettuce and carrots. Shopping at Kroger's the following day became imperative.

If you work every night, it's probably easy to establish a diurnal routine. It's harder when you work five out of every seven nights, like I did. What do you do during the night off? The problem is compounded when the nights off occur at irregular intervals. After three months, I had not quite solved the problem. And now, for only the second time, I was confronted with two consecutive nights off. What to some might seem a welcomed opportunity, to me percolated as a nagging dilemma.

After eating, I wrote in my journal and read the latest issue of *The New Republic*, the subscription, a gift from my father. I watched the TV news until the report of the weekly body count from Vietnam.. The ratio of enemy dead to American dead magically remained at ten to one, the figure cited by experts as guaranteeing ultimate victory. I stared at the cover of a Steinbeck novel and eventually put it aside unopened. I finally settled down with a *Playboy*. In the wee hours of the morning, I stripped off my clothes and lay in bed. Soon, I addressed my sexual tension, but the relief was at best only partial; I needed the real thing.

I awoke in time to attend church, but the prospect of traveling by bus to the Unitarian Church did not appeal. I had only attended twice in three months, something I had failed to disclose to my mother, who often expressed in her letters the hope that I had found a good church. Because I usually worked Saturday nights, Sunday mornings were typically a time for sleep. That morning, instead of church, I went to the Hungry Bird Café and nursed a cup of coffee through the entire Sunday *Post-Dispatch*.

Early in the afternoon, I took my dirty clothes to the neighborhood laundromat. My building had a washing machine and dryer in the basement, a musty room of wires, pipes, cobwebs and peculiar smells. However, the machines were either in use or more commonly broken when I needed them. The last time I had tried to use them I had encountered my neighbor bent over the open door of the washer - bleached hair cascading over her face, a bruise visible on her thigh below short shorts, a basket of dirty clothes at her side - cussing extravagantly.

After the laundromat, I went to the grocery store. Because I had two bags full of food, I rode the bus home. I got off at the stop, turned the corner and saw an ambulance and congregation of people in front of my apartment building. When I got there, I asked a man in the crowd what had happened. He told me that someone had been stabbed.

Shit! I should have taken Mr. Thompson seriously.

Pushing through the crowd, I got to the stoop. I set my bags down and opened the door. Mr. Thompson stood at the bottom of the stairs, looking up at a stretcher, which was laboriously making its way down, an ambulance attendant at each end. When they reached the hallway, I saw that there was a woman on the stretcher, her face contorted in pain. But she was old not young. It was Mrs. Thompson. Involuntarily, I expelled a sigh of relief. Mr. Thompson saw me and clutched my arm.

"They want to take her to City Hospital. I want her to go to Firmin Desloge. We have the Medicare. She'll die at City. Don't let them take her there. Please, doctor."

"Okay, Mr. Thompson, right now we need to get out of the way so they can take her out."

100

We stood aside. I held the door open with one hand and kept the other on his shoulder, gently steadying him. We followed the stretcher onto the stoop and watched the attendants load her into the back of the ambulance. Some of the curious pressed forward to get a better look, only to be waved back by the attendants.

"Please, don't let them take her to City Hospital."

The attendants were familiar, although I could not recall their names. One remained in the back with Mrs. Thompson. With Mr. Thompson pleading at my side, I approached the other as he was closing the door. Initially annoyed at the interruption, he seemed to recognize me, and his face relaxed a bit.

"I work in the ER at City. She's my neighbor. What happened?"

He studied me momentarily and glanced at Mr. Thompson, who was blubbering away beside me. He looked back at me. I must have passed muster.

"Thought you looked familiar. She took a nasty fall. Broke her hip. Vital signs are okay."

"Damn! Too bad. You know she has Parkinson's."

Mr. Thompson pulled on my arm. "Tell him! Tell him!"

The attendant nodded towards the old man. "Yes, he told us that."

"He wants you to take her to Firmin Desloge. Can you do that?"

"Yeah, he mentioned that a few times." The sarcasm was evident, but he appeared to be deliberating. "We're supposed to transport to City." He paused and looked again at Mr. Thompson. "Okay, we can take her to Firmin Desloge, if that's where she usually goes."

"Thanks." I said.

"Mister Thompson you can ride up front with me." The attendant said.

Instead of relaxing his grip on my arm, Mr. Thompson tightened it. "Aren't you coming, too?"

"No, they don't need me, she's in good hands." I moved my arm in a subtle effort to detach myself, but he clung more tightly.

"No, we need you. You know us. Please come."

Damn, I didn't need this. I looked at him. White hair was plastered against his scalp. Tears streaked his aged face. Lips quivered, and spittle gathered at the corners of his mouth. Eyes burned like coals in the dark ashes of his desperation.

This was crazy. I shifted my gaze to the attendant who stood impatiently. I shrugged my shoulders, a gesture of surrender.

"You can ride in the back, if you don't mind it being tight." The attendant reopened the door, and I climbed in.

I spent the next six hours with Mr. Thompson at Firmin Desloge Hospital. Mostly, I sat in a waiting room. Mumbling and crying, he paced and sat, paced and sat. Every hour or so, I accompanied him to the restroom. Repeatedly, I reassured him that nowadays broken hips could be fixed. She would walk again. I tried to distract him, asking about his work as a shoe repairman, about how he had met his wife, about growing up in south St. Louis, about the great Cardinal teams of the '30s, about the construction of the arch. Nothing seemed to work. We received occasional reports from a doctor or nurse. Surgery was planned for a day or two. A doctor said something about her heart, which neither of us understood. When we briefly saw her, she was sleeping peacefully. If only they could do the same for her husband.

102

Mr. Thompson finally calmed down enough to call his son in Columbia. I had to explain most of it to the son. He set out immediately. When he arrived two hours later, I left. The buses had stopped running, so I had to take a cab. That night I slept soundly.

The next morning, I remembered my groceries on the stoop. Of course, they were gone, and no one I spoke to recalled seeing them. So, off I went to the grocery store. My wallet was taking a big hit.

That afternoon, Mr. Thompson's son brought him back to the apartment. The old man was doing much better emotionally but was physically exhausted. The son thanked me profusely. Mrs. Thompson had surgery the next day, and it went well. But she never returned to the apartment. The Thompsons moved to Columbia, and I never heard from them again.

After a two-night hiatus, I returned to work Monday. The other senior resident had duty that shift; he was quite different from Hawkins. Dr. Morland pretty much ignored me; I don't think he even knew my name. That was fine with me. He seemed satisfied that I did my job: shuffling patients into and out of rooms, transporting them to wards or x-ray, cleaning up blood and gore, assisting with procedures, mixing plaster for casting. He had thanked me once after I helped restrain a particularly belligerent drunk during a laceration repair. Dr. Morland would sometimes flirt with a couple of the nurses, and I heard that he took one on an evening Mississippi River cruise.

I recorded a lot of my St. Louis experiences in a journal. That's how I've been able to recall things decades later. You get everything in an ER like City's, from the ones who arrive dead from a shooting or stabbing or traffic accident to the ones who come in with a hang nail. There was always a steady stream of coughs, sore throats, rashes, belly aches, headaches, back aches and sprained ankles. Then there were the heart attacks, strokes, GI bleeders, venereal infections, asthma attacks, drug overdoses and diabetic comas. I particularly remember the little kids brought in convulsing from acute lead poisoning. "I just can't keep him from eating the plaster crumbling off the wall," a distraught mother would say. There seemed to be a lot of women with cuts, bruises and even fractures from running into doors or falling down stairs. Often a concerned husband, boyfriend or father hovered over the injured woman. Years after I left the ER I figured out that doors and stairs had been among the least of her worries.

Occasionally, a fight would break out in the ER. Once, in the waiting room a woman started beating her husband with a large handbag. Threats were common fare. Everyone who worked there had been the target at some time of verbal abuse. We lived with it. A full-time security guard was on duty every shift. Between altercations, the regular night-shift guard, an overweight middle-aged guy, would sit in the waiting room, chewing tobacco and reading paperback westerns. Apparently, he was an alderman's brother. One morning, before I left to go home, he asked me if I wanted a juicy piece. It took me a few seconds to realize that he was not offering me chewing gum.

Tuesday night I would face Hawkins. Avoiding him for eight hours would be virtually impossible. I considered calling in sick. I decided that would be acting like the coward he thought I was. Maybe he would forget my comment. Yeah right, maybe the Cardinals would concede the World Series to the Red Sox.

At the beginning of the shift, I was in the waiting room, straightening things up. I returned a one-legged rag doll and a three-wheeled dump truck to the small toy box and neatly stacked old Readers' Digests and Field and Stream magazines on a table. It had probably been a long time since some of our patients had seen a field or a stream.

"Mr. Blanchard, could I have word with you?"

Startled, I turned towards the familiar voice to find Hawkins leaning over the reception desk, his face close to the round hole in the window, his eyes fixed on me. Mr. Blanchard? This could be worse than I expected. I balled up the hamburger wrapper I had just picked up and tossed it in the waste can. I followed him down the hall to the supply room.

"Mr. Blanchard," he started once we were inside the all too small space. "I trust you have had time to think about what you said to me the other night." He appeared calm, almost subdued.

This was a different approach than I had anticipated. Did he expect me to apologize? I smelled coffee on his breath. There was a dark mole I had not noticed before on the side of his neck. I realized he was waiting for a reply. An apology might get me off easy.

"What did I say?"

As I watched, his face transformed: the sneer emerged, eyebrows crept downward, ears inched upwards. The beast was escaping from its lair. Strangely, I felt relieved.

He brought his right hand up, as if to hit me. But it stopped, and he pointed a finger at me, which came within an inch of my chest.

"You pinko bastard! Don't get smart with me. You know exactly what I'm talking about. It's bad enough that while brave boys are dying for our country in a damn jungle, you and your ilk are enjoying the easy life here, giving aid and comfort to the enemy." He paused to take a breath. A drop of saliva inched down his chin. "Don't you ever say anything like that to me again. You're already getting a bad report from me, but if you insult me again, I'll do my best to see that you are fired. I could do it, too. Do you understand?"

Could he really get me fired? I had received positive one- and two-month evaluations from my supervisor. Keep up the good work, he had said. And Hawkins was generally disliked by the ER staff. How much weight could he carry? This was an empty threat, right? I looked at the IV bottles on the shelf behind him and didn't say anything.

"Good, you understand."

He moved to get around me. I moved to let him pass. I remained there for a minute or two after he left.

About 3am a man carried a semi-conscious teenage girl into the waiting room, placed her on a chair and left. Oblivious, the guard sat in the corner, smoking a cigarette and reading his book. After a few minutes, a man waiting to be seen went to the reception desk and expressed concern about the pool of blood that had formed under the new arrival's chair. This immediately set things in motion; we quickly discovered that she was an "AB." During my very first shift in the ER, I had learned that AB was short for abortion. Specifically, it referred to a woman who was suffering a complication of one.

After I finished cleaning up the blood in the waiting room, I checked with the team that was working on the AB in the major trauma room. She was in bad shape. I could not tell if she was conscious. An oxygen mask covered her nose and mouth; her cheeks blended in with the white sheet. Blood flowed into one arm and saline into the other. Her feet were in stirrups, legs splayed apart, with a muttering Hawkins hunched between them, dropping bloody surgical sponges onto the floor. This, I did not want to watch, so I went to help an intern extract a peanut from a kid's nostril.

Soon, a nurse came to say that they needed me to help with the AB. Back in the trauma room I found a blood-splattered Hawkins talking to a doctor whom I quickly learned was the Ob/Gyn resident on call.

"We're pouring blood into her, but we can't keep up with what she's losing. We've given her four units, and her pressure is sixty over zero, pulse is one eighty. She's going down the tubes without an emergency hysterectomy." His face suggested ambivalence about whether she deserved this heroic effort.

The Ob/Gyn resident said something that I didn't catch. Standing beside him, a guy with a crew cut I pegged as a med student shifted his feet awkwardly.

Hawkins spied me. "There you are. Help Dr Petry and his med student get her upstairs to the ER." He peeled off the bloody gloves, threw them in a bucket and left.

I did what he told me to do. When I returned to the emergency department, I had a lot of blood to clean up. Later, I heard that she had not made it.

We spent the next few hours gradually whittling down the patient backlog that had accumulated when so many staff members had tended to the AB. Around six o'clock, Beth asked me to put a man who had been triaged to low priority in a room and find out more about his trouble sleeping. This wasn't part of my job description, but I was occasionally asked to do it. I complied.

He was an 18-year old who looked like the sidewalk outside Mack's Tavern on a Sunday morning. Peering through blood-shot eyes, he told me that he had not been able to sleep since his mother died a week ago. Cancer. He couldn't stop thinking about her. His sister, an LPN, told him about a red capsule that would help him sleep, and he wanted to try it. He didn't like to take medicine, but he was desperate. On the ER sheet, I recorded his blood pressure, pulse rate and temperature, and in the space for chief complaint wrote, 'Insomnia, mother died, wants a red capsule.'

"I'm really sorry about your mother. The doctor will be in soon to see you."

"Thanks man. God bless you."

A few minutes later I saw Hawkins standing in the hall outside the exam room, scowling at the sheet I had completed. He spotted me before I could duck into a room.

"Neville, is this your shit?"

I walked over to where he was festering. "I did the intake on him."

"So now you're a nurse's aide, or maybe even a med student. Moving up in the world, aren't you?"

"Beth asked me to get some info on him. That's all."

"And he told you his mother died and he needs something for sleep." The sneer was in full bloom.

"Yeah, he seems to be having a rough time."

"What a damn tragedy. There must be some kind of terrible epidemic in his family, cholera or something." He thrust a thin hospital chart at me. "You didn't notice that he was seen last Wednesday by Dr. Jordan. It seems his sister died, and he needed something for sleep." He paused for dramatic effect. "She gave him a script for thirty Seconals. Do you know what Seconal is?"

"I've heard of it."

"You've heard of it." His mouth curled into the geometric shape of pure contempt. "It's a popular drug of abuse. On the street it's known as red devil; you see, because it's a red capsule. He's a drug addict, you ass-hole, and he's going to be out of here so fast his head won't stop spinning for a week." With that he turned, opened the door and entered the room.

108

Hell, I hadn't seen any chart. I only had the single sheet for this visit, and I wrote down what the patient told me like I was supposed to do.

Sure enough, in less than a minute the guy came out of the room, but he didn't go quietly. He yelled obscenities and threats all the way down the hall, through the waiting room and out the door, his "You'll get yours, you god-damned son of a bitch doctor" ricocheting off the walls. More power to you, pal. I thought.

During the shift change, I was helping Stan, a day-shift orderly, restock the trauma room when a nurse burst in.

"Quick, we need this room. Something bad has happened to Dr. Hawkins."

I became aware of a lot of noisy commotion in the hall, and within a few seconds, Beth and an intern came in followed by a stretcher propelled by a security guard. I could see only fragments of the figure on the stretcher. The room was instantly filled with people and sounds.

"He's still breathing." "He's lost lots of blood." "Stabbed in the abdomen." "We need an IV, stat." "What's his pressure?" "Get the crash cart."

I inched along the wall and made it to the door. In the hall I met a white-faced, trembling receptionist.

"What happened?"

"A patient came in and said there was someone out in the parking lot bleeding. It was Dr. Hawkins."

I went down the hall and leaned against the door of the supply room and tried to think through the fog in my brain. Should I go home? In a few minutes, a nurse came out of the trauma room and saw me.

"Orderly, go upstairs and get three units of O negative blood, stat."

109

In the blood bank, the technician handed me the three units. "That's all we have of O negative right now. There was a real run on the stuff during the night."

I thought of the AB, and a vision of Hawkins peeling off bloody gloves at her bedside appeared.

"I've requested more blood from Firmin Desloge and the Red Cross, but it'll be twenty to thirty minutes at the soonest before it's here. I'll type his blood, but that'll take a while."

I took the blood downstairs, went into the room and handed the bags to the nurse. This time I stayed. There was a breathing tube in Hawkins' mouth attached to an Ambu bag, which an intern was rhythmically compressing. IV bottles dangled over his head, and within a minute two bags of blood joined them. Morland and the attending physician huddled over his body, apparently doing something in his abdomen. There was a lot of blood.

"I can't see the damned aorta, too much blood. Dammit, get the suction down here. Right here."

I heard the loud slurping sound and watched red fluid flow through the plastic tube into the jar on the floor under the table.

"What's his pressure?"

"I palpate fifty." A nurse responded.

"We're going to lose him if we can't get this bleeding stopped." Morland said.

I went outside and stood in the hall. Except for the drama in the trauma room, the ER was at a standstill, something I had not seen before. In the waiting room a policeman talked to the security guard. Patients had been taken somewhere. Staff members not involved in the heroic efforts stood in the hall or sat in the reception area, looking glum.

In a few minutes, the nurse came out again. "Is the blood here yet?"

110

"No."

"Okay," she said. "We need someone with O negative blood to donate right now. Who's O negative?"

I contemplated a spot of blood on the tiled floor. I had donated once in college during a blood drive. It had not been pleasant. I looked at the nurse. "I'm O negative; I'll do it."

Within a minute the blood bank technician had a big needle in my arm, and a few minutes later my blood had filled a plastic bag. When I sat up I became woozy, so I lay there for a while, staring at a gray ceiling.

When I could stand up without getting dizzy, I went out in the hall. Immediately, I knew that it hadn't worked; Hawkins had died. As I headed through the empty waiting room to go home, the nurse called to me. I turned to her.

"Bill, I'm sorry to have to ask you this, but would you be willing to help Stan clean up? I know you're off duty, but Dr. Hawkins' wife will be here soon. She knows he's been injured but doesn't know he's died. Dr. Anderson will tell her when she arrives. If she wants to see him, we don't want to make it any harder for her."

Outside the hospital, I saw the cops milling around. A clot of them congregated near Hawkins' Mustang. On the pavement, a line of crimson spots led to the ER door. I looked at the tiny spot of blood under the band aid on my arm. I headed towards the street and saw a cop stop a car that had turned into the ER circle. While he talked to the driver, the passenger side door opened; a woman in a pale green dress got out and started running towards the ER, a look of terror on her face. I watched her until she disappeared inside.

When I had entered the trauma room, Stan was sweeping stuff into a pile on the floor.

111

"Watch out for needles." He said.

I walked over to the table on which Hawkins lay naked. A suture line tracked across his abdomen where they had opened him up and then closed him. There wasn't as much blood as I expected. While I stood there, a fly landed on the tip of his nose. I watched it, perched there in the center of that dead face. Then I shooed it away with a wave of my hand. I went over to the sink, got a clean wash cloth from the cabinet, wet it under the faucet, squirted soap on it, and started to cleanse his body.

Helen, 2008

"I'll get it."

As he pushed his chair away from the table, he looked across the top of the cereal box. His son's dark eyes looked back at him over the whiteness of the up-tilted bowl that concealed most of his small face.

"We need to leave in five minutes."

On his way to the wall phone he heard Harriet's jubilant voice pierce the murmurings from the kitchen television. "CNN has called North Carolina for Obama."

"Great! Icing on the cake." He responded, and watched Marty place the bowl on the table and direct a milky smile his way. Checking caller ID, he reached for the phone. "Hello, Grandma." He said cheerfully. "It's a great day for the country."

The voice that greeted him was anything but cheerful. "Gene, I'm afraid I'm calling with sad news. Your grandfather died last night. He passed peacefully in his sleep."

"But I don't want to go with Great-gran to vote. Miss Oakley will miss me if I'm not there." A drop spilled from a watery eye onto his brown cheek as the boy looked first at his mother and then his father.

Across the table from his son, Gene spoke. "Now Marty, we've been through this before. Miss Oakley knows you will be a little late for school today."

"Yes Honey, Miss Oakley knows that you're going to help your great-gran vote." Harriet leaned forward and brushed a curl from her son's forehead. "Daddy will drop you off at school like usual. You'll only be a little late. You won't miss much at all." She

113

turned to her husband. "Can you manage? I need to run; my first patient is scheduled in thirty minutes."

"Sure, we can handle it." He looked at his son. "Can't we, Marty?"

The boy peered into his half full bowl of soggy cereal. "Uh huh."

The dark-skinned woman stood up, stepped over to her son, bent down and planted a noisy kiss in his mini Afro. "Luv ya." She then circled to her husband, who turned his face upward to receive the brief kiss on his lips. "Luv ya, too."

Marty looked up at his mother. "Mommy, aren't you gonna vote?"

"You bet, Honey. I've waited years for this day." She gave him a big smile.

"When?" Her husband asked.

"I'll get away at lunch."

"There'll probably be a line."

"I've freed my schedule until two, when I give a lecture. I'll have plenty of time. This little ole southern black girl is gonna exercise her citizen's right." Her exaggerated accent danced over the breakfast table. She moved towards the kitchen. "You'll vote after you drop Marty off?"

"Yeah, they know I'll be late."

"Okay. You guys take good care of Great-gran and savor the day. I should be home by six."

Helen waited for them on the bench near the front door, enclosed in her light coat, handbag in her lap, autumn sunlight silver on her uncovered head. Before Gene stopped the car, she was moving towards it, and he had to hustle to get out and around to the other side to open the door and assist her.

114

"Hey, Grandma. Sorry we're late; the traffic was heavier than I expected."

At the open car door, the old woman paused to catch her breath. "You don't really need to do this. The van is taking folks to the polls several times during the day."

"We want to, Grandma. Marty will remember this all his life. So will I."

Helen's eyes found his. "I hope so," she said softly. "I hope so."

After she had settled into the passenger seat, Helen turned her head towards the back where her great-grandson was buckled into his booster seat. "Hi, Martin, how are you this fine morning?"

"Okay." He replied to the top of her gray head and returned to his dinosaur book.

When he stopped at the red light, Gene glanced at his grandma who still seemed to be breathing heavily. "Are you okay, Grandma?" She took medicine for heart trouble: congestive heart failure and atrial fibrillation. Harriet had explained it to him.

"I'm fine." When the car started moving again, she asked "Your mother's working at the polls today, at E.K. Powe?"

"Yes, she expects to be there all day. The campaign wants an observer at every precinct, you know, to make sure there's no funny business."

"Oh yes, good idea. I could tell you stories about Durham elections."

"I bet you could." He again briefly glanced at her and then looked back at the road. They were creeping along Main Street, past the boarded-up windows and graffiti-laden sides of buildings. They passed a house where a client had lived. It looked deserted. He had not been able to keep the man out of prison but had

115

succeeded in getting a lighter sentence. In Public Defender work, you valued those little victories, or you didn't last long.

"What was the first presidential election you voted in, Grandma?"

Helen gazed through the windshield, as if seeing something far away. "1940, in Philadelphia. In 1944 your grandfather and I voted for Roosevelt, over at E.K. Powe School, where your mother is right now. That's where we voted the first time here. And the second time, too; in 1948, we voted for Wallace."

"Wallace! You couldn't have voted for Wallace in '48; he didn't run until '68. I'm pretty sure of that. But you would never have voted for Wallace, anyway."

"Oh no, not that Wallace, the other Wallace, the good one."

"Oh yes, I remember, the Progressive Party. Thurmond was the Dixiecrat, Truman, the Democrat and Dewey, the Republican. Truman won, a big surprise."

"Yes." She continued to stare straight ahead. "Truman was alright; I liked him better than your grandfather did. He did integrate the army. That may not seem like much now, but it was a big thing back then. Most people 'round here hated that. They thought it would mongrelize the white race."

Gene chuckled. "Well, they were right, it did. Look at me and Harriet; look at Marty." He paused. "Look at Obama."

"Don't joke about that, Gene. Martin's not a mongrel. He's a wonderful blessing."

"Obama's like me. He's like me, isn't he, Daddy?" The eager voice came from the back seat.

"Yes, Honey, he sure is; he's just like you."

To his grandmother Gene said, "I'm sorry; I know it's not a joke. But we have come a long way haven't we. And you did so much over the years to make things better: the co-op, Head Start, the Friends School, the Civil Rights work. You and Grandpa, both of you. Harriet and I are so proud and thankful for what you have done." He paused and when she did not immediately respond, continued, "And the irony is that what those bigots in the past were so worried about is happening, and that's good, it's part of the solution."

"Yes, you're right, we've come a long way." He strained to hear her words over the belching of a passing truck.

He turned a corner; the church where his grandma voted was just ahead. An assortment of campaign signs ushered them to it. "So, you first voted in Durham in 1944." He pulled into the parking lot and aimed for the spot closest to the door. "That was before Dad was born." He regretted it as soon as he had said it.

He parked the car and called over his shoulder, "Okay Marty, we're here. Time to help Great-gran vote."

As Gene helped his grandmother get out of the car, she gathered her coat around her frail frame and said, "I wish he could be here today to see this."

"Me too, Grandma, me too."

"That's a trump, Helen. Are you sure you're void in diamonds?" Mildred, not the most tolerant of bridge partners, eyed her from across the table.

"Oh, sorry." Flustered, Helen picked up the card she had just laid on the table, returned it to the fan of cards she held in her hand, and placed another on the table. "There, I did have a diamond." Suddenly, her heart was beating hard and fast, like it had for a while the day before.

"Well, now we know where the four of trumps is." Kathryn observed lightly.

117

"Are you okay, Helen? You seem rather scatter-brained today." Mildred produced the ace and swept the small pile of cards to her turf, arranging them into a stack beside her glass of red wine. On the book shelf behind Mildred, Kathryn's covey of descendants watched the action from their picture frames. On the adjacent wall, a cherubic girl lifted a flower to a smiling young woman, in the domestic tranquility of Kathryn's cherished Renoir print. Once upon a time, Helen's husband had given lectures on Impressionist artists.

To Helen's left, Agnes said, "I think she's worried about the election. She's worried about her boy. She's afraid the polls are wrong. She remembers Truman in '48."

"I remember Truman in '48." Kathryn laughed.

Helen looked at Agnes and suppressed the urge to react to the "boy." Agnes had only recently moved into the retirement home. In the past month, she had been included in the weekly bridge game to replace a woman who had suffered a stroke. For Helen, she was like the grackles that would infest the yard when she and Will wanted to watch cardinals or robins. She had put up with people like Agnes all her life and was frankly worn out with the effort. Still, this was not the time for conflict.

Scatter- brained? Probably. She had been distracted when she misplayed the card. Yes, she was worried about the election; she had seen enough racism through the years to be skeptical of the predictions. But that's not what had distracted her. She had been remembering the morning, not so much the voting, but her return to the home.

"Do you have time to come in and see Grandpa?" She had asked Gene when he dropped her off. No, he had a 10 o'clock meeting with a client, but he was looking forward to seeing Grandpa on Saturday. Gene and his family would be eating lunch with her in four days. Janet would be there, too, from Greensboro. It would be good to see Janet. It would be good for Will to see Janet. Yes, it would.

Kathryn continued. "If that's what's botherin' you, you have nothin' to worry about. Obama's gonna win. No doubt about it. Hell, even I voted for him."

"You didn't!" Agnes stared at her bridge partner. "How could you, a southern lady? How could you?" She nodded towards Helen. "I can understand Helen; she's a Yankee, but you were born and bred in the South."

"Southern, northern, what difference does that make? Anyway, Helen's lived in Durham for near 'bout seventy years. Isn't that right?" Kathryn did not wait for Helen's assent. "The other guy's too old, and that woman is an idiot. She's a disgrace to us all."

"Well, all I know is that my Carl Lee would be turnin' over in his grave if he knew a colored was runnin' for president." Chest heaving, Agnes slumped back in her chair and glared through thick glasses at the cards in her hand.

"Well I hate to think what acrobatics he'll be doin' tonight when the colored wins." Kathryn embraced sarcasm.

"Enough! Back to bridge. This is why I never discuss politics or religion." Mildred tossed the king of diamonds onto the table.

Triumphantly, Kathryn thumped the three of hearts on top of it. "There!"

"Damn, a singleton." Momentarily deflated, Mildred looked across at her partner. "Why couldn't you have the singleton?" Then her face softened. "How's Will doin' today?"

Helen's heart beat was slowing; her breathing, easier. "The same."

Yes, the same. He had sat in the easy chair across from her, remnants of tuna fish smeared on the bib tied around his neck, music from a Mozart piano sonata tickling the air. On the wall over his head hung his favorite photograph, the one with baby Janet in Helen's lap, Billy standing beside her, holding a toy truck, and Will, behind them, straight and strong, his smile like sunlight. There he had sat inert and vacant while she narrated the events of her morning. Yes, the same.

Gene detached himself and found his wife in the happy crowd, talking with two nurses from the clinic. Behind her, a large screen, displayed running totals of popular and electoral votes beneath the talking heads of CNN.

"Don't you think it's time to get Marty home?" He shouted over the music and the din of voices. "Where is he, anyway?"

Wordlessly, Harriet pointed, and Gene spied his son. He was gyrating, possibly in time to the music, with a boy and girl in a small space between clots of adult celebrants.

"He's not going to want to leave." She shouted back.

"What do you think?"

"You're right, we need to get him home. He's going to have a hard enough time getting to sleep."

"He's not the only one." Gene laughed and navigated towards his son.

A few minutes later they stepped from the turbulent heat of celebration into the cool night air.

"Put your jacket on, Marty." Harriet said, and then lifted her head to peer at the myriad specks of light that decorated the black sky. "Wow, what a night."

"Mister Blanchard. Mister Blanchard." A middle-aged man attired in the iconic Obama Hope t-shirt approached them, his right hand extended, his left holding a bottle of Lowenbrau. "It's Gene, isn't it?"

Gene shook hands with the vaguely familiar man while Harriet told him that she would take Marty to the car, and not to be too long. "Yes, I'm Gene Blanchard."

"You probably don't remember me. I'm Don Watkins. I worked with your dad at the school. I teach American History." His breath hung in alcoholic puffs in the air.

"Yes, sure, I remember. You were at the funeral." Gene paused and then added, "Dad always spoke highly of you."

The man shivered slightly. "That means a lot to me. Your dad was a wonderful teacher and a wonderful man. You know, he was a mentor to me, took me under his wing when I started, helped me through some rough times in those first few years." He gazed beyond Gene towards the banquet hall door; a pair of revelers was exiting.

"Yes, he enjoyed helping younger teachers."

"I just finished rereading his collection of stories about his experiences in the St. Louis ER. Wonderful writing.

"Yes, he was particularly proud of that collection."

Don Watkins shifted awkwardly. "How are ya'll doing? Your aunt, your grandmother, your mother?"

Gene wasn't surprised by the omission; his grandfather had not been at the funeral. "We're doing okay, about as well as you could expect. We miss him a lot. My son doesn't quite understand why his grandpa isn't here anymore. Like the rest of us, he's struggling to deal with it."

"I know it's rough." Don Watkins paused and then, in a somewhat different tone, said, "I hope you can enjoy the moment tonight. It's an historic occasion."

"Oh yes, it's exciting." Gene was ready to join his wife and son in the car, but there was something he had wondered about for a while, so he asked. "How are the kids doing? Especially the ones in the class, you know, the class where he died?"

"Well, they've all received counseling, of course. That's still going on for some of them. I think in general they're doing okay. Kids are resilient, but when your teacher drops dead in front of you, it's something you don't forget."

"No, you don't." Gene reached out his right hand. "Mister Watkins, it's good seeing you. Thanks for the kind words about my father. Take care."

Four years earlier, Helen and Will Blanchard had watched election returns in their apartment in the retirement home, with disappointment. Even then, the Alzheimer's had been nibbling at his brain - the annoying memory lapses, puzzling spells of confusion, embarrassing moments of irritability – although they didn't know it then. That was when they were still visiting their friend from the old neighborhood, in Memory Care. After one visit, Will had said to Helen, "If I ever get like that, just shoot me." She had grimaced, this from a man who had probably never shot a gun in his life. It wouldn't come to that, would it?

The rarely used TV in Will's Memory Care room was on, the sound low. Will sat on the bed, the plain white t-shirt hanging loosely, the diaper secure around his loins, his bare, hairless legs motionless against the pale sheet, his feet sheathed in lovingly knitted red socks. The woman's voice from the TV was a whisper.

"The polls won't close for another two hours on the west coast, but he's won Pennsylvania, Ohio and Florida, so they're saying he'll be the new president." Facing his bed, Helen spoke from the easy chair into the void.

122

Two weeks before while she was feeding him lunch, he had suddenly uttered her name. Since then, nothing. Would she ever hear it spoken from his lips again? She gazed at his head; his ears had grown longer through the years, but his nose was the same. The skin was dry and creviced under the gray stubble. She had not shaved him in two days. How many times had she stroked those cheeks, kissed those lips?

She switched off the TV with the remote and looked again at her husband. What was left inside that beloved head? Inside the head - suddenly, that brought the tragic reality back to her. An aneurysm, they said. It suddenly burst, they said. Like a balloon, they said. Had it a long time, they said. It just decided to pop right then, in front of his class. Dead before he hit the floor, they said. What was it like to be dead before you hit the floor? What was it like to be dead before you died?

Helen shook her head to clear her mind and focus on what she needed to do.

Helen opened her hand bag, reached inside and rummaged around until she found what she wanted. She held the wad of tissue paper in her hand. With her other hand, she flattened the tissue; her fingers did not work as well as they used to. She looked at the small pills, white against the pink paper, and slowly counted them - fifteen. Two weeks of saving a pill instead of placing it in her mouth and swallowing. "Be careful, Grandma, never take more than one a day." Harriet had warned her. "An overdose could be very dangerous."

Yes, even death, she had learned when she used the computer in the library. Kathryn had shown her how. "You should use the Internet." Her friend had said. "There's all kinds of interesting things."

She looked from the pills to her husband and then to the half empty glass of water on the bedside table. As she looked at the glass, a scene emerged from the tangle of memories. A father and his son played catch in the front yard, the baseball going back and forth. "When the ball is down here hold the glove like this. When it's up here hold the glove like this. That's right." The ball flew back and forth, back and forth, smacking into each glove with the confident sound of a future.

Helen arose and placed the pink tissue and the white pills on the table beside the glass. "Time for bed." She bent down and enclosed Will's legs in her arms. "Okay, help me here, honey." She swung the legs onto the bed, as his body turned. She straightened up and gently pressed her hands down on his chest.

He complied.

She pulled the sheet and light blanket up to cover his chest and crossed his arms over the blanket. She bent over and touched her lips to his. When she straightened, his eyes, gray like the eastern sky at twilight, stared upwards at the print of Caravaggio's *Calling of Matthew*, which Bill had placed on the ceiling.

Helen looked at her husband's face for a moment. Then she picked up the tissue, reached for her bag, and poured the pills into it. She walked to the door, turned out the light, opened the door, and passed out of their life.

A Dead Boy

He was dead, no question about that. The father had been right. The mother clutched the pale naked body, reminding me of the Renaissance Pieta I had once seen in a museum. Her tear-tracked face folded into the curly blond hair; her eyes filled with the knowing, not quite focused on me. I confirmed the silence of the small chest with the ritual application of the stethoscope, a tool of my trade.

I had joined mother and dead son in the cramped, dingy back seat of the worn-out Chevy soon after the thin man with the wispy goatee and long pony tail had appeared at the front desk of the clinic and said, "I need the doctor, I have a dead boy out in the car."

After Jean, my office assistant, interrupted my weekly exposure to the recitation of Mabel Potter's myriad ailments with this news, I found the man on the stoop of the cinder block clinic building, where he was peering down at the September dust. It didn't take him long to tell me about it: How he had got in the car and begun to back down to the road when he felt the bump; he had hit something. Because he thought the boy was in the trailer with his mother, grandmother and baby sister, he didn't think about his son. Some animal had ventured into the yard at just the wrong time. That's what he was thinking as he climbed out of the car and until he discovered his 3-year old David lying motionless under the bumper, beside the wheel. He knew about mouth-to-mouth and had tried that while his wife had pushed on the boy's chest, but their efforts had been of no use. It had happened about an hour before. They lived up Rocky Ridge Hollow and wanted the doctor to see him before they took him back home and buried him.

"He was delivered by a midwife, and we never had a birth certificate on him," the father said as he gazed towards sun-soaked Barrow Mountain, beyond the house tops of the town. "We figured he needed a death certificate, you know, to show that he had ever lived." The sound of his voice, like the flow and eddies of a woeful breeze.

The father was young, probably about my age. He wore a faded sweat-stained t-shirt, and his dusty jeans hung loosely. Brown feet filled insubstantial sandals, unusual foot-wear for men in those parts. With an "I'm very sorry," I touched his bare arm, to establish contact, healer to sufferer, father to father.

He did not respond, and we stood silently together on the stoop, enveloped by the chorus of insects in the adjacent field, gazing into the distance, until he pointed to the car at the other end of the clinic parking lot and said, "He's over there."

My first experience with a dead child had occurred during the third year of medical school, and for months afterwards, I could close my eyes and see her bloated body, ravaged by the leukemia and its futile treatment, the grayish clouds of skin like the sky of an impending storm. Over the ensuing years of training, I had seen other dead children; their images gradually diffused into mist beyond the easy reach of memory. It was a necessary part of being a doctor.

In the car I told the mother how sorry I was and how this was such a terrible thing to happen. She held her dead son tightly to her body and briefly looked at my face, my impotent words rebounding from her eyes. After listening to the chest, I asked her to loosen her grip a bit and turn him so that I could see more of him. She complied, and I was able to get a good look at the body, to feel his arms and legs, push on his belly and palpate his head. The only blemish was a shallow bloodless gash on the top of a bluish lump above his right eye, hardly an explanation for a dead child. But this trivial wound must have concealed a storm of damage inside the skull. After finishing the examination, I looked at the familiar parts of the little boy body and struggled to control the fear that surged like a blizzard gale on a mountain top.

From the front seat a whimpering sound pulled me back; I became aware of an older woman sitting on the passenger side, holding a baby. Despair saturated the face that turned to me. The infant she cradled, clad only in a diaper, slept in peaceful oblivion.

"Are you his grandmother?"

She nodded silently and with the tremor of a sob turned to look at the baby, a tear falling from her down-turned face.

My attention returned to the mother, who had again gathered the dead son to her body, as if to restore him to safety. Laying my hand on a shoulder, I felt her heat through the fabric of the dress. "Are you going to be okay?" I watched her and waited. When she did not respond after a moment, I asked if there was anything I could do to help. A barely perceptible shake of her head answered.

Exiting the car, I welcomed the breeze on my face. I asked the father, who had stood by the open door while I had been in the car, to come with me into my office, where he gave me the information necessary to fill out the death certificate.

I said the usual things that doctors offer in such situations, and he told me that the grief was awful but that they would be okay. "We're strong people," he spoke into my words of solace. He left the clinic; the ghost of his sorrow lingering in my office. On the certificate, I wrote 'accidental head trauma' as the cause of David Hibbert's death; I recorded a date of birth that was ten days before my son's day of birth.

After he left and before returning to Mabel's complaints, I called home. Barbara answered.

"How's Danny?"

"He's fine." Surprise in her voice and after a pause, "Is something wrong? Are you alright?"

"Yeah, just wanted to check." I told her I'd see her that night and hung up, feeling a bit foolish but relieved.

That evening I told Barbara about the dead boy. I read three books to Danny before bedtime instead of the usual two, and for the first time since we had moved to Hampton, I stayed with him in his bed. He quickly fell asleep, and I lay there curled into the music of his breathing. As I dozed off, the phone rang, and I had to go to the clinic to sew up a laceration, which bled profusely.

The phone call from the chief medical examiner in Raleigh came a week later, when the image of the dead boy in his mother's arms intruded less often into my thoughts and the gnawing anxiety had begun to subside.

Yes, I replied, I had signed the death certificate. No, I had not realized that David Hibbert's death qualified as a medical examiner's case and that I should have arranged for the body to be sent to the medical examiner fifty miles away in Asheville. In cases of sudden unexpected death in children, explained the chief, autopsies often need to be performed. As he reminded me of what I knew from my medical school and residency training, I felt embarrassed. I had overlooked the necessity of a medical forensic investigation of David's death. How could I have made such a mistake?

But even as I silently berated myself, another reaction, a countervailing force gathered in the roiling of my mind, the insistence that there had been no need for further investigation;

128

things had happened just as the father had described. The man on the phone was doing his job, but I was the one who had seen the mother cradling her dead boy, witnessed the grandmother's grief, listened to the father's telling of the terrible accident, felt the suffering. I had done my job as a physician. To the man on the phone, I acknowledged my error and apologized, offering the meager excuse that I had only been in practice for three months and had not encountered such a situation before.

He commiserated, but into my solidifying defenses, he spoke. "You recorded the cause of death as accidental head trauma. How did you determine that?"

Damn him. As I related the events that had been told me and described the lump on the forehead, I realized that my words were like leaves in the wind. Clearly, I had minimal objective evidence on which to base my assessment. I had blown it. Mercifully, his purpose in calling was not primarily to admonish me.

"We have some reason to be concerned about this death," he explained. "Our computer analysis found a match for information on David's death certificate with a case about two years ago in Watauga County, north of you. A little girl, three years old, last name Hibbert, died from a fall into an old well. There were some inconsistencies in the story the father told, so we looked into it, an autopsy and everything. We finally signed her death out as unintentional, but the local ME remained a bit uneasy about it. He asked the county social services staff to keep an eye on the family; they had a one-year old boy. A couple of weeks later when the social worker went by to check on the family, they had disappeared, no sign of life at all. Neighbors a mile down the road told her the house had been empty for over a week and they had no idea where the family had gone. The guy they rented from lived in Boone and didn't even know they had left."

Hunched at my office desk across from the chair where a grieving father had sat a week before, assuring me that they were strong people, I listened to the chief ME. He paused, and I dreaded what was coming next.

"You indicated on the death certificate that he was born in Watauga County, but the state has no record of a birth certificate."

Arousing myself, I stood up and walked the few steps to the window. The phone cord barely reached. Through the foliage on the river bank, I could glimpse patches of the churning waters of the French Broad. "Yes, the father mentioned that there was no birth certificate. A midwife delivered him, I assumed at home, but I didn't ask." The oppressive air of the office absorbed the sound of my voice. A robin stood motionless on an island of grass in the shade of a maple tree.

The ME continued. "An old woman used to deliver babies in Watauga; it was illegal, but the sheriff didn't do much about it. I heard that she died about a year ago." He paused and then said, "I'm thinking that it's the same family. David was the baby two years ago. Two sudden child deaths in one family raise a lot of concern."

I agreed that it could be the same family. But I didn't want to consider the implications of that possibility. Either the parents had suffered the unbearable, the accidental loss of two children, or one or both had somehow intentionally caused the deaths through neglect or abuse. Was this the worst luck imaginable, or something else even more awful? Victim or villain, whom had I encountered? While I watched, the bird took wing and disappeared into the greenery of the river bank.

The chief ME asked about David's family, and I told him the little I knew. They lived in a remote, particularly mountainous area of the county, where I had not yet been. My mention of the baby produced a momentary silence; I could sense him adding this disturbing plank to the edifice of his suspicions.

"We'll need to get more information about this." He seemed to have made a decision. "We need to find out if it's the same family. We'll have the county sheriff and social services department look into the family to see if there's been anything suspicious. Someone from the Asheville ME office will probably visit the family. We hate to do it, but we may need to exhume the body for an autopsy. When another child might be in danger, we must be especially vigilant." He stopped. His impeccable reasoning collided with my replaying of the father's description of his futile efforts to revive his son, leaving my mind littered with the wreckage of certitude.

He finally broke the silence. "You say they took the body back home for burial."

"Yes, that's what he said they were going to do."

After the call ended, it took some time in the office for me to rally myself to return to the patients who awaited me that afternoon. I hope that I made no serious mistakes.

That evening, conflicting emotions and competing allegiances ate at me. Because of confidentiality I could not go into any detail with Barbara about what was bothering me.

"Something's come up about the boy's death," was all I could tell her.

We had known that there would be times when my work would infect our family life, but that didn't make it any easier. Her late-night back massage eased the physical tension but did little to relieve the anguish in my mind. In the early morning hours, sleep

131

finally rescued me from visions of what I had actually seen and from what I could not avoid imagining.

The next day was a Saturday, and during the half day clinic I deliberated about whether or not to visit the Hibberts. By the time I finished with my last patient, I had yielded to the not so rational need to see them again. What did I expect to get out of it? Answers? Reassurance? Expiation?

Checking with the operator, I found the Hibberts had no phone, not unusual for families in remote areas of the mountains. I faced the task of locating them. Jean, who had lived all her life in town, advised me to get directions from Bascomb Morgan; he ran a general store where the road to Rocky Ridge Hollow branched off the county road. She figured he would know all the folks who lived up the hollow.

Under a mid-afternoon sky that was gradually collecting clouds, I found Morgan's store. In front of the wooden building stood two old style pumps that offered a choice of gasoline grades at five cents more per gallon than what was available fifteen miles away in town. Plastered on the front of the store and hanging from the edges of the galley roof, signs in various stages of decline advertised R.C. Cola, Camel cigarettes and an assortment of other products.

I parked my Bronco between a pick-up truck and twenty-year old Ford and climbed out, my shoes crunching the bottle caps that littered the sunbaked ground. As I ascended the steps to the galley, I nodded to the old man who sat on a wooden bench under a Wonder Bread sign and beside a basket of freshly dug potatoes. Inside I found Bascomb Morgan handing a bag of groceries across the counter to a young woman. I waited until she left and then introduced myself as the new doctor in Hampton. Emitting the scent of stale cigarettes, the paunchy middle-aged man extended a meaty hand across the counter.

"Glad to meetcha, Doc. I've heard good things aboutcha. You doctored my cousin Alfred a while back, fixed him up real good." He paused and then, "What brings you to these parts?"

He knew who I was asking about immediately. "Those hippies," he said with a half-smile and no hint of rancor. "They live in a trailer up the hollow, about a mile past Dewey Fulton's place, rent from old man Johnson. He lives in town now."

He told me that the younger woman came in occasionally to buy food: canned meat and vegetables, sugar, flour, the usual. She paid with food stamps. "Cute little kids," he added. They hadn't been around very long, moved in early in the summer, he said, too late to put in a garden. Dewey's wife had taken by some tomatoes, corn and other vegetables. "They keep pretty much to themselves. I don't know for sure what he does. Heard he might be hired to cut tobacco down the valley, but really can't say for sure." He stopped and then asked, "One of the kids sick?"

He didn't seem to know that one of the kids was dead, and I didn't tell him. I dodged the question, soon thanked him and climbed into the Bronco to head up the narrow road that coiled into Rocky Ridge Hollow.

Accompanied by a dry creek bed on one side, the road rose steadily through a mixed pine and hard wood forest, decorated with splashes of early autumn colors and punctuated periodically by houses, mobile homes and small patches of farm land. Above the trees, clouds effaced the sun, shrouding my journey in extended shadow.

As I drove, I continued to rehearse various scenarios for the visit. The closer I drew the more I doubted that my inner turmoil would in any way be relieved by the visit. It seemed increasingly

133

naïve to think that getting a feel for the family in their home environment and perhaps hearing about the previous loss of a daughter would provide clarifying illumination.

By the time I saw the trailer that Bascomb Morgan had described, I was debating whether to turn around and go home, to allow the ceaseless trickle of time to eventually douse this fire, as it had extinguished past flames of distress. Only I knew this would take longer. But something about that trailer, silhouetted against the graying afternoon, beckoned me. I would see the suffering family again.

However, that was not to be. When I turned into the dirt driveway and pulled up the short incline to the shelf of bare earth beside the trailer, a blanket of solitude enveloped me. With the motor still running, I sat and studied the scene, slowly absorbing the reality. Turning from the abandoned trailer, I peered across a field of tall grass that climbed a hill, yielding to pine trees, which dissolved in a low-lying cloud.

I cut the engine and got out. Looking at the trailer I offered a hopeless 'Hello, anybody home?' into the growing breeze. I heard a rattling sound and watched a squirrel scamper over the slanted metal roof and jump onto a tree beyond the end of the dwelling. Resting on cinder blocks, the trailer appeared to be approaching the end of its longevity. I walked to the only door and found it dented and deformed, padlocked precariously to an insubstantial metal frame. I could easily have entered but didn't.

Instead I walked in the dry grass around the structure, noting the dents and bruises, the rust and peeling paint and the fractured glass in a back window, the hole incompletely occluded by a yellowed cloth, probably a diaper. At the back of the trailer between the roots of the squirrel's tree something in the dirt caught my eye. I reached down and picked up a toy dump truck with a missing wheel. Except for that I found nothing to indicate recent human presence. The place was stripped bare, skeletal, desolate in the gathering gloom.

I walked in wider circles around the yard, and then into the field and later into the woods on the other side of the Bronco, searching for a mound of soft dirt, a patch of bare earth, a cross, an arrangement of stones, a cluster of flowers, anything. I found nothing.

Aware of the impending storm, I returned to the Bronco. I stood behind it and gazed down the rutted driveway to the pavement below. This was where he had said it happened.

Reaching into myself, I recreated the scene, saw David running from the front of the trailer, his little legs churning, his thin chest heaving with the exertion. Where was he heading: Some bird or squirrel in the woods, his father, a pet dog, or was it an aimless little boy romp, inexplicable to any observing adult, a uniquely childhood pleasure? But as I watched him propel himself towards his death, the image faded, and he disappeared. I saw instead newly fallen leaves swirling in the dust, driven by the wind across the driveway and against the trailer. Heavy with the burden of knowledge, I turned back, the first drop falling on my cheek as I opened the door.

Faulkner's Hamlet

Listening to the night sounds at the open window of his rented room, Labove gazed at the oak that etched its full-bodied imprint on the lavender of the Western sky. Confidence flowed into him like breeze through leaves on robust limbs; he felt the doubts of recent weeks vanish. "Yes, I can do it."

Journal Entry, Jacob Labove, Monday, September 25, 1897, 7:15 pm

The school house is Will Varner's old livery stable. I have been working on it for the past month with intermittent help from some of the older boys in Faulkner's Hamlet who could not come up with satisfactory excuses to avoid the labor. We procured cast-off desks and a few old books and slates from the school in Jefferson. It finally looks more like a school than a stable; although the odor of horses lingers.

This morning fourteen children showed up for the first day, if you can call a fifteen-year old boy almost as big as me, a child. The youngest was six, and he wet his pants in the middle of the morning. Fortunately, his older sister was there and took him home. They soon returned; he had on a dirty brown dress and was miserable from humiliation for the rest of the day. With the warm weather, the girls wore light cotton dresses, and the boys wore shirts and pants or overalls. All but two of the children were barefoot. Some of the little ones seemed bright and eager; the older ones were more sullen and suspicious. Among the girls was Varner's daughter, who is said to be thirteen. They must mature early in northern Mississippi.

Even before I could start class, a fight broke out between two boys. Apparently, there is bad blood between the families. I ended it quickly and did not spare either miscreant the force of my fists. They are already learning that I am determined to maintain order. I face prodigious challenges in this benighted place, but I am up to it.

I succeeded in completing the lessons I had planned for each age group. None of them knows much of anything, so I am starting from scratch. The little ones seemed more receptive and interested in learning, and several of them may even be able to master reading and writing. The older boys are probably hopeless. If I get them to learn simple arithmetic, that will be an accomplishment. Except for Varner's daughter, the older girls did a lot of giggling and looking at the boys. Varner's daughter, Eula is her name, is a different one entirely. She sat in serene silence, oblivious to the activity around her, exuding an aura of imperial placidity.

Journal Entry, Jacob Labove, Monday, October 18, 1897, 9:30 pm

We started the fourth week of school today, and I am cautiously encouraged. Most days I have between twelve and fifteen students; some come almost every day, others only occasionally. Poor little Silas Tull fell in the creek and drowned. I called off classes the day of the funeral. The cotton is all picked, so attendance has improved recently. Beulah Quick got married, and her husband won't let her come any more. It's just as well; she riled up the boys. Discipline has been no problem since I bloodied Hiram Bookwright's nose when he pulled down Ethan Houston's pants.

Most of the children who come regularly have learned the alphabet and can count to ten. A few can count to twenty, and Bo Snopes can spell his first name. They prefer history over arithmetic. They like to hear about Robert E. Lee and Jefferson Davis, although they sometimes get confused about exactly who won the war. Bayard Sartoris keeps insisting that his granpa whipped the whole Yankee army. Today, I tried to explain the difference between Abe Lincoln and the devil, but I didn't make much progress on that one. They learn about the devil real early around here.

Eula Varner is there almost every day. Her brother brings her each morning in the carriage and picks her up in the afternoon. In between, she is a palpable presence; her body absorbs the space that it occupies with languid indifference. Today, I looked down at the letters she had printed on her slate and could not help but notice her breasts under the thin fabric. She is a distraction; that one is. Each morning I find myself hoping that she won't show up, and then I see her silhouetted in the school house door.

It is unseasonably hot tonight, and there is no breeze through my window. The full moon brightens the sky, and Varner's store across the way casts a shadow on the dry dirt. The large oak behind the store has not yet shed its leaves. I hear the drummer in the room next door; he has a woman in there. How did he manage to get her by the usually vigilant Mrs. Littlejohn? My mind is restless tonight. Earlier in the evening I read Keats' "Lamia." I was not soothed. I yearn for a dreamless sleep.

It was unseasonably hot in Faulkner's Hamlet, even in the shade on the gallery of Varner's store. Three men sat in that inadequate shade. The youngest one repeatedly fanned his bare head with a yellowed wide-brimmed hat. He was a sewing machine salesman who came to the Hamlet every six months or so and stayed a few days at Mrs. Littlejohn's boarding house. He was known to be a good salesman. Most of the women around those parts had purchased a machine in recent years; he was working on the few who hadn't. The women also still had the brooms and brushes and kitchen pots and pans that he had peddled a few years back. Yes, he was effective selling things to country housewives who didn't know they needed them. He was a talker, too. Ratliff was his name.

"I see Faulkner's Hamlet's got itself a school since I was here last."

Armistid was the man tilting the middle chair back against the worn unpainted front of the store. Much older than Ratliff, he carried in his left hip a Yankee musket ball from Shiloh. He wore once-blue overalls, a faded gray short-sleeved cotton shirt and a hat similar to the one Ratliff waved around, only more sweat-stained. His face was brown and sun-leathered under the hat, and his jaws incessantly worked the plug. Regularly, dark fluid squirted from his mouth onto the wooden floor of the gallery, to congeal in the stagnant dust.

"Yup."

"Well, how 'bout that." The salesman tilted his chair against the storefront while continuing the rhythmic beating of the still air. "Who's the teacher?"

The third man grunted. He was dressed much like Armisted, except that he was bare-headed. Little tufts of gray hair ringed his bald head. He was thin, wrinkled and old. He sat hunched forward, and his right hand moved methodically up and down a stick that he held in his other hand. Slivers of wood fell from the stick to the gallery floor at his feet; his hand partially concealed the knife. After Ratliff spoke, he raised his head and peered at Littlejohn's across the dirt road. He kept on whittling, as if the hand and knife were fused by an implacable rhythm independent of the rest of him.

"Young feller from that college in Oxford."

"A man?" Ratliff expressed surprise.

"That's what I said."

"Jist wanted to make sure." Ratliff peered out from the shade into the density of the late morning heat. He raised his free hand to wave at a solitary man hunched over the mule end of a wagon loaded with cotton bales that was perturbing the dust in its slow transit by the store. The salesman seemed to chuckle to himself. "Well, well, well. How 'bout that, a man teacher from the college right here in the Hamlet. Y'all getting' cosmopolitan, sure 'nough." His yellow hat flogged the gallery air in utter futility.

"I heard he was raised in Jackson." Armisted shifted the plug from one cheek to the other.

"Well, well, a city boy teachin' school in Faulkner's Hamlet. Whadya know 'bout that." Ratliff's hat suddenly stopped its repetitive motion and came to rest on the right knee of his creased store-bought pants. To give the working arm a rest, he took the hat in the other hand and resumed the assault on the inert air.

The sewing machine salesman was not one to tolerate silence. "I reckon it's good for the youngins 'round these parts to learn readin', 'ritin' and 'rithmetic."

Armisted moved slightly in his tilted chair and aimed a dark stream at the stained plank by the heel of his boot. "Don't see no use for it. Not knowin' how never did me no harm, as I can see."

Ratliff laughed. "That's debatable. Yes, that's debatable. You can't even read that sign over there that says Littlejohn's, can ya?"

"Don't hafta read it. I know that's Littlejohn's, been Littlejohn's for near 'bout twenty years."

"Well, let's say you was new to the Hamlet, jist come inta town for the first time and wanted to know where to get a fine meal and lay yer head down for the night. You'd wanna know that's the boardin' house, wouldn't ya?"

"Hell, this wouldn't be no place I'd ever come to if I wasn't already here." Armisted added another deposit to the gummed puddle on the gallery floor. "You the only feller I know who comes 'round the Hamlet who don't live in these parts, and you ain't got to read to know 'bout Littlejohn's." He paused and looked at the gray weather-beaten structure across the way, his mouth working hard on the tobacco. "You even know 'nough 'bout Littlejohn's to get that discount."

Ratliff stopped beating the air and looked at the old man beside him. He chuckled. "Some folks 'round here don't know half the things they think they know." He looked back at the frame house where he spent three or four pleasurable nights every six months or so and resumed fanning his bare head. "Well, I say it won't hurt these youngins now to learn how to read and write and count. You can't deny, knowin' how to count can be mighty useful. Times are changin'. You know some folks 'round here ain't as honest as folks used to be." Ratliff paused and chuckled again. "Say, that reminds me, how's Will Varner's clerk gettin' 'long?"

Winterbottom stopped whittling, leaned to the side and turned his head to look into the store. He could hear Flem Snopes moving in the dark interior. He grunted. "Right common, I reckon."

Ratliff looked across Armisted to Winterbottom. "Seems like the last time I was here you had borrowed five dollars from Flem Snopes."

Winterbottom's hand was moving up and down the stick again. "Yup."

"You're a braver man than me; I wouldn't borrow a burnt match from that feller."

"Didn't need no burnt match. That five bucks come in handy."

"I bet it did. But still I'd jist as soon set down to eat with a rattlesnake as borrow anything from Flem Snopes." Ratliff paused and then asked. "Have ya paid it back yet?"

"Nope."

"No?"

Winterbottom's stick was getting thin. "He ain't said nothin' 'bout that five bucks. I jist give him four bits every Friday, and he seems satisfied. He calls it somethin' I don't recall right now."

"Interest?"

"Yeah, that's it."

The salesman stopped fanning momentarily and gazed past the boarding house into the distance where a hawk circled in the sky. "Yup, I think it's a good thing those youngins is learnin' that 'rithmetic."

Ratliff listened to the knife blade cut into the dwindling wood for a while. Then he shifted in his seat and asked, "That man teacher keepin' his pants on?"

Armisted looked at him from under his decrepit hat. "He's still alive, ain't he?"

"Glad to hear it."

Journal Entry, Jacob Labove, Monday, November 15, 1897, 11:45 pm

I am a weak and tormented man. Tonight, I read Byron's "She walks in Beauty", but that didn't help. Then I read "Song of Solomon"; that didn't help either. If I sleep, I'll dream about forbidden flesh and will awaken engorged with shame and will not be able to stop myself. When she recites her letters, I am enthralled; my legs tremble, and my heart beats wildly in my chest. I am obsessed. Oh Lord, deliver me from this wickedness!

Waiting at the road for her brother to come get her in the carriage, she pulled the coat tightly around her body as protection against the wind. "Damn you, Jody," she muttered into the encroaching darkness. Shivering, she turned and headed back to the school house, the glow of the wood stove beckoning through the window. After she reentered the room, she stopped just inside the door and peered into the waning light. She could see Mr. Labove kneeling at her desk, his bare head resting on the wooden seat. Slowly, she approached the desk, and as she drew closer, she heard the moaning. Curious, she stopped by the kneeling form.

"Whatcha doin' with my chair?" Her voice punctured the sound of his misery.

The teacher's head jerked up, and he stared into her shadowed, inscrutable face. His hands clutched the desk, and he struggled to stand. Pressing the coat to her body, the girl stepped back from her teacher. Tears etching his face, he staggered to his feet and lunged for her.

"Oh Eula!"

She stepped back and raised her arms. "You git away from me!"

He grasped each arm with trembling hands and pulled her to his body. "Eula, Eula, Eula, please!"

Encircled, she felt his heat through her coat and dress. Twisting and turning her body, she wrenched her right arm free and struck him hard in the face. "You stop pawin' me! Stop it!"

Feeling his strength dissolve, she pushed him away and turned to escape the room. At the door, she looked back at the crumpled, sobbing heap in the dirt. Slowly, she walked through the doorway and out to the road to wait for her brother.

While Labove was still lying in the school house dirt, he heard the sound of a horse, the creaking of carriage wheels and the

144

murmur of voices. Lifting himself from the dirt, he sat on her seat. Becalmed by the finality of surrender, he waited for Jody. The outside sounds subsided, and heat from the stove in the corner of the room gradually succumbed to the advancing cold. Shivering, he aroused himself from the stupor of submission and moved to the doorway to peer into the darkness of the empty road.

'He's gone to get the gun.'

Standing in the school house doorway, the teacher waited until he realized that the brother could have made the trip to the old plantation house and back several times, and even could have assembled a posse of men if he so desired.

'He's waiting for me at the store.'

Slowly, Labove walked the half mile to the boarding house where he had lived for three months. With each step, he anticipated the sudden appearance of the avenging brother, of the enraged mob, but the nocturnal silence was interrupted only by the occasional hoot of an owl and bark of a dog. Varner's store stood black in the moonlight. Lights glimmered in the frame houses scattered along the deserted road. The hanging lantern glowed orange on Littlejohn's porch, illuminating his way home. He entered, stood in the parlor and looked into the dining room; he saw the place set for his supper and heard Mrs Littlejohn moving in the kitchen.

'She doesn't know.'

Climbing the stairs, he reached his room. It was undisturbed. He pulled the chair over to the window and sat in the darkness, and he waited.

'It'll be any time now. Then it'll be over.'

For hours he sat hunched into the deepening cold and watched the clouds move across the full moon, casting black shapes on the packed ruts of the road. As he waited, he studied the

145

oak behind the store, naked now of its leaves, the indomitable trunk thrusting into the sky, the wind caressing the bare limbs. A broken branch pointed earth-ward. Suddenly it came to him, what the interminable waiting meant, and he knew the humiliation was complete.

She climbed into the carriage, settled on the seat behind her brother and pulled the coat around her body. "Where ya been? I'm cold."

Jody flicked the reins, and the horse moved forward. "Quit yer fussin', ya should be thankful I come to get ya. Wouldn't hurt ya none to walk home once in a while."

"You know paw don't want me to do that with all those boys 'round."

"Ain't nobody gonna mess with Will Varner's daughter 'round here."

Shivering in the back seat of the carriage, Eula heard the wind blowing through the skeletal tree limbs; she looked up at the yellow moon in the black sky. She thought about the heat that awaited her from the fireplace in her bedroom. They rode home in silence.

From the gallery, the two old men watched the figure of the man and horse move up the road from the old livery stable.

"Mighty peculiar seein' 'im over here this time a day." Armisted commented.

Winterbottom sliced into the stick with the knife blade. "Yup."

They watched as the big man rode the gray gelding up to Littlejohn's fence, dismounted and tied the reins to a post.

"Do you reckon he's…?"

146

"Naw, not in broad daylight."

The man ascended the stairs, strode across the porch, paused briefly at the door to remove his hat, and entered the boarding house.

"Mighty peculiar, I say."

Armisted hunched forward in the chair against the cool of the morning breeze and sent a brown stream to the plank floor. The hip where the Yankee had plugged him ached. Beside him, Winterbottom worked steadily on the stick.

In a few minutes, Will Varner came out of Littlejohn's followed by the landlady. Standing on the porch, she watched him descend the stairs, pass by his horse and cross over to the store. By the time he was climbing the three steps to the gallery, she had reentered her house.

"Howdy, boys."

"Mornin' Mr. Will."

"Out early, Mr. Will."

Will Varner stood just outside the door of his store and looked at the two men who sat on the gallery. "Either of you fellers seen anything of that school teacher this mornin'?"

"Can't say that I have."

"Me neither." Winterbottom took another swipe at the stick. "Is he missin'?"

Varner looked over at Littlejohn's and then back at the two men. "Didn't show up at the school this mornin'. The chil'rin got kinda rowdy and roused up ole lady Carrothers over at her place. She sent her boy up to the house to bother me 'bout it." He paused and looked again at the boarding house. "Harriet heard him come in last night, later than usual. Didn't eat no supper. Didn't see him for breakfast. His room is cleaned out; left a five dollar bill on the bed. Harriet says it's probably for next week's rent and meals.

147

Says he always pays in advance." Varner turned to move into the store. "I'll see if Flem knows anything 'bout this."

"If anybody knows anything, that'd be the one."

"Yer right 'bout that." Winterbottom shifted in his chair. "Don't see why that Jackson feller would pay for somethin' it don't look like he's fixin' to use."

"Yeah. Maybe he left a little somethin' to make up for leavin' so sudden."

"Wonder what spooked 'im?"

"Ha! Reckon he messed with somebody he shouldn't uv messed with."

Varner came out of the store and started down the steps.

"Flem see anything, Mr. Will?"

Varner stopped at the bottom of the steps and turned to the men. "Says he saw a feller toting a carpet bag up the road before sun up. Musta been him."

"Couldn't uv gotten far. You gonna go after 'im. Mr. Will?"

"Why would I wanna do that? He's due two weeks pay." He turned back to head across the road. "Next time I'll get a woman teacher. They not as likely to run off this way."

"Sounds right smart to me." Armisted spat on the floor and rubbed his hip

Note: Did you recognize that the date of Lebove's first journal entry was William Faulkner's date of birth? If you have not read Faulkner's *The Hamlet* go read it now. He told the story of teacher Labove and Eula Varner far better than I ever could. When you finish with Faulkner's novel, be sure to come back to my stories.

The Man Who Felt Terrible

If only he could go back nine months and undo it all: the room overlooking the white sand, the breeze coming through the window, the patch of moonlight on the dark water, the seductive music of the waves. "How could you forget the diaphragm?" The comforting caress, "It's okay." But it wasn't okay, and he knew the past could not be changed.

The day that would change Kevin Waller's life started early. Ringing emerged from the relentless beating of the wind-blown rain on the window. It ceased with the incisive slash of lightning and sonorous thunder. He lay there waiting to see if it was real, or part of a dream. He heard it again; groaning he rolled onto his side and reached for the phone. The bedside digital clock offered a scarlet 2:31.

"Hello."

"Is this the doctor?" The voice was male, old, unfamiliar.

"This is Doctor Waller."

"Doctor, you've got to help me. I feel terrible. It's got a hold of me."

"Okay, wait. Who is this?"

"Wilbur Bowman. Doctor, you've got to do somethin'. I can't stand it."

Wilbur Bowman. He knew a lot of Bowmans but could not recall a Wilbur. "Okay Mister Bowman, tell me what's bothering you."

"Like I said, Doctor, it's takin' hold of me and won't let me go."

"Mister Bowman, have I seen you before as a patient?"

"No."

"Who's your regular doctor?"

"I ain't got no doctor. Last one I saw was ole Doc Sams; he's been dead a long time. But I need one now. Can't you help me?"

"Okay, do you have any medical problems? Heart trouble? Sugar diabetes? High blood pressure? Lung trouble?"

"No, I ain't got none of them that I know of. But somethin' bad's got me now and won't let up."

"What's it like?"

"It's awful." The caller paused. "Ain't you gonna help me?"

"Mister Bowman, I need to get more information." He sighed into the darkness. "Do you have pain? Are you hurting anywhere?"

"No, please, Doctor, you've gotta…"

The doctor interrupted him. "Any chest pain? Any tightness or pressure in your chest?"

"No, Doctor, I…"

"Any trouble breathing?"

"No."

"Do you feel weak? Do you feel dizzy or like you're going to faint?"

"No."

"Can you move your arms and legs okay?"

"Yes."

"Are you having any trouble with your stomach or bowels? Any abdominal pain? Vomiting? Diarrhea?"

"No, none of that. Ain't you gonna help me?"

Alice moaned beside him. He tried to keep the frustration out of his voice. "Did you feel okay when you went to bed last night?"

150

"Yes."

"Do you take any medicine?

"No."

"Do you have someone there with you?"

"Just Baxter."

"Baxter?"

"Yes, Baxter, my dog. He's layin' right here by my chair."

There was a flash of lightning followed by a blast of thunder that devolved in a long rumble. There was silence on the line.

"Hello, Mister Bowman, are you still there?"

"Yes." His voice was shaky.

"Where do you live?"

"Up Willow Creek."

Damn, the doctor thought, at least ten miles over winding mountain roads. "Is there a neighbor who can come over and help you?"

"Oh no, not in this weather, in the middle of the night. There's nobody close-by; I live at the end of the road." He paused. Can't you come and give me a shot or somethin'? I feel terrible."

The doctor took a deep breath. "Mister Bowman, I'm sorry you feel bad right now, but I don't think there's anything serious wrong. You're not having a heart attack or stroke." He paused and took another breath. Ponderously, Alice moved, shifting the mattress. Wind drove rain against the window above his head. "Sometimes Mister Bowman, we all get anxious and frightened in the night, especially when it's storming. I think you'll feel better in a little while. Maybe, if you drink a glass of milk and pet Baxter, it'll help."

"You're not gonna come out and see me?"

"No, that's not necessary. You're going to be okay. But if you want, I can see you in the clinic first thing in the morning. We'll be open at eight, and you won't need an appointment. Just come on in." He paused. Over the phone the man's breathing sounded like the wind outside. "Goodbye, Mister Bowman." He hung up and lay back on the bed. "Damn."

"Who's that?" His wife's arm landed on his bare chest. A slice of lightning revealed her bulk under the sheet.

"Some crazy old man."

Lying in the bed, with his wife's arm heavy on his chest and the tempest raging outside, Kevin Waller waited for sleep. But he had to review the encounter with the distraught Wilbur Bowman to reassure himself that he had not missed anything, that the old man was not really sick. He reminded himself that if he saw everyone who called in the middle of the night, he would get little sleep. Most of his night calls were not true emergencies, and he did get up when he thought it was important. Just last night he had gone to the clinic at two in the morning to take care of a sick baby. After three years of practice in the small town, he had become adept at distinguishing the few calls that required immediate attention from the many false alarms. If only it was that simple; in recent weeks he had found himself lying in bed long after the false alarms had ended, waiting for sleep to rescue him.

Under the weight of Alice's arm, he turned onto his side and watched the artistry of lightning through the far window, the dark lattice of the window intermittently silhouetted against the liquid silver outside. Red numbers compounded on the bedside clock.

He could not avoid the intruding memories: the long ago ticking of the clock in his bedroom, the melancholic nights of his childhood, the longing and the tears, the silence from his mother's room. And he thought of Lawrence, his new daddy, she said, but never his daddy, bringing into his life a cheerful eagerness, but also the noises, moans and giggles, the rhythmic movements of his mother's bed, the nocturnal sounds that became worse than the silences they replaced. After a time, there were new night sounds: Larry his brother, but never really his brother, the crying, his mother feeding him, changing his diaper, singing to him.

Under the weight of the arm and the assault of the lightning and thunder, he couldn't suppress it, couldn't keep it away, the coming reality, and he was captive to the night, when loss was most intensely felt and change most deeply feared.

Finally, the lightning faded, the thunder receded, the wind relented and the rain subsided, and with his wife breathing endlessly beside him, he watched the dawning of the day slowly reveal the crib against the wall.

By morning, the rain had stopped. The breeze that entered the open window and stirred the dining room curtain brought the scent of spring wetness and the recurrent call of a bobwhite. As he spooned a mouthful of soggy Cheerios, Kevin Waller watched the Today Show on the small TV. The form of his pregnant wife passed in front of the screen. He watched her settle into the other chair by the table. She bit into her toast and chewed in silence. She took a swallow of milk, looked at him and smiled, the white film of milk on her lip like a moustache. He returned the smile. It could happen anytime now, he knew. She was ready; the bag had been packed for weeks.

He became aware that she had spoken. She was looking at him, a little bemused, waiting. He reached back to retrieve the question that had fluttered by him initially like a butterfly.

"Did you get a call last night during the storm?"

"Yes."

"I didn't think I was dreaming." A crumb bobbed between her lips. "Nothing serious?"

"Nothing serious."

On the TV, Katie Couric was interviewing a woman, a pretty one, almost as cute as Katie. The woman was talking about her husband, a pilot in the military. He was bombing Serbia. The young wife admitted that she worried about him, but she was proud of him for serving his country, doing what he was trained to do. Kevin Waller grunted in rebuttal. A picture appeared on the screen; it showed the woman dressed in white, her husband in a uniform, a handsome guy. The wedding had occurred just before he had left to drop bombs.

The doctor turned away from the screen to inspect his wife. Watching her chew and swallow, he wondered if the brownish hue that pregnancy had imparted to her face would return to the preferable rosy glow after she gave birth to their son.

Another face flickered before him, as it occasionally did, the relic of a distant memory. The man's face had long ago lost any precision of detail, any physical identity. However, he always knew who it was, and the ethereal image invariably became joined by the more distinct image of his weeping mother.

His gaze shifted from his wife back to the TV. Katie and the proud bride had disappeared, to be replaced by the image of smoke billowing from a bombed building. He remembered how, as a boy, he would watch *Green Beret* over and over until he finally became old enough to realize how foolish he was to think that he would find his father in a movie about Vietnam.

Grimacing, his wife rubbed the large mound of belly through the fabric of her robe. "He's kicking the soccer ball again."

The expectant father looked out the window at the redbud petals clustered on the grass. A squirrel bounced across the lawn, spraying water droplets in its wake. He swallowed the last spoonful of cereal.

"You remember that I have a doctor's appointment at three?"

"Yes." He looked at her. She could no longer fit behind the wheel and still reach the accelerator and brake. "I told Bonnie that I'd be gone this afternoon. I should be finished by one or one-thirty. We should be there in plenty of time." Her obstetrician was an hour away.

"I hope she keeps me. I'm almost a week overdue."

"I know."

A few minutes later he stepped out the front door into the warmth of the new day. The sun dissected the clouds over Ash Mountain. Reflected light from the moist grass created a silver carpet at his feet. Wet faces of pansies turned up to greet him.

It had been such a day in May when the man in the uniform had driven the black car with the gold writing on its side into the drive-way. From the sandbox, where he had been positioning his toy soldiers in the sand fort, he watched the man take off the hat that policemen wore and walk slowly to the house. He looked like one of his plastic soldiers had suddenly enlarged and turned into flesh and blood. Then he had heard the unforgettable sound and had seen his mother on the porch crumble into the man, and he had first experienced the terror, the terror that no six-year old should ever suffer, that no thirty-three-year old should suffer. But he had, and he still did.

After Christmas, when he had first seen the ultrasound shadow of his son, he had struggled to contain the resurgent fear.

Watching him from the exam table, Alice's smile had disappeared, and he had never been able to explain it to her, or to himself.

He stood in the wet grass of his front yard and tucked the gray image of his son into a pocket of his mind. Deciding to walk the ten minutes to the clinic, he started down the hill.

Then he was on another hill, dandelion gold sprinkled through the grass. He was astride towering shoulders, his small arms clutching his father's head. The gentle hand came and nudged his hands upward. "Hey Kev, I need to see where we're going." As his father ran down the hill, he held on tightly and saw his mother below, her face turned to them. His mother and father kneeled before him; an orange butterfly fluttered nearby. Tears filled his mother's eyes, as his father spoke. "Daddy's going away for a while; you'll need to be the man of the family until I get back."

On Main Street, he came upon Homer Bowman sweeping water from the sidewalk in front of the Five and Dime.

"How ya doin', Doc?"

"Fine, Homer. And you?"

"Can't complain. How's the missus? Still waiting?"

"Yeah."

Behind Homer, the store window exhibited a large poster. A smiling young woman sat, a boy on one side, presenting a box of candy, a girl on the other, holding a bouquet of flowers. A beaming man stood behind the woman, a hand on her shoulder. The joys of Mother's Day, the poster proclaimed. Kevin Waller reminded himself that he needed to send a card.

"I know how it is; all mine came late. Told Mabel that she had some elephant blood in her." The store-keeper laughed. "Helluva storm last night. Do any damage at your place?"

"Nothing bad, a few limbs down. Flowers bent over, nothing that won't heal." Homer's grin reminded him of his night-time call. "Do you know a Wilbur Bowman?"

Homer stopped sweeping; the smile was gone, his eyes had narrowed, and his mouth seemed to struggle for words. "Wilbur Bowman was my father." He paused and took a deep breath. "He's been dead ten years. Funny you should bring him up. Pa died ten years ago today. Mabel and I are goin' up to Willow Creek Church this evenin' to decorate his grave."

Kevin Waller shifted uncomfortably; he had not expected this. "I'm sorry to bring it up, Homer. It was some other Wilbur Bowman I got a call from in the middle of the night." He gazed down Main Street in the direction of the clinic and started moving forward. A car honked in the street; a drop of water from the store's awning fell on his head.

"What?" The question halted the doctor. "I know all the Bowmans 'round here. Most are kin to me one way or another, and there ain't no other Wilbur Bowman." The store keeper looked intently at his doctor. "Must've been some other Bowman. There's Dewey up Rocky Point. He'd be one to call a doctor in the middle of the night." His face relaxed a bit.

"No, it wasn't him. I know him well." The doctor felt the awkwardness and wanted to move on, but something intrigued him, that led him to say, "Your father's buried in the Willow Creek Church cemetery."

"Yup. Ma is too. They lived up Willow Creek in the last house on Beaver Springs Road. That's where they raised us kids and a bunch of tobacco. When Ma died, Mabel and I wanted him to come to town to live with us, but he wouldn't hear of it. Lived up there by himself, except for his old dog."

157

Despite the warmth of the sun, Doctor Waller shivered. Shifting his gaze across the street, he saw Buddy Faulk leave the café. Buddy waved and called to him. The doctor stared at the deputy sheriff and did not respond. His eyes returned to Homer who stood motionless, holding the broom, studying something in the distance.

"What did he die of, your father?" He could not conceal the twitch in his voice.

"Don't know for sure. Doctor we had here then said it was probably his heart. But he never had no heart trouble that we knew of. Pa didn't like doctors. No offense, Doc; he didn't know you. Hadn't seen one in years. He was shot in the stomach at the Battle of the Bulge, spent three months in an army hospital. Never wanted to have nothin' to do with doctors after that." He paused and stared past Doctor Waller. "It was Sunday mornin'. We went to get him for church, Mabel and me. We found him slumped over in his chair. His dog was sittin' there beside him, kinda moanin' and frettin' a bit." He stopped again, moved his right hand over his mouth, and then resumed. "Funny thing, Doc, the phone was in his lap. Mabel and I figured he was tryin' to call us when he died." Homer stopped, passed the broom from his left hand to his right, and looked up at the sky.

Kevin Waller turned away and mumbled, "I guess I got the name wrong." The sun was hot on his neck where beads of sweat were collecting. His legs shook, and a weight on his chest made breathing difficult. He looked up Main Street and saw the cars and pickups congregating at the clinic. As he moved towards refuge, the cell phone buzzed in his pocket, and he dug it out.

"Hello."

"Kevin, I think it's started; my water broke."

"Okay Honey, I'll be there right away."

About the time Homer Bowman was placing flowers on a grave in the Willow Creek Church cemetery, Kevin Waller was looking into the face of his son for the first time. As he locked onto the alert eyes of the newborn, he remembered the smile that had spread across Homer's face when he had turned on the sun-splashed sidewalk, still holding the phone in his hand, and had said, "Homer, I'm going to be a father."

Snake

She told me that I didn't have to go. She gave me the chance, but I didn't take her up on it. "You don't have to go on the camping trip, you know," Maw said from the kitchen where she was cooking pancakes. I sat at the table, looking out at the morning sunshine and the blue sky over the roof of Lee's house, and felt safe. I could handle it. Anyway, my buddies were going, and I didn't want to be left out.

Beside me on the ground, Lee's snoring merges with the night sounds beyond the tent. How could he go to sleep so fast? Above me, the canvas is barely visible in the dark. Visions of Superman and Mickey Mantle flicker in my mind. How I wish I could actually see their posters on the wall of my room right now and know that Maw was in her room. I hear rustling in the underbrush outside. Fearing the danger coiled in the forest, I shrink deeper into the hot sleeping bag. Why did Biff have to tell that story?

Before the trip we heard from the older scouts about Biff's war stories. "Just ask him what he did in the war," one advised. While roasting marshmallows over the campfire, Roy asked him, and the assistant scoutmaster jumped at the chance to impress us tenderfoot scouts on our first camping trip. Five eager boys leaned with anticipation into the ring of light. Not being real keen on war stories, I hung back just out of the circle. My father had died fighting on Iwo Jima. The end of Biff's cigarette glowed red from the other side of the fire as he began to tell it.

"You never knew in the fighting when some fool thing would happen that you'd never forget if you lived through it. It was a couple of weeks after we'd landed on Omaha Beach, and we had driven the Krauts out of Normandy and were pushing them

160

towards Paris. Every so often they'd stop and fight us, but mainly they were retreating. Most of the French folks had cleared out, so there were a lot of abandoned farms and houses about. We had to be careful because sometimes enemy snipers would hide in the houses or barns and take pot shots at us. Our platoon would stop and clean them out; we had to blow up a right smart number of houses to get rid of them. I reckon those French farmers were pretty pissed off when they came back and found their homesteads a pile of rubble. But then we were fighting for them, saving their butts."

Biff paused to pull on his cigarette while we laughed about the French butts. Henry cut a loud one, and we laughed again. When Biff told him he needed to go clean out his britches, we laughed some more. I thought about what Maw would have said about Biff's mouth.

"One hot sunny day we came upon a deserted farmhouse. We didn't draw no fire, so we figured it was empty, but we weren't sure what was in the field on the other side. Sarge split us up and sent most around the front of the house. Me and Bud Fuller from Mississippi, he sent around the back. Bud was a good ole boy. I had won two bits off him playing blackjack on our ship crossing over to Normandy.

"Poor Bud's luck plumb ran out that day we went back of that farmhouse. He was running right there beside me, and then suddenly I heard a scream and he disappeared, like the earth just sucked him right up. One second he was there. The very next second he was gone. I stopped running and looked over to where he'd been. I could hear this god-awful yelling and screaming down in the ground. I tell you, I've never heard such suffering, either before or since, and I sure hope I never do again. When I moved closer I could see this jagged hole that he'd fallen into, and then I figured out what had happened. Poor ole Bud had run across a rotten board that couldn't hold him up and had fallen into the old well that the board was covering up.

"I eased on over to the hole and called down to him. I sure didn't want to get close enough to fall in myself. By then the other fellows had come around to see what was keeping us. I realized Bud's yelling was quieting down, but I didn't know if that was good or bad. Since Bud wasn't making so much noise down there, I could hear something else, a rustling and rattling sound that sent shivers up and down my spine. Soon, we didn't hear Bud no more at all; it was only that other noise, like something in a frenzy."

Biff was a hazy dark form through the smoke. An owl hooted in the distance. On the log beside me, Lee sucked marshmallow stickiness from his fingers. My stomach felt like clothes in Maw's washing machine, going around and around.

"It took us a good while to get Bud out of that hell hole. We finally got a heavy chain with a big hook on the end of it from a supply truck that was going up the road. We had to throw that thing down there a slew of times before we finally snagged Bud and was able to haul him up. When we pulled him out of that hole we saw that he was swelled about three times normal, but that wasn't the worst of it by a long shot. He was covered by a dozen or so rattlesnakes, slithering on him and still biting the poor man. I'd never seen a sight like it. Some of the guys took to retching and puking and turning green. When the snakes let go and commenced to crawling on the ground, Sarge swung his M1 around and blasted them bastards to mush. Me and a couple of others guys started doing the same thing, and soon they were all dead, like poor Bud. Ham Hawke from Tennessee dropped a grenade down that hole and blew them others to hell.

"I got detailed to accompany the body back to Caen, where Bud was buried in the military cemetery. I couldn't stand to look at him because I kept seeing those snakes hanging on. But a lot of folks from headquarters came by to see the man who had been bitten to death by the snakes. He was kind of a celebrity, the poor guy.

"I joined back up with the platoon a few days later. A couple weeks after that we were drinking wine and dancing with the mademoiselles in Paris, but I had a hard time getting Bud out of my mind. It still scares me to think how close I came to falling down that well and getting ate by those snakes."

Dry wood crackled in the low flames, and insects hummed in the surrounding trees. Biff flicked his cigarette stump in an orange arch into the embers. Huddled tightly into myself, I watched my blackened marshmallow shrivel into the dense coals. I thought of the hug Maw had given me before I climbed into the back of the troop truck. "Have fun," she had said.

Stirring beside me, Lee broke the silence. "Do you think there's some in these here woods?"

Biff thought about that while thrusting a sharpened stick into the soft whiteness of a marshmallow. "I reckon there's some in these parts."

In the tent, I shudder into the endless night. I have an additional problem: I need to pee. Why did I drink that Kool-aid? I cannot suppress it all night. I'll either go in the sleeping bag or have to go outside. What a choice! I feel the wetness in my eyes and am now glad that Lee is asleep. But I know that if I wet the sleeping bag, he'll find out, and Maw will discover it when I get home. She knows that smell. I can't put it off any longer.

I'm outside the tent; as fast as I can, I have my willy out and piss into the blackness just beyond the tent. My pee hisses into the earth. Turning quickly to get back to the tent, I see a dark form by its entrance.

"Can't sleep?"

"No sir."

"Come sit by the fire."

So, I sit on the log beside Biff, watching crimson coals that do not warm my body. I remember how Maw bends over the bed each night to kiss my forehead. Biff moves closer on the log, and the heat penetrates my jeans. Maybe I hear a rustling in the grass beyond the dying embers.

"Frankie, want to stay in my tent tonight?"

Yes, I'll be safe there.

An Unhappy Woman

Sylvia Pritchard was an unhappy woman.

Sylvia was unhappy for several reasons. Most obviously, a victim of multiple sclerosis, she was confined to a wheelchair. Weakness in her arms and hands made it difficult for her to attend to many daily tasks. She needed assistance with dressing, and bathing, and using the bathroom, and getting from wheelchair to bed, and from bed to wheelchair. She could still feed herself but not without spilling food on her clothes. Food preparation and house cleaning challenged her. The slow but steady decline in strength and the increasing frequency of the stabbing pains in her hands and feet accentuated her unhappiness. Bladder accidents occurred more often. She dreaded the prospect of a catheter. Yes, anyone would agree that Sylvia Pritchard had reason to be unhappy.

Another reason for her unhappiness: She had married the wrong man. Her mother, her brother, her sister, and most of her friends had warned her against the marriage. Even back then, it had been generally known that Jesse Pritchard was 'bad to drink.' This communal knowledge had only solidified over the years. His reputation certainly could not have escaped young Sylvia. After all, she had graduated near the top of her high school class. Perhaps she thought that she could change him, a dubious proposition. In any case, if she had thought that, she had failed.

After marriage, Sylvia had worked in the shoe factory in a town, twenty-five miles from her home. This had ended within five years because of the symptoms of MS. She didn't know then that she had a disease she had barely heard of. She just knew that her hands and feet were sometimes numb and sometimes painful, that she occasionally saw double, and that she had episodes of severe dizziness. And she was always tired. It took another two years before the neurologist in still another town farther away made the diagnosis and informed her of the absence of effective treatment. It took longer for her to receive Medicaid and still longer before she qualified for disability payments. The neurologist did not accept Medicaid and had little interest in providing charity care to a poor Appalachian woman. The general practitioner in Pineville, the county seat two large mountains away from her home, didn't seem to know much about MS.

Jesse's employment history featured extended stretches of unemployment punctuated by brief jobs working tobacco or cutting timber. The older he got, the fewer jobs he had. He spent long hours playing poker and pool with his drinking buddies and frequenting the town's lone tavern. Rumors occasionally surfaced in town of a moonshine operation, but most folks discounted this, convinced that Jesse lacked the work ethic necessary for such an enterprise.

Sylvia and Jesse lived two miles from the small cluster of buildings that comprised the village of Laurel, in a house that Jesse had inherited by default. His father had long-ago disappeared; his mother had died of cancer, and his older sister had left for parts unknown. When his brother was run over by a train while passed out on the railroad track, Jesse had been left alone in the family homestead. The wooden structure had once been a farm house, but any semblance of a farm had vanished, the land slowly reverting to its primitive state. Jesse had needed someone to take care of the place, and himself.

The anti- Jesse sentiments of Sylvia's family intensified over the years as her disability progressed. Her brother Haskell and sister-in-law Beth owned and managed the hardware store in town. For years they urged her to leave her dead-beat husband and live with them, with no success. Sylvia had married for better or worse, and apparently, she had accepted the worse, much to the distress of those who cared about her.

Ambivalence characterized her mother's approach to Sylvia's domestic situation, perhaps because of the mother's complicated relationship with her now deceased husband. At times, she advised her daughter to leave; at other times, she insisted that Sylvia persevere with wifely duties, without specifying what those might entail for a disabled wife. Despite the contradictory messages, her mother was devoted to Sylva, over the years visiting her almost every day. She timed her visits to avoid Jesse, which turned out to be relatively easy.

Sylvia's younger, unmarried, and probably lesbian sister had also offered her a refuge from marital troubles, to no avail. Amber lived alone in a spacious home with modern amenities. In addition to working as a secretary for an insurance firm in Pineville, she raised goats, capitalizing on the growing demand for goats' milk among the urban gentry. After completing college, Amber had returned to her hometown, aspiring to teach in the local grade school. She blamed the rejection of her application on narrow-minded opposition to her 'independent life style.'

In contrast to her estrangement from the town folks and uneasy relationship with Haskell and Beth, Amber was committed to helping Sylvia as much as she could. Quickly learning that cash ended up being converted to alcohol or gambled away, she directed her financial assistance to special appliances in the bathroom and kitchen that eased her sister's burden a bit. She and Haskell made sure that bills were paid, but they could not prevent Jesse from drinking up much of the disability income.

Sylvia and Jesse did not have close neighbors. Connie and Claude Summers lived about a quarter of a mile away, and Melissa

Higgins lived the same distance away on the other side. Connie had taught fifth grade in the local school for decades. Claude had retired from a job on the railroad, and the couple enjoyed traveling to country music venues. The Grand Ole Opry was a favorite destination. When home, Connie would visit her former student. To Claude and others, she voiced criticism of Jesse, asserting that "something needs to be done." She once complained to the county Department of Social Services, but nothing came of that.

Melissa was an outsider who had arrived a few years back, the new owner of a foreclosed farm. She had been accompanied by a man, assumed to be a husband, but he had not been seen in a long time. Melissa had become a farmer, raising tobacco (which she didn't smoke) and chickens. Unquestionably, she worked hard. "She worked like a man," folks said. The farm seemed a success. She kept to herself, but she did develop a friendship with Amber. This may be why she became so helpful to Sylvia. Melissa did the chores that a husband usually performed. She cut wood, keeping Sylvia well supplied with pieces for the stove in the kitchen. Claude had previously provided this service and had objected when Melissa started encroaching on his domain, but only a bit. Rheumatism bothered him.

The presence of a wood burning stove surprised Melissa, who appreciated her electric range and knew that Amber would have purchased one for her sister, if asked. Once when Melissa had chopped a load of wood, Sylvia indicated that she would welcome a new stove but that Jesse insisted on keeping the old one. He had not explained why. Perhaps, she speculated to Melissa, it had something to do with pleasant childhood memories. Melissa had chalked up his opposition as another black mark against a lousy husband.

In the summer, Connie and Melissa kept Sylvia stocked with fresh produce from their gardens and provided canned vegetables that lasted deep into the winter. Haskell brought groceries from the store in Laurel each week.

When Sylvia became dependent on a wheel chair Haskell bought a special van to transport her. She didn't go many places any more, but when she did, he took her. No one ever heard him complain about that. Complaints about her no-good husband, folks heard a lot.

Every Sunday, Sylvia attended a Baptist church outside of town with her mother, Haskell and Beth, and their daughter Grace, soon headed for college, never to return to live in Laurel. But that was in the future. Grace frequently helped out with her disabled aunt, particularly after contact with her other aunt had been restricted. At church, Sylvia sang the hymns, listened to the preaching, and joined in with an "Amen" at the appropriate times. When folks told her that they prayed for her, she thanked them.

On pretty days after the service, Haskell would navigate her wheelchair over the uneven ground to their father's grave in the church cemetery. Later she would eat a mid-day meal with her brother's family and then return home, where her husband might still be sleeping off his hangover.

After years of declining health, Sylvia expressed some hope in the newly opened clinic in Laurel. Gabe Reynolds, the nurse practitioner who staffed the clinic, took her on as a special project. Soon after his arrival in Laurel, he made a home visit to meet Sylvia accompanied by Haskell. In his training, Gabe had learned the importance of assessing the home environment of a disabled patient. In preparation for seeing Sylvia, he had read about MS. He was pleased to see the ramp to the porch and the front door wide enough to accommodate a wheel-chair. He was surprised, however, to encounter a pool table occupying most of the front room.

"Welcome to the world of Jesse Pritchard." Haskell commented sarcastically.

In the kitchen, Gabe noted the wood burning stove and voiced concern about the hazard. Having grown up in a small town in eastern North Carolina where such stoves were plentiful, he knew of the danger of fire, especially in wintertime.

"Yeah, we're worried about that. They don't need it for heat, but she won't let us replace it. I don't understand why."

They found Sylvia in a brightly lit back room, settled in her manual wheelchair, knitting something with blue yarn, and watching her favorite soap opera. Gabe offered to wait until the show was over. No, they could cut the TV off; nothing much happened from one day to the next, or, for that matter, from one week to the next, she explained.

Haskell grunted in response to this and said. "You must rate. She never cuts it off when it's just me."

Perhaps because he started by complimenting her knitting, Sylvia and Gabe hit it off from the beginning. She answered his questions about her recent health. He checked her blood pressure, listened to her heart and lungs, and noted the hyperactive reflexes in her knees, typical of MS. He talked about things that might help her. Having received an ear-full about her husband on the way to Sylvia's home, Gabe cautiously inquired about him.

"He's sorry he couldn't be here to meet you, but he had something important to do."

Haskell grunted in disgust, and she looked at him, a flicker of reproach in her eyes.

Gabe quickly responded, "I'm sorry to miss him, I look forward to meeting him soon."

"Yes," she said.

"I do have one more question. It looks like you can get around in the house pretty well, except for the front room. That pool table must make it hard for your wheelchair."

"Oh, I don't go in there. That's for Jesse and his friends." She looked down at the ball of yarn in her lap.

Another grunt, which Sylvia ignored. She started working the needles slowly and said, "I can't knit like I used to. My fingers don't work too well."

"You do fine, Honey." Haskell patted her hands and looked at Gabe. "She's made real pretty sweaters for everybody in the family."

In the van, heading back to town, Haskell thanked Gabe for the visit. "I think she took to you, Doc."

"I'm glad, but you know I'm not a doctor; I'm a specially trained nurse who can do some things doctors do."

"Okay, right. I get it. I don't claim to understand exactly what you are professionally, but I do know you got on well with my sister. We're glad you're here. She's received little medical care for a long time." He paused and when Gabe did not respond, continued, "You get the picture about this worthless husband. I don't know how she puts up with it. He's hardly ever home, and when he is, he's in there with his no-good buddies, drinking, filling the air with cigarette smoke, playing pool, cussing up a storm, and making a big racket." He paused again and then said, "She's so unhappy there. She'd be much better off with us."

While growing up, Gabe had been recognized as a bright boy. Teachers encouraged him to aim for college, and he did. After earning a nursing degree, he worked for three years in a hospital, where he met his wife, a social worker. Then, he completed the family nurse practitioner program in Chapel Hill. Soon, Gabe, Paula and their infant daughter moved into a mountain-side home half way between Laurel and Pineville, and he started practicing at the new clinic.

Gabe grew into the responsibilities quickly. He found less and less need to consult with his supervising physician, who practiced in Pineville. 'Doc Gabe' became a popular and valued addition to the community. After a while he stopped correcting folks about the doc.

Within a few weeks, Gabe had replaced Sylvia's old wheelchair with a motorized one and arranged for her to receive home health services. A trained aide visited daily, augmenting the assistance provided by family members and neighbors. Sylvia started taking a multivitamin tablet and a pill to help with muscle spasms. Life improved for Sylvia, but she still had MS and all the impairments and frustrations that imparted. She remained unable to do many things other 40-year old women could do with ease.

Haskell transported Sylvia to the clinic for her appointments. Gabe had offered to see Sylvia in her home to save her the inconvenience of trips to the clinic, but she valued the clinic visits. They gave her an opportunity to see people and catch up on community news in the waiting room.

In his first few visits with Sylvia, Gabe learned some things about her that surprised him. She read a wide range of books obtained from the bookmobile. American history particularly interested her. She listened to the radio and watched TV, and not just soap operas. She kept up with national and international affairs. She complained about Reagan. Gabe wasn't a fan of the president either. Once Sylvia asked him if he knew that Edgar Degas had become blind late in life. No, he did not know that. He struggled to recall who Edgar Degas was. He began looking forward to her visits and scheduled them more frequently than they probably needed to be.

About a year after they met, Sylvia Pritchard gave Gabe a pink sweater she had knitted for his daughter. "It's not very good," she said. "I hope she likes it."

That night, Paula held the sweater and said, "That was nice of her." She didn't comment on the defects in the knitting.

Several weeks later, on a cool autumn day while the sweater still fit, Paula took Abby to visit Sylvia. "Sylvia was delighted. It made her day." Paula told Gabe that evening.

At another visit, Sylvia handed Gabe a folded sheet of paper and said, "You don't need to read it now."

Later that day during a break between patients, he unfolded the paper and read the short hand-written poem. He didn't know much about poetry, but it vaguely reminded him of a poem they had studied in high school. Emily Dickinson, he thought that was the name.

At the next visit, he thanked her for the poem and asked if she had written others. Yes, she had a notebook full. He said that he would like to read more, but he never did get to read any more of her poetry.

Although he knew it made her uncomfortable, Gabe sometimes asked her how things were going with Jesse. The words varied, but the response was the same: okay, alright, like usual. Once she said, "He's had a rough life. He does the best he can." Once she complained that his friends were a bad influence. Another time, she said, "I know my family doesn't like him, but they don't know him like I do."

173

On one visit, Gabe took the plunge and asked if Jesse had ever hurt her.

Appearing offended, she reacted quickly. "You mean, hit me."

"Yes, or done something physical that hurt you."

"Oh no, he would never do anything like that. I'm his wife."

Sylvia's health care provider first encountered her husband around two o'clock on a Sunday morning. When the night policeman contacted Gabe about an injured drunk, his first inclination was to send him to the emergency room twenty-five miles away. But Gabe changed his mind when he heard who it was. He drove the twenty minutes over the winding highway to the clinic, where he found Jesse Pritchard with a gash on his forehead that needed suturing. The circumstances of the injury were murky. Jesse was in no condition for an intelligible conversation. Gabe repaired the laceration and persuaded the policeman to keep Jesse in the one-room city hall for the remainder of the night. Sylvia didn't need to be disturbed at that hour, although Gabe suspected that such a disturbance was not unusual.

Jesse did not return for removal of the stitches. Sylvia later told Gabe that Buster had taken them out with his pocket knife.

Gabe's next encounter with Jesse occurred a few months later when he showed up at the clinic one morning with a painful, swollen right hand. Gabe had already heard about the fight in the tavern the night before. Jesse had a broken bone in his hand. A boxer's fracture, it was called, but Gabe didn't tell him that. He didn't want to dignify the situation. The hungover man was in no mood for a discussion of his wife, his behavior, or anything else. Gabe placed a splint on the hand and wrist, wrapping it tightly with

174

an ACE bandage. "You'll need to keep the splint on for two to three weeks, and I want to see you back in three days." Maybe then, he could have a meaningful conversation about Sylvia.

Gabe next saw Jesse a week later when he stopped by Junior Norton's place, one of the two gas stations in Laurel. Trying to stay neutral in local rivalries, he took turns buying from each station. Jesse sat outside on the bench, leaning against the cinder block building, smoking a cigarette, a beer can at his side, a cue stick in his left hand, and no splint on his right hand. Gabe told Junior to fill it up, walked over and sat on the bench.

"Hello, Jesse."

"How ya doin', Doc?"

"Fine, and you?"

"Can't complain."

"Glad to hear it." He looked at Sylvia's husband. Jesse was only a few years older than his wife but appeared much older. Gabe could see the pink scar, partially concealed by the brim of the Atlanta Braves cap. "Playing pool?"

"Nah, I'm waitin' to play the winner. Those two are so lousy, it'll take 'em all evenin'." Jesse flicked the cigarette butt onto the broken pavement.

Gabe could hear the clatter of balls inside. "I see you're not using your splint."

Jesse took a swig of beer and set the can back between the two men. "Don't need to. Hand don't hurt no more."

"Good." He eyed the purplish discoloration of skin on the pinky side of the hand and wrist. "It still might be a good idea to wear it a while longer."

"Can't, don't know where it is."

Gabe gazed across the street at the hardware store and then watched Junior put the cap back on the gas tank and move to clean the windshield. "How's Sylvia doing?"

Jesse chuckled. "Like usual, Doc. Feisty as ever."

Feisty? Gabe would never have considered Sylvia feisty. But then he remembered her response to his inquiry about domestic violence. "What do you mean, feisty?"

"Doc, I hear ya got a wife, too, so ya know they can get to naggin' pretty bad." Jesse reached into his shirt pocket and pulled out a crumpled package of cigarettes.

Gabe waited a bit before he asked, "What do you do when she nags?"

"I leave. I got better things to do than listen to her bitchin'."

Again, he waited a bit and then said, "You ever get rough with her?"

Jesse turned to face him. "No way, Doc. I ain't that kinda guy. I saw too much of that with the old man. Finally, I whacked him with a chunk of stove wood to keep him from chokin' ma. The next day he was gone for good. I promised my ma I'd never treat a woman that way, and I never have. I know I'm no perfect husband, far from it, but don't lay that on me." Jesse spat on the ground and lit a cigarette.

Gabe believed him; at least he very much wanted to believe him.

Neither man spoke for a while. Junior finished wiping the windshield and came over to Gabe. "Want me to check the oil?"

"No, thanks. I'll pay in a minute."

"You know your credit's good, Doc." Junior went inside.

Gabe could hear him teasing a pool player about how bad he was. Gabe said. "It would be good if you could come to the clinic with her for an appointment."

176

Jesse grunted. "Nah, Doc, can't do that. That brother of hers takes her, and me and him don't get along. Now, if I could take her in my pick-up over there, I'd do it. But it ain't easy on her."

Gabe glanced at the heavily dented truck parked in the grass beside the railroad track. He knew Jesse's license was suspended. Sometimes, he had trouble understanding the enforcement of law in Pine County.

"Doc, she likes ya a lot. Says you've helped her." Jesse paused. "But she's still right pitiful. That MS is a bad one. It sure makes her unhappy. It gets me down too. Sometimes, she gets so low I can't stand to be 'round her."

Gabe needed to head home. "Jesse, glad we had this conversation. Good luck with the pool game." He stood up and entered the building to pay for the gas.

During his next visit with Sylvia, Gabe asked if she wished Jesse would be around the house more. She looked at him and said, "No, not really. He's around more than people think. It's hard for him to be around me sometimes. I know that. Maybe I remind him of his ma during her last days. You know he dropped out of school to tend to her."

"I didn't know that."

"I just wish he'd hang out with a better class of people."

The phone rang at five-thirty on a Sunday morning in the middle of January, arousing Gabe from a pleasant dream.

He answered the bedside phone reflexively. "Hello." Sleep clogged his mind.

"Doc Gabe, this is the sheriff, sorry to bother you so early, but I have some bad news."

"Wait... wait a minute. Let me wake up completely." After a few seconds, "Okay, Sheriff, go ahead."

"I hate to have to tell you this, but Sylvia and Jesse Pritchard over at Laurel died last night. Their house burned down."

"What... No, that can't be. No." He stopped and swung his legs over the side of the bed. Paula sat up in bed behind him and began to rub his back, the way he liked. Darkness permeated the room. "No... No... Sylvia dead. Are you sure?" This could not be happening. Less than a minute earlier, he had been blissfully sleeping.

"Yes, sorry to say, and her husband too." The sheriff paused and then said, "He tried to save her."

"Tried to save her?"

"Yeah, rushed into that burnin' house before Buster Ramsey could stop him. They'd been drinkin' at that bar across the state line, and Buster was bringin' him home. Even before Buster completely stopped, Jesse was outa the truck and runnin' to the house. Buster said he was hollerin' Sylvia's name over and over. Buster said Jesse ran right into that fire. Never seen nothin' like it. Buster went up the road to the neighbors, Claude Summer's place, to call it in. But Claude had seen the fire and already contacted Riley Duval in Laurel to send the fire truck." The sheriff stopped.

Gabe sat, silent, devastated. Paula hugged him from behind. "I'm so sorry, Honey."

The sheriff resumed. "By the time the fire truck and volunteers got there, it was pretty much destroyed." The sheriff paused again and then said. "Not sure what started it, but they had an old stove. Those things are bad to start fires. Every winter we have several, but most of the time people get out. I reckon with her condition, you know, in a wheelchair and all. "

178

"Yes, I know." Gabe found his voice. "Sheriff, this is a terrible shock." He released a sob and wiped his eyes with his fingers. Paula handed him a tissue. "Thanks."

"Doc, I'm sorry to be the bearer of..."

Gabe interrupted. "Sheriff, do you know... do you know... does Sylvia's family know about this?"

"Yeah, they do. All of them were there at the end, except the mother. As you'd expect they were all upset. Haskell was fit to be tied. I think the other gal was gonna tell the mother. She's probably done that by now."

Gabe did not want to listen to the sheriff any more. He wanted to be holding his wife. "Thanks for letting me know, sheriff." He hung up. "Damn!"

He looked at the alarm clock. The phone call had lasted less than five minutes. So much can change in such a short period of time. Gabe had dealt with death on numerous occasions, but this felt much different.

Gabe and Paula hugged each other. "Life can be cruel," he muttered. "I can't imagine the pain of dying in a fire." After a while, he pulled away and said, "I need to go to Laurel to see what I can do."

"Yes, I know.

Before he left, Gabe went into his daughter's room and looked at her. She slept peacefully, her arm around Jerry the stuffed giraffe.

Gabe spent most of that day in Laurel. Sylvia's family had gathered at Haskell's home. Within hours, they were inundated with food. Gabe ended up stationed at the door, accepting food and condolences, deflecting well-wishers, explaining that at this time the family wanted to grieve in private.

179

The tragedy dominated the talk of the town. Sylvia's death generated the expected sentiments; folks knew how to feel about it and what to say about it. A terrible way to die, but her suffering was over, and she was in a better place, they said. "She's gone home to Jesus," was a common refrain. Her death in no way challenged their basic assumptions and beliefs about the workings of the world.

In contrast, Jesse's death generated a complicated mix of reactions. His rescue attempt elicited almost universal surprise. "Who would have thought it," was a commonly expressed response. Some considered his heroic action at the end of a wasted life to have conferred a measure of redemption. Others echoed the verdict, bitterly pronounced by Haskell: "If he'd been home where he belonged this never would have happened." Yes, feelings about Jesse were decidedly mixed.

Late that afternoon, before he left for home, Gabe had a moment alone with Amber.

"I'm struggling to process him giving his life to try to save her. That turns everything I thought about him upside down." Amber looked at Gabe. "Did we misjudge him?"

"I don't know." He paused. "Jesse made it hard to see the good in him. I think your sister saw it."

Jesse's body lay unclaimed in the funeral home in Pineville. Eventually, it was cremated.

Sylvia's funeral service was held in the church where she had worshiped for years. The crowd overflowed the sanctuary, with many mourners standing outside under a gray sky in the cold mist. Some probably could not hear what the pastor said or the choir sang. But they were familiar with Baptist funeral practices.

The ornate casket was closed, unusual for funerals in the community, but understandable in this case.

After they watched the casket lowered into a muddy grave beside her father's, Gabe and Paula headed to their car. Gabe was stopped by the pastor, a young man about his age. Paula continued to the car.

"I wanted to introduce myself." The pastor started. "I'm Avery Humphrey. I live in Pineville and serve three churches in the area."

"Gabe Reynolds. I'm glad to meet you, Reverend Humphrey." They shook hands.

"I've heard a lot of good things about you from members of my flock. Haskell speaks highly of you, and I hear you meant a lot to Sylvia. Thank you for what you have done and are doing."

"Sylvia meant a lot to me too. I miss her." Gabe paused and looked back to where men were shoveling soggy dirt into the grave. "I appreciate your kind words."

"Sylvia was a child of the Lord. He works in mysterious ways. Ours is not to understand but only to accept. Her suffering on this earth has ended. She is with God. She is no longer unhappy. Praise the Lord."

Gabe shifted his gaze to the reverend, who was smiling at him, an irksome smile. The mist had changed to light rain, and the wind had picked up, a miserable winter day.

"Reverend, I don't think we can know for sure what's in another person's mind, but I think Sylvia would still want to be living with us here on earth, if she had her way. I don't think she was that unhappy at all. Goodbye."

When Gabe got into the car he found that Paula had removed her coat. He saw the green sweater with the uneven sleeves that she wore. He smiled at her. "Let's go get Abby."

All of this happened over thirty years ago. We left Pine County two years after Sylvia and Jesse died and moved to Goldsboro, a small city near my hometown. Paula and I wanted a better school system for Abby, and I wanted more time with my family. I practiced with a family medicine group, and Paula worked for the county social services department. Abby is a lawyer in Raleigh.

After we left, we returned to Pine County a few times to visit friends, but we have not been back there for many years. Laurel has changed, and not for the better. Haskell died, and Amber and Melissa moved away. I hear that marijuana now grows where Amber's goats grazed. The clinic has been closed for several months. Pine County has been hit hard by the opioid crisis.

Paula and I retired a year ago, and we enjoy spending time with our two grandchildren and traveling. I have started writing about my experiences as a nurse practitioner. This is Sylvia's story, so I wrote it in the third person.

Over the years, I have become familiar with the poetry of Emily Dickinson. On occasion, I take out a well-worn piece of paper and read the hand-written poem, titled "An Unhappy Woman." I think Sylvia perfectly captured Emily Dickinson's sense of irony.

The Healing

He was crouched behind the log, his rifle lying in the mud at his side, his pack heavy and wet on his back, the crotch of his brown cotton pants soaked. His entire body trembled, and his hands clutched his head below the helmet. Tears rolled down his cheeks, and he sobbed uncontrollably. The noise engulfed him, shouts of men in English and Spanish, mixed with the steady hammering of gunshots and the frequent explosions of cannon fire. Aware of legs moving rapidly on the other side of the log, he registered the dreaded familiar voice calling repeatedly for them to charge. Gradually, the furious sounds of battle receded, and he was left amidst the stillness of the despoiled jungle with the pounding of his heart within his heaving chest.

Then Randolph Lewis the third was lying on a bed, hot and wet from the sweat of his frenzy, gazing into the early morning light that entered the single window and hearing the chirping of birds. The tentacles of the nightmare released him, and his breathing slowed and became regular. It took him a moment to realize where he was. He saw his trunk against the wall by the bureau, and the desk and wooden chair closer to the bed. A lamp sat on a smaller table by the bed, the lampshade light blue, with a design that resembled clouds. Rolling onto his back, he stared at the motionless fan suspended from the ceiling. Sounds of birds outside flowed through the walls and filled the still air of the room.

He thought of his mother and Loretta. They would be up by now, each engrossed in her devotional. Closing his eyes, he saw the two faces through the oily film of the train window, each pinched and stern and dry-eyed, each framed by the flat black hair, identical in expression and judgment, one older, one younger, both implacable in the dense Tennessee air of summer.

June 22, 1902

I am writing in the early morning, having suffered the nocturnal visitation that has haunted me so regularly since that fateful day in the wretched jungle nine months ago. I pray that the course of recovery upon which I am now embarking will deliver me from this miserable punishment and restore me, a whole man, to the two women whom I am destined to serve. I arrived late last night at Harris Springs Fountain of Health, the train being delayed at several points along the way. The prolonged journey was quite unpleasant. Deprived again of peaceful sleep, I face the new day with the weariness of the preceding night unrelieved.

Hunched over the table, a faded brown robe hanging loosely on his thin body, Randolph stopped writing and dipped his pen in the inkwell. A knock on the door followed by a cheerful female voice startled him.

"Seven o'clock, Mister Lewis, time to get up."

He stared at the door. Sunshine slanting through the window cast an orange rectangle on its dark wood.

"Mister Lewis, time to get up." The voice called again to him through the orange glow.

He laid the pen on the table and felt the muscles of his hand relax. "Yes, thank you." The strength of his voice surprised him. As he sat motionlessly looking at the door, he heard the voice again, fainter this time.

"Seven o'clock, Mister Watkins, time to get up."

Hearing a noise behind him, he turned to the window. A bird, perched on the sill, seemed to be peering into the room. Randolph was struck by the intensity of the bird's apparent interest. When he stood to move closer to the window, the bird flew away, circled the garden below, and disappeared into the green fullness of a tree. Randolph was left with the unaccustomed anticipation of a new day.

Freshly shaved, Randolph descended the spiral staircase to the large hall on the first floor. He stood in the hallway and looked at the oil paintings on the walls, pastoral scenes, a mountain landscape, a portrait of an old woman dressed in black. He recognized the door to the dining room where he had eaten a late supper the night before. After hesitating, he opened the door. A gray-haired colored man, wearing a servant's jacket, was placing plates on the long table. Sunlight streamed through the windows on the east side, turning the china pieces on the table to gold.

The colored man stopped and bowed slightly towards Randolph. "Good morning, Mister Lewis. Breakfast will be served at seven thirty."

Randolph recognized him as the driver of the carriage that had picked him up at the train depot the night before. Ezra, he thought that was the name, but he wasn't sure. He looked from the servant to the grandfather clock that stood in the far corner of the room. Five minutes. The man moved towards him.

"You can wait in the parlor across the hall. Doctor Aqualine and the others will be here promptly at the half hour." The two men stood together inside the dining room doorway, and the older one gestured with his white-gloved hand to the double doors across the hallway.

Randolph crossed the hall, pushed open the doors and entered the parlor. On the opposite side of the room, he saw a fireplace. He looked at the mantle. Immediately, his breathing became constricted; his heart pounded in his chest. His legs shook; he swayed and almost fell to the floor. He turned his head quickly from the scene, and a blue chair swam before his eyes. Gasping for air, he staggered to the chair and collapsed into it. Beads of sweat erupted along his hairline. Tightly closing his eyes and clasping his shaking hands in front of his surging chest, he struggled to control the panic that had seized him. He hunched forward in the chair, elbows on his knees; his trembling hands cradled his whirling, throbbing head.

After a time, he began to breathe easier, and the shaking diminished. His arms and legs felt stronger, and his heart beat slowed. He opened his eyes, careful to avert them from what was above the fireplace. He was regaining control. It had not been a bad one. He heard the sound of the double doors open, followed by a man's voice.

"Excuse me, breakfast is ready."

Randolph turned his head and saw a tall figure standing inside the doorway. The man was young, about his own age. Dressed in a light green shirt and tan trousers he leaned on a cane that he held in his right hand.

"Are you all right?" The man took several steps towards him, the cane taping on the wooden floor. "You look white as a ghost." He moved closer. Randolph peered up at him. "And you're drenched in sweat. Should I get the doctor?"

Randolph weakly waved a hand. "Oh no, I'm just a bit hungry, and the heat is taxing." His voice quivered.

"Yes, the heat here can be oppressive, if you're not used to it." The man stood by Randolph's chair, a look of concern on his face. He shifted his cane to his left hand and extended his right one. "Name's Watkins, Lucius Watkins from Little Rock."

Randolph pushed down on each arm of the chair and struggled to his feet. He steadied himself before taking the other man's hand. It was firm and dry in his moist palm.

"Ra... Randolph Lewis, from Brownsville, Tennessee." Looking past the other man into the hall, he fought an urge to flee to his room.

"You must be in Turner's room. We're neighbors upstairs." Lucius paused and then continued. "Left early yesterday morning. Amazing recovery. Had some kind of heart trouble, chest pains, terrible palpitations. Left a new man." He paused again, shifted the cane to his right hand and took a step back. "The waters do wonders. I've been here three days, sitting in the water and drinking it, sixty-four ounces a day. Glad they have the indoor facilities." He chuckled. "My knee's much better. I'll be tossing this cane away in a day or two, and a few days after that I'll be running races. Took a bullet in the ole knee following Teddy Roosevelt up San Juan Hill. Hurt like the devil. Could hardly walk. But now it's almost like new." He looked down at his right leg and stamped his foot on the floor. "Were you in the war?"

Randolph looked at the foot that had thumped the floor and took a deep breath. "Th... the Ph... Philippines." He hesitated and then said, "I s... saw action at Ca... Cagayan." Raising his head, he avoided Lucius' face.

Lucius laughed and slapped Randolph's right shoulder. "We beat those bastards from one end to the other, didn't we?" He turned toward the doorway. "Let's eat breakfast."

The middle-aged, portly, neatly bearded man sitting across from him leaned forward and said, "Stick out your tongue."

He complied.

187

The doctor peered at the tongue. "Ah ha." He grasped Randolph's right wrist and looked at the large watch at the end of the gold chain. "Tachycardia." He removed the stethoscope from a side pocket of his white coat. "Unbutton your shirt, please, Mister Lewis." The doctor placed its cupped end on his patient's bare chest and listened for a short time. "Uh huh." He returned the instrument to his pocket, leaned back in the chair, crossed his legs and cleared his throat.

"Mister Lewis, you've had a bit of bad luck in the war. Nervous exhaustion. Not uncommon. We've treated many cases here at the Fountain of Health, with satisfactory outcomes. The successful regimen for this condition consists of three baths a day for thirty minutes each in the hot mineral springs, and the ingestion of sixteen ounces of water four times a day. That's what I recommend for you. The mineral water works internally and externally to purge your system of distress and restore your vitality." The doctor spoke quickly, gazing at a point on the wall behind his patient. "The meals we serve are specially designed to assist with the recovery. I'll see you here in the office each morning at ten o'clock to monitor your progress. I anticipate a stay of ten days."

Doctor Aqualine looked at the young man and then stood up. Randolph followed. They shook hands.

The doctor turned toward the door of the office and then paused. "You know, we only have five patients here at a time. That's so we can give you the necessary attention. You met the other four at breakfast. As you know, we only accept men. We find that the delicate female constitution is incompatible with the potent waters of Harris Springs." The doctor stepped toward the door.

Randolph took a breath and stammered. "That's what we wanted." He paused and took another breath. "M... m... mo...mother and I."

Doctor Aqualine turned back to him. "Your mother, you say. Yes, I see." He looked at his patient. "What is your matrimonial state?"

"I... I'm... I'm be... betrothed."

"Excellent, excellent." The older man laughed and clapped his patient on the shoulder. "A good wife is a blessing and a comfort to a man. Yes, indeed, a true treasure." He paused and then continued, "How long have you known her?"

"All... all my life."

"Wonderful. You know what you're getting, hey. And when's the big day?"

"Wh... wh... when I get well. Wh... when I get settled back in Br... Brownsville. You know, have some prospects"

"Well, Mister Lewis, we'll get you back to your women in tip-top shape." The doctor clapped Randolph on the shoulder again. "You're free to associate with the other patients as much or as little as you wish. The important thing is to avoid agitation and allow the medicinal waters to heal you." With his hand on an arm, the doctor guided the younger man towards the door. "You've met Ezra. Then there's Lizzie, his wife, the cook. You probably won't see much of her." The doctor momentarily stopped moving and turned to his patient. "And there's Dove, my daughter; she's my assistant. She woke you up this morning." He paused again and then asked, "Do you like birds, Mister Lewis?"

"B... birds? Well, yes, I gu... guess so."

"Good. We have a lot around here, many different kinds. Dove seems to attract them. She loves to watch them and tend to them." He looked intently into the face of his patient. "We find

189

birds to be very beneficial to the healing process. I recommend that you spend time each day with our birds, Mister Lewis."

Randolph had taken his first bath in the mineral water and had just finished lunch. Standing in the shadows on the back porch, he gazed into the ponderous heat of the afternoon and considered going to his room to try taking a nap. Maybe today, he could have a restful sleep.

"Hello, Mister Lewis. Welcome to my garden."

The voice emerged from the chorus of birds, clear and melodious. He saw her. In a long white dress, she stood in the grass between the porch steps and a rose bush, her face turned up to him, golden ringlets of hair undulant in the gentle breeze.

"Would you like to join me for a walk in the garden?"

Speechless, he moved down the stairs. Then they were walking in the grass between the flower beds and bird baths, under the trees. Feeling her closeness, he struggled to calm the pounding of his heart. They stopped beside a weeping willow.

"Do you like birds, Mister Lewis?" She looked up at him. He felt tremors in his legs and steadied himself.

"Yes." The sturdy sound of his voice surprised him.

"What's your favorite?"

"Well." He saw a flash of red among the green of a tree. "Cardinal."

"Oh, we have lots of those." She enthused. "See, there's one in the magnolia, and one on the grass over there by the peonies, and another in that bird bath." She pointed. "Those are the males, of course." She laughed. Then she pointed again. "Look, in the sweet gum, over there, a female. They have less red." Her gaze returned to him.

A bird splashed in a nearby marble bath, spraying water on the surrounding flowers. Randolph breathed the scent of lilacs and felt the warmth of the sun on his bare head. He looked at her face.

She turned away from him, extended her arm and swept it expansively in front of her. "Of course, we have all kinds of birds. See the meadow lark over there, and the wren by the porch, and the white-throat swallow near the mums. Mister Lewis, you can see dozens of different types of birds. They're all safe here."

Darkness had fallen, and the birds were asleep. In his room, Randolph Lewis sat within the circle of light cast by the lamp and reread the journal entry that he had just completed. The creaking of the overhead fan merged with the steady chirping of the crickets outside the walls; the periodic croaking of a bullfrog contributed to the concert. He didn't often make two entries on the same day, but he wanted to record the experiences of his first day at the Fountain of Health.

He stood and moved from the orbit of light to the window; he looked down into the garden. The full moon etched tree silhouettes on the ground. For the first time in months, his body felt relaxed, his mind at ease. He turned from the window and re-entered the light. Bending over the table, he stared at the leather-bound journal open to the page, filled with the record of his day. He turned the page, picked up the pen, dipped the tip through the round mouth into the black liquid, and boldly wrote across the white space, 'Dare I hope for relief from the anguish that afflicts me?'

The lamp was off, and he stood in the room, his bare body white in the moonlight flowing through the window. As he put on the nightshirt, he thought of Loretta. He lay down on the bed aware of his weariness.

191

"**Mister** Lewis, I'm pleased with the condition of your tongue and the strength and regularity of your pulse today. We have made good progress during the first day of therapy." The doctor stood up and moved towards the door. Randolph followed him. They shook hands at the doorway, and Randolph turned to leave. "By the way, Mister Lewis, did any of your people serve in the war?"

Randolph stopped but did not turn back to the doctor. "Th... the w... war?"

"Yes, the War for Southern Independence."

Immediately, his heart was beating rapidly; his chest was tight. He hoped the trembling of his legs was not noticeable. Struggling for control, he stammered, "yes". He felt the doctor waiting, watching him. "Gr... Grandfather Lewis d... died at Vicksburg. Gr... Grandfather Molder was killed at Antietam." His face averted from the doctor, Randolph closed his eyes; he could see the portraits at home, the one of his father's father in the parlor, the one of his mother's father in the dining room. He had grown up in their perpetual presence, his mother the devoted priestess of their legacies.

Then he became aware that Doctor Aqualine was talking, pride clearly in his voice. "My father, the colonel, died at Shiloh. His portrait is in the parlor. You've no doubt seen it. You should take a look at his sword; it's on the mantle over the fireplace under the portrait."

Days passed quickly for Randolph far from Brownsville. He drank the mineral water, bathed in the hot springs on the grounds of the old plantation manor, ate the nutritious food, sat in

192

the shade of the porch, and walked in the garden with Dove Aqualine. Each night he recorded his progress in the journal.

June 27, 1902
I am writing by the light of the lamp, at the end of my fifth day at the Fountain of Health. There are encouraging signs that the therapeutic regimen is having its intended effects on my affliction. While my nightly repose is by no means peaceful, the frequency and intensity of the distressing dreams have diminished noticeably, and I have observed an easing of the spells of agitation that so cruelly seize me during the day. The doctor expresses confidence in my recovery. Indeed, it appears that the waters are exerting a salutary effect. The quantities of water excreted with such regularity suggest a quite thorough cleansing of the system.

A noteworthy sign of my progress is the regularity with which I engage in discourse with my fellow residents of the Fountain of Health. In particular, Mr. Watkins, the son of a Little Rock haberdasher, has proven to be an attentive companion. He was quite liberal in his praise when he learned that I interrupted my studies at the university in Knoxville to volunteer my service in the war with Spain. He was most especially impressed with the role Mother played in this sacrifice. Mr. Watkins freely admitted that he volunteered out of boredom with his job in the haberdashery shop despite his mother's extreme protestation of the decision. Such a maternal attitude is strange to me. Mr. Watkins is now walking without a cane and with a barely discernable limp. He will leave in two days, a healed man.

Today, Dr. Aqualine made inquiries regarding certain family affairs. His interest in such sensitive matters engendered some unease in my mind but did not provoke the distress that I would have expected. The interview touched briefly on Father's unfortunate problem with whiskey and his sudden disappearance. The doctor expressed regret at the loss of Grandfather Molder's plantation after the war and offered quite impassioned testimony about the evils of Reconstruction. He expressed confidence that my Southern blood will assure me success in life.

My slight discomfort from the interview with the doctor was quickly assuaged by the first of two walks in the garden. I must acknowledge that these happy events have become the highlights of the day. My companion on these walks calms my soul and does much to relieve my habitual melancholia. She is a simple girl who seems unencumbered by the worries of the world. Rather, she manifests a joyous disposition acquired by a life of innocence among the flowers, the trees and the birds. I find myself thinking of her more and more.

The night is far advanced, and it is time to retire. I feel that I will find rest tonight. I must remember to write Mother and Loretta tomorrow. I have been shamefully negligent. They are anxious about my condition, and I should communicate the favorable progress to them.

"**Mister** Lewis, the birds are active today, don't you think?"

"Yes, they are." As they walked along the line of oaks at the edge of the garden, he was much more aware of her presence at his side than of the birds. A sprig of verbena adorned her hair. She breathed deeply, inhaling the fragrance of honeysuckle; beneath the fabric of the dress her bosom rose. He quickly looked away. A bird flew by and landed on a nearby branch. It reminded him of the mystery.

"Miss Aqualine, there is a particular bird that perplexes me."

"A bird that perplexes you, Mister Lewis?"

"Yes, each morning when you knock on my door, I notice it at the window, looking into the room. I'm certain it's the same bird, a brown bird, I don't know what kind. I have a strange feeling about it." He slowed his pace to stay beside her and waited for her response. They moved into the shade of an oak tree.

Finally she said, "Mister Lewis, birds are like people in certain ways. I have observed that they have favorite places, places where they feel comfortable, safe. The window sill of your room may be such a refuge for your bird." She stopped moving and turned toward him. "Mister Lewis, we have a place of healing for wounded men, and we have a sanctuary for birds."

They resumed walking. Randolph felt privileged, as if he had been entrusted with a special confidence. It gave him courage.

"Miss Aqualine, forgive me, could I ask you a question of a rather personal nature?"

"What do you want to know, Mister Lewis?"

"Have you always lived here, at the Fountain of Health?"

"Oh yes, I was born here, but it wasn't the Fountain of Health then."

"What was it?"

"Just a house." She paused. "It has been in Father's family for many years. After the war, we lost most of the land."

Randolph waited for her to continue, when she didn't, he spoke. "Could I inquire, Miss Aqualine, about your mother?"

"She died when I was born."

"I'm very sorry, Miss Aqualine, please forgive my insensitivity."

"No, that's all right, Mister Lewis." She paused and then continued. "I was raised by grandmother Aqualine. Grandmother passed when I was sixteen. I miss her very much."

They walked in silence under the trees, sunshine falling intermittently on them, birds fluttering overhead. Randolph wanted to know more.

"What has your schooling been?"

"Oh, I attended the school in Harris Springs. Father wanted me to go to the women's college in Little Rock, but I couldn't leave my garden." She stopped and turned to him. "Mister Lewis, I have everything I want right here."

On the following day, Randolph received a letter. He stood in his room looking through the window into the afternoon tranquility of the garden. He watched Dove move among the flowers and trees, her whiteness accentuated by the variegated colors around her. While he observed her, she reached out to a red bird that splashed in a birdbath; the bird flew to her, landing on the outstretched hand. With the bird perched on her hand, she slowly moved behind a bush, disappearing from his view. Turning from the window, his attention returned to the letter on the table. Sighing, he sat in the chair, picked up the letter, and read it again.

June 22, 1902
Dear Randolph,

Your mother and I hope that you arrived without incident at the Fountain of Health. We are confident that you will diligently apply yourself to the task of resolving your unfortunate condition. As you know, your mother deserves a son who can attend to her needs as she ages, and I, as your intended, deserve a husband who can fully meet the responsibilities inherent in that role.

Yesterday, your mother was exhausted by the stress of your departure. Consequently, she spent the remainder of the day resting. This morning she had regained her strength sufficiently to allow the two of us to visit Mr. Peters to discuss your future employment. Quite frankly, he expressed concern regarding a propensity for nervous instability that he has perceived in you since your return from the war. Your mother and I reassured him that your stay at the highly respected Fountain of Health in Arkansas would alleviate any such indisposition. Your mother reminded Mr. Peters that as a very young man he served in your late grandfather's regiment. I am pleased to report to you that our visit was successful; Mr. Peters has generously agreed to take you on as a teller in the bank. Your mother and I are confident that this welcomed news will inspire you to a complete recovery.

In recent weeks, you have on occasion discussed the possibility of resuming your studies at the University of Tennessee. Your mother and I do not believe that this course of action is in your best interest at this time. We are concerned that in your current state you would be inordinately susceptible to the inevitable temptations of university and big city life. If this is a disappointment to you, rest assured that we strongly support the eventual completion of a course of study conducive to success in business.

Randolph, be comforted in the knowledge that your mother and I pray constantly for your restoration.

Your Betrothed,
Loretta

Hunched over the table, he stared at her name. A visage materialized to hover like a cold mist in the constricted air above the letter. He felt wound like a tight ball of twine.

When he heard the bird outside the room, the apparition dissolved. He folded the letter, stood up from the table, and turned to face the window. As he gazed into the garden, he felt the unraveling of tension in his body, his hand relaxed, and the released letter floated to the floor.

For the first time, one morning the knock on the door and Dove's cheerful voice awakened Randolph from sleep. After answering her call, he lay peacefully on the cool dry sheet, with only a vague residue of an unpleasant dream. He listened for the faint repetition of her voice at Lucius Watkins' door, but he was disappointed. Then he remembered that Lucius was leaving that day.

After his first mineral water bath of the day, Randolph sat in the shade of the back porch, a book of Lord Byron's poetry open in his lap. Two men sat nearby discussing an article in the newspaper about a new saw mill in Harris Springs. His mind was on neither poetry nor saw mills; he was waiting for Dove. Soon, he smelled honeysuckle and turned to see her standing beside his chair, smiling down at him. He arose.

"Good morning, Mister Lewis."

"Good morning, Miss Aqualine."

"Another beautiful day."

"Yes," he said. Turning to gaze into the garden, he added, "Mister Watkins left early."

"Yes, he took the first train." She looked into the garden. "I guess he was eager to get home." She paused and then exclaimed, "Oh look, there's a new chipping sparrow." She sparkled with excitement as she pointed to a bird perched on the nearby railing of the porch. The bird was staring at her.

Randolph studied the new bird; he had a strange sensation about it. He felt like he knew the bird, but he was certain that he had never seen it before. "It seems to have a defective wing," he observed.

"Yes," she replied, "a wound from a hawk." She turned to Randolph. "Unfortunately, sometimes birds fight like men do. The water in the bird baths will heal it in a few days." She spoke with confidence. "Mister Lewis, are you ready for our morning walk in the garden?"

On the morning of his last full day at the Fountain of Health, Randolph Lewis awakened to the sound of birds outside his room, to the sight of sunlight streaming through his window, and to a fullness in his loins. Astonished, he tentatively explored under the nightshirt, confirming a state that he had not known for many months. His hand slowly stroked his enlarged manhood as he lay on the dry sheet.

"Mister Lewis, time to get up; it's seven o'clock."

Randolph waited for the guilt, for the self-recrimination, but he felt only anticipation, a vigor. And it came easy and satisfying, as it never had before.

A little later, Randolph entered the parlor. Across the room, he saw the portrait of the doctor's father, dressed in Confederate gray, the eyes staring back at him. His gaze dropped to the sword, the ornate handle, the golden blade naked and exposed before its sheath. Hearing a sort of whimper, he turned and saw another man, standing by the blue chair. The man was young and seemed unsteady, shaky.

Confidently, Randolph reached him in two strides and extended his right hand. "Randolph Lewis," he said with alacrity. "We're neighbors upstairs." The man's grip was weak in his hand, the palm moist and cold. The man looked at the floor. "I'm from Brownsville, Tennessee, heading home tomorrow, a new man."

The man raised his eyes; Randolph saw the tears. "I... I... I'm Hu... Hubert Mu... Mumsford, Ri... Ripley, Mis... Mississippi."

Randolph clasped the other man's trembling shoulder with his hand. "Let's go eat breakfast, Mister Mumsford."

On their last walk together, Dove and Randolph left the garden and strolled arm in arm amidst the tall oaks. Sunlight penetrated the dense canopy of leaves in narrow golden beams. Birds rustled in the branches overhead and squirrels scampered over the carpet of moss. As they walked, she told him how her grandmother had convinced her grandfather not to cut the trees down to create more cotton fields. But now her father only owned a small patch of the forest, and she rarely ventured from the garden.

Soon they came to a large open area. They stopped beside a road where deep wagon tracks carved into the sunbaked earth. Dove tightened her hold on his arm; Randolph felt her body stiffen. Across the road, he saw dozens of tree stumps. Limbs and dead leaves littered the ground like body parts on a battlefield. Beyond the clearing, he saw men moving. A team of horses slowly dragged a pair of logs over the ravaged land. As he watched, a tree swayed and then crashed to the ground; the earth seemed to respond with a tremor. Dove shuddered, and he felt the heat of her body against his arm. He barely heard her quivering voice.

"Mister Lewis, please, let's go back."

"Certainly."

He freed his right arm from her grip, circled her waist with it, and hugged her to him. They began to turn together back to the woods, but she uttered a cry, pulled away from him, and rushed into the scarred road. She stumbled in a rut, the bottom of her dress dragged in the dirt, and she almost fell. Randolph watched her bend over and gently lift something small and brown from the road; he realized what it was.

Sobbing, she caressed the stiff body. Randolph enveloped her in his arms, and she laid her head against his chest and cried convulsively. Continuing to hold her, he slowly guided her from the road into the sanctuary of trees. After her sobbing had subsided, he detached himself and with a stick dug a small grave.

Later, they leaned against a tree trunk; he looked into her tear-stained face and told her everything. He told her about his terrors, about his disgrace in the Philippines, about his grandfathers, about his father, about his mother, and about Loretta.

She gently stroked the side of his flushed face and said to him, "You're a brave man, Randolph. Your burden has been lifted, and you are free."

On his last night, he stood naked in the darkness of the room and gazed through the window into the shadows of the garden below. The whiteness of a lily shined like a bright star in the darkness. The birds slept.

He lay on the bed, the sheet cool on his body. He fell asleep easily. Then he had wings; he was soaring above the treetops. The sunlight sparkled on his body. Looking down, he saw the colors of the flowers and the green of the grass, and then he saw the white figure reaching up to him. He flew towards the beacon of life.

After his bath, Hubert Mumsford found Dove Aqualine on the back porch. Although he had walked with her the day before, he was still a bit afraid of her. She smiled at him, and he gathered his courage.

"I'm sorry I missed Mister Lewis this morning. I wanted to say goodbye."

"Yes, he left very early, took the first train. He was eager to get home." She smiled at him and then turned to look into the garden. She exclaimed with excitement, "Look, you can see the new cardinal, over there on the low branch of the weeping willow. He's rather shy, but he'll be braver in a few days."

Last Meal

"Okay Morrow, here it is."

The outside door of the slot slid open.

"You sure you don't want some other kind? There's lots of flavors." The slot door shut.

The prisoner heard the soft chuckle. Opening the inside door, he saw the bowl in the slot but did not remove it. "Is it vanilla?"

"Yup, that's what it is." Another chuckle.

As Morrow removed the bowl from the slot, looked out the small window of the cell door at the three guards: Hogan, a nigger, and a thin wiry dark-skinned guy with a goatee, a Mexican.

The spic had been by several times with Hogan, and Morrow had seen him once in the yard. The nigger had been around a long time, but Morrow had never spoken to him. The mongrels would remember his silence, his defiance. He talked to Hogan and some of the other whites, but not much. From the way the guard sometimes looked at him, looked at the niggers and wet-backs, and a few things he said when no one else could hear, he figured that Hogan was a supporter. Morrow knew there were a lot of his kind in the prison, on both sides of the bars, warriors for the white race, members of the Aryan Brotherhood or other patriotic organizations. However, he didn't have much contact with them; he was special. He knew it, and they knew it.

The bowl was cold in his hands; the ice cream had melted a bit, but there was still a white mound of it. Sitting on his chair, he pulled the spoon out of the mound and watched the hole it left slowly disappear in the pure whiteness. The ice cream was smooth and sweet in his mouth.

"When will it be ready, Papaw?"

"Not much longer. It's getting thicker."

He could tell. The rhythmic cranking was slowing, a good sign. He had turned the handle first, when it was easy. But his arm had tired, and his grandfather had taken over. It would be ready soon, ready to eat.

Tommy sat on the porch with his legs dangling over the side. Light from the bulb overhead cast shadows on the wood floor. His distorted shape extended across the yellowed earth to melt into the darkness beyond. Over the tobacco plants at the edge of the western sky, a touch of pink lingered like a palm print on glass. In the dark woods across the road where the blackberries ripened, firefly lights flickered. Bullitt sat panting at the foot of the steps, his tail stirring the dust.

"Papaw.

"Yeah, Tommy." The deep voice emerged from the sound of the churn.

"Why'd my daddy have to get killed?"

With the squeaking of the crank, the boy heard the incessant clicking of crickets and the occasional hoot of an owl. Bullitt lowered his head and rested it on the bottom step.

"Tommy, I know it's hard. Your daddy had to do his duty. Sometimes, you have to fight for what you believe in if you're a man. You'll understand some day."

The boy heard his grandmother moving inside the house. He swatted at a mosquito.

"Papaw, I wish I lived with you and Mamaw all the time."

"Why's that?"

The cranking had stopped; he could almost taste the cold sweetness. "I don't like Lester."

205

A dog barked in the distance; Bullitt raised his head and growled. Down by the pond, a bullfrog croaked.

"It takes a while to get used to a new daddy." Papaw lifted the cylinder from the ice and set it on the porch.

"He ain't my daddy." The boy felt the twinge in his back where Lester had hit him with the belt the day before he left to visit his grandparents on the farm. "He's mean to me."

"Well, Tommy, I think she's done." The boy watched the shadow stand up, arch its back and stretch arms over its head. His grandfather picked up the container of ice cream. "Let's see what Mamaw says."

The boy scrambled to his feet and rushed to open the screen door.

Morrow sat on the wooden chair, holding the bowl that was empty except for a little white puddle in the bottom. Slowly, he scanned the cell: The blanket folded on the bed where he had slept for the last time, books and magazines stacked under the sink and beside the commode. Toilet paper dangled just above the floor; the next guy could use it. The spider was motionless in the web that extended from the commode to the wall; gone was the fly that had been ensnarled in the silken trap.

After he was gone, they would take down the Confederate flag that hung on the wall over the bed and the poster of William Pierce brandishing the *Turner Diaries* on the opposite wall. He knew his mother would throw all his stuff away. The bitch.

Like dust on a country road, quiet had settled over the cell block, an unusual quiet for death row, but then this would be an unusual night, one that would be remembered. Lifting the bowl to his lips, the condemned man swallowed the last drop of the white liquid.

Tommy lay in the bed where his mother had slept as a girl. Had she listened to the night sounds outside the open window and felt the breeze on her bare arms and legs? What had she thought about? Had she ever thought about the son she would have?

Tommy was aware that his Mamaw was standing in the doorway watching him. Then she was bending over the bed. He could smell her; he loved the smell of his Mamaw.

"Have you said your prayers?"

"Yes ma'am."

She kissed him on his forehead. "Good night, my Darling."

"Mamaw, could I live with you and Papaw all the time?"

"I don't know; we'll see. Right now, you need to go to sleep. You've had a busy day, and tomorrow you'll help Papaw fix the fences."

As he drifted off to sleep, Tommy Morrow savored the lingering taste of the vanilla ice cream that he had made with his Papaw.

The silence suddenly ended with a bang in the corridor, a mop in a bucket. They liked to make a racket cleaning the halls when the inmates were trying to sleep. Sleep, now that was another thing Morrow would never do again. No, he realized that wasn't right; sleep was what he would soon be doing forever. Eternal sleep: that didn't seem so bad.

He heard more clanging outside the cell, like the noise of a distant train, a long time ago.

Lester had gone, leaving just the two of them again, and Tommy was glad. It was near the end of the sixth grade. "Here's ten bucks." She'd said. "Go to the picture show. Stop by the Tastee

Freeze for a cone on the way home. Don't get home before eleven." She had smiled at him. Usually, she would do this on Friday or Saturday night, and Pete and Harvey would go with him. But on Wednesday night he had to go alone. He saw "Superman" for the second time.

The night was warm, and he licked rapidly to keep up with the melting chocolate ice cream. Not wanting to get home too early, he took his time. The moon was hidden by clouds. Dark buildings loomed beside him, and the street lights were widely spaced. His shadow elongated as he walked from the light into the darkness, until it disappeared for a while, to reappear behind him. The sidewalk had ended; the ground was uneven. Occasionally, a car passed on the street; he wanted to be home. In the distance, he heard the clanging of freight cars on the tracks, and then suddenly they appeared right in front of him: two of them, bigger than him, probably seventh or eighth graders.

"Hey white boy, whacha doin'?"

The light of the street lamp behind Tommy illuminated the black faces. Frightened, he did what they told him to do. He gave them the money he had left, the two dollars and 63 cents. He turned his pockets inside out to prove that he didn't have any more. The bigger boy grabbed his hand and shoved the ice cream cone into his face. They walked away laughing about the chicken-shit white boy. Tommy ran.

When he reached his street and saw the beat-up Ford under the street light in front of the house, he stopped running. The house was dark. He stood by the tree in the Sawyer's yard. His heart beat fast in his chest; he gulped air. Melted ice cream and tears dripped from his cheeks onto his shirt. He wiped the sticky mess from his face with the shirt and watched the house. An owl hooted. Insects buzzed in the darkness. A truck shifted gears out on the highway.

Light seeped between closed curtains from the house across the way.

After a while, the front door of his house opened, and a man came down the steps and into the light of the street lamp. A stranger, he wore a t-shirt and jeans; the cigarette tip glowed against his dark face. The man got into the Ford, started the engine and drove off, the muffler rumbling into the distance. A dog barked.

Tommy waited a few more minutes in the Sawyer's yard before entering his house. His mother was in her room. He called through the closed door to tell her he was home.

She never asked about the chocolate stains on his shirt; he never asked about the man.

That summer, Tommy, Pete and Harvey caught a nigger boy in Granger Park and beat the crap out of him. But that had not rinsed away the taste of shame.

Although Morrow hated to think about that night, he recognized it as a turning point; his real education had begun that night. That was when he started learning about the big difference between the way things were and the way things should be. That was when he first began to sense what he needed to do to make things right.

"Hey Morrow, are ya ready to fry in hell for all time?"

He stood up and set the empty bowl on the bed and thought about responding, but it was only Murdock. Murdock was next in line to die. Morrow had only contempt for the shit-for-brains white trash who had killed a policeman during a liquor store stick-up. What a waste. Men like Murdock were too dumb to channel their legitimate anger into something productive, something that would rescue the white race from oppression and restore it to its rightful place. Whites like Murdock were too blind to see it; they were pitiful. Sometimes, Morrow thought they deserved being victims.

No, he would not answer; Murdock wasn't worth it. Morrow would save it until the end, when he had the right audience. He would have his say, and no one who heard it would forget the grand finale of his legacy.

Murdock's taunts meant nothing to Morrow. Killing a cop was meaningless compared to what he had done. Morrow had been five blocks away when he heard the explosion. It was louder than he had expected. Exhilaration had surged through him. That had been his downfall; he had deviated from his plan. He had intended to get as far away as possible, to watch it all on the news, reveling in his achievement, in the blow he had struck for freedom and against government oppression, but he had wanted to see for himself. He had driven by the destroyed court house, to see the smoke in the air, to see the chaos, the hysteria, to hear the screaming, to witness the destruction and suffering, to experience the victory in one battle of a long war. It had gone against his discipline, his years of training in the marines, his time in the Persian Gulf War. If he had stuck to the plan, he would still be free, still be fighting the war. But he had made peace with himself over the mistake. He was still fighting; he had become a symbol, a symbol of resistance, a symbol of patriotism. Soon, he would become a martyr. They would get no satisfaction from killing him. He would die unrepentant, cursing tyranny and celebrating eventual triumph.

Murdock had given up, and quiet again enveloped the cell block. Ready for what was to come, even a bit impatient, Morrow stood by the door of his cell and listened to the silence. Slowly, he became aware of a sound, a soft snoring. He realized that it was coming from Washington's cell next door. He was surprised that

210

this irritated him; he thought that he was beyond being bothered by Washington anymore. But Washington sleeping on such a momentous occasion annoyed him; he couldn't help it. The goddamned nigger had always been a pain in the ass. He had been the one prisoner who had seemed indifferent to Morrow. He had shown Morrow no hatred, no respect, no nothing. He was the one who just didn't give a damn one way or another. It had bothered Morrow, and it still did. The spook was only in for killing his wife and the guy she was cheating on him with. What gave him the right to be so arrogant? But that wasn't really it. Morrow couldn't hide it from himself, even on this special night. It wasn't anything the bastard did or didn't do; it was whom he reminded him of.

Physically and emotionally beaten, Morrow lay impotent in the tortuous dust of a North Carolina summer and stared in fear at the black face that leered over his. He was overwhelmed by the stink of nigger. Red-rimmed constricted pupils bore into him. Spittle from the twisted mouth of the drill sergeant sprayed his face, mixing with his sweat and tears, as he cowered helplessly under the assault.

"You worthless white trash. You ain't no marine; you're a piece of shit, a fuckin' piece of shit. I knew a pissant piece of Southern white trash named Morrow in Nam. You even look like him, probably your no-good daddy, he was. Got shot in the back one day, running from the gooks. We was all better off with the yellow-bellied coward dead. But I tell you somethin', you fuckin' piece of shit, you ain't gonna get off that easy. I'm gonna make a marine outa you or you'll die tryin'. Now, get off that ground and climb that wall or I'm gonna really get pissed at you."

Morrow had climbed the wall that day in boot camp, and he had never forgotten that sergeant and what he had said about his daddy.

Annoyed with himself, Morrow moved away from the door so he could no longer hear Washington's snoring. He did not want to be thinking about the humiliation of boot camp at a time like this. Instead, he thought about the first blow he had struck for the white race.

Standing on the walk-way, Morrow faced his Papaw and his Mamaw. An occasional person passed the three of them on the way to or from the court house. Noise from afternoon traffic flickered in the background. Pale in the bleak winter sky, the sun imprinted their shadows into the moribund grass. Boiling inside, Morrow glared at the building behind his grandfather: 'God-damn that Jew banker, god-damn that Jew judge.' He had seen the county court house in the town square since he'd been a little boy. Now, he was realizing what it represented.

The old man reached up and put a tremulous hand on his grandson's shoulder. Morrow looked down into his Papaw's eyes, sucked into the sun-leathered face. He would never see him alive again. He would see him in his coffin six months later. Because he was in some damn desert in Iraq, watching dark-skinned mutants piss in the sand, he didn't get to his Mamaw's funeral six months after that.

"Tommy, let's go get some ice cream at the Tastee Freeze."

"No Papaw, I can't; I've got to get back to Lejeune. I only got a day off."

His grandfather squeezed Tommy's arm. The old man didn't say anything. He had fought the Japs in the Pacific, and he was mighty proud that his grandson was a marine.

But the grandson did not go directly back to Lejeune.

The sheriff looked at Morrow through the bars of the cell. He was a little man, but at least he was white, unlike one of the deputies who had arrested him. Morrow figured the world had really gone to hell when they had nigger deputy sheriffs in little towns in North Carolina.

"You could be in a passel of trouble, boy."

The 'boy' pissed Morrow off, and he glared back at the sheriff. He clinched his right fist at his side; it hurt from smashing into the Mexican's face. But the pain felt good; he was glad he had slugged the bastard. He wanted to slug the sheriff, but he knew he'd be in big trouble if he did that. Morrow could tell that the sheriff had something to say.

"You're Luther and Paulette Parker's grandson, Lilly's boy? He stopped, and Morrow saw the little smile play around his mouth. "I remember ole Lilly from school."

Morrow struggled to keep from rearranging the smug face with his fists. He had nothing but disgust for his mother, but he always resented another man's acknowledgement of what she was. Morrow stared into the eyes of the sheriff, who soon looked at the cell wall behind his prisoner.

"Terrible thing about what's happened to your grandparents, terrible thing. It ain't right." The sheriff sighed and shook his head. "Fine folks. I've known 'em all my life." He looked at Morrow. Morrow didn't say anything; he wanted to see what was in it for him when it played out.

"When's the auction?"

"Day after tomorrow." Morrow spat it out.

"Yup, the bank don't waste no time." The sheriff shifted his eyes again to peer into the cell. "I hear Supreme Pork is fixin' to buy it and turn it into a hog farm." He grunted in disgust. "Just what we need 'round here, more hogs."

Morrow waited.

"Where're Luther and Paulette stayin' now?"

"They have an apartment over on First Street."

"That's a shame, a cryin' shame."

They both knew about First Street; it was where white trash lived. It was the kind of place where Morrow's mother would live. The sheriff must have thought so too.

"What's Lilly doin' now?"

"Last I heard she was in Raleigh. We don't stay in touch much."

"Reckon not." The sheriff shifted his feet, looked Morrow in the eyes and frowned. "Getting' in a fight in a bar don't help your grandparents none."

Morrow remained silent.

"Some folks in the bar say you were kinda provoked."

Yeah, Morrow thought, he was provoked. Some greasy, shit-assed spic was talking to a white girl at the bar. He was way too friendly with her. It wasn't right, even if she was white trash. He didn't say anything to the sheriff. He was okay with where the conversation was going.

"There's been a lot of 'em comin' into these parts in recent years. Not long ago, ten or twenty years back, you hardly ever saw a Mexican 'round here. Now, the streets are full of 'em. They're the only ones who'll work in these chicken packin' plants. Many of 'em are illegal, I reckon, but the businessmen don't want you shippin' off their workers. The Mexicans cause trouble some times." The sheriff paused and shifted on his feet. "But that don't give you cause to start fights in bars."

Morrow stared back at the sheriff. He knew this was the crucial part; either he was in trouble or he was not. The sheriff was deciding what to do with him. Morrow was damned if he was going to kiss his ass. He didn't say anything.

After waiting a while, the sheriff spoke. "Luther and Paulette have had enough trouble without any aggravation from you. For their sake, I'm not gonna charge you with anything this time. You can stay here in jail and sober up. There's a Greyhound that comes through at seven in the mornin'. You be on it. Remember, if you come back here, you behave yourself. You've used up all my good will."

Later that night, as he sobered up in the county jail in the basement of the court house, Tommy Morrow shed tears for the last time in his life.

Morrow found himself in a room that he had often envisioned. A gurney occupied the center. Soon, he would be stretched out on it. It looked comfortable. He didn't remember getting to the room, but he figured he must have walked. His hands and feet were in chains, but he could still take small steps. Five other men were in the room: Hogan and two other white guards, a man in a white coat, and one in a suit and tie. The room had only one door. There was a small table on one side of the gurney and a sink on the other side. An entire wall consisted of a dark glass. Morrow knew who watched from the other side of that window. They sought closure; he chuckled silently. Such self-deception, he would haunt them forever.

He thought of the window in his bedroom in the old farmhouse, the peach tree outside, the mourning doves, the night-time owl. Shaking his head, he cleared his mind of distraction.

The man in the suit was speaking; it sounded official. Morrow recognized it, his crime, the murder of seventeen people. Sometimes, he didn't quite believe he had really done it.

"Thomas Morrow, do have any last words?" The suit was looking at him. A smile flickered on Hogan's mouth; he figured what was coming. Morrow looked into the black window and slowly shook his head. It wasn't quite time yet.

The condemned man lay on his back strapped to the table. He saw the doctor with the syringes. He felt the stick in his arm. As he watched the needle pierce the IV tubing, he knew it was time. He opened his mouth to speak, but instead, he tasted the sweet residue of vanilla ice cream. He heard the steady clicking of crickets and the insistent croaking of a frog. Breeze from an open window caressed his arm, and he saw the moon between the clouds over the tobacco field. As he became drowsy, he could smell his Mamaw, feel her lips on his forehead and taste the sweetness of life in his mouth, just before it passed from him.

Note: After Timothy McVey was executed for the Oklahoma City bombing, I read that his last meal had consisted of his favorite ice cream, mint chocolate chip. This was sobering to me because mint chocolate chip was and still is my granddaughter's and my favorite ice cream. When she was small, Ellie and I shared a special pleasure in eating it together, a spoonful for Ellie and a spoonful for Grampa, one for Ellie and one for Grampa, and so on, until the delicious stuff was gone. This disquieting connection with a terrorist led me to wonder what if any experiences McVey had had with grandparents. Instead of searching biographical material on the Internet, I decided to see where my imagination would take me. In my attempt to explore the mind of a racist mass murderer, I again used the highly offensive word and some vile language. Morrow's attitudes and actions are abhorrent; but in the hell of this depravity does a remnant of the little grandson endure, a seed of redemption?

In the Park

He observed her, the striking woman - young, tall, long black hair, creamy chocolate skin, a blue blouse, a multicolored skirt - supervising a group of children, frolicking by the fountain, probably a kindergarten class, maybe first graders.

The old man sat in the tranquility of the spring morning and watched her graceful interactions with the children. As he watched her, his gaze penetrated the surface beauty to expose the bruises. He visualized her sprawled on the floor, crying in pain, pleading not to be hit again. Discomforted, he looked away.

As was his custom in this season, he sat under the greenery of the trees near a bed of flowers. On this morning, he was reading the new biography of Harry Truman, *The Wall Street Journal* folded on the bench at his side. The intermittent call of a bobwhite descended from a nearby tree. He looked up into the branches, and beyond the leaves; across the park he saw the top of his apartment building, protruding into the blue sky.

He had lived on the seventh floor for twenty years; for the last two of those years, he had lived alone. From his front window, he could look down at Rittenhouse Square. For part of the year, he saw green tree tops. For a few weeks each year, he saw the reds, oranges and yellows of autumn. And for part of the year, he could easily peer past the bare branches to the gray ground and perceive tiny human figures. Through the years, he had witnessed the life of the park.

He stared at the sky; it had been the same blue when they had put Wilma in the ground. Even after two years, so many images reignited the memories, brought back the sadness. During the years of their marriage, he had always expected to die first, even after her illness began. But this had soon changed. Despite

218

the medications, the surgery, and the best efforts of a battalion of doctors, the sickness had gradually transformed into the dying, and then one agonizing form of suffering had been replaced by a deeper despair. He had been powerless to stop it.

The old man heard the rhythmic sound of shoes striking the ground and felt the breeze of rapid movement. He looked from the sky to the bare back of the young man who had just jogged by his bench. The jogger passed an on-coming young man, this one dressed in a dark suit. He carried a briefcase and talked on a cell phone, a man in a hurry also. The old man watched him, absorbed in his world, oblivious to the teeming life around him. He had once been a young man in a hurry, but now he sat and observed what the busy men and women in their fine clothes, with their briefcases and cell phones, did not see: the homeless hunched on park benches, the babies in strollers, young lovers hand in hand, two Asian women engrossed in conversation.

As he often did, he wondered if anyone he saw in the park had been his patient. *That old man looks vaguely familiar. Did I take out his gallbladder? The woman with the poodle, did I remove her breast? Probably not. I can't remember faces. Maybe if I could see the scars.* No one had ever come up to him in the park and said, "Doctor Pickens, you probably don't remember me, but you saved my life."

Niles Pickens had retired from the medical school faculty ten years ago. He had been a general surgeon. He had thrived as a surgeon and a teacher, especially in the '60s and '70s. His teaching rounds and lectures had been legendary, and his days had been filled with the diverse challenges of subduing disease. He had worked skillfully and at times heroically, inside damaged bodies, exploring, removing, repairing, healing. Indeed, he had been a master with his hands, a man with few peers.

219

Change had come, slowly at first, then more rapidly, as specialization eroded his professional temple. His younger colleagues had increasingly narrowed their therapeutic focus. He had become encircled by experts in particular organs: the colon, the gallbladder, the breast. As had the patients, the students and residents had gradually gravitated to the specialists, and there had been little left for him to do. He and Wilma had retired together. A large banquet had honored the distinguished professor and the devoted nursing director of pediatric services.

In recent years Dr. Pickens had thought less and less about his profession. Early in retirement, he had returned to the medical center for clinical conferences and to engage with former colleagues and students. But he noticed that they rarely invited him into their offices, and when he conversed with them in the hallways, their eyes and voices suggested a need to attend to more important matters. His visits had dwindled and eventually stopped.

He had had Wilma then. They had spent the retirement years together as they had envisioned: visiting children and grandchildren, traveling in Europe, taking leisurely walks, learning pottery and ballroom dance, attending concerts and plays. But there had been far too few of those years.

"Cool tie, dude."

Mildly annoyed, the retired doctor looked up. The boy had flashed by on roller blades and was looking back at him grinning. The boy had on earphones; his hair was green. Sunlight glittered on the small ring of metal in his nose. Dr. Pickens watched him glide over the uneven pavement and recede into the life of the park.

Every day for over forty years, Niles Pickens had worn a bow tie to work; it had been his trademark. His father, a druggist in north Philadelphia, had also worn a bow tie. Like his father's ties, his were of the old type that needed to be tied. He had dozens, a drawer full. They had accumulated over the years, gifts from patients, colleagues and friends. Each morning before he went to work, Wilma picked the tie that he would wear that day. He continued to wear a tie; every morning he tied the bow, and every night he untied it when he was ready for bed. He tolerated the occasional comments the ties attracted in the park.

As he watched the green-haired skater disappear, Dr. Pickens noticed an old man walking slowly towards his bench. The man looked familiar. He struggled to place him, and then surprised, he recognized him as the retired stockbroker who lived with his wife on the same floor of the apartment building. *What's his name?* He studied the other man. He and Wilma had played bridge with the man and his wife, a short fat woman who had chattered endlessly. *He's changed, lost weight, looks bad. He's been sick.* And then the realization: *He is sick.* His neighbor was suddenly exposed, cracked open like a hard-boiled egg. Dr. Pickens recognized the old adversary; he saw the ugly yellow mass enclosing the bowel in deadly embrace. As he watched, the doomed man turned onto another path and slowly disappeared. The doctor exhaled in relief.

After Wilma had died, Dr. Pickens had been inundated with food, mostly from the widows in his building. He had eventually thrown away the casseroles, pies and cakes that had accumulated to slowly decay in his crowded and neglected kitchen. But the food had continued to arrive for months, delivered by solicitous and consoling women, the aroma of chocolate mixed with the odor of perfume. In the face of his indifference, the widows had finally turned to other pursuits.

For a while, he had accepted offers from neighbors and former colleagues to dine. He had eaten supper on one occasion with the retired stockbroker and his wife; it had been a painful affair. He had eventually stopped accepting such invitations, and they had eventually stopped coming. He had turned inward, seeking solitude and protection in a routinized existence.

By noon, the shade from the trees had disappeared, and he was sitting in the sunshine. Tiny droplets of sweat collected along his hairline, which he periodically blotted with the handkerchief that he carried in a pocket of his trousers. He had read two chapters of the biography and finished the newspaper. He had stopped often to watch someone in the park, to dissect through the skin, to probe the inner being, to lay bare the secrets.

He returned to his apartment and ate a tuna sandwich and banana for lunch. He had mail, a letter from Joan, his daughter in Denver. Knowing what it contained, he laid it unopened on the table. She had called the week before. Her voice had been more insistent than usual, her concern palpable, annoying.

"Dad, we worry about you; it's been two years. You need to get out more, travel. We want you to come visit. You could make a big trip out of it, see Niles and Gretchen in Chicago, Dave and me here, and then swing down to Santa Fe to see Jamie. You haven't seen him since the funeral." Listening passively, he had waited for her to finish.

Perhaps, he would read the letter tonight, with his glass of wine. Traveling held no interest for him. He didn't want to visit his daughter or his older son, and the thought of seeing his other son, the artist and massage therapist, was disagreeable. Jamie had been one of the few sources of discord with Wilma, and since her death his youngest child had rarely been in his thoughts. Long ago, Dr. Pickens had learned to avoid the things that he could not control.

As was his custom, after lunch he lay on his side of the bed, his open right hand resting in the empty space of the other side. He fell asleep listening to Mahler's *The Tragical,* with the distant murmur of city in the background.

In mid-afternoon, he walked around the corner to the Civil War museum where it was quiet. He was slowly making his way through letters written by Union soldiers during the Peninsula campaign. His great-grandfather had been wounded at Williamsburg. After briefly exchanging pleasantries about the spring weather with the museum director, he was relieved to find the reading room empty.

Late afternoon found Dr. Pickens again in the park. The rhythms of the park changed during the course of the day. Now there were more people, particularly children, and thus more noise, more bustle. He knew the regulars, the ones who stayed to frolic or to talk or to sit and read or just to sit and watch, as he did. He also knew the ones who passed quickly through on their daily journeys from one place to another and back again. Many of them he knew well, very well, though he had never spoken to them.

He was watching for one person in particular, hoping that he would see her again. And then he saw, a girl, probably eleven or twelve. He had noticed her in the park often in recent days, late in the afternoon. She always had a rabbit with her, on a leash, a big white rabbit that hopped along beside her. She reminded him of someone he knew long-ago. He had never seen her talk to anyone in the park. As he watched her walk across the grass, he realized why he had never seen her smile. *She has diabetes; she's different from the other girls in her school. She resents the insulin shots she must take and the diet she must follow. Her parents work long hours, and she's left with a nanny who bores her. The rabbit is an Easter present intended to relieve her loneliness. She takes good care of her pet, but she's still unhappy.* As he watched her pass by his bench, he thought of calling to her, to comment on the rabbit, but he did not do so.

A man and a boy threw a baseball back and forth on a sunlit patch of grass near his bench. The ball created a thud when it landed in a glove. The boy wore a Phillies t-shirt and looked to be about ten. He threw with a fluid over-hand motion. Dr. Pickens watched the father and son play catch. *I haven't thrown a baseball in fifty years.*

He had played first base on his high school team. He had been a good player. His interest in playing baseball in college had succumbed to the rigors of his pre-med studies. Years ago, he had taken the boys to see the Phillies play, when he had the time. Jamie had played on a Little League team. But that had not lasted long; he had given it up and moved on to some other temporary interest. 'He's trying out different things.' Wilma had tried to explain. *I guess that's what he's still doing.*

He watched the father and his son. *Maybe if I had spent more time with him.* Dr. Pickens frowned and turned away from the man and boy to look at tulips by the fountain.

He was annoyed that he had allowed Joan's unread letter to intrude into his thoughts. To regain control, he stared into the reds and pinks of the Rhododendrons across the walkway. In a while, his gaze was interrupted by the frail figure of a woman, a park regular. As he watched her slowly trudge along, the doctor studied the condition of her decomposing liver. *It wont be long now.*

There was a line at Houlahan's; because he did not want to wait, he ate at a new restaurant around the corner on Walnut Street. As usual, he ate prudently, selecting the grilled chicken with rice and spinach. The waitress was young, pretty, dark-haired; she showered him with smiles and attention. He studied the bulge of her breasts under the thin blouse and inspected her amply exposed legs.

He thought of another attractive dark-haired girl, a lifetime ago, and afternoons at the drugstore, evening walks in the park, Friday night sock hops. Departing from his usual practice, he left a generous tip. Turning back for a last look as he was leaving, he visualized the tiny growth in her right ovary. He carried an unwanted burden into the waning sunlight.

In the deepening shadows of twilight, he sat with his back to the noisy street, looking into the inner sanctum of the park. Usually, it was his favorite time of the day, but he was vaguely disquieted. Across the walkway from him, two men sat on a bench, the intimacy subtle but unmistakable. He had seen this couple in the park on other evenings. He had watched them strolling casually together and sitting in quiet conversation and had been bothered by something ill-defined. As he studied the pair in the diminishing light, it came to him. *The older one is infected. He loves his partner and wants to protect him.* He studied the men. *They've had an argument.*

As Dr. Pickens observed the two men, he momentarily thought of Jamie, but he really did not want to be further disturbed this evening. He watched a squirrel scamper across the grass and effortlessly climb a tree.

As he sat and peered into the subsiding light, he became aware of another couple, more conventional and less inhibited than the gay men. The teenagers were entwined on a blanket in the deep shadows near the bushes. He did not see them well, but he recognized them; he had seen them before in the park and had noted their care-free adolescent love. But now he observed that they bore a burden; something had changed. As he considered their future, he felt a twinge of sadness. *What's the matter with me?*

Redirecting his thoughts to a Union soldier's letter to his wife that he had read that afternoon, he wondered if the man had survived to return to her.

The arrival of a man who sat at the other end of his bench interrupted his thoughts. He easily recognized the man as a bum, probably homeless but not one of the park regulars. Unavoidably, Dr. Pickens was familiar with the homeless men and women who frequented the Rittenhouse Square area. He saw them daily and endured their repeated requests, at times almost demands, for money. He refused to submit to panhandling. But he did not ignore the homeless; he knew most of them very well. They were constant sources of discovery. As he sat in the park and observed them, their stories unfolded before his eyes. This man, however, who loudly occupied part of his bench, was a stranger.

"I got me some new shoes. Don't they look good? Brand new. Fit real good, comfortable. Got them today. Don't they look good, my new shoes?"

At first, Dr. Pickens thought the man was talking to him. He looked at the derelict and realized that he was not talking to anyone in particular. Maintaining a steady commentary on his shoes, the bum turned his head from side to side like a preacher exhorting his congregation.

Most people who walked by the bench ignored the man, relatively oblivious to the antics of the homeless. A few of those passing by eyed him with disdain. After a few minutes, the gay men left, the older one sending the bum a look of reproach.

The bum continued to talk loudly about his shoes. Dr. Pickens studied him with rising interest. *Who is this guy? Why the obsession with his shoes? What's he doing here? What's his story?*

In the deepening shadows of twilight, the doctor gazed at the stranger intently, his mind open, inquisitive, receptive. The man was tall, thin, middle-aged, his long, tangled hair streaked with gray. Bushy black eyebrows hovered over yellow eyes. His nose was big and deformed, a red glob affixed to a leathered, creviced face. Black stubble littered his cheeks. His voice arose from deep within his chest, and words tumbled out of his mouth like rotten fruit from an overturned garbage can. A jagged gray scar disfigured the left side of his neck. He wore a tattered jacket vest over a long-sleeved shirt that might once have been white. His left hand lacked an index finger, and his twisted knuckles looked like knotted tree roots. His wore loose, baggy gray pants, the bottoms caked with mud. He wore no socks, and on his feet, he had filthy lace-less sneakers.

Got them from a dumpster. The doctor concluded as he watched and waited.

"Look at my new shoes, brand new. Don't they look good?" The man talked tirelessly into the still air of the dying day, impervious to the incisive gaze of the old surgeon.

Perplexed and disappointed, Dr. Pickens turned his eyes away to peer into the darkness of the bushes. The teenagers were gone. He stood up and looked one last time at the object of his futile examination. Still nothing. Frustrated, he made his way along the path towards the park exit closest to his building.

Suddenly, he heard the barking behind him and was turning around when the dog slammed into his left leg. His leg buckled, and he fell to the ground. The doctor lay stunned, conscious of pain in his left knee.

"Damn," he muttered.

After lying on the ground for a moment, he struggled to sit up. The leg hurt, but he made it to a sitting position. Nothing else seemed to be hurting. He smelled the man before he heard him and heard him before he felt the touch on his left shoulder. He recoiled.

227

"Damn dogs. They shouldn't let 'em in the park." And then, "You okay, doc?"

The fallen man slowly turned to his benefactor and came face to face with the bum who had occupied his park bench and now was bending down to him. The stench was awful.

"Let me help ya there."

The doctor felt a tugging in his left armpit. He resisted it.

"No, wait. Let me rest a bit."

"Okay doc, you the boss."

Dr. Pickens sucked in some air and carefully flexed his painful knee, it moved, a good sign. He pressed both hands on the dirt path and began to push himself up. Pain shot through the knee, and he groaned.

"Okay, take it easy, doc; let me help ya."

The bum had a hand under each armpit and was lifting the fallen man. The doctor struggled to get his legs under his body, to take on his weight. He was almost up, but his left knee gave way. The bum caught him before he fell again.

"I gotcha, hold on, take it easy." And then, "Rest a bit before ya try to walk."

"Okay, good idea." The doctor leaned heavily into the other man. His silk shirt pressed against the bum's jacket. The unraveled bow tie fell to the ground.

They clutched each other in an awkward embrace. The doctor was vaguely aware of figures moving in the shadows. A man passed by, and then a man and a woman walked by, glanced at the strange couple and then turned away. Nobody stopped. Feeling less pain, Dr Pickens yearned for escape. He wanted desperately to be home, in the comforting solitude of his apartment.

"Ready to give it a try?"

"Yeah."

Together, they took a couple of steps

"Okay, good, now where to?"

"Over there, I live across the street."

"No problem, we'll get there."

And they did. By the time they reached the park exit, the doctor was walking with only slight assistance from his helper. From the entrance of the building, the doorman saw them and hurried across the street to rescue the doctor.

"You okay, Doctor Pickens?" The uniformed man looked at the doctor and then at the bum. "Is he botherin' you?"

"No, no, I fell and he helped me."

"Oh. Okay." Then he said, "Let me help you across the street." And to the bum, "I've got him now."

"Wait." Dr. Pickens said just before stepping into the empty street. He turned from the doorman to the bum and extended his right hand. "I want to thank you."

The bum shook his hand. The doctor held the coarse hand in his and looked into the yellow eyes, aware of the unaccustomed touch of another person. The man let go of the doctor's hand and turned to re-enter the park.

"Wait, what's your name?"

The man turned back to face the doctor. "Joe, my name's Joe."

"Thanks, Joe."

"Sure doc, no problem. You take care." The man disappeared into the darkness of the park.

"Doc, you better check to make sure you got your wallet before he gets very far."

He made no effort to check the back pocket of his soiled trousers. "Thanks, I still have it."

The doorman helped the old man into the lobby. He was walking on his own. The knee hurt, and he knew it would bother him for a few days, but there was no serious damage.

Outside the elevator, the doorman asked, "Do you want me to go up with you?"

"No, I'm okay, thanks."

Late that evening, Niles Pickens sat in his recliner, an ice pack on his left knee that was extended in front of him. Joan's letter lay open in his lap; there was a half-filled glass of Chardonnay beside him. As he held the phone to his ear, he looked again at the four smiling faces in the framed photograph that stood beside the wine glass. He had dug it out of a box in his bedroom closet and had wiped the dust off the glass. For years, it had been on the desk of his hospital office. *The children were so care-free and Wilma, so alive.* He listened to the periodic sound. He decided that he would give it one more ring.

"Hello."

He paused, looked at the letter in his lap, and said, "Hello Jamie, it's Dad."

Note: I wrote the next two stories for Ellie, but I hope they have appeal for children of all ages, even those who receive Social Security. Ellie, my wife Cokie, and I are avid fans of the Harry Potter series. Ellie and I have read the books and seen the movies together. For years we played "Harry Potter," making all kinds of magical things happen when we pointed our stick wands and gave commands. A fallen tree was a basilisk, a gray cloud, the death eater mark, a bird in flight, a snowy owl, a white towel swinging on a clothes line, a dementor, the shaggy-haired guy at the McDonald's counter, an Auror. One day, as Ginny and Ron, we stood on a wooden bridge over a creek in Rock Bridge State Park and watched a rather large turtle paddle upstream. We cast a spell to protect it from the troll we knew lurked in wait under the bridge, thus did a story germinate.

I marvel at J.K. Rowling's genius in creating a magical world that has captivated millions of readers. As someone who has received so much from my reading over many decades, I deeply appreciate her success in introducing so many to the wonders of the imagination and the joys of reading. Thank you, Ms. Rowling.

Pylon is my parody of William Faulkner's writing that won the 1998 Faux Faulkner prize sponsored by the University of Mississippi and Jack Daniels Distillery.

The Forest Adventure of Ginny and Ron

On a late summer morning, a red-headed teenager grumbled in frustration as she worked up a sweat in the disorganized front yard of the humble Weasley homestead in rural England. The youngest Weasley child had been instructed by her mother to rid the yard of pesky doxies, and Ginny Weasley was angry. It was not fair. While she chased the silly, elusive creatures around the tall grass, full bushes and ample trees that surrounded the Burrow, Ron, who should have been helping her, was practicing his Quidditch skills in the field across the pond. Hoping to become the keeper for the Gryffindor Quidditch team in the upcoming school year, Ron was vigorously fending off bludgers, which the twins, George and Fred, were firing at him. No, it wasn't fair at all. Ginny also had aspirations of making the Gryffindor Quidditch team. Why was Ron allowed to practice while she had to pursue hateful little doxies that scurried just out of her reach, emitting high-pitched hideous laughter?

Ginny's knowledge that she could easily dispense all of the awful doxies by using a simple spell enhanced her frustration. Yes, she could wave her wand in a circle around the yard while pronouncing "doxievanishaway" and all the pests would immediately disappear. But no, because of that stupid rule against under-age wizardry, she could not use magic outside the grounds of Hogwarts School. Compounding her frustration, Ginny knew that her mother could use the same spell to clean out the doxies, thus saving her harried daughter from this onerous task.

"It builds character." Yes, Mrs Weasley had said that to explain why Ginny had to expunge the doxies without the use of magic.

"Character," she muttered as she lunged for a particularly nasty doxie. Feeling oppressed, Ginny Weasley was angry, angry at her mother, angry at her brothers, angry at the world in general. Ginny stopped to wipe the sweat from her brow with the hem of her light cotton robe. When she looked up something caught her eye, a sparkle of red against the blue sky. As she watched, the scarlet speck became larger and larger, until it materialized as a big red owl that landed on the ground at her feet. Although Ginny had only seen the owl once before, she recognized the bird as Rubravian, Albus Dombledore's owl. What a surprise!

She reached down and removed the envelope that Rubravian held in his beak. Then the big red owl spread his wings and flew back into the sky, rapidly disappearing from sight. Ginny studied the envelope that she held in her hand. Recognizing the official Hogwarts seal, she tore it open with eager anticipation.

After quickly reading Dumbledore's neat script, she gave a loud cry of joy and leaped into the air. Her three brothers across the pond stopped to stare at her. Ignoring them she raced into the house.

"Mother, Mother," Ginny shouted, as she swept through the front door and collided with a broom that was magically sweeping the living room floor.

Mrs. Weasley hurried out of the kitchen where she had been brewing a pot of beetle-nut stew. "What is the matter? What has happened?" Mrs. Weasley's inclination was immediately to fear that something bad had happened to a family member every time there was commotion of any sort. This habit kept her in an almost perpetual state of apprehension.

Ginny rushed to her flustered mother and thrust the note from the Hogwarts headmaster into the startled face. "Dumbledore is sending me on a special mission." Ginny stopped to catch her breath and then continued. "Me, a special mission for Dumbledore! Me, a special mission!"

"Calm down, Ginny, calm down, please. What are you talking about?" The short, dumpy, red-haired woman snatched the paper from her daughter's hand and started to read it. By the time she had finished, her face radiated profound worry and disapproval.

"The idea of that foolish old man sending two children into Rock Bridge Forest is preposterous! That's a dangerous place. There are all kinds of evil things lurking in those dark woods." Her eyes narrowed as she peered at her daughter. "I will not permit it."

"Mum, Ginny, what's going on?" George, Fred and Ron burst into the room, speaking in unison, their summer robes ballooning behind them.

Their mother glared at them. "Nothing that concerns you. Go back outside and play that silly game."

Indignant, Ron began to reply, but he was preempted by his sister. "It does concern Ron, too. Dumbledore says for him to go with me."

"Go with you. What are you talking about?" Ron approached the two witches and reached for the note in his mother's hand. Mrs. Weasley jerked her hand away and hid the note behind her back.

Ginny looked at Ron and began to explain. "Dumbledore sent a note via Rubravian, instructing us to go immediately to the wooden bridge at the center of Rock Bridge Forest and then to await further orders."

"Wow, that's neat! Rock Bridge Forest!" Ron exclaimed.

"But you're not going!" Mrs. Weasley bellowed.

"But… but, Mum."

Ginny interrupted her stammering brother. "Mum, Dumbledore is our headmaster, we must obey him. You always say that we must do what he asks us to do, and he's asking us to go on this mission. It must be important, and there must be some special reason why he is asking Ron and me to do it. And he has suspended the rule against under-age magic for us. We can take our wands and use magic if we need to. So, we will be perfectly safe."

"Yippee!" Ron reacted to the wonderful news about the use of magic.

Mrs. Weasley remained intransigent. "You're supposed to obey your mother, too. I say you're not going. What would your father say if I allowed you to go and something bad happened?"

"Dad would let us go because he knows that Dumbledore would never ask us to do something that could hurt us," Ron reasoned.

"Yeah." A hopeful Ginny added.

"They've got you there, Mum." Fred chimed in. "I'll tell you what. Why don't George and I go with them just to keep them out of trouble? We'll make sure nothing bad happens to them."

"Good idea," agreed George.

In unison, Ginny and Ron turned on the twins. "You're forgetting that Dumbledore did not instruct you to go, just Ron and me. If he had wanted you two to go also, he would have included you in the note, but he didn't," Ginny responded resolutely.

"Okay." Fred retreated. "But I bet when you get in the forest, you'll wish we were with you. We've had more training in Defense Against the **Dark Arts** than you have."

"Well, we've had enough for Dumbledore to trust us with an important mission," Ron replied.

"Mum, what are you going to do?" George inquired. "Time is wasting." Four pairs of eyes peered expectantly at the angry matriarch.

With a deep sigh, Mrs. Weasley relented. She brought her hand from behind her back and gave the note to Ron. He read it quickly, a smile spreading over his flushed face.

"It's against my better judgment, but I agree that Dumbledore would never knowingly put you in danger."

Ron and Ginny cheered loudly. Their mother observed them sternly. "You better be careful. If you get killed, I'll never speak to you again." All four teenagers laughed heartily while their mother continued to scowl.

Ron referred to the note. "It says that we must get to the bridge before sunset today. That means we must hurry. It is a long way from the Rock Bridge at the edge of the forest to the wooden bridge in the center of the forest." He paused and then resumed. "I wonder what he wants us to do at the bridge."

"I guess we'll find out when we get there," Ginny responded.

"You'll need to eat a big lunch before you go." Mrs. Weasley turned and bustled into the kitchen.

Ginny and Ron followed her, to find heaping bowls of stew and large mugs of butterbeer magically awaiting them on the table. They gulped down their lunch and stood up, raring to depart. Mrs. Weasley flicked her wand and uttered a spell. Two large broccoli and pineapple sandwiches and a jug of butterbeer suddenly hovered in the air beside them.

"Take these as a snack," Mrs. Weasley advised.

"No Mum, we need to go fast, so we'll have to travel light," Ron resisted.

"At least take some butterbeer."

"We won't need it, Mum. We won't get thirsty," Ginny assured her.

"You'll be sorry," Mrs. Weasley muttered.

"How are we going to get there? It's a long way," Ginny inquired pensively.

His eyes sparkling with opportunity, Ron replied. "I guess we'll have to apparate." Ron was frequently eager to apparate, although he had never actually done it.

"Oh, no you don't," His mother vehemently objected. "You don't know how to do that yet. If you try to apparate at your level of training, you'll get swinched, and that really hurts. How will you be able to get through Rock Bridge Forest if you leave one of your legs here? Have you thought of that? And what would I do with an extra arm or leg that you left behind? It would just be in the way."

"Oh Mum," Ron whined.

"You can take the portkey at the pond."

Down by the pond, Mrs. Weasley and the twins watched as the two adventurers placed their hands on the old worn-out boot that stuck out of the mud at the water's edge.

"Don't get your feet wet," Mrs. Weasley admonished the travelers. "Be careful," she added anxiously.

With their hands on the boot, Ginny and Ron looked at each other and together said, "Rock Bridge Forest".

After the brief sensation of rapid transit through a thick cloud, the sister and brother found themselves staring at a large granite formation that arched over a stream of water. They recognized Rock Bridge, the entrance to the forest, the forest that they had heard about but had never seen, and certainly had never entered. Now, they would experience it for themselves.

Hesitantly, wands in hand and ready, they approached the Rock Bridge on a narrow pathway that wound among tall trees. When they came to the entrance of the tunnel in the rock, they saw that the path continued alongside the creek under the bridge. They shivered in the cold air. In the darkness of the stone tunnel, Ron commanded, "Luminous." The end of his wand magically burst into light, illuminating the uneven rocky walkway at their feet. They slowly made their way along the trail, keeping the sunlight at the other end of the tunnel always in view. When they reached the other side of the rock underpass, they welcomed the warmth and light of the sun and marveled at the panoply of color that greeted them and the chorus of birds serenading them from the treetops.

Ron smiled and tucked his wand into the sleeve of his robe. "This isn't scary at all," he observed confidently.

"Still we need to be careful." Ginny relaxed her grip on her wand but kept it poised in her hand. "Remember, Dumbledore said in the note to stay on the path, never to leave it for any reason."

Suddenly, something black swooped down, fluttered in the air just over their heads and then soared back into the sky. Instinctively, they ducked their heads and then peered up at their attacker. Ron jerked out his wand and pointed it at the sky.

"A bat."

"Yeah."

"They won't hurt us."

"I hope not."

They climbed a gentle hill, being careful to stay on the trail. Rocks rimmed the trail; interspersed among the rocks beautiful flowers of all kinds: lilies, tulips, pansies, violets, sunflowers, roses and many others bloomed. Ginny wanted to stop and pick some purple flowers, but because that would require that she leave the path, she didn't do it.

Soon they attained a flat place, and the path passed a small pond. Strange looking duck-like animals swam on the surface, watching the two humans with keen interest. Then they noticed that the ground on each side of the path was gradually turning to mud. Soon they were in the middle of a swamp, the path the only dry ground.

"I've heard that if you step in that yucky stuff, you'll be stuck forever and not even counter-spells of Dumbledore will get you out," Ron warned. Despite the hot humid air from the bog, Ginny shivered.

"Aren't there supposed to be big snakes in this forest?" Ginny asked fearfully.

"Yea, that's what I've heard. But don't worry; I know how to deal with snakes."

"How?"

"It's a freezing spell. You'll learn it this year at Hogwarts. You point your wand at the snake and say "Freezeoserpentiosa" and the snake freezes, can't move. We did it in Defense Against the **Dark Arts** class. Neville messed up and made his own hair turn to ice, but the rest of us did it fine after a few tries. Hermione did it the first time, of course." Ron grunted with a mixture of disgust and envy.

"Freezeoserpentiosa?"

"Yea, that's it. Just say it over and over to practice."

"So, do you just leave the snake frozen? Can you make it so the snake will move again?"

"Sure. All you have to say is "Unfreezeoserpentiosa." But I don't know why you would ever want to unfreeze a snake. To me, the only good snake is a frozen one," Ron chuckled.

239

Eventually, the path left the swamp and coursed along the top of a cliff. Looking over the edge to the distant creek below, Ginny shuddered. "I don't like high places," she complained.

"No problem." Ron waved his wand over the side of the ledge and said "Flatenoutodandelosis." Suddenly, a completely flat field of dandelions replaced the steep valley.

"Wow," exclaimed Ginny with relief. "That's much better."

"Be careful, don't try to walk on that field; it's not real. It's only an illusion. The valley is still there; you just can't see it. If you step over there, you will fall into the creek."

"Thanks for warning me. Will I learn how to create illusions this year too?"

"Yep."

After a while, they left the ledge and no longer needed the illusion of a flat field. Ginny was getting tired; her legs were aching and weary, and worse than that, she was thirsty. She thought of that jug of butterbeer that she had refused. She would love to have a deep swig of that now, but she would never admit it to her mother.

They walked through a forest of tall trees, which allowed limited sunlight to penetrate to the ground. The air was cooler, and the light dimmer, heralding the approaching sunset. They had not reached the wooden bridge. Would they get there in time?

Ginny saw a strange shape on the ground up ahead. It looked like a big tree that had been blown over and was lying on the ground. As they drew closer, she stared at it with growing anxiety. Then suddenly, she shrieked, "There's a giant snake!"

"Where?" Ron quickly scanned both sides of the trail, his wand poised in his hand. Ginny pointed a trembling finger. "I see it," he said with alarm.

240

Together, they slowly inched along the path toward the snake, never taking their eyes off the creature.

"It's not moving. It doesn't see us. But we must walk right in front of it; it will see us then for sure," Ginny whispered.

"No, it's frozen," Ron announced, relaxing the tension in his body. "Someone came by here and froze it."

"Thank goodness." Ginny released the breath that she had been fearfully holding for almost a minute. "It sure is huge, at least 20 meters long. It could swallow you whole. Look at its eyes, and the tongue is out. It looks like it was getting ready to bite something."

"Yes, whoever froze it did it just in time. Ron looked at his sister, a smile flickering around his mouth. "Should we unfreeze it?"

"Oh, no!" she gasped.

They passed by the frozen giant snake and continued down the path. A few minutes later the adventurers encountered a large tree that had been blown over; the trunk blocked the path.

"I guess we'll have to climb over it." Ron approached the obstacle.

"No, we can't. That would mean leaving the trail. Something bad will happen," Ginny cautioned.

"Blimey, you think so?" Ron was skeptical.

"Yeah. I think Dumbledore wants us to stay on the trail. That means keep our feet on the ground."

"Okay, but what are we going to do? I don't know any spells for removing dead trees from paths."

"You don't?" Ginny almost giggled. "Let me try."

She moved in front of her older brother, pointed her wand at the thick trunk that obstructed the path, and said "Trunkusamputationala." Suddenly, the part of the trunk that

241

blocked the path disappeared, and the trunk looked like it had been cleanly cleaved in two, with a piece removed.

Dumb-founded, Ron starred at the transected tree trunk. "Where did you learn that?" he finally stammered.

"Herbology."

"Herbology?"

"Yes, trees are just big herbs. We learned how to trim herbs, you know, cut them up. Really Ron, you should pay attention more in Herbology." Ginny knew that Ron disliked Herbology and could not help reminding him of her superior knowledge of the field.

Turning away from her to pass between the two sections of the trunk, Ron muttered gruffly, "Let's go; we don't have much time."

Indeed, there was not much time left. Daylight was waning; the air was cooling. Unmistakable signs of impending evening were evident. Voices of birds rose from the trees in anticipation of the coming slumber. Bats fluttered in the air above the heads of the travelers, reminding them of the nocturnal creatures that prefer darkness. Once, a heavy rustle in the underbrush attracted their attention, and they glimpsed a large form cantering through the woods.

"Ron, was that a Centaur?"

"I think so."

"Will they hurt us?"

"Not if we stay on the trail."

"How much further?"

"I don't know."

"I'm tired and thirsty."

"Me, too."

They walked on the trail beside the creek, listening to the water gurgling over the rocks and lapping at the shore.

"There's something up ahead." Ginny's voice punctured the forest sounds.

Hovering over the creek, a vague, ghostly form slowly emerged from the deepening gloom of the late afternoon. As they moved towards it, the form gradually gave shape to a wooden bridge, and they realized that they had reached their destination. When they paused a few feet from the end of the bridge, Ron spoke softly.

"One thing I haven't mentioned before. I've heard that there is a troll who lives under this bridge. I don't know, maybe it's not true."

"A troll!" Ginny gasped in horror. "Why didn't you tell me?"

"I was afraid you wouldn't come. Anyway, it may not be true."

"A troll!"

"Trolls don't scare me very much. Don't forget, I defeated a troll in the girl's bathroom my first year at Hogwarts."

"Yea, but you had help from Harry and Hermione."

"Well, that's true." Ron sighed and looked at the bridge. He didn't feel very brave now at all. "What should we do? The note said to go to the middle of the bridge and wait for further instructions." He thought he detected a whiff of troll body odor in the air but decided not to mention that.

Ginny moved forward onto the bridge. "Okay, let's do it." Ron followed his sister to the middle of the bridge where they stopped and looked around.

"What do we do now?"

"We wait, I guess."

"Do you hear something?" Ron whispered.

"Yea, it sounds like snoring," she whispered.

"Something really big is snoring. Like a troll." Ron shuddered.

"Well, if he's snoring, that means he's asleep. Let's make sure he stays asleep."

"Good idea."

In a few minutes, they heard fluttering overhead. Looking up, they thought it was a bat. But then Ginny could barely discern a familiar scarlet form against the gray sky. "Rubravian," she proclaimed more loudly than she intended.

"Shuuush. Quiet, remember," Ron admonished.

In a few seconds, Dumbledore's owl was perched on the bridge railing beside the two adventurers, who were overjoyed to see him. Ginny removed the envelope from the bird's beak, and they both bent forward into the diminishing light to read the headmaster's message.

*Look into the water and you will see a precious
animal that deserves your protection. Enclose him
in a concealment charm so he may evade the
danger that lurks under the bridge and can continue
on his journey. The wizarding community thanks
you.*

Ron and Ginny looked at each other and then turned to peer into the murky darkness of the water.

"I wonder what animal it is."

"I hope we'll be able to see it."

"Look, there's something in the water. What is it?" Ginny was pointing at the creek, excitement in her voice.

244

"Yes, I see it. Blimey! It's a turtle. Yes, a turtle, swimming in the water. Quick, we need to use the concealment charm. Do you know it?" Ron was excited, his voice rising dangerously.

"Yes," Ginny answered.

Together, they pointed their wands at the turtle that was rapidly approaching the bridge. They had little time to protect the reptile. "Concealioterrapinophilia," they called in unison. The turtle suddenly disappeared from view.

"We did it!" They shouted in celebration. Invisible, the turtle would swim beneath the bridge, escaping the fatal grasp of the hungry troll. But now the two humans faced great peril.

"We did something else, too," Ron announced anxiously. The slumbering monster had awakened.

Suddenly, the terrible stench of troll breath permeated the air. They heard the unmistakable rumble of troll emerging from under the bridge. Then they saw the bald gray head of the beast slowly rising from the other side of the bridge, and then two beady black eyes were staring straight at them. The ugly head rose further revealing the snot-drenched nose and then the gaping mouth, filled with razor sharp teeth and a giant meaty tongue. Paralyzed, their wands immobilized at their sides, they watched in horror as the hungry mouth opened still wider, and the awful head moved towards them prepared to bite huge chunks out of the bridge and consume their trembling bodies.

Then miraculously, they each felt something grasp their robes at the back of the neck and lift them into the air, away from the bridge and into the sunset-streaked sky over the dark, receding forest. Ginny looked up into the large belly of a bird and recognized Fawkes, Dumbledore's majestic phoenix, who had come to their rescue just in time. Ginny knew that Dumbledore would not allow anything bad to happen to them.

Soon, they were at the portkey outside Rock Bridge Forest, and a little while later they found themselves releasing their grip on the old boot by their pond. Ron and Ginny looked away from the pond into the growing darkness to see their mother, father and twin brothers running jubilantly towards them to welcome them home. They had completed their mission.

Green Magic

Several days later the euphoric glow of the forest adventure was still engulfing Ginny and Ron as Mr. and Mrs. Weasley saw them off to school at platform 9 and ¾. They passed from the muggle world into the wizardry realm with the anxious admonitions of their mother to be careful vibrating in their ears. Barely had they settled into a compartment of the Hogwarts Express with their best friends, Hermione Granger and Harry Potter, when the excited Ron started to describe their recent adventure.

Hermione soon interrupted the frenetic recitation with an exclamation of astonishment, "Wait a minute, you mean Dumbledore gave you permission to use magic?"

"Yes, and we sure needed it; we would never have survived the terrors of Rock Bridge Forest without our magic. I used many of the spells we learned in Defense Against the **Dark Arts** class," Ron replied proudly.

Hermione's expression changed from a look of surprise to one of perplexed frustration. "I sure could have used magic this summer; it would have saved a lot of time and hard work. Not to mention these awful calluses." She held out her hands, palms up to display thickened skin.

Ginny inspected her friend's abused hands with sympathy. "What did you do?"

"I spent most of the summer helping my mum and pop build a new house. Believe me, at times I was tempted to wave my wand and say 'homebemade,' but I would remember the rule against underage magic and stifle the impulse."

"Poor you," Harry injected with a note of sarcasm. "I would much rather spend my summer building a house than being persecuted by Dudley and his repulsive pals. Sometimes, it was all I could do to keep from turning them into pigs."

"We are all so sorry that you have to suffer through summers with such miserable muggles, Harry," Ginny commiserated. Harry gave her a wan smile; Ginny's face immediately became as red as her hair, and she turned to look out the window.

"Yeah, Harry," Ron added, but he was eager to return to the story, launching an animated description of their arrival at the Rock Bridge via portkey.

Since the adventure, Ron had almost incessantly recounted his exploits in Rock Bridge Forest to anyone willing to listen, and even to those like Fred and George who were increasingly loath to hear another retelling of the well-worn tale. With dwindling tolerance, Ginny endured her brother's escalating exaggerations; with each repetition the forest was darker and more menacing, the bats more aggressive, the serpents larger, the bridge more foreboding, and the troll more horrible. If anything, Ron's energetic narration to Harry and Hermione inflated the dangers even more. But when Ginny tried on occasion to inject a moderating amendment to the over-heated description, she was quickly rebuffed by her brother. Finally, with a self-congratulatory smile, Ron ended the tale and settled back into his seat to receive praise from his friends.

"Wow!" Genuinely impressed, Hermione continued, "Weren't you afraid?"

Ron responded quickly, "Not really."

"Don't be silly, Ron. We were both terrified. You know it. Stop showing off." Ginny directed a withering look towards her brother. Tired of his pomposity regarding the whole experience, she was ready to put it all to rest.

"Well maybe we were a bit scared. You know it was dark and gloomy, and Rock Bridge Forest does have rather a sinister reputation. But I was confident that we could handle the mission. And we did."

"Yeah, with Fawkes' help. He saved us."

"Well, that was all part of Dumbledore's plan, wasn't it?" Ron's face wore a smug expression. "And he chose us."

A pensive Harry ended his silence. "Yeah, Dumbledore showed a lot of faith in you two, and you delivered." Ron beamed proudly, and Ginny blushed again. "However, it seems to me the real question involves the turtle. Why was the turtle so important? What does it mean that Dumbledore would risk your lives to get a turtle past a troll? There must be something special about that turtle."

"That's right," agreed Hermione. "What's with the Turtle?"

"Well, I dunno. I haven't thought much about that," replied a somewhat deflated Ron.

The Great Hall of Hogwarts Castle reverberated with the frenzied activity of hundreds of newly-arrived students. The four friends joined their house-mates at the Gryffindor table in a cacophony of happy reunions. Neville rather sheepishly wore a polka-dotted chartreuse cap, knitted by his grandmother, and Parvati and Lavender proudly displayed emerald bracelets that supposedly repelled obnoxious boys. Within minutes, Ron was surrounded by spell-bound second year students captivated by his narrative of the recent forest adventure.

Furtively, Harry glanced at the Ravenclaw table and recognized the familiar head of lush black hair; his heart beat increased. Shifting his gaze to the darker side of the hall, he identified the pale face of Draco Malfoy. Across the sea of

249

youthful ebullience, their eyes momentarily locked, and the characteristic smirk spread over the Slytherin's visage. With a melancholy sigh, Harry turned his attention to Hermione's overly didactic explanation of the mechanics of house-building to a bemused Nearly Headless Nick.

After the ghost escaped to caper with Peeves, Harry remarked to Hermione, "Wonder who the guy in that green robe is, sitting at the faculty table beside Snape."

"Well, duh, a new faculty member, I guess."

"Yeah, I figured that much," an exasperated Harry retorted. "What do you think he teaches?"

"Don't know. But he does look rather distinguished in that spectacular robe. Don't you think?"

"Nah, I think he looks kinda silly."

Hermione smiled and poked her friend with an elbow. "You're just jealous because your ole robe is drab and black."

"Well blimey, that's the way wizards' robes are supposed to be." Harry turned away to find Ron at his side. Hermione strolled over to give Angelina Johnson her opinion of the Herbology textbook.

"Who's the new bloke in the faculty?" Ron inquired.

"Don't know. Hermione thinks he's distinguished."

"She would. Looks kinda silly to me."

"Yup."

Dumbledore arose from the faculty table at the head of the Great Hall and stretched out his robed arms. Quiet gradually descended on the audience of students. After the first years had been suitably distributed into their houses by the Sorting Hat, an array of sumptuous food suddenly materialized on the tables, and students eagerly attacked the mounds of roasted potatoes, broccoli, peas, carrots, joints of pork and lamb, thick chunks of tender beef, succulent slivers of chicken, fragons of freshly baked bread, sloggerts of savory sauces and pitchers of pumpkin juice. Choclairs and blueberromas topped off the feast. All over the hall students caressed their distended bellies, emitted contented sighs of over-satiation and collectively produced a near concert of sonorous burping.

The Hogwarts Headmaster again rose and launched into his customary welcoming speech; he reviewed some school rules and highlighted his expectations for the coming year. He acknowledged the returning faculty individually and then turned his attention to the single new addition to the faculty.

"It gives me great pleasure," Dumbledore intoned in his deep voice, rich in both authority and kindness, "to introduce our Defense Against the **Dark Arts** Instructor, Professor Liam Dennehy." He paused for the polite applause to end and then continued, "As you may have surmised, Professor Dennehy is a native of Ireland, where he has lived for many years. Professor Dennehy has most recently taught at the Cashel School of Wizardry in the Emerald Isle. Before that he served as the very successful coach of the Irish National Quidditch Team, and before that he excelled as the star goaltender for the team."

An excited Ron nudged Harry and whispered into his ear. "Blimey, I've heard of him. He was one of the best keepers ever. He holds the record for most shutouts in international competition."

"Shush!"

"Shush yourself, Hermione. This is wonderful."

"Quiet both of you; Dumbledore is telling us more about him." Harry was trying to listen intently to the Headmaster. He well knew the crucial importance of this faculty positions.

"I well remember Professor Dennehy when he was an exchange student at Hogwarts years ago; I was a young faculty member then." The Headmaster smiled at the thought that he had once been young. "Even as a student, his skills as a Quidditch player were much in evidence." Dumbledore turned to the new professor and continued, "We are very fortunate to have you with us." He turned back to the students. "Please join me in welcoming professor Dennehy. I trust that you will honor him by devoting to his expert instruction the energy and hard work that it deserves."

With his exquisite green robes flowing around him, the new teacher arose and bowed into the enthusiastic clapping of the Hogwarts student body.

'A student years ago, I wonder if he knew Tom Riddle,' a thoughtful Harry Potter mused to himself.

Indeed, Liam Dennehy had known Tom Riddle, much to the Irishman's misfortune. They had both arrived at Hogwarts in the same year. Because of his Irish brogue and different cultural background, Liam had been an oddity at first. But his personality and skills in the class room and on the Quidditch pitch had quickly earned him popularity among the other students, in contrast to the brooding, insular Riddle. Unlike most of the other students, Riddle resented Liam for his Irishness, considering him akin to a mudblood. As Riddle increasingly embraced the **Dark Arts**, it was probably inevitable that Liam would become a target of his malevolence. One day when the Irish boy was swimming in the lake with friends, the opportunistic Riddle took advantage of his temporarily defenseless enemy and placed a powerful spell on him, a spell that he had only recently perfected but one that would profoundly affect Liam's life.

A few minutes into their first Defense Against the **Dark Arts** class, Ron leaned over to Harry and whispered, "He talks funny."

"Of course he does, he's Irish."

The familiar "shush" sounded behind them, and Ron turned to glare at Hermione.

By the end of that first class, the three friends had positive feelings about their new professor and optimistically anticipated learning a lot in the coming year. "He's good. He knows his stuff." Hermione offered her assessment, and her two companions agreed.

As the three moved towards the door, they were interrupted by the now familiar distinctively Irish voice. "Mr. Weasley, could I speak with you for a moment?"

They turned around, and Ron stammered, "Ur, yes sir." He looked at Harry and Hermione, who stared at him with a mixture of concern and amusement. 'What has he done now?' They each were thinking.

Ron looked at them with an expression of apprehension. "You guys don't wait for me; I'll catch up with you."

In the hallway outside the classroom, Hermione and Harry were accosted by the smirking Draco Malfoy, who was flanked as usual by the hulking cretins, Crabbe and Goyle.

"Potter and Granger," Draco snarled through his teeth. "Don't you think old Dumbledore has finally gone daft on us?" Crabbe and Goyle snorted.

Harry's fist tightened around his wand, but he remained silent, moving to the side to pass by his adversaries. Hermione could not ignore the insult, however.

"What do you mean?"

Draco sneered at her. "Well, as a mudblood, I would not expect you to be upset, but Potter here is supposed to be a pure blood."

Hermione moved angrily towards Draco, but Harry quickly interposed himself between them and firmly placed a restraining hand on Hermione's arm. "Watch it Malfoy; you're skating on thin ice. Hermione has mastered more magic than you'll ever know."

"Is that so, Potter? We'll see about that someday, I'm sure. But the issue now is the obvious negligence of our esteemed Headmaster, isn't it?" Crabbe and Goyle grunted in assent.

Hermione grew even more irate. "What do you mean by that, Malfoy?"

"Well, it's obvious, isn't it? He's hired someone who is incompetent to teach us Defense Against the **Dark Arts**." Draco's pale face radiated a smug arrogance. "How could someone from the miserable island of Ireland know anything about defense against the **Dark Arts**? That place is full of backward, ignorant, dirty lowlife who can barely grow potatoes, much less perform magic. The old man's finally gone off his rocker, and he's endangering all of us. My father is going to be very upset when he hears what Dumbledore has done. He's on the Hogwarts board of directors, you know. I bet there'll be some big changes around here soon." With a particularly nasty sneer, Draco finished his diatribe. Crabbe and Goyle laughed maliciously.

Hermione lashed back. "I trust Dumbledore. If he hired Professor Dennehy, he must be very good. I think today's lesson went well. He knows his stuff. I don't care if he is Irish. Why are you so prejudiced against people who are different from you?"

"Well, the mudblood spea…"

"Shut up, Malfoy." Harry pulled Hermione around the three Slytherins and propelled her down the hall. "Let's go, Hermione. You know it's pointless to argue with those idiots."

"But he'll harm Dumbledore."

"No, he won't. Dumbledore can deal with the likes of Lucius Malfoy."

Meanwhile, back in the classroom, Ron, alone with the new teacher, wondered what he had done wrong. But he relaxed a bit when he saw the smile on Professor Dennehy's weathered face.

"Mr. Weasley, I believe you have a younger sister. I think she has a class with me this afternoon." Professor Dennehy stopped and gazed at Ron.

Ron waited a bit to see if more was coming and then responded, "Yes, Ginny."

The teacher resumed in a soothing voice. "I would like for you and Ginny to come visit me in my office tonight, if that is possible."

"Ur, well, okay."

"Would 7 o'clock be convenient?"

"Yes sir, I guess so. That's after supper, and we'll be doing homework." Knowing this was only half true, Ron felt a pang of guilt. Ginny would be doing homework, but he would be talking Quidditch with the guys or maybe playing chess with Dean Thomas or reading the Daily Prophet. Homework would be one of the last things he would likely be doing. However, the professor didn't need to know that.

During supper, the four friends speculated about why the new teacher had invited Ron and Ginny to his office. Hermione speculated that Professor Dennehy had heard about Ron's penchant for mischief and wanted to elicit his sister's help to keep him out of trouble. "Rubbish!" Ron responded to that. Harry was mystified by the invitation, figuring that Ron had not yet had enough time to get into any trouble. Whatever the reason, they would find out soon.

At 7 o'clock the siblings stood outside the new teacher's office door. Ron's knock was answered with a broguish "come in." They found their new instructor still clad in his dazzling green robe. In fact, most of the things in the room radiated one or another shade of green. A model of hospitality, Professor Dennehy seated Ron and Ginny in unusually comfortable chairs and even served them butterbeer, a rare treat within the walls of Hogswarts. He asked about the health of their parents and reported the Irish wizarding community widely respected Mr. Weasley's efforts in the Ministry to better understand Muggle culture. A few minutes of such pleasantries assuaged Ron and Ginny's anxieties about the visit. Their gracious host sat across a small desk from them, sipping butterbeer and smiling benignly. In a picture on the wall behind him, a little green man with a funny hat seemed to be dancing some type of jig.

"So, I understand that the two of you had quite an experience in Rock Bridge Forest recently."

Ron responded eagerly, "Yes, we sure did."

"Tell me about it." And the professor settled back in his chair to listen to Ron's rendition of the adventure.

When Ron finished, Professor Dennehy seemed to be deep in thought, and the brother and sister waited with rising anticipation for him to comment. Finally, the teacher spoke. "So, it appears that the point was to get that turtle past the troll who lived under the bridge."

"Yeah, I guess so." Ron sounded a bit disappointed. He had never thought much about the turtle, too busy basking in the glory of their achievement. First Harry and now Professor Dennehy seemed more focused on the turtle than his exploits.

"Getting the turtle safely past the troll was very important to Professor Dumbledore," Professor Dennehy continued.

Pre-empting her brother, Ginny replied, "Yes, he sent us on a really scary mission, so the turtle must have been important. I don't know why it was so important. I've wondered about that."

"Yes, you completed a frightening mission successfully. You should be quite proud of that. I know Dumbledore is very grateful to you." Professor Dennehy paused and then added, "So am I." He smiled again at the siblings and stood up. "Well, I expect you are eager to get back to your homework." He did not miss Ginny's bemused glance at her brother. "Thank you for visiting with me tonight and telling me about your adventure. I am quite impressed with your bravery and your talents." He walked them to the door and shook hands with each. "Goodnight."

After exiting the room, Ron looked at his sister. "That was weird."

"Sure was. I don't think I've ever shaken hands with a professor before."

"Me neither." Uncharacteristically thoughtful, Ron continued, "He seems to have a thing about turtles."

"Yeah, did you notice that statue of a turtle on his mantle?"

"Who ever heard of someone having a statue of a turtle?"

At the end of the first week of study, Professor Dennehy announced in class that he would be teaching Irish dance one evening a week to any students who were interested. "It's purely voluntary." He assured them, and then added, "It's great fun and good exercise."

The boys uniformly greeted the offer with disdain but some of the girls, including Hermione and Ginny, were interested enough to attend the first class. Soon captivated by the new activity, references to jigs, reels, and hornpipe increasingly recurred in their conversations.

The dance pupils convinced Professor Dennehy to provide two lessons a week, which they eagerly anticipated. Only a dozen girls participated, all but two of whom were Gryffindors. No Slytherin girls were involved, to the relief of Hermione and Ginny. Despite constant derision from their male peers and many of their female mates, their commitment to learning Irish dance continued to strengthen. "Twinkle toes," "Real witches and wizards don't dance," "Why are you wasting time on such nonsense?" "The Irish are backward folks," were some of the milder reproaches directed towards the Irish dancers. But they persevered.

Late in an evening several weeks after the term started, Dumbledore and Professor Dennehy sat comfortably in the Headmaster's office sipping vintage Elfinwine from the year 1451. Fawkes slumbered on his perch overhead, and most of the former headmasters slept in their portraits. But old Maximus Elderberry, a renowned insomniac, shifted fitfully, drawing occasional looks of irritation from the current resident of the office. After staring for a time at his restless predecessor, Dumbledore returned his gaze to his friend.

"And how are the kids?"

Attired in his green robe, Liam Dennehy leaned forward to set his empty wine glass on Dumbledore's ornate table. "Fine. Colleen works for the Irish Ministry of Magic, in the Division for Amicable Relations with England."

"So, she has her work cut out for her." Dumbledore chuckled.

"Yes, she does, but she reports they're making progress."

"An optimist." Dumbledore sipped more wine. "And I see in the sports news that your son stars on the Quidditch team, a chip off the old block, so to speak."

"Yes, Malachi is doing quite well. You know they won the World Cup last year. I'm very proud of him."

"And well you should be." Dumbledore directed an annoyed glance at Maximus, who had just emitted a heavy sigh. "Sorry to keep you up, Maximus; maybe you would have better luck trying to sleep in one of your other portraits, like the one in Germany."

"No bother, Dumbledore. No bother at all."

Muttering "What a nuisance," Dumbledore turned back to Liam. "And how is Bridget?"

"Well, at the moment she's in Bolivia, doing research on some root of a rare jungle vine. There's a potion derived from the root that she's interested in."

Dumbledore looked solemnly at the younger man. "To possibly use for your condition?"

Liam glanced up at the sleeping Phoenix, and his expression became somber. "Yes, she still has hope. I've pretty much resigned myself to it. You know it's been so many years. But she won't give up. Being an expert on potions and antidotes, she's still looking for something that reverses the curse." He stopped and cracked a small smile. "She likes to visit London now and then, still thinks Diagon Alley is one of the best places to shop in the world." He paused to grin. "She says she'd like to go shopping there without having to leave her husband at home or carry a big turtle in her bag."

"Yes, I can understand that, and I can understand her determination to find a cure. One of the biggest disappointments of my life is my failure to find a way to undo that spell. You know, Liam, I don't like to fail, especially when it comes to wizarding."

"I know, Dumbledore, you've done everything you can, and I really appreciate that. I'm sure that my freedom from the affliction while at Hogwarts is due to your powers as a wizard, all the charms and protective spells you put around the place."

"Maybe so." Dumbledore sighed and took another sip of wine. "I'm just frustrated that a student could come up with a spell that I have not been able to reverse."

"So, you still think that Tom Riddle did it?"

"Yes, I'm sure of it. He was obsessed with the **Dark Arts** as a student. He was becoming Voldemort while he was here. You were one of his first victims." Dumbledore looked at the portrait of Maximus, who nodded sadly in agreement.

"Tom Riddle is Voldemort. I had heard that rumor. You believe it?"

"It's no rumor, Liam; there's no doubt. Tom Riddle and Voldemort are one and the same."

"I know that he never liked me. I figured it was because I was Irish. A lot of the Slytherins seemed to hold that against me, but he was the worst. I never could understand the depth of his animosity."

"You were everything that he wasn't, Liam. I think it started as jealousy, and then it became much more malignant. The **Dark Arts** create a very powerful attraction, particularly for someone who is socially isolated and has a weak self-image to begin with. But that's enough with the pop psychology."

Liam stood up and walked around to the back of his chair; he slammed a fist into the palm of his other hand. "Dumbledore, I think I know when it happened, when he put the spell on me. I was swimming in the lake with some other guys from Gryffindor. Suddenly, I felt funny, and that's when I saw the turtle, swimming along beside me. I felt this overwhelming attraction for the turtle. After that I worked so hard to create the turtle as my animagus. I have never realized it before; the spell and the turtle are intimately connected. The turtle offered relief from the effects of the spell. It makes sense." He sat back down and awaited the Headmaster's response.

"Yes, I think you're right."

The two men sat in silence, listening to the snores of the former headmasters and the periodic burps of the only one who was still awake. It was very late, and Liam knew that he should leave. But then he remembered.

"I forgot what I came by to do, Dumbledore."

"Oh." The Headmaster answered rather wearily.

"I want to thank you for what you did to get the turtle past that troll. You must have a lot of confidence in Ron and Ginny to give them such a risky mission."

"There was no risk to it, but they did perform admirably. Although, I must say the Weasley lad has milked it for all it's worth."

"No risk! They were saved by Fawkes in the nick of time."

"Yes, that's true, but they had back-up. Ron and Ginny were never in any danger at all. I was with them in the forest. I took care of a bothersome serpent. When they were on the bridge I was nearby on the bank. Of course, they couldn't see me, but I was prepared to intervene. It turns out they did very well. I didn't need to stupefy the troll."

"But why go to all that trouble? You knew the troll was there and could have eaten the turtle. You could have easily handled the troll in many different ways. Why put the Weasley kids to so much trouble?"

"Trouble!" Dumbledore laughed. "Do they consider it trouble? I gave them an opportunity to be heroes, and they rose to the occasion, splendidly I might add. Those two needed a little boost to their egos. They come from a good wizarding family, but a poor family. They lack the material things that many of our students have and sometimes get teased for that. They tend to be overshadowed by their older siblings, especially George and Fred, who, as you have probably observed, are quite notorious. Ron is overshadowed by Harry Potter and Ginny, by Hermione Granger. As you well know, Harry is unique, and Hermione is one of the most brilliant students we have had here in a long time. I gave Ron and Ginny a mission, and they accomplished it. Good for them. I could have taken care of the problem myself, very easily as you say. But I like this way better, don't you?"

"I marvel at your wisdom, Dumbledore, and your compassion." Liam stood up and moved to the door. He turned and said "Thank you for the help you gave the turtle. It was obviously very important to me. Goodnight."

The passing days grew shorter and cooler as Hogwarts students were engrossed in their studies. Defense Against the **Dark Arts** quickly became Harry's favorite course. He and most other students considered Professor Dennehy a superb teacher who explained things clearly, provided plenty of practical opportunities to perfect new skills, and exhibited remarkable patience, while maintaining high standards. Malfoy and his consorts still grumbled about his "incompetence," but their complaints increasingly fell on deaf ears.

Gryffindor won their first Quidditch match of the year when Harry snatched the Golden Snitch in time to give them a razor-thin 200 to190 point victory over Hufflepuff. After the match there was little jubilation among the Gryffindor players; almost all of their frustrations were directed to Ron, who had been the keeper and had allowed far too many Quaffles to pass through the goal. As most of the players trudged back to Gryffindor Tower, Alicia Sinnert, the Quidditch captain, talked about finding a new keeper.

Enmeshed in self-recrimination, a disconsolate Ron lagged behind his teammates. He repulsed Harry's effort to console him. "Leave me alone," he angrily retorted.

As Ron walked slowly down the empty hallway, a green-robed figure stepped out of the shadows and called to him. "Mr. Weasley, could I have a brief word with you?"

"Uh, hello, Professor Dennehy."

The teacher came up to Ron. "Congratulations on your victory, a hard-fought, well-played match."

"No thanks to me." Ron stared at the floor. "I stunk."

"Come, come, you exaggerate. This was your first match as keeper, I believe. I know the first few times I played keeper on the Gryffindor team, I wasn't good at all. I recall that we lost our first match. My mates were plenty upset with me."

"You couldn't have been as bad as me."

"Don't get down on yourself, Ron. You'll get better quickly. It takes time and intense practice and hard work; I know you have that in you."

Ron perked up a bit. "You think so?"

"I know so." The teacher started to stroll towards Gryffindor Tower, and Ron followed. "Care for a little advice from an old retired keeper?"

Ron's spirits swiftly rose. At a time when he would have willingly accepted advice about how to improve his Quidditch skills from Neville, he was being offered advice by one of the greatest keepers of all time. "Yes sir."

"Well, I noticed you seem to watch the Chasers and Beaters a lot. I can understand. I watched them too much at first, too. But try not to do it so much. Keep your eye on the Quaffle; that's what you have to stop. You're quick; you have good reflexes. I think you'll find that watching the Quaffle will make a difference."

"Thanks professor, I'll do that."

Three weeks later, after a particularly vigorous Quidditch practice, Alicia spoke to Ron. "You're doing much better, Weasley. I'm gonna let you play keeper against Ravenclaw. Don't let us down."

A week after his late-night conversation with the Headmaster, Professor Dennehy asked Harry to come around to his office in the evening. Harry settled into one of the easy chairs and accepted a flagon of butterbeer. With some amusement he watched the fancy footwork of the little green man in the painting. 'Hermione and Ginny think they can learn to do that. Ha!' The thought amused him.

The professor sat across the table from Harry, a serious expression on his face. "Thanks for coming to see me tonight, Harry; I know you are busy, with your studies and with Quidditch and all." He paused and looked at Harry's forehead. "I have struggled a lot about whether or not to tell you what I am about to tell you." He laughed lightly. "Obviously, I have decided to tell you." He stopped again and peered at his hands clenched before him on the table. Disquieted, Harry shifted in the chair. "I'm telling you my story because I know that Voldemort has a special interest in you, an interest that, shall we say, is not benevolent." He paused and looked into Harry's eyes.

"Yes sir. We could say that." Harry was increasingly discomforted.

"Because of that, I believe it is in your best interest to know everything you can about Voldemort to better defend yourself, and, I might add, the rest of us."

Harry's gaze shifted to the statue of the turtle on the mantle, and suddenly he knew that the mystery of the turtle would soon be revealed to him.

"Many years ago when I was a student here, another student, a student named Tom Riddle, put a curse on me." The professor noted Harry's reaction to the name and then continued. "Despite the efforts of Dumbledore, my wife, a world-renowned expert on antidotes, and others to reverse the spell, it still affects me. Whenever I am anywhere within the boundaries of England, except on the grounds of Hogwarts, my skin breaks out with a terribly painful, itchy rash that is unbearable. Nothing helps but leaving England or finding refuge at Hogwarts. Years ago, before I knew I was afflicted with this curse I became enamored with turtles. It was a strange experience, which I didn't understand until last week when I talked with Dumbledore. I was swimming in the lake and saw a turtle. Suddenly, I wanted to be a turtle. For the rest of that year, I worked hard to become an animagus. When school was over for the year, I started for Hogsmeade to catch the Knight bus to Holyhead in Wales, where I would take the ferry to Dublin. But all of a sudden when I left the grounds of Hogwarts I was covered with this terrible rash. I was in agony. I had to escape. For the first time, I was able to morph into a turtle, and the rash vanished. That was the first I knew about the curse. As you can imagine, traveling as a turtle was slow going. Several times, I transformed back into my human form, but each time the rash was awful. I had to abandon my trunk, and it took me three weeks to make it to Holyhead. I sneaked onto the ferry, but as soon as we cast off from the dock, I transformed myself and was free of the rash. My parents were beside themselves with worry by the time I got home."

"Wow, that's terrible, professor." Harry rubbed his forehead. "It doesn't affect you at Hogwarts?"

"No, I'm fine at Hogwarts, but anywhere else in England, it's pure torture. I completed my studies here and traveled between Hogwarts and Holyhead as a turtle. I got used to it."

"But professor, you were a star Quidditch keeper and then the coach. How did you play Quidditch in England?"

"Ah yes, Quidditch." Professor Dennehy sighed. "I never played Quidditch in England, except here at Hogwarts. We didn't play much in England anyway. You know, because of the unfortunate antipathy between Ireland and England. When we did have to play in England I would discover that I had pulled a hamstring or such and couldn't play. When I became coach, I convinced the National Team to boycott England as a protest against centuries of mistreatment. I'm not proud of that little maneuver, I must admit. But the hamstring ploy didn't work when I was no longer playing." He stopped and watched his student's reaction to all of this.

Harry processed these startling revelations in silence and then suddenly experienced an epiphany. "So, you were the turtle that Ron and Ginny saved from the troll."

For the first time Professor Dennehy smiled. "Yes, exactly." His countenance once again became somber. "But Harry, I ask you not to disclose any of this to anyone, even your best friends. I wanted you to know because of your unique connection to Voldemort. Dumbledore is the only other one here who knows, and I would like to keep it that way."

"Certainly professor, your secret is safe with me."

Late one dreary autumn afternoon the four friends were laboring in Hagrid's pumpkin patch. They were not happy.

"Why'd he grow so many of these things this year? There are at least three times more pumpkins than last year," Ron complained.

"He said something about needing a lot of pumpkin juice," Hermione responded.

"What's he going do with so much pumpkin juice? I've never known him to drink it." Ginny looked perplexed.

"Yeah, me neither," her brother agreed.

"Where did he go this time?" Harry wheezed as he hoisted a huge pumpkin and began lugging it to the porch of the gamekeeper's cottage.

"Don't know. I reckon he's gone to the same place he's gone every other time he's disappeared for three or four days this year." Ron struggled with another giant pumpkin.

Hermione wiped clods of dirt from her hands as she paused to rest. "I think he goes into the Forbidden Forest."

"Whatever for?" Ginny had returned from the porch where she had deposited a pumpkin and peered dejectedly at the number of big round orange objects that remained attached to the vines covering the ground.

"You know Hagrid; he's probably tending to some other giant spider." Burdened with a pumpkin, Ron lurched towards the porch.

"Why did he insist that we pick these monsters today instead of waiting a few days until he got back from wherever he's made off to? Then he could do this work." Harry brushed dried leaves from the front of the sweater that Mrs. Weasley had given him the preceding Christmas.

"He said he didn't want the pumpkins to get too ripe; it would make the juice bitter." Ginny bent down to lift another pumpkin. "And he told us not to use magic to move the pumpkins. That might make the juice bitter, too."

"Bitter! Pumpkin juice bitter! Pumpkin juice is supposed to be bitter," Ron snorted.

Except for the occasional groan, they worked silently in the gathering gloom of the dying day. Hermione broke the silence. "I have a theory. Do you want to hear my theory?"

"No, but I bet we will anyway," Ron retorted.

Eager for an opportunity to rest, Harry stood up and said, "Let's hear it."

"Well, you know how every time Hagrid comes back from being gone for a few days, he has bruises and cuts all over him."

"Yeah, he's probably off wrestling some giant," Ron responded sarcastically.

"You may be righter about that than you realize. Except I don't believe it's a giant, and I don't think he's tending to a spider." She paused for dramatic effect. "I think it's a dragon."

"What! Dumbledore clearly told him not to fool with any more dragons," Harry countered.

"Yeah, but you know Hagrid and dragons, Harry. And I found in my reading last week that baby Hungarian Horntails love to drink pumpkin juice. And they are the only dragons that give birth to live young. Other dragons lay eggs."

"So what?" A skeptical Ron snapped. "Do you think Hagrid is providing maternity care to some pregnant Hungarian Horntail?"

"Yes, that's exactly what I think."

"Blimey! You mean we're wrestling with these Hagrid-size pumpkins so he can feed some baby dragon?" Ron swore in disgust.

"I said it's only a theory, Ron."

Moments later, as the Gryffindors worked to transport the few remaining pumpkins to the porch, four robed figures emerged from the grayness; each held an outstretched wand. Harry readily recognized the voice that dripped with contempt.

"What have we here, Gryffindor servants, laboring in the pumpkin patch for their dear master, Hagrid the Horrible."

Harry also recognized the snorts of agreement that followed these repugnant words. "Hello, Malfoy and Crabbe and Goyle, and yes, it must be Pansy Parkinson. Have you come from the warmth of your Slytherin cauldron to help us pick pumpkins?" Harry's voice could drip with sarcasm when he wanted it to.

"Don't be ridiculous, Potter. That's peasant work. Mudblood work." He derisively pointed his wand at Hermione. "Crabbe, Goyle, what do we see over there?" Malfoy nodded in the direction of a large log.

"Wands, Draco; I see wands," Goyle grunted. "Four wands."

"Well, wasn't that stupid of them."

"Sure was. Them Gryffindors ain't very smart, are they Draco?" Oblivious to the utter irony of his statement, Crabbe smirked.

For once, Harry was inclined to agree with the dumb oaf. He had been uneasy when Ron had suggested that they lay down their wands. But he went along; it made lifting and carrying the pumpkins much easier. But he sure regretted the decision now. He could sense Ron beside him, rigid with rage. Ginny and Hermione appeared to be equally as angry. They each knew they were in a tough jam; at the moment their wands were too far away to be of any use.

Malfoy spoke again. "So, what should we do with 'em?"

"Let's turn 'em into pumpkins," Pansy Parkinson suggested.

"No, too good for them."

"Let's freeze 'em. You know, turn 'em into statues, where they can't move." Crabbe laughed.

"Yeah, we could do that. Goyle, what do you say?"

"I remember when Weasley put that spell on himself and up-chucked them slugs for hours. That was one of the funniest things I ever saw. We could do that to them."

Ron gulped and looked longingly at his wand.

"Don't try it, Ron." Harry whispered.

"Good idea, Goyle." With his wand poised, Malfoy paused and contemplated the opportunities for a few seconds. "Let's turn 'em into rats. That's what they are. Yeah, rats it is."

Ginny and Hermione looked at each other out of the corner of their eyes, and Hermione whispered, "jig."

With four wands pointed malevolently at the four friends, Malfoy began to pronounce the spell. But then Ron became aware that Hermione and Ginny were rhythmically moving up and down. It was like jumping but wasn't jumping. Their bodies were tight, with arms straight at their sides. Their eyes focused straight ahead, and strange smiles appeared on their faces. 'They're dancing! The idiots are dancing.' An embarrassed Ron thought.

Watching Malfoy, Harry unexpectedly observed his nemesis stop in mid-curse to stare open-mouthed at the two Gryffindor witches. His companions seemed similarly mesmerized. Harry turned to look at Hermione and Ginny, peering incredulously at their rapidly moving feet, which appeared to be flying effortlessly over the heavy vines and rutted earth. 'Dancing! They're dancing.' He realized with amazement.

When Harry turned back to the Slytherins, he saw that Malfoy's face was changing. It was becoming pointed; his ears were enlarging, and Malfoy's body was shrinking and becoming contorted. Harry stared in utter astonishment; before his very eyes, Malfoy was turning into, into a…a… yes, he was turning into a rat. With incredulity, he looked at Goyle, whose face was a sickly green; something was erupting from his mouth, something slimy and gray. While he watched, the writhing thing fell to the ground, to be followed immediately by an identical thing oozing between Goyle's trembling lips. Harry looked at Pansy Parkinson, who was rapidly assuming an all too familiar orange round shape. Beside her, Crabbe stood rigidly, an extended arm pointing an impotent wand, an ugly hulking statue.

Hermione and Ginny stopped dancing and looked proudly at each other.

"WWWWhat happened? HHHHow did you do that?" A flabbergasted Ron stammered.

"We danced a jig," His sister tried to be nonchalant.

"But it was magic. Look what you did to them." Ron pointed to a large ugly black rat, scampering among the pumpkin vines. "That's Malfoy." The rat emitted a hideous screech and ran behind a large fencepost.

"Yeah, it's an improvement; don't you think?" Hermione giggled.

For once Ron ignored the chance to ridicule Malfoy. "Your dancing did that. It's magic! Irish dance is magic!" His face reflected a look of pure wonder.

"I guess so." Hermione seemed somewhat uncertain.

"Did you know this would happen?" Harry asked eagerly. "Did you mean to do that to them? Did you know you were performing magic?"

Hermione and Ginny looked at each other and hesitated. "Well, it's hard to explain." Hermione started.

Ginny interrupted, "I just got an overwhelming urge to dance right before Malfoy started the spell."

"Me too, I felt like dancing a jig, and I did, and this is what happened." With the sweep of her hand, Hermione encompassed the Pansy pumpkin, the Crabbe statue and the miserable Goyle, who was constantly vomiting slugs into the mist. The Malfoy rat remained hidden behind the post.

"So, you didn't know Irish dance was magic?" Harry pressed the two witches.

"No, nothing like this has happened before when we danced," Hermoine acknowledged. "But then we have never danced when we were being threatened."

"Professor Dennehy never mentioned anything about doing magic with Irish dance. We dance because we love it," Ginny added.

Ron walked over to the frozen Crabbe and pushed on his forehead. The statue toppled over and bounced on the ground.

Hermione approached the pumpkin Pansy. "Pansy dear, you look so, so, so..."

"Orange," Ron contributed.

Ginny peered with revulsion at the bug-eyed, green-faced, slug-puking Goyle and whispered into his ear without a shred of sympathy. "You poor boy."

"How long will the spell last?" Ron asked.

"I have no idea," Hermione replied. "Probably not long enough."

The four Slytherins did make it to Defense Against the **Dark Arts** class the next day. Pansy's skin exhibited an orange tinge. Crabbe moved with a certain jerky inflexibility. Goyle burped with annoying regularity. Malfoy's ears seemed a bit long and floppy. Each seemed very subdued. They uttered no snide comments about an incompetent professor.

That day, Harry and Ron stayed after class to talk to the instructor.

"What can I do for you lads?" Professor Dennehy inquired cheerfully.

"Uh, well, uh, you see, it's like this, sir, is it too late to start Irish dance lessons?" Ron finally got it out.

The professor grinned. "Are you lads interested in learning Irish dance?"

"Yes sir, we are," Harry responded.

"Well, wonderful. I could hold special tutorials for you and any of your friends who are interested. I would love to have some boys involved. It's great fun."

"Uh, yeah, well, sure, great fun. That's what we heard sir," Ron stammered.

"How about Friday afternoons, say 4 o'clock?" Professor Dennehy offered.

"Yes sir. I think that'll work for us. Thank you, professor." Harry turned to leave.

"I'm looking forward to it." Professor Dennehy seemed excited. "By the way, what made you change your minds about Irish dance? It has not escaped my attention that you lads have, let us say, not been exactly complimentary of the activity."

"Well, sir, we uh, you see…"

Harry interrupted. "We didn't know it was magic, sir"

"Magic? What makes you think it's magic?"

"We saw it do magic."

"And when did you see this, Ron?"

"Uh, yesterday, sir. We were in a bit of a jam, and Ginny and Hermione danced and got us out of the jam."

"Very interesting. And is this why you want to learn to dance, to do magic?"

"Yes sir, of course." Ron considered it a strange question.

Professor Dennehy frowned. "I'm sorry to disappoint you, but it doesn't work that way. If you learn Irish dance in order to use it for magic, it will not be magical."

"Uh, say that again, sir."

"Irish dance is only magical if you learn it for pure fun and enjoyment. You cannot use it as a means to an end. It's an end in itself. If the reason you want to learn Irish dance is to do magic, it will not do magic. Hermione and Ginny could do magic because they love to dance. They did not even know dancing could have magical effects. It is true that dancing a jig can get you out of a jam, but only if you dance for the joy of it." Observing the glum faces before him, he paused and then added, "I'm sorry, boys, you can learn to dance, and I hope you do, but you will not perform any magic with it. Your motivation is all wrong."

Out in the hall, Ron said, "It galls me that Hermione and Ginny can do magic that we will never be able to do."

"Bummer!" agreed Harry.

Pile On

Knowing knows before hearing hears, recollection exudes from the congealed entanglement, emasculate in the indomitable odor of mansweat; remembering before knowing: hands splayed on bended knees, semicrouched in rapt immobility, forwardleaning into the ponderous nocturnal autumn air, in furious anticipation of arrested inertia, incipient savagery, luminous in the brooding dusk-dark; displayed in partisan ceremony before the assembled throng, protuberantly congregated with fluctuant fascination for imminent apotheosis, for tumescent glory, to be consummated on an immaculate gridiron of intractable temerity, enclosed within the insensate entreating pleas of exuberantly fleshed, lascivious, pomponned, post-pubescent mammarian splendor; forwardmoving peremptorily with the sound, an inviolate sonorous command, refusing abnegation, compelling allegiance, doomed in primordial obdurate masculinity; receiving the thrusted leather oblong not-trophy, neither chalice, but rather palpable symbol of insatiable honor, impregnable, invincible but ephemeral; visceral thrusted, arms engulfing as a lover's embrace, but futile; forwardmoving with escalating fury inexorably toward the armor-clad foe, nonapparitional, voracious, implacable and girded for the assault in resplendent triumph; arrested in stark, abrupt and utter abrogation of motion, profound dissolution, defunctive, sudden and complete; and now cohered with the hard, immutable, incorrigible earth; with the penetrant whistling infiltrating through the laboriously unlimbering extrication of virile man-flesh to the abject fury of disembodied surrender; and then, with resolute, indubitable, authoritative finality, the hearing, "second down."

Non-fiction

Note: In the first three non-fiction pieces, I have changed the names, except for those of the nurses.

"It Passed from Me"

My next patient was Bertha Higgins, an old woman I had not seen before. I knew when I went into the exam room that whatever was wrong with her would likely be bad. Before I had entered the room, Kathy, the nurse practitioner, had pulled me aside in the hallway to tell me that Bertha's daughter, with whom she lived, was concerned that her mother had become "puny" in recent weeks. A few days earlier the daughter had found blood on her mother's bed sheet. Alarmed, she had badgered her mother into reluctantly acknowledging "a little bleeding down there." Bertha had refused to see a doctor but had become so weak that she could no longer resist her insistent daughter. Against her will, she had been carried into the clinic by a grandson. Kathy had pricked her finger and obtained blood for a red cell count, which we could measure with a centrifuge in the clinic. Bertha's hematocrit was 18%, less than half the normal value. She had severe anemia and urgently needed a blood transfusion, which would involve a trip to the hospital, over fifty miles of winding mountain roads.

When I entered the room, I found my new patient lying on her side on the exam table, her face turned to the wall. Sickness scented the air. Her daughter, whom I recognized, hovered over her head and greeted me with a grave expression. For months I had been fighting a losing battle to get Hazel Flynn to take her high blood pressure and diabetes pills. I wondered if I would have any more success caring for her mother.

The medical history came entirely from the daughter. Repeatedly, Bertha muttered to the wall that she didn't want to be there and begged to be taken home at once.

I soon learned that Bertha Higgins had rarely been ill and had not seen a doctor in years. All eight of her children had been delivered at home by a granny woman. In recent weeks, she had been getting weaker but did not seem to have pain anywhere. The absence of chest pain was reassuring; despite the anemia, her heart muscle seemed to be getting enough oxygen. Hazel wasn't sure whether the bleeding was coming from the bladder, vagina or rectum. After admitting its presence, her mother had refused to discuss the bleeding any further.

It rapidly became evident that any examination would be difficult and quite limited. Despite the heat of a North Carolina August day, Bertha wore several layers of clothing and was not about to remove any of them for me. Somehow, I needed to examine her rectum; I wanted to get her co-operation, if possible. Establishing eye contact might be helpful. With some difficulty, Kathy, Hazel and I turned Bertha on the table so that I could see her wrinkled grimacing face enshrouded by the waxy pallor of anemia. While staring at the ceiling, she let me know that, except for her long dead husband, no man had ever touched her "down there."

With much imploring and reassurance, Kathy and Hazel finally convinced her to allow me to displace sticky undergarments with my hand and gently insert an index finger into her rectum. Bertha wailed in protest. The finger immediately encountered a hard, immobile mass, which to me could only be one thing, rectal cancer. I removed my finger and peeled off the glove, turning my back to conceal the blood from Hazel's eyes.

Giving bad news is never easy; I needed a moment to compose myself. Kathy and I exited the room, leaving patient and daughter to their mutual misery. Kathy and I were not surprised by my finding; unfortunately, rectal cancer was a common cause of bleeding and anemia in the elderly. We needed to convince Bertha to go to the hospital for a blood transfusion, diagnostic work-up and treatment of the mass.

When we returned to the room, things had calmed down a bit. A subdued Bertha was propped into a sitting position by her daughter, who talked to her softly. Hazel looked up at me with a "what do you think, doc?"

I started with the immediate need for a transfusion to treat the "low blood." That had little effect. I took a deep breath and told them about the growth in the rectum. At the mention of a growth, Hazel gasped and clutched her mother's arm. Kathy put an arm around Hazel's shoulders. There was no noticeable response from Bertha, who stared at the floor.

Pausing, I glanced out the window of the former bedroom in the old farm house that had been converted into a clinic. Sunlight sparkled on the tassels of nearby tobacco plants. I looked back at my patient and waited for the question, "Is it cancer?" When it did not come, I resumed, informing them that we needed a small piece of the growth to determine for sure what it was. Even though I knew what it was, a tissue diagnosis was necessary before any definitive treatment could be given.

This time the response was immediate: Bertha's eyes tore into my face as she declared with finality that she would not be cut on, because if she had cancer, cutting on it would spread it all over her body, resulting in an agonizing death. Such had been the fate of her mother and her sister and a bunch of other folks she knew about, and she wasn't going to let it happen to her. If she had

278

cancer, she would trust her fate to the Lord. She stopped, breathless, but her eyes continued to resist me, while Hazel's head nodded in vigorous agreement.

The reaction was not unexpected; the belief that cutting on a cancer made it worse was prevalent in the rural Appalachian community where I practiced medicine. This misconception often defied my best invocations of medical science. Any effort to convince Bertha and Hazel of the merits of a biopsy much less surgery would be futile. I tried anyway. I emphasized the seriousness of Bertha's condition, but Hazel had now joined with her mother in a determination to escape the clinic as fast as possible. I was the one talking to the wall. There would be no trip to the hospital, no transfusion, no biopsy, and no treatment. Bertha Higgins headed home to die.

While Hazel's son carried his grandmother out of the clinic to his pick-up truck, Kathy pressed a bottle of iron pills into Hazel's hands, with instructions to give her mother one pill three times a day. If we couldn't do anything about the cancer, we might be able to make her feel better temporarily by treating the anemia. It was a long-shot. Hazel said that she would try to get the pills into her mother and, through the tears streaking down her face, thanked us for our time. Kathy, ever the optimist, told her to bring Bertha back in a month for a hematocrit recheck. But I didn't expect to see Bertha Higgins again; I knew she would be dead soon.

Thus, I was surprised when she showed up with her daughter a month later. Just before I entered the exam room, a beaming Kathy told me that Bertha had a hematocrit of 36%, a dramatic improvement, another surprise.

In the room, I found Bertha sitting on the table, color in the sagging flesh of her cheeks and something alive in her eyes that I had not seen there a month before. From the chair beside the table, Hazel expressed joy at the good news about the blood test and proudly reported that her mother had taken the iron and felt much better.

From her perch on the table, Bertha announced that the Lord had cured her. Concealing my skepticism, I replied that I was pleased that she felt better but added that I needed to examine her rectum again. Bertha quickly assured me that "it ain't there no more; it passed from me." To my surprise, she told me that I could check for myself if I was a "doubting Thomas," and without protest she lay down on the table, submitting to the exam. I pulled on the glove, inserted my finger and found an empty rectum; the mass was gone. Astonished, I pushed the finger into her as far as it would go; Bertha grunted Nothing! I pulled out and looked at the finger - no blood.

Before I could collect my thoughts, Bertha was telling me about it: how she went to church, and the congregation prayed over her, and she felt it pass from her, and she knew the Lord had blessed her and made her whole again. She ended with an emphatic "Praise the Lord."

Hazel looked at me expectantly, and when I confirmed that the growth was gone, she gave a "Hallelujah" and rushed to embrace her mother.

With a toothless grin that seemed to proclaim the power of her God, Bertha said, "I told you so." So she had, and I rejoiced with her at her good fortune, but I was mighty perplexed.

Although I practiced in the mountain community for another two years, I never saw Bertha Higgins again. I kept up with her through Hazel, who came in periodically for treatment of her medical problems. "Momma" was always doing fine, with no recurrence of bleeding or feeling puny.

It has been over forty years since I saw Bertha Higgins, and I expect that she has been long dead, from either rectal cancer or something else. For a long time, I didn't know what to make of the experience. Initially, I wondered if I had been wrong about what I had felt in her rectum; maybe it had been a mass of feces that had later passed. But this explanation did not fit with what I had found on the first exam or with the bleeding and anemia. I could not avoid the reality that a cancer, which had bled enough to cause life-threatening anemia, had disappeared with no medical treatment.

Bertha and her daughter were convinced that the Lord had cured her during the church prayer meeting. In her subsequent visits to the clinic, Hazel frequently referred to the "miracle." As a disciple of science, I rejected such a notion; miracles were not a part of my creed. I was confident of some rational explanation consistent with the truths of biology. I just didn't know what it could be, and that bothered me.

Until the emergence of what we consider modern scientific medicine in the nineteenth century, explanations of illness and therapeutic interventions had involved an intimate mix of natural and supernatural processes. The ancient Greeks attributed sickness to the displeasure of the gods on Mt. Olympus and the imbalance of humors in the body. Seventeenth-century English physicians saw divine punishment of sin manifested in the devastating epidemics of plague that recurrently ravished the country. Through the centuries, religious principles and practices infused the healing arts. Pre-modern physicians generally made little or no distinction between the spiritual and the physical, the mind and the body.

The dichotomy between physicality and spirituality, which characterizes modern medicine, evolved over the past one hundred and fifty years, as scientific discoveries progressively grounded disease causation and therapeutic strategies in the natural world. With increasing knowledge of viruses, inflammation, autoimmunity, atherogenesis, carcinogenesis and other disease mechanisms, and with the development of effective treatments based on this knowledge, physicians less and less invoked metaphysical concepts or supernatural forces to explain illness. Body and soul became progressively disconnected, one the domain of medicine, the other the domain of religion.

Yet, many people have not embraced the physical/spiritual division of modern medicine, but see the supernatural, in the form of divine power, enmeshed in the processes of health, sickness, healing and dying. The concept of illness as either divine punishment or a test of faith remains relatively common. Old women in rural Appalachia are not the only sick persons who turn to prayer for healing or who attribute cures to "the Lord." Unlike Bertha Higgins, many combine prayer with modern therapeutics when faced with the crisis of serious illness, an affirmation of the pre-modern unity of the physical and spiritual. Sometimes, the sick use religious beliefs and prayer as a substitute for modern medicine. For Bertha Higgins, this approach seemed to be successful. For others, the outcome is quite different.

Several years after Bertha Higgins' "miracle", I was practicing in Chapel Hill, North Carolina. Late one Friday afternoon Carol Dawkins, a fifty-year old woman, came to the clinic because of severe headache, shortness of breath and progressive weakness. When I examined her, I quickly discovered her secret: Her left breast had been replaced by a large rotting mass. I had never seen a cancer of the breast so far advanced.

I admitted her to the hospital immediately, and x-rays and blood tests soon confirmed my suspicion: The cancer had spread throughout her body. Her condition was so bad that I didn't know if she would survive the weekend. She did. In fact, she lived another six months before succumbing to her cancer. She was a fighter. From the time she first entered the hospital, she wanted aggressive treatment, a desire completely discordant with her apparent prolonged neglect of the cancer. I was mighty perplexed.

That first weekend she was in the hospital, I spent a lot of time with Carol Dawkins. For the most part, I listened to her story.

She had grown up in a little town in North Carolina and had married her high school sweetheart when he returned from World War II. Having experienced war, he was burdened by memories that she could never comprehend. Over the years, they moved from town to town, as he lost job after job, gradually descending into alcoholism. She returned to school, earned a master's degree and for the last few years of the marriage was the sole breadwinner, working as a high school music teacher. Along the way, she found comfort in religion and became a charismatic Christian.

She finally separated from her husband, and the week the divorce was finalized he entered the hospital with alcoholic liver disease. He died a few days late. She blamed herself. On the day of his funeral, she discovered a lump in her left breast. Exactly one year and one day after she found the lump she came to me, seeking medical care for her cancer.

Over the weekend, between the x-rays, blood tests, morphine shots, and the first dose of chemotherapy, she told me what that last year had been like. She had known that the lump was cancer from the beginning. She watched it slowly get bigger, day after day, week after week, until one day a tiny red hole appeared in the skin over her lump. During the following weeks, she watched the hole enlarge and the malevolent tissue emerge from her body and relentlessly expand. All this time, she prayed for it to stop getting bigger, for it to go away. She never told anyone about the cancer, not her fellow teachers when they expressed concern about her pale skin and weakness, not even her two daughters when they begged her to see a doctor.

She explained it to me: she had been in mourning and could not attend to her own medical needs until the one-year period of mourning had ended. It was a religious belief, she said, a religious belief that was all-important to her, a religious belief that I didn't understand then, and don't understand now. It was a religious belief that killed her.

In the hospital, Carol quickly became notorious among the staff as the well-educated patient who had "neglected" her cancer. The cancer and radiation specialists often referred to her "denial." The chaplain who visited with her knew of no official religious belief that could account for her behavior; he attributed it to "guilt" over the divorce and subsequent death of her husband. Her own pastor agreed; she was seeking expiation, atonement.

As for me, anger soon replaced my initial shock, anger directed not at Carol but at the religion that had victimized her. But as I interacted with her over the ensuing weeks, I realized that she never saw herself as a victim. She never expressed regret over the delay; she never saw any contradiction between her behavior during the twelve months of mourning and her intense desire to live. For her, it was all part of God's plan, and she accepted it. Carol Dawkins wanted to live; she did not want to die, but a higher spiritual call superseded her instinct for self-preservation

---

Recent years have seen a resurgence of interest among healthcare professionals in spirituality and a rethinking of the prevailing mind/body dichotomy. Much of this interest derives from the findings of studies that regular church attendance is

284

associated with increased longevity and decreased rates of a variety of diseases. According to this research, the apparent health benefits of church attendance are not explained by socioeconomic status or lifestyle factors, such as cigarette smoking, alcohol use and physical activity. Researchers are now trying to determine what it is about church attendance that confers the protective effects. Is it social support? Religious beliefs? Spirituality? A combination of factors? This research grapples with the challenges of how to conceptualize and measure spirituality.

Concurrent with this research focus on spirituality, healthcare professionals are realizing that many patients expect attention to spiritual as well as physical needs in the management of their medical problems. This has led to considerations of the role of prayer in the healing process. Questions of whether physicians should pray with patients and whether prayer improves disease outcomes are increasingly discussed in medical journals and at medical conferences. Such discussions, rare as recently as thirty years ago, have now been featured in popular magazines and television talk shows. Whenever I hear about these discussions, I think of Carol Dawkins.

I also think about sitting at the bedside of an old man whom I had known for years. He was dying; medical science had nothing more to offer him. We were alone; his wife puttered in the kitchen of the home that he had built for her over fifty years before. We had talked for a while, and he appeared to be dozing. It was time for me to leave. When I shifted my chair and started to stand up, he opened his eyes and looked into mine. After a few seconds, he asked me to pray with him. A pillar of his church, he was a devoutly religious man. He had often talked to me of his beliefs and in recent days had told me that he was ready to join his God. The day before, I had knelt with his wife, their children and their grandchildren in this same room while his pastor had prayed for the Lord's will to be done.

After my patient asked me to pray with him, I took his hand, thin from age and disease, in mine and closed my eyes. In the silence, I tried to reconnect with the God of my youth, to resurrect a long-lost sense of the sacred. I waited and I hoped. I felt the cool bony flesh of his hand. I heard his shallow breaths. I tried to pray, but nothing was there; all I could do was hope that my friend's wish would soon come true.

With my eyes still closed, I heard his fragile voice break the silence. I heard him express thanks for his life, for his family, for his many blessings. He asked for forgiveness of his sins. He asked for strength to face the time he had left on earth. Then I heard him ask his God to bless his doctor. My dying patient was praying for me. After a pause, we said "Amen" together.

Early the next morning, his wife called to tell me that he had died during the night.

During my years of practice as a family physician, the spiritual values of patients and their family members were at times essential elements of my experiences with them. I listened to their prayers, discussed with them the meaning of illness, suffering and dying, and connected them with rabbis, priests and ministers who could provide more spiritual care than I could. Usually, diseases took their expected courses: Patients with the common cold recovered. Patients with metastatic lung cancer died. Sometimes surprises occurred: a patient expected to get well died; a patient expected to die lived.

At times as a physician, I made a difference in such outcomes, but all too often I didn't. From what I saw, neither the patient's spirituality nor the presence or absence of prayer affected eventual life or death outcomes. Religious or otherwise highly spiritual patients did not seem to live longer or recover quicker.

However, prayer and spirituality frequently did affect patients' experiences with sickness and suffering and the meaning they derived from such experiences. Often, I saw religious faith or other forms of spirituality provide comfort and a measure of peace to dying patients and their families. For Carol Dawkins, religious beliefs and prayer eased the burdens of her final weeks and gave her strength to face death. But I also saw a 90-year old man, trapped in a prolonged hell of dying, curse the God he had worshipped all his life.

One of my most remarkable experiences involved a colleague at the medical school where I taught for 37 years. At age 59 he vomited up blood and was subsequently found to have cancer of the esophagus, a particularly nasty disease. At that time, fewer than 5% of patients afflicted with this form of cancer were alive five years after diagnosis. He had surgery, but two years later a large mass in his abdomen announced the dreaded recurrence. This time he had radiation therapy; however, a year later he showed up with pain, weight loss and jaundice from a liver riddled with cancer. His chances of living another six months were dismal. An eternal fighter, he opted for aggressive chemotherapy, which offered at best a small chance of a partial, temporary remission.

He lived free of cancer for another 30 years, teaching medical students well into his eighties. He remained an atheist until the day he died. There were no prayers involved in his cure, yet his robust spirit served him well. A strong believer in the power of the human mind, he repeatedly talked to his cancer, telling it that he hated it, telling it to die, to go away. It did.

In thinking about my practice experiences, I have come to realize that I missed many opportunities to address the spiritual needs of patients who entrusted their care to me. I could have done much more. So many times, I did not value their prayers, explore the personal meaning of their suffering, or even refer them to professional sources of spiritual support and comfort. I can cite reasons for my failures: time pressures of a busy practice, insensitivity to the subtle opportunities, preoccupation with the challenges of medical complexities, emotional depletion, and discomfort with certain religious beliefs and practices. Whatever the reasons, intellectually, emotionally or spiritually, I often fell short of meeting my patients' needs. Reflecting on my experiences with patients has inevitably brought me to my own contemplation of what "spirituality" means.

I grew up in a strongly religious family. The Presbyterian Church functioned at the center of our family life. I gradually rejected basic principles of Christian theology, progressing from a superficial adolescent rebellion against parental authority, through a deepening skepticism fueled by increasing attraction to the rationalism and objectivity of science, to a sustained estrangement from the religion of my childhood. The notion of an omnipotent, omniscient, omnipresent deity became alien to my understanding of the world and the human condition. For years, I thought little about spirituality, as I lived my life somewhere in the philosophical niche between agnosticism and atheism.

While I remain disconnected from my Christian roots, my sense of the immaterial, the metaphysical and the transcendent has evolved and, I would like to think, has broadened and deepened over the years. With less humanistic faith in reason and more skepticism about science and technology, increasingly I have become aware of something that could be called the spiritual.

I think this is what the physician-author-poet William Carlos Williams, in his essay "The Practice," described as "a glimpse of something, from time to time, which shows us a presence has just brushed past us, some rare thing... We can't name it." As for Williams, experiences with my patients have been crucial to this developing consciousness.

Of all the things I saw as a physician, the disappearance of Bertha Higgins' cancer presents the most enduring mystery. It most dramatically challenges rational explanation. After all, my patient who told his metastatic cancer to go away also received powerful drugs. While virtually unheard of, his recovery was consistent with scientific understanding.

From time to time through the years, I have thought of Bertha Higgins. I have replayed the events over and over, questioning whether I really felt a mass or whether I really found an empty rectum, wondering whether it could have been anything other than a cancer. But I've never been able to talk myself out of the reality of her cancer and its disappearance.

As the years passed, the disappearance of her cancer has bothered me less and less. While not accepting her explanation, I have come to accept the event as a source of wonder, even as a source of hope. Maybe, Bertha's "cure" is a window into something that transcends the rational, the measurable, something indefinable but real. Someday medical science might explain this presence, solving the mystery. But maybe not, and that's okay with me.

Blind Beulah

I killed Blind Beulah. I didn't shoot her or stab her or poison her. I did not intend to kill her; I intended to help her. It happened this way.

In the summer of 1972, I moved to a tiny town in the mountains of North Carolina to live and practice medicine. Soon after I arrived, I heard about Beulah, and soon after I heard about her, I met her.

Accompanied by the nurse Linda, I drove to Beulah's home, located at the edge of town. With the help of community volunteers, Linda had spent most of the previous year organizing the clinic where I now worked: procuring a vacant building, acquiring supplies, assembling a staff, and hustling funding from the Appalachian Regional Commission. She had also attended, the best she could, to some of the most urgent healthcare needs in a community long devoid of any healthcare professional. This had included periodic visits to check on Beulah, a woman of uncertain age, but most likely somewhere north of 80 years, who lived alone and qualified as somewhat of a town character.

On a hot August day, we navigated a deeply rutted, sunbaked dirt road to Beulah's home, shaded by a copse of pines and abutting the foot of a mountain. A small plot of lush bean, squash and tomato plants occupied a splash of sunlight in front of the long-ago painted wooden shack. The remaining front yard consisted of a discordant mix of grass, weeds and rocks. What looked like a decaying wooden barrel lay beside a near-by pine tree. Farther back, a pyramid of chopped wood loomed in the shadows. We climbed the three uneven plank steps to the small porch, empty except for a rusted set of bed springs that leaned precariously against the front of the house.

"I've asked them to get rid of that several times." Linda addressed her frustration to the springs. The "they" referred to a middle-aged couple who lived down the road from Beulah and helped her out with the garden, wood chopping, weekly delivery of groceries and other odd jobs.

Standing just outside the screen door, Linda loudly announced our presence. After waiting a while she repeated the announcement, and I heard a faint response from the dark innards of the shack.

We entered the dusky interior of Beulah's home. It took a few seconds for my eyes to transition from the outside brightness to the inner gloom. As forms took shape, I noted the few objects in her living room. A yellow black-speckled ribbon hung from the ceiling, dangling at head level. On further inspection, this became a strip of fly-paper studded with the bodies of victims, which I carefully avoided as I moved around the room. The furniture consisted of two stuffed chairs and a television on a small table, with rabbit ears laying on their sides and the screen blinking a jumble of diagonal lines. I realized that the TV emitted a barely audible droning buzz. On three of the four walls hung calendars, which displayed farmers working in fields, but each showed a different month, and the years ranged from 1961 to 1967. On the front wall, a small plastic Jesus hung on a wooden cross. Two unscreened windows faced each other across the sparse room, which distinctly smelled of old age. I soon discovered that quite a few flies had escaped the fate of their unlucky cousins.

Beulah emerged from the kitchen, a tall slightly stooped woman whose layers of clothing could not conceal her thinness. She walked slowly but with confidence and invited us to have a seat. We ignored the invitation, and Linda introduced me. Beulah's eyes roamed the room but then focused on a spot near me when I offered my "Hello, glad to meet you."

Beulah's home consisted of a living room, kitchen, bedroom and small bathroom, the latter a bit of a pleasant surprise. Outhouses still served the poorest of my patients. The absence of doors made our safety inspection easier. A round tub filled at least half of the bathroom, squeezing the tiny sink into one corner and a floridly stained commode into another. The somewhat messy kitchen featured a wood burning stove and a 1930s vintage refrigerator. A few dirty dishes littered the small table that occupied the center of the room. The bedroom featured a ragged quilt on the bed, and small objects I could not identify covered the top of a bedside bureau. Generally, things seemed in pretty good order, considering that an elderly blind lady lived here alone. While almost as ancient and decrepit as its inhabitant, the place appeared relatively safe, with nothing under foot that could trip her.

On that visit, we spent about twenty minutes with Beulah. I brought my black bag, and she consented to have me check her pulse and blood pressure. Each registered normal. But she declined any further examination. Linda later reported that on previous visits she had never gotten any further with an examination. Beulah seemed pleased that we had visited but didn't say much, providing brief answers to our questions and offering no complaints about anything. She appeared a bit relieved to have us depart.

We left, each with a mess of newly picked green beans and three robust red tomatoes. On the way back to the clinic, Linda finished telling me what she knew about Beulah.

According to her daughter, who intermittently lived in town, Beulah had lost her vision rather quickly about ten years earlier. The daughter had dragged her to an eye doctor who had said that nothing could be done about the loss of vision. He had given them a diagnosis, which the daughter could not remember.

Beulah had lived alone since the daughter and a son had left home decades earlier. Linda had never heard of any husband. Beulah had assured Linda that she had no health problems and took no medication. She had adjusted to her blindness and professed contentment with her life. Long-time residents in the town knew her as 'Blind Beulah' and considered her a bit of an irascible recluse. This didn't stop some of them from helping her out in little ways when the need arose. It takes a village to raise a child, and this village apparently collaborated to tend to a blind old lady.

Over the next year, I made two home visits to Beulah, each pretty much a repetition of the first visit: brief answers, no complaints, no meaningful examination, and no interest in an extended visit. The clinic nurse checked on her more frequently, with similar results. Beulah resolutely protected her privacy and independence.

The inevitable decline began during my second year of practice. I started getting disturbing reports from the nurse and the neighbors: food left out to spoil, a stick of wood in the refrigerator, more dirt on the floor and cobwebs in the corners, episodes of memory lapses and confusion. My visit confirmed her deteriorating mental status. Then she started falling. I sutured a laceration of her left leg and one on her forehead in consecutive months. Once, she lay on the floor in a pool of urine for hours before the neighbor discovered her.

Beulah's daughter expressed concern but offered little assistance. She struggled to manage her own affairs. Beulah's exhausted neighbors had reached their limit. We hauled in a large sofa and arranged for Beulah's teenage granddaughter to spend the night with her. That didn't work. Beulah complained bitterly, and the granddaughter liked boys, booze and pot more than she liked tending to her declining grandmother. She exited after a few days, cursing "the hateful old woman."

Beulah's son lived several hundred miles away in Wilmington, North Carolina and habitually visited once a year for a day or two. Apparently, he did not get along with his mother. When I finally contacted him by phone he expressed little interest, attributing her problems to old age and senility, as if that solved them. The Department of Social Services became involved, but Beulah threatened the visiting social worker with a pistol, which markedly cooled the department's interest.

Things reached a crisis. Clearly, she could no longer live alone, and no one could or would live with her. Beulah had never qualified for Social Security, and she had meager financial resources. We succeeded in obtaining Medicaid coverage for her, which would pay for nursing home care. She furiously opposed nursing home placement, and her daughter equivocated for several weeks as conditions became increasingly desperate. I silently wished that her death would relieve us of this burden, but to no avail. Finally, the daughter relented to my entreaties, consenting to involuntary nursing home placement of her incompetent mother. Her brother had already washed his hands of the situation, telling me to do whatever I thought best.

We arranged placement in a nursing home, sixty miles away in Asheville. On the fateful day, the local ambulance arrived with Beulah's daughter to transport her to the home. As expected, Beulah pitched a fit, venting her impotent fury with abject wails. With considerable difficulty, the attendants loaded her onto the stretcher and strapped her in, with her constant lamentations piercing the air.

As they carried her across the threshold of her home, her cries suddenly stopped, and she became silent, completely unresponsive to all stimuli. The ambulance attendant called me, and I went to check on her. I found her unconscious on the stretcher, her mouth gaping open, her sightless eyes staring at the blue sky, apparently, the victim of a stroke. So, instead of the nursing home, she went to a hospital in Asheville, where she died the next day without regaining consciousness.

Many town folks attended her funeral three days later, most of whom had probably not seen her in years. On occasion, I attended funerals of patients, but I did not attend Beulah's. Apparently, neither did her son. He called me from Wilmington the day of the funeral and cussed me out, the terrible doctor who had "killed" his mother. In contrast, Beulah's tranquilized daughter thanked me for the care I had provided her mother. She left town with her latest boyfriend a few days after the funeral, and I never saw her again.

My family moved away two years later. Before leaving, I traveled down the dirt road to Beulah's home. I stood in the clumps of grass amidst the beer cans and cigarette butts and stared at it, vacant since the day of her dramatic departure. It had not changed much since my first visit. Three boards nailed across the doorway punctuated the darkness that emerged from inside. Only a child or small animal could have entered, but I had no interest in going in, anyway.

A glint of something from a patch of dirt caught my eye; I looked down and saw a condom. Near-by, something else on the ground attracted my attention, the plastic Jesus partially covered by dirt. I studied it for a while and thought of picking it up, but I left it there in the dirt where Beulah's garden had once thrived.

I have needed to tell this story for a long time, the story of how I came to kill Blind Beulah.

Note: This story qualifies as creative nonfiction. The events occurred well over 40 years ago, and I do not claim to be completely accurate with respect to some of the dialogue or details. But the accusation by Beulah's son that I killed her is seared into my memory.

Prostrate Trouble

"Doc, my prostrate's botherin' me."

I knew about the "prostrate" and the frequent confusion of two words, identical except for the presence or absence of a single letter. I had stopped trying to correct patients.

Odell Norris looked like he had just stepped out of a Thomas Hart Benton painting and into my exam room: the elongated face, leathery skin with a perpetual farmer's tan, eyes recessed beneath prominent brows, ears that extended from his Atlanta Braves baseball cap to the angle of his jaw, tufts of gray hairs peeking out of his nostrils, yellowed teeth partially concealed by thin, dry lips. He wore a faded blue shirt, and the gnarled, calloused hands that emerged from the sleeves seemed a bit too big for the rest of him. Bib overalls linked this 1970s Appalachian farmer to his 1930s Midwestern ancestor popularized by Benton. He exuded nervousness.

"How's your prostate bothering you?" I asked.

"It's been givin' me trouble."

"Okay, what kind of trouble are you having? How do you know it's your prostate?"

"It's prostrate trouble, Doc. I can tell."

Was there a hint of frustration in his voice? Okay, time to abandon the open-ended questions I had been urged to use in medical school and begin to dissect this self-diagnosis. "Does it hurt when you pee?"

"No."

"Do you have pain in your privates or lower back?"

"No."

"Do you suddenly have to pee real bad and have trouble holding it?"

297

"No."

"Have you been peeing more than usual?"

"No, peein' ain't a problem."

Prostate trouble, but peeing is not a problem. That was unusual. "Have you been feeling hot, having fever, or sometimes feeling cold, having chills?"

"No, Doc, none of that. It's my prostrate." Now, more than a hint of frustration.

"Okay, I'm trying to figure out exactly how your prostate is bothering you. Are you feeling sick in any way?"

"No, Doc, I don't feel sick. It's prostrate trouble." He rarely made eye contact and mostly looked down at or near his boots. He shifted in the chair and emitted a prolonged sigh. Obviously, we were not connecting.

"How long has your prostate been bothering you?"

This seemed to revive him. "About a month or so."

"That long?"

'Yeah, but not every day."

"How frequently?"

"I reckon maybe two, three times a week."

"Two or three times a week?"

"Yeah."

"How long does it last?"

"About ten minutes or so. Not long, it goes away"

"And then it doesn't bother you anymore?"

"No, it don't 'til the next time."

"Can it happen at any time, or does it occur at a particular time of the day?"

"In the mornin', when I wake up."

"Any other time?"

'A coupla times in the night."

This made no sense. Stumped, I looked at him in silence for a few seconds while he scanned the room, his eyes finally resting on a poster about childhood immunizations on the wall behind me. It sure didn't sound like prostate trouble to me, but I decided to check his urine anyway. "Could you pee in a cup for me?"

"I reckon, if you want me to."

I scribbled an order for a urinalysis with microscopic examination and handed it to him. "Take this out and give it to the nurse. She'll give you a cup to pee in. The bathroom is down the hall. Then when you're finished give the cup to the nurse and come back here." I paused and noticed the prominent knuckles of his left hand as it gripped his left knee through the overalls. "When was the last time you saw a doctor?"

"A few years ago, I saw Doctor Shultz in Newport. I got a fish hook caught in my finger. Damn fool thing."

"When was the last time you had a check-up, a physical exam?"

"Don't know, maybe when I had my 'pendix out a while back."

I looked at the sheet of paper that had been filled out at the front desk, the beginning of a medical chart for a new patient. "You're 67?"

"Yup."

"Okay, while you're here I'll check you over. When you come back to the room get undressed and put on this gown, open to the back." I pulled a gown out of a drawer and handed it to the skeptical farmer with prostrate trouble.

In the meantime, I saw another patient, who was fortunately much less perplexing than Mr. Norris. Before returning to him, I checked with the lab; his urinalysis was normal, no white cells in the urine, no sign of infection. No surprise there.

His physical examination revealed nothing abnormal. Given his extensive sun exposure, his skin was remarkably free of worrisome lesions. On rectal exam, his prostate was big, consistent with his age but showed no signs of infection or malignancy. I left the room while he dressed and stood in the hallway, deliberating over what to tell him. I had no idea what his prostrate trouble was. I knew that his prostate was not the problem.

I sat across from him in the exam room. His cap was back on, and small beads of sweat had formed beside his long ears. "Mister Norris, your prostate seems to be in good shape. As you may know, the prostate tends to get bigger as men get older. Yours is bigger than it used to be, but it doesn't seem to be causing any trouble that I can find. No sign of infection or cancer." I stopped and waited for a response.

He looked into my eyes for the first time. His lips trembled a bit as he said "My wife died a year ago, and I ain't been with no other woman. I don't understand it."

"I'm sorry your wife died. I know you must miss her."

"I do." He paused and then said "It ain't natural to be getting my courage back at this time of life."

It finally hit me, what his prostate trouble was. Among Appalachian men, "courage" was slang for sexual potency. Men occasionally complained of losing their courage, but this was the first complaint of a return of courage I had encountered. I struggled to stop the smile that tickled my lips. This bothered my patient a lot, and I needed to take it seriously. I carefully formulated my next statement. "You're concerned because your manhood sometimes is hard when you wake up in the morning, and then it soon goes away, probably after you take a good piss."

He looked at me with a mixture of surprise and embarrassment. "Why yeah, Doc, that's what I've been tellin' ya. Prostrate trouble."

Trying to suppress the grin, I looked from his face to the end of the exam table where minutes before he had bent over while I probed his rectum with a gloved finger. No wonder he had seemed mystified. When I had things under control, I looked at him again and said. "I'm sorry that it took me so long to understand." I paused and he waited, his face relaxing a bit, and the tension in his hands diminishing. "I'm curious. Why did you think this was a prostate problem?"

"Like you said, I knew older men could have prostrate trouble. My pa did. When I started having this problem in the mornin' and a few times in the night, I naturally thought of my prostrate. What else could it be?"

"Let me ask you this, Mister Norris. Years ago, when you were a lot younger did you have erections like this, I mean your manhood getting hard in the morning and sometimes at night?"

"Oh yeah, a lot of times. Right regular."

"Did you think that was prostate trouble back then?"

"Oh no, it was natural back then."

"Well, it's still natural now. Men your age and even older can have this happen, and it doesn't mean anything is wrong. It's not prostate trouble. In fact, it shows that you're still pretty healthy." Giving good news was fun; I welcomed the infrequent opportunities.

For the first time, a smile played around his mouth. "Really, Doc, you don't say."

Really, what you are experiencing is very natural and completely normal."

A grin exploded across his face. "Thanks so much, Doc, that's a load off my mind."

I saw some pretty sick folks later that day in the clinic, but I occasionally chuckled about the man with prostrate trouble. Momentarily, at the end of the visit I had considered suggesting to him another way he could get a load off, so to speak. But I decided not to go there.

That was long ago. I'm now five years older than Odell Norris was when his prostrate bothered him. I'm pleased that occasionally in the morning and even at night my prostrate bothers me.

Sissy

Randy and I went to school together, first grade through high school. But in this case 'together' is misleading. I do not remember ever talking with him. It's almost a statistical certainty that we exchanged a word or two. I just don't recall it. I had a rather large group of friends in elementary school: Andy, Lee, Mike, Billy, Joey and others, but not Randy. He was said to be an only child, but other than that I knew nothing about his home life. What I remember about Randy is that he was a sissy. Being a sissy in grade school in Durham, North Carolina in the 1950s was not a good thing. It may not be a good thing in 2018.

For boys in elementary school, particularly in the upper grades (fourth through sixth), sports were a big deal. Most of us avidly supported either the Blue Devils or the Tar Heels, with a few Wolfpack and Demon Deacon fans in the mix. I was a Blue Devil, and to this day I cannot root for Carolina under any circumstance. If they played the Taliban in a basketball game, I would face an existential crisis. In early spring of the sixth grade, I suffered misery for days after the hated Tar Heels completed an undefeated season by beating Wilt Chamberlain and the Kansas Jayhawks for the NCAA basketball championship.

Randy's lack of interest in sports spared him that particular misery, but it endowed him with a more enduring fate. At recess he was invariably the last boy chosen for any sports team, whether the game was flag football in the fall, basketball in the winter, or softball in the spring. On the football field and basketball court, he was a stationary presence in the midst of frenzied action, never touching the ball unless it accidently hit him. In softball, he always batted last, a guaranteed strikeout victim, and he was customarily planted in right field where he could do the least damage. A ball hit in his direction pretty much assured the hitter of a home run, unless the neighboring center fielder was particularly fleet of foot and strong of arm. On one occasion Randy's bat actually made contact with the softball, which slowly rolled in the direction of the pitcher. This achievement elicited a loud cheer from teammates, a mix of surprise, sarcasm and perhaps support. I don't recall whether he made it safely to first base. Randy did not exactly run; he had more of a bovine amble.

Randy was responsible for my most embarrassing moment in the fifth grade. While I ran with the football past his usually immobile form, Randy somehow reached out and removed the flag from my back pocket. As the only boy in flag football history to be 'tackled' by Randy, I suffered unmerciful teasing by my classmates. I would have far preferred repeated trips to the principal's office to this humiliation.

During the athletic events that were so important to most of us, I would occasionally notice Randy standing to the side of the action, wistfully looking across the playground at the girls doing their thing. I recall having the sense that Randy was in the wrong place.

I have only vague memories of Randy in the classroom. I could not tell you if he was smart or a good speller, or good at arithmetic or art. He was one of those docile, obedient students whom busy teachers loved to have in a class and male peers resented.

Randy was a prime target for bullying in grade school, but interestingly, I don't remember that happening. Maybe it did; we certainly had some bullies. In retrospect, I suspect that Randy's extreme vulnerability, his utter defenselessness, paradoxically protected him. You won no glory from beating him up. Most of the girls could have done that. He was probably picked on and ridiculed, but primarily he was ignored. He was there, but he wasn't there.

After we left grade school, I have little memory of Randy. Rough kids from the wrong side of town lurked in the halls and playground of the junior high we attended. He was probably bullied there. I was.

By high school, Randy had grown into a Pillsbury Dough Boy type guy and was generally considered to be "queer." That must have been very unpleasant for him; gay support groups did not exist back then. But I have no knowledge of what his life was like. I never saw him at school football or basketball games, sock-hops, proms, school plays, movie theaters, Tops Drive-in or any of the other teen hangouts. He wasn't in the school clubs I was in. But then it was a big school; we had over 500 in our graduating class.

My wife and I met in the ninth grade in a new school. She was the teacher's pet, straight A student and hall monitor. I was a desultory student and football jock who walked funny. We graduated from high school together. We did not attend our tenth- or twenty-year reunions but did attend our thirtieth. We had a great time reconnecting with folks we had not seen in decades. I'm pretty sure Randy was not there.

At our fortieth reunion, hair was grayer, heads were balder, bellies were bigger, body parts were droopier, and more of our classmates had died. Randy's name appeared on the list of the deceased. I commented on this to a classmate who lived in Durham and had helped organize the reunion. With more than the suggestion of a smirk, he reported that Randy's mother had said he died of cancer but everyone knew he died of AIDS.

I know nothing about Randy's life. I don't know what he did to put food on the table and a roof over his head. I don't know if he got married or had kids or had a partner. I don't know if he

305

came out of the closet, stayed in the closet, or was ever even in the closet.

I hope that Randy loved and was loved in return. I hope that he experienced the joys of friendship. I hope that Randy hit a home run: wrote a novel, painted a masterpiece, preached a sermon, won a court case, cured a patient, made a scientific discovery, designed a building, taught a student to read, ran a marathon, laid a stone walkway, flew an airplane, cooked a delicious meal or ... . I hope that he achieved an enduring self-awareness and self-acceptance from fully living in a world of wonder and woe. I hope that he enjoyed a measure of the happiness that I have experienced.

When I hear the claim that the "gay life style" is a choice I think of Randy. As a boy Randy was different from the rest of us. Of course, each of us was different in some way, but his difference was more consequential. I doubt that Randy chose to be different in a way that isolated him and exposed him to ridicule. I think Randy was gay, but I don't know for sure, and I don't care. It's true that we make choices along the way in life, some we are proud of, some we regret. Randy was a boy when I was a boy. He needed a friend back then. I'm sorry that I chose not to be his friend.

Personhood: The Beginning and the End

"Life begins at conception. Abortion is murder." I often hear these opinions from people who want the government to force women to continue unwanted pregnancies against their will. Allegedly, medical science provides "proof" of this claim about the onset of human life.

Is this true?

Actually, science has determined that human life began hundreds of thousands of years ago and has persisted in a continuum since then. There is human life in a tube of blood. There is human life in a culture of skin cells designed to grow new skin for a badly burned patient. There is human life in the sperm and egg cells before they unite in the process of fertilization (conception). There is human life in the placenta, but no effort is made to maintain this life after the birth of a baby.

What the opponents of abortion rights seem to mean is that individual, specific human life (personhood) begins at the time of conception. This claim is based on the scientific fact that a new, unique genome is created with fertilization. The resulting fertilized egg (zygote) contains a unique set of genes, a unique array of DNA. Thus, DNA in a never-before arrangement in a living human cell purportedly equals personhood. So the argument goes.

Is this true?

Our brain is the human organ that most definitively distinguishes us from other animals. From a scientific perspective, humanity and brain function are inextricably wedded. Any consideration of personhood must address the role of the brain.

Late in the evening of February 1, 2015, my brother-in-law Aram was found unconscious on the floor of his home by his son-in-law. EMTs were summoned, and they transported Aram to a hospital where he was determined to be deeply comatose. An MRI revealed that he had suffered a massive hemorrhage into his brain with severe, irreversible brain damage. He was placed on a ventilator.

My sister Janis was 120 miles away, attending to our mother who had undergone surgery earlier that day. Janis arrived at the hospital in the early morning hours and learned of the hopeless prognosis. After discussion with their son and daughter, she decided to discontinue "life support." Aram's higher brain centers were destroyed. What made Aram, Aram was gone; his personhood had ended. After the ventilator was disconnected, Aram's breathing and heart beat gradually slowed, and within a few hours they stopped.

Clearly, his family and medical professionals considered Aram's life to have ended even though billions of cells in his body, containing his unique DNA, were still living. Medically, when determining the end of personhood, the status of brain function is the crucial factor, not the presence of unique DNA in living cells. Personhood depends on brain function. Every day in this and other countries physicians discontinue life support for patients like Aram despite the presence of "human life" in their bodies. Unique DNA in a living human cell does not equal personhood.

We should use the same scientific criteria to determine when personhood begins that we use to determine when personhood ends.

There is no brain function in the zygote formed at conception. It will be months after conception before a level of brain function has developed in the fetus that exceeds that which Aram had when "life support" was discontinued. We know a lot about fetal development, but we don't know exactly when the fetal brain reaches a level of function consistent with personhood. Based on my understanding of the science, this most likely occurs around 21 to 23 weeks of gestation. Over 99% of all abortions are completed before this time. Half of all abortions are performed in the first 2 months of gestation. Abortions at or after 21 weeks are almost always necessitated by serious medical problems with the fetus or mother or both. Murder is the intentional killing of a human being. Abortion rarely if ever involves killing a human being, as defined medically.

(Despite their extremist rhetoric, many opponents of abortion-rights clearly do not really believe that abortion is murder. Candidate Trump's assertion that abortion should be legally prohibited and that a woman who had one should be punished provoked an immediate outcry from leading anti-abortion activists and organizations. The prohibition, they heartily endorsed, but the idea of punishing the woman, they vehemently opposed. Obviously, this makes no sense when the woman has willingly participated in killing a human being. Not punishing a woman for doing to an eight-week old fetus what she would be vigorously punished for doing to an eight-week old baby clearly acknowledges the major difference in the biologic and moral status of the two. When do we not punish a person for murder? When it is not murder!)

Not only is it unscientific, defining a specific human life as unique DNA in a living cell is problematic in other ways. In 1991, Mike, a friend of mine, developed kidney failure. Fortunately, he received a transplanted kidney that sustained his life for 20 years. Sadly, he died of complications of cancer that was probably enabled and hastened by the medication required to prevent rejection of the kidney.

The "donor" of Mike's kidney was a young person who died in an automobile accident. But, did the donor really die in the

309

accident? Not if you believe that unique DNA in a living cell equals personhood. For 20 years, Mike's kidney consisted of millions of living cells that contained the donor's DNA. Was the donor still alive? Most abortion-rights opponents would scoff at this question and consider it ridiculous and irrelevant. However, they cannot evade the implications of their own logic. If the zygote is a living person because of the presence of unique DNA in a single living cell, then certainly a healthy kidney comprised of millions of living cells with unique DNA has a credible claim for personhood.

There is an effort in this country to legally establish personhood as beginning at conception. Consider the possible unintended consequences of such legal action. The implications are mindboggling, independent of the egregious violation of a woman's right to privacy and to control her reproductive function. Insurance companies could use the logic informing this law to deny life insurance payments when the deceased was an organ donor, claiming that the person still lived. This would have a major chilling effect on the willingness of persons to register to donate organs. Because they would still meet criteria for personhood, patients like Aram would be maintained on life support for extended periods of time, generating immense financial and emotional costs.

Henrietta Lacks was a poor young black woman who died at Johns Hopkins Hospital in 1951. But did she really die? Her cells continue to live 60+ years later in the form of HeLa cells. For years, these cells have been used extensively in medical research, contributing to advances in medical knowledge and treatments. HeLa cells derive from the cervical cancer that killed Henrietta. These cells turned out to have the unique property of "immortality." Unlike other cells they did not eventually die when

310

cultured but continued to divide and proliferate. Her cells and her DNA (although heavily mutated) live on. Is Henrietta Lacks therefore immortal?

The assertion that medical science has proven that a human life begins at conception is easily refuted by the position of numerous medical and scientific organizations on the issue. Despite pressure from "pro-life" groups to do so, the American Medical Association, the American Academy of Family Physicians, the American College of Obstetrics and Gynecology, the American Academy of Pediatrics, the American College of Physicians, the American Public Health Association and many other scientific organizations have refused to endorse the claim that life begins at conception. In fact, these organizations submitted *amicus curiae* briefs to the Supreme Court opposing a Missouri law that asserted that life begins at conception.

Based on my knowledge of the relevant science, I believe that the product of conception (zygote) has the potential to become a human being, a person. This potential is actualized if the fetus makes it to approximately 21 to 23 weeks of gestation. (We know that at least half of all products of conception are lost in the first few weeks after fertilization, usually because of serious genetic or morphologic defects incompatible with continued development. Nature is a most prolific abortionist.) Because of the potential to become a human being, the fetus has value. Physicians expend considerable energy and resources attending to the fetus as well as the pregnant woman. I was privileged to provide prenatal care and to deliver babies for years. However, I believe that a fetus' potential to become a person does not trump a woman's basic human right of self-determination. Depriving a woman of the right to control her reproductive capacity denies her human agency, subverts her humanity, diminishes her personhood. Our commitment to human rights requires vigilance in protecting her freedom to decide what to do when faced with a problem pregnancy and assuring her legal access to safe abortion services if she chooses to terminate.

As a physician, I am committed to scientific inquiry; I support the appropriate practices, applications and interpretations of science. I am greatly disturbed when science is misappropriated or distorted for ideological purposes. People are entitled to their conviction that life begins at conception, but they are not entitled to impose their conviction on others. They are certainly not entitled to abuse science to serve their agenda.

A Credit to His Race

"He's a credit to his race." Growing up in the segregated South, I heard this statement on occasion. It was always said about a black man, almost always by a white man. It was intended as praise, but even as a child I vaguely sensed the double-sided nature of this "compliment."

The current concerns about micro-aggressions suffered by African-Americans and other minorities recall this characterization, which I consider an earlier micro-aggression. This micro-aggression co-existed with a host of horrific macro-aggressions and reflected attitudes about race that fueled oppression. To explain, I provide some personal history.

From my earliest memories until my mid-teens, racial segregation festered as a constant backdrop to my life. It rarely impacted me directly, but it persistently reminded me of the way things were: lily white restaurants and movie theaters and swimming pools and church congregations, colored people in the back of the bus, separate and clearly unequal schools, and the frequent use of the N-word. White children called black adults by their first name. I was ridiculed once by a buddy for responding to his Negro maid with a "yes, ma'am." The sirs and ma'ams instilled into southern children were reserved for white adults. A pervasive system preserved white supremacy by enforcing social control at multiple levels, ranging from the separate public water fountains and toilets to the sign on the outskirts of Smithfield, North Carolina that proclaimed "Welcome to Ku Klux Klan country." When the tactics of the White Citizens Council, the "respectable" façade of the Klan, failed to maintain racial order, overt violence targeted uppity blacks who challenged the white power structure.

313

My home town of Durham, North Carolina prided itself on being enlightened and progressive in terms of race relations. Durham boasted a small but solid black middle class and was home to the nation's largest black insurance company as well as to the "liberal" Duke University. But this reputation did not stop a jury of white men from acquitting in ten minutes a white bus driver of the puny charge of manslaughter for shooting a black World War II veteran who refused to move to the back of the bus. Neither did this reputation prevent the assault by a racist mob on participants at a 1948 rally for the presidential candidate, Henry Wallace, who advocated racial integration. Sadly, Durham **was** more progressive than many southern cities.

When I started the ninth grade five years after the Supreme Court declared school segregation unconstitutional, Durham initiated the slow process of school integration. One of the half dozen black students who attended previously all white schools showed up in my home room. I well remember the entourage of police officers and photographers who accompanied her on the first day of class. My tiny face appeared in the background of white faces in the front-page photo in the afternoon paper that featured a frightened Anita sitting in the front row.

I had no contact with the only black ninth grade student in the school. I saw her eating lunch alone in the cafeteria day after day. I never saw her on the playground during recess, and I never saw any fellow student talk to her during the entire year. I'm fairly sure she suffered insults and indignities, but even if she didn't, the social ostracism would have been oppressive.

Anita stuck it out, and four years later she was one of two black students in our graduating class of 500. Indeed, Anita was a credit to her race, the human race.

Durham congratulated itself on smoothly integrating schools, and compared to many places, this self-satisfaction was warranted. That first year, the handful of minimally integrated schools received an occasional bomb threat. We would troop out to the playground and look at the school, waiting for it to blow up. It never did. That was about the extent of overt opposition to integration. However, within 10 years many white students were attending private schools, and the public schools had become predominantly black and increasingly deprived of vital resources.

As with school desegregation, integration of other aspects of Durham public life proceeded with less conflict than in many other southern cities. Protests at various business establishments resulted in threats, angry confrontations, arrests and occasional violence. A few businesses closed rather than serve black customers. A white high school friend was hassled by some classmates because he participated in local civil rights protests. But by the time the federal Civil Rights Law passed, the reality of desegregation was accepted in Durham, albeit grudgingly by many whites. Progress brought repercussions, however. For example, all public swimming pools permanently closed.

Having grown up in the Philadelphia area, with black classmates and friends, my parents were always uncomfortable with racial segregation. After the end of World War II, they remained in Durham because my father had obtained what in many ways was his ideal job. He worked as a medical illustrator at Duke University Medical Center for 42 years. Early in his career he, so to speak, dodged a bullet. He befriended the black photographer who had been hired by his department to take photographs of black patients with interesting abnormalities. One evening he and my mother had Graham, the black photographer, over to their small apartment to eat dinner. Several days later my father was called into his boss' office. The conversation went something like this:

"Bob, I hear that you and Hildur had Graham over for dinner. Is that right?"

"Yes, that's right."

"Well, if the powers that be in the hospital find out about this, I will be forced to fire Graham. I may be able to save your job. I don't know. Personally, I don't care if you socialize with him, but you need to realize that you are in the South, and this type of behavior is not tolerated by a lot of people. When you do this, you are taking big risks, and you are jeopardizing Graham's wellbeing."

Apparently, the powers that be did not discover my father's transgression, but my father was smacked in the face by the awful reality of racial segregation.

My parents clearly communicated their opposition to segregation in numerous ways. They did not allow my brother, sister or me to use the N-word, and much to my embarrassment, they corrected our friends when they used it. My parents treated Negroes with respect, using mister and misses when referring to them. My father volunteered to register blacks to vote. In the early sixties my father unsuccessfully tried to arrange dialogue between members of our church and a black church. For his efforts, he was told by a fellow church elder to "take your family and go join a nigger church."

"He is a credit to his race." I never heard this said about Martin Luther King Jr. or any other civil rights leader. I heard it said about the black minister who preached prayerful submission to white authority with the promise of eventual heavenly rewards. I heard it said about the black banker who raised money to repair broken playground equipment at a black school when the school

316

board refused to pay for the repairs with taxpayers' money. I heard it said about a black athlete who would never have taken a knee during the singing of the National Anthem. (The 1960s Mohammad Ali was the antithesis of a credit to his race.) Negroes who were credits to their race did not rock the boat, did not challenge the status quo. They played by the rules set by whites. They were considered role models for other blacks.

But the problem with this "compliment" goes further than that. Based on the perceived inadequacy of "the colored," it was an indictment of a race. The black race was uplifted by the culturally sanctioned achievement of an individual. A black person represented race in a way that a white person did not. White worth did not depend on the qualities or behavior of individual whites, black worth did. Whiteness embodied intrinsic social value. The black person who did something laudable in the eyes of whites was exceptional and provided some hope for the redemption of an inferior people.

One day in the mid-sixties, I was watching a St Louis Cardinal baseball game on TV with my friend Andy and his father. The announcers lauded the recently retired Stan Musial, praising his personal integrity and his contributions to charities in St Louis.

I said "Stan Musial is a credit to his race." Surprised and annoyed, Andy's father glared at me with disdain and angrily informed me that the white race is exceptional and does not need credit from anyone.

Okay, I admit it, nothing in the preceding paragraph is true except that I had a friend named Andy. I never watched a TV game with his father, and I made no such comment about Stan Musial. I never made such a statement about any white person, but I wish I had. I don't know that Andy's father specifically would have responded in this imagined way, but I'm certain many white adults would have.

While we have made considerable progress since my childhood, clearly racism still infests our society. Sadly, it takes obvious forms, such as the despicable actions of self-avowed white supremacists. But what about the subtle yet damaging micro-aggressions experienced by racial minorities?

Torch-bearing Klansmen in Charlottesville, Virginia evoke condemnation from many Americans (but not the president). However, the white woman repelled by blatant displays of racism turns to her husband after watching an African-American athlete interviewed on TV and says "He's certainly well spoken." A well-meaning college professor tells a black student "I was pleasantly surprised by how good your paper was." A white student asks a black student why she chose to attend the University of Missouri rather than Lincoln University, historically, an all-black school. In a sociology class, when the discussion turns to urban crime and drug use, white students look to their black classmates as experts on the subjects.

These are examples of racial insensitivity based on stereotyping provided by students at an open forum on race relations held on the University of Missouri-Columbia campus in December, 2014. Are they manifestations of racism? I don't think that's the appropriate question. The important question is how we change attitudes and beliefs that engender such hurtful micro-aggressions and obstruct racial equality and justice.

In the context of segregation, the statement that a black person was a credit to his race would seem a benign and perhaps even welcomed respite. But it functioned as an insidious expression of racial prejudices that validated oppression. Unfortunately, its progenies survive as micro-aggressions that

318

impede our pursuit of racial understanding and harmony. By being less obvious, these subtle racial offenses may be even more damaging than flagrant demonstrations of racism.

Acknowledgements

Special thanks to Cokie, my life companion, for her proof-reading and constructive criticism and for taking care of me. I thank our sons Kevin and Russell and granddaughter Ellie for the unmeasurable riches they have brought to my life. Creative writing seminars led by Trudy Lewis and Speer Morgan, faculty members in the English Department of the University of Missouri-Columbia, have been valuable to me. I thank them and other seminar participants for their helpful critiques of earlier versions of some of my stories. Thanks to members of my writing group, Roy Fox, Gordon Christensen and Marvin Feldman, for their helpful comments and suggestions. Thanks to countless friends and colleagues who have stimulated, challenged and nurtured me through the years. Thanks to my patients and their families who taught me so much about living and loving, enduring and prevailing. Special thanks to my parents for everything.

Made in United States
Troutdale, OR
04/07/2024

19022314R00195